A DETECTIVE INSPECTC

STALKING THE RIPPER

JACK GATLAND

Copyright © 2022 by Jack Gatland / Tony Lee
All rights reserved.

This book or parts thereof may not be reproduced in any form or by any electronic or mechanical means, including information storage and retrieval systems without written permission from the author, unless for the use of brief quotations in a book review.

This is a work of fiction. Names, characters, places and incidents are either the product of the author's imagination or are used fictitiously, and any resemblance to actual persons, living or dead, business establishments, places of learning, events or locales is entirely coincidental.

Published by Hooded Man Media.

First Edition: July 2022

PRAISE FOR JACK GATLAND

'This is one of those books that will keep you up past your bedtime, as each chapter lures you into reading just one more.'

'This book was excellent! A great plot which kept you guessing until the end.'

'Couldn't put it down, fast paced with twists and turns.'

'The story was captivating, good plot, twists you never saw and really likeable characters. Can't wait for the next one!'

'I got sucked into this book from the very first page, thoroughly enjoyed it, can't wait for the next one.'

'Totally addictive. Thoroughly recommend.'

'Moves at a fast pace and carries you along with it.'

'Just couldn't put this book down, from the first page to the last one it kept you wondering what would happen next.'

Before LETTER FROM THE DEAD...
There was

LIQUIDATE
THE PROFITS

Learn the story of what *really* happened to DI Declan Walsh, while at Mile End!

An EXCLUSIVE PREQUEL, completely free to anyone who joins the Declan Walsh Reader's Club!

Join at www.subscribepage.com/jackgatland

Also by Jack Gatland

DI DECLAN WALSH BOOKS

LETTER FROM THE DEAD

MURDER OF ANGELS

HUNTER HUNTED

WHISPER FOR THE REAPER

TO HUNT A MAGPIE

A RITUAL FOR THE DYING

KILLING THE MUSIC

A DINNER TO DIE FOR

BEHIND THE WIRE

HEAVY IS THE CROWN

STALKING THE RIPPER

A QUIVER OF SORROWS

MURDER BY MISTLETOE

BENEATH THE BODIES

ELLIE RECKLESS BOOKS

PAINT THE DEAD

STEAL THE GOLD

HUNT THE PREY

TOM MARLOWE BOOKS

SLEEPING SOLDIERS

TARGET LOCKED

COVERT ACTION

DAMIAN LUCAS BOOKS

THE LIONHEART CURSE

STANDALONE BOOKS

THE BOARDROOM

AS TONY LEE

DODGE & TWIST

For Mum, who inspired me to write.

For Tracy, who inspires me to write.

CONTENTS

PROLOGUE

HELEN CROME HADN'T PRECISELY WORKED OUT THE MOMENT the man had started following her, but by the time she reached the western end of Eastcheap, the road that led from Monument Station towards Tower Hill to the east, she'd clocked him a couple of times in the reflections of windows, each time keeping his distance, matching her speed, and keeping himself to himself.

Helen had been out with friends after work that evening, which was strange, as, in her late thirties, Helen had never really found herself a solid social group, preferring to flit around regular meeting spots in the City. She hated travelling, especially on the underground during the summer, where the hot and sweaty of London seemed to congregate, and, as she worked nearby in Fenchurch Street, she found it incredibly easy to go to City talks after work. And, with parents living in Bamburgh, way up north in Northumbria, she didn't really have much to hurry home to.

She didn't even have a *cat*.

She'd been at a bar on Eastcheap tonight; a 'music'

themed one, with vinyl albums above the drinks. She couldn't remember the name of the place, and all she knew about it was there'd been some singer electrocute himself to death on stage there about five months earlier—she only knew this because the man hosting the talk had made a joke about testing the microphone before he spoke into it. The talk had been about Britpop and the rise of independent music in the nineties, and Helen had gone to it because she liked a couple of the bands mentioned. And, unlike some of the audience, Helen was just old enough to actually remember the bands when they first appeared. She recalled the *Oasis* versus *Blur* 'battle of the bands' single competition back in August 1995; she'd only been around eleven at the time, but it'd made the news. She'd been team *Blur* then, although in the years following, this had changed.

However, half the audience in the bar tonight hadn't been alive when it happened, and there was a part of Helen that almost resented this, feeling like they were tourists, hitching a ride on a part of her life very special to her. And, at the end, when the talk finished at nine pm, she'd decided not to hang around afterwards, in what they called the "networking" part of the evening and had made her way out of the side entrance, deciding an early night was called for, and making her way quickly to the City Thameslink on Ludgate Hill. It was a long walk, almost a mile, but it was a straight one, the bulk of the journey along Cannon Street.

And, as it was a nice late August night, she'd had no problem with it.

Until she spotted the stalker.

He was young, in his early twenties. Blond, shaggy hair and an olive-green ex-army jacket, he looked like he could have been in *Oasis*, or any of the bands at the time, and he'd been at the talk, standing near the bar. Helen recalled seeing him at one point, but had paid no interest to him. Although she was single, and he was pretty good looking, he was obviously at least fifteen years or more younger than her, and Helen had no false expectations on how such a conversation would go. And she wasn't—what did they call them?—a *Cougar*, no matter what she thought.

And so she'd carried on west, hoping it was just a simple and innocent coincidence he was following her; after all, Cannon Street led to its self-named train station, or Mansion House, or even St Paul's. There was every reason he would travel this route on his own way home.

Still, there were ways to check this, she considered.

As she walked down Cannon Street on the north pavement, past Cannon Street Station on her left and across the road, she stopped in front of a stone and glass building situated just past St Swithin's Lane. It wasn't an extraordinary building, but it had a small part of London history there, as, in a little portico built out of the stone wall and behind tempered glass, was a small, regular block of limestone. Above it, chiselled into the wall, were three words.

THE LONDON STONE

Helen had walked past the stone many times over the years, and she'd spent her time reading the inscription beside it, explaining how the stone was thought to have been a Roman milestone, from which all distances in Britain were measured; she'd even been to talks in London where strange old men in vintage clothing suggested this was possibly the stone that Excalibur itself had been pulled out, with scholars and academics claiming the act itself had been performed in nearby St Paul's, although more as a ruler "striking the stone with a sword" to announce their, well, *rulership*.

But, as far as Helen was concerned, this was just a stone.

And, for the moment, it was a very convenient way to pause and read the plaque beside it, killing time, waiting for the blond stalker to walk past.

He hadn't.

And, as Helen glanced right, she saw the man was examining the window of a closed coffee and doughnuts shop about fifty metres away, oblivious, so it seemed, to the woman staring warily at him.

Deciding to test her theory out more, Helen continued to walk down Cannon Street, picking up her pace and moving on, now past St Paul's Cathedral on her right, pausing for a moment on the steps to look up at the building. It was dark, and the lights around the cathedral lit it up in an ethereal white, standing out against the evening sky. It was truly beautiful, and Helen stood for a moment to bask in the glory, while also checking for any signs of her stalker.

Who was gone.

With a breath of relief, Helen chuckled. *She'd actually believed he'd been following her.* Poor man probably hadn't even noticed her. With a definitely more relaxed attitude, Helen started west once more, pausing as she approached Ave Maria Lane, as a sudden urge for a burger hit her. It wasn't even nine-thirty in the evening yet, but she hadn't eaten before she'd attended the talk. There were a couple of burger restaurants across the road, and she considered turning and walking back—

The stalker had returned.

As Helen had glanced back to one restaurant, she saw

him, strolling past St Paul's, still following her, although at a slightly further distance.

With a slow groan, Helen turned back to Ava Maria Lane, crossing it quickly, moving on. She considered looking for a policeman, or waving a police car down; she'd seen a couple pass on her walk, but what would she say? That she'd become spooked by some poor bugger taking the same path as her? She needed to be sure before she called anyone.

By now she was at the start of Ludgate Hill, and the Thameslink station was visible in the distance, but although she'd be safe on a train, Helen didn't want to catch one. She worried about what would happen after she got off, when she was alone on the other side; this might give the blond stalker an idea where she lived, and she needed proof of her suspicions first. So, deciding on the spur of the moment to change her route, she doubled back on herself, walking the ten steps backwards to Ava Maria Lane, turning north up it.

This diversion had brought her closer to the man now, and as she turned up the street and walked swiftly now, she glanced into the windows of the buildings to her right, noting that he too had now sped up.

What was his game?

To her left now was an old, red-brick building, wrought-iron gates in front of an archway, wide enough for vehicles, although none seemed to be welcome there, shown by a black sign reading PRIVATE PROPERTY - PLEASE DO NOT ENTER. Helen knew this was Amen Court, as she'd once attended a housewarming party there. The pedestrian gate was open and, without a second thought, Helen quickly nipped in through the entrance, passing under and through the archway as quickly as she could. The surrounding buildings up to this point had all been businesses, and most were closed at this time of night, but Amen Court was residential; if she started screaming or shouting for help, she knew she could find at least one or two people to open a window, to see what was going on, if only to shout out to *keep the bloody noise down.*

And, more importantly, she knew Amen Court was a U-shape that led around to an entrance twenty to thirty metres back; by following this, she was doubling back on herself without the man spying on her realising, and, by the time he entered the court, she would be back out onto Ava Maria Lane and heading back to City Thameslink as fast as she could.

As she reached the corner where the road turned to the left, she paused, watching behind, just out of sight. She expected to see the man enter after her. However, after a couple of moments, nobody appeared.

Helen fought the urge to walk back; there was every chance the potential stalker had expected her to do this and was now waiting on the street, watching both entrances. She'd possibly even trapped herself in the process.

Cursing her stupidity, she followed the path around; to her right was a high, brick wall, stained and darkened by years of London life, the glow from a gas lamp in the middle the only light, but she wasn't looking at it. Instead, she was already watching the road ahead, as it turned left, back out into the lane.

What if he'd second-guessed her and was down the road?

Helen started rummaging through her bag now, as running was possibly not even an option anymore. She needed a weapon. Pulling out a small can of deodorant, she weighed it in her hand. It was half-full, enough to spray into a face. It wasn't mace, though, or any kind of pepper spray; somehow, she needed to *weaponise* it.

In the bottom of her handbag was a cheap plastic lighter; a throwback to the days when she used to smoke. She hadn't for over a year now, but the lighter had never left the bag. Helen remembered a TV show she'd seen, where someone had used a spray deodorant as a flamethrower, the lighter creating a jet of flame that was short, but effective. Holding it up, Helen wondered whether she was about to burn herself badly by doing this, but at the same time felt this could still be a better result than what was waiting for her.

What was waiting for you. Listen to yourself.

Helen had to chuckle at the thought; she didn't even know if the man *was* following her. And what if he did fancy her? What if he was too shy to say anything? This poor bugger was about to lose his eyebrows because he didn't have the balls to speak to—

She stopped as she turned into the last part of Amen Court's three roadways.

There, at the end of the street, only ten metres away, was the blond man.

'Are you alright?' he shouted down at her.

'*Am I alright?*' Helen couldn't help but be incredulous at this. 'Am *I* alright? *You're* the one following me!'

The man paused at this, thrown by the accusation. Then, seeing the lighter and can of spray in Helen's hands, he held up his own hands in a sudden, horrified realisation.

'Oh, God, no,' he said, walking towards her. 'I'm sorry, I didn't realise you hadn't recognised me. I'm Taylor, Jodie's brother.'

Helen didn't know a Jodie, and she sure as hell didn't know a Taylor.

'I don't know who you are,' she said. 'Stay back.'

The man, now identified as Taylor, carried on towards her, slowly, hands raised.

'We met at the Greenwich thing!' he protested. 'We—well, surely you can't forget how we—'

He stopped, now only a couple of paces from Helen.

'Oh God,' he whispered. 'You're not Roisin.'

'No, I'm not Ro-*sheen*,' Helen replied, mimicking the way Taylor had spoken the name; part in irritation, but also with a little amusement at the situation. Or, more accurately, amusement at the now obviously uncomfortable and reddening Taylor.

'I'm so sorry,' he mumbled now, his hands lowering. 'I saw you at the talk and I thought you were—I mean, *she* was blanking me.'

'So you thought you'd follow me?'

'You kept looking back, I thought it was a game. I thought you—*she*—wanted...' Taylor trailed off as he realised the hole he was digging was now way above his head.

'You thought you'd stalk a woman who, from the sounds of things, wanted to avoid you.'

'I—no, *you* wanted to avoid me. I don't know about Roisin.'

'Well, here's a clue,' Helen hissed. 'Maybe don't stalk her next time you meet.'

Taylor nodded, still red from the embarrassment of the moment.

'Now I see you close though, I can see you're not her,' he tried a small smile. 'You're—'

'Older?' Helen meant it as a joke, but it came out bitter.

Taylor shook his head at this.

'I was going to say more attractive,' he continued, and Helen now inwardly groaned.

He was trying it on.

But, at the back of her mind, Helen thought *why not? He's a good-looking man, and you have the upper ground here.*

Because he's like half your age.

Helen remembered something about sexual peaks and flushed at the thought, but before she could reply to the compliment, Taylor's expression changed, becoming more urgent, more intense, and he darted forward, grasping at her arm.

It was a knee-jerk reaction. As he moved in, Helen instinctively flicked the lighter, pressing down on the cap of the deodorant as she did so, the two items creating a microsecond of flame that flashed out in the night, engulfing Taylor's face as he yelped, staggering back. The flame hadn't been long enough to cause any damage, but Helen hoped it'd been enough to dissuade the young man from trying that again. Maybe singe an eyebrow hair or two, even.

'Are you *insane?*' he hissed.

'You were grabbing me!' Helen replied, confused at his angry response, and now worried she'd misread the situation.

In reply, Taylor pointed angrily behind her.

'I was pulling you away from *that!*' he snapped, and Helen glanced around momentarily to see what he pointed at, worried still this was a lure, something to take her attention away.

Behind her, against the wall and dangling down from the gas lamp attached to it, was a shape in the darkness, hanging from what looked to be a rope of some kind. It took Helen a moment to realise what it was.

A man.

'How did you miss it?' Taylor asked, once more grabbing Helen, pulling her back, as if worried the hanged man would leap up and attack. 'You literally walked past it.'

'I was too busy watching for you,' Helen replied, half accusingly, but distracted as she allowed herself to be moved. 'Is that—'

'Yeah,' Taylor looked around the windows of the Court now, moving towards the body. 'Call the police.'

'We should call an ambulance,' Helen wavered. 'He might need—'

'What this guy needs is a morgue,' Taylor commented, now close enough to examine the body. It was that of a middle-aged man, maybe in his late fifties or early sixties. He had shaved, balding hair, the stubble no more than a couple of days' worth, and there were a couple of obvious shaving cuts on the side, most likely from where the man had shaved himself, possibly with a shaking hand. He wore a cotton bomber jacket, cheap and navy blue, black jeans and what looked like unbranded trainers. He was average in weight; his neck was bunched up because of the rope, but he looked to be slimmer than he appeared here. His eyes were open still, and half rolled up into his head, his tongue out and hanging to his side.

'Urgh,' Taylor pinched his nose. 'He's pissed himself. Or worse. The black jeans hid it.'

'What's that around his neck?' Helen asked, pointing at what looked to be a piece of card, a long piece of string tied to two corners, and looped around his neck behind the noose.

Taylor squinted up.

'It says "justice",' he whispered, looking back at Helen.

'Justice for what?'

'Justice for something that isn't our concern,' Taylor waved at her. 'Police.'

Helen nodded, finally pulling out her phone and dialling 999. She'd half expected to be making this call earlier, but for other reasons.

And, as Taylor examined the body closer, wincing at the smell, Helen phoned the police.

1

DINNER DATED

Declan Walsh had found himself in a variety of life or death situations in the year he'd been stationed at the Temple Inn, or "Last Chance Saloon" Command Unit, within the City of London's boundaries, but this was by far one of the most excruciating ones so far, he had to admit.

Leaning back in his chair and loosening his tie, he forced a smile as he looked across the table towards the teal-coloured booth facing him. Billy Fitzwarren was, as ever on point, clothes wise; his deep blue three-piece suit was obviously fitted at great expense, the paisley shirt worth more than Declan's suit in total, and the gold-flecked tie likely flecked with actual gold.

Beside him was Andrade Estrada, his black hair tousled to perfection, his black suit and tie making him look more like a model on his lunch break than an undertaker. Or, at least, a *really* sexy undertaker.

Finally, opposite Andrade was Anjli Kapoor, still in her workwear, which in this instance was a navy blue suit and white blouse, her black hair pulled back into a ponytail, a minimal amount of makeup placed on hurriedly before arriving.

Currently, Billy was telling a story of how he and Andrade met, possibly for the second time that evening, and definitely for the fifth or sixth time since they'd started dating.

'That's a great story,' Declan said when Billy eventually finished, still looking at Anjli, beside him, almost able to mimic it word for word by now. 'Superb.'

Anjli, in her defence, seemed happier to be there than Declan was, and sipped at a red wine slowly, before replying.

'Gets better every time we hear it,' she nodded. 'Can't wait until the next time.'

Billy, sitting across from Declan, glanced at her, his face falling as she spoke.

'I've told you the story before?' he asked in mild, almost hurt surprise.

'In fairness,' Declan interrupted, nodding over to Andrade as he continued talking to Billy, 'You met Andrade during an investigation, you told us about the meeting in the briefing, and it became an item of public and police record, so telling us the "how we met" story is always going to suffer by repetition.'

Billy grinned.

'Yeah, I forget it was in a briefing,' he said as he looked back at Andrade, now reaching for Billy's hand and giving it a squeeze. 'I can't even believe it's been a month.'

And I can't believe we've just heard the story for a fifth time, Declan thought to himself as he scanned his eye around the restaurant, urgently looking for the waiter.

They had planned it for weeks; the first meeting of Billy's new beau, but Declan had assumed he'd just turn up to a pub gathering, or they'd walk into the office one day and Andrade would be sitting on the desk, talking to Billy.

Declan hadn't even considered that this simple act of connection would have to be performed during a *double date*, interspersed between small talk and conversational oneupmanship.

Not that Declan was uncomfortable with dates; he'd been with Anjli Kapoor for a couple of months now, and they'd been on several during that time. But, having been housemates before they became a couple, Declan and Anjli weren't that fussed about them.

At least, he *hoped* Anjli hadn't been fussed about them.

Now, he was wondering whether Anjli *had* been fussed about them, maybe *had* wanted more dates, and maybe he'd let her down.

And now everyone was watching him.

'Sorry?' he sheepishly replied.

'You zoned out,' Anjli replied, hiding a smile.

'Oh, sorry. I was worrying about Jess.'

It was a boilerplate answer; his daughter, now sixteen and starting her A' Levels in a couple of weeks, wasn't in any trouble at all, but they didn't know that.

'Oh?' Anjli looked concerned. 'Is she okay?'

Shit. Anjli would, of course, know that.

'Yeah, just being a father,' Declan waved a hand. 'And we're not here to talk about me, we're here to talk about these two.'

Billy flushed.

'We were just talking about how this is long overdue,' he said. 'You know, how we never go out.'

Declan went to reply, to contradict this statement, reminding Billy that they always had dinners, usually because their cases went into the night and a quick meal around the corner was often the best they could get, when he felt a slight tap on his shin from Anjli, and knew this was her reminder that as far as Andrade was concerned, they *didn't* all meet up. There was a reason it'd taken a month for them to get to this dinner, and Billy had claimed it was because of workload.

'Yes,' he replied, stone faced. 'We should go out more. Damn our constant and unending workload. That keeps us in the office. All the time.'

To be honest, Declan was also feeling a little overwhelmed; they were eating at *The Ivy Asia*, an opulent restaurant on New Change, across the road from St Paul's Cathedral, and one that genuinely felt out of Declan's comfort zone.

The incredible night view aside, intricately painted Chinese dragons snaked their way across the ceiling, as the floor beneath them was created from what looked to be shards of illuminated jade. And, to add more pressure, a statue, or rather a fully armoured mannequin of what Declan assumed was a Samurai warrior, faced him from across the floor, as if daring him to say anything.

And it wasn't just the decor; while struggling with his chopsticks, Declan had noticed a couple of television actors in the restaurant. The original Ivy was a known haunt for celebrities, and it seemed this carried on elsewhere.

The place wasn't cheap, but the food had been excellent. Declan was dreading the bill. The starters had cost almost twenty pounds alone, the main course further above that, and the wines Billy had chosen were from a list that began with three-figure numbers.

'There's a chap over there,' he whispered, indicating a

balding man with ginger hair. 'He's really familiar. I'm sure we've been on a case together, but I don't want to say hello until I can work out what case it was.'

Anjli looked over at the man, and before she could stop herself, snorted out a loud laugh. As several of the other diners glanced across at her, she stifled another snort, looking back at the table.

'He plays a copper on TV,' she said. 'Maybe you were going on a TV case together?'

Declan groaned.

'That'll be it,' he replied.

'Maybe he'll want to go on a case with you, though?' Anjli, finding a loose thread here, was pulling on it with glee. 'Maybe you could punch a priest, or disrupt Parliament...'

'The priest was over a year ago,' Declan smiled back, but it didn't reach the eyes. 'And Parliament probably won't let me back in, now Charles bloody Baker is in charge—'

He stopped, looking over at Andrade, now staring at his food, but obviously listening intently. This had been one reason for the delay in double dating, as Andrade had first approached Billy a few weeks earlier on the orders of his higher-ups at the Colombian Embassy; they wanted someone with Charles Baker's ear, now that he was Prime Minister, and thought the City of Police Unit that had saved his life, and the Detective Inspector seen with him on TV would be a good place to start.

It didn't take long for them to realise Baker didn't really want to be seen with the Last Chance Saloon, especially as they had more dirt on him than he had on them, and most likely went for alternative options.

Luckily, Andrade was able to bypass any issues with this, and kept seeing Billy after his "mission" was dropped.

Declan had worried about this, his years in the Royal Military Police giving him a cynical view on such connections, but even though he still had his suspicions, and Monroe also felt the same way, when looking at Billy and Andrade together, the two of them seemed happy enough.

'Anyway,' he changed the subject again. 'How are things for you two?'

'Oh, we can't complain,' Billy glanced across shyly at Andrade.

'And the sex is absolutely—' Andrade began, but was interrupted by Anjli, coughing suddenly.

'Sorry,' she said, grasping for her glass of water. 'I think the carrot went down the wrong way—*what?*'

The question was aimed at Andrade and Billy who, while she'd spoken, had both broken out in laughter. As they calmed down, Billy pulled a crisp and obviously prepared earlier ten-pound-note out of his pocket, passing it to his boyfriend.

'You win,' he said graciously, before looking back at Declan. 'I'd bet that you'd be the one to get embarrassed first if we talked about sex, but Andrade reckoned Anjli was more innocent than she made out to be.'

'Oh, they're doing fine,' Declan patted Anjli's hand. 'They're making bets on us. The only thing likely to break them apart right now—'

'Is a sudden *fatality*,' Anjli hissed, more embarrassed than angry, gripping a chopstick with a force not usually used with kitchen utensils of such a style, following this up with a chuckle, shaking her head.

'Bastards.'

'Hey, we don't get to share our work day together,' Billy shrugged. 'We have to make amusement when we can.'

'If it makes you feel better, your boss, Mister Monroe? He was the one to interrupt when we did the same thing to him and Doctor Marcos,' Andrade smiled.

'Yeah, not much fazes Rosanna Marcos,' Declan nodded, before going 'wait, when did you see them?'

'Two weeks ago,' Billy leaned back in his chair, expecting a row. 'We offered you a date before, but you couldn't make it. Not our fault you're more popular than Monroe.'

He paled as he realised what he'd said.

'Although don't tell him I said that.'

'As long as you remember to invite De'Geer and Davey at some point,' Declan laughed, and once more found himself staring at blank faces. 'Now what?'

'De'Geer and Davey aren't a thing,' Anjli said. 'They had a couple of dates, but it fizzled out ages ago.'

'So why's he always hanging around with her?' Declan was confused.

'Because he wants to be a forensic officer?' Anjli smiled as she replied. 'I mean, he's been doing night courses for over six months.'

'I didn't realise it hadn't worked out,' Declan shook his head. The unrequited love for DC Joanne Davey that PC Morten De'Geer had begun the moment he met her in Hurley, while they hunted the *Red Reaper*.

'Davey is a little busy anyway,' Billy shrugged. 'What with following Marcos around, and the therapy sessions—'

'Therapy sessions?' Declan raised an eyebrow at this. 'I know we're hard to work with, but I didn't think *she'd* need to seek help?'

Billy's face took on a more serious expression.

'I don't know what it's for, most likely all the bloody

bodies she works with. And by that I mean bloody as an expletive, not that the bodies are all, you know, icky.'

'How do you know she has therapy then, if she hasn't told you about it?'

'I was working late last week, and she brought him around,' Billy replied. 'Giving him a bit of a tour before they went to one of the interview rooms.'

'Interview rooms?'

Billy shrugged.

'I got the impression she's so busy, he has to come to her for the sessions,' he explained. 'And I'm guessing forensics isn't the best place to do something personal like that. So, they used one of the interview rooms, as it was quiet, and at that time of the night could be undisturbed. I think she wanted to use the briefing room, but was aware I'd see them through the glass.'

He considered this.

'Nice guy, didn't say much, explained he was a doctor and there in a professional capacity but didn't want to know anything about anyone, then followed Davey upstairs.'

'He probably didn't want to speak to anyone who could alter his diagnosis of Davey,' Declan suggested.

'Oh yes? And you're an expert on this, are you?' Anjli smiled.

'Lizzie sent Jess to therapy after the *Red Reaper* case,' Declan replied. 'Only a couple of sessions, just to be sure, but she, the therapist, didn't want anyone around who could affect the sessions.'

'And your then-pissed-off ex-wife would definitely affect those sessions,' Anjli nodded. 'Especially as she'd banned you from seeing Jess at the time.'

Declan thought back to the start of the year. When his

daughter had almost been murdered by a serial killer, Liz had overreacted, in Jess' words, banning Declan from being near his daughter. It took weeks to calm her back down, and in the end it was the advice of a murderer, waiting for trial, that convinced her to allow Declan access again, pointing out that Jess was going to follow in his footsteps, no matter what she tried.

Declan felt a twinge of guilt; this was the first time he'd thought of ex-DI Theresa Martinez in a while. He made a mental note to check in on her, and another mental note not to tell Anjli; she already knew Declan had a crush on Martinez from years earlier.

'Anyway,' he said, desperately trying to change the subject. 'We were talking about De'Geer, and the fact Davey wasn't interested in his advances.'

'Don't worry, I know someone who'd soothe his brow,' Billy winked. 'And by soothing his brow, I mean—'

'We all know what you mean,' Declan was the one to interrupt this time. 'And it has to be either that coroner we met during the Kelsey case, or—'

He stopped.

'Bloody hell, it's PC Cooper, isn't it?'

Anjli grinned.

'We like to call it "Coopergeer",' she said. 'You know, like "Bennifer."'

Declan frowned.

'But that's Ben Affleck and J-Lo,' he replied. 'It's the first names. Ben and Jennifer. We'd have to call it Morten and...'

He trailed off.

'What the bloody hell is Cooper's first name?' he asked.

'You don't know her first name?' Anjli was amused at this. 'She's been here since May and you...'

She also trailed off as realisation struck her.

'Shit.'

Billy shook his head at both of them.

'Disgusting,' he replied, as if appalled by this. 'She's made you mugs of teas and everything.'

'Go on then, what is it?' Declan folded his arms.

'Well, I know it starts with an *E*,' Billy pulled his phone out.

'Oh, no, we're not having you google her or anything,' Anjli took the phone away, placing it onto the table. 'Come on, cyber-king, what's her name?'

Billy opened and shut his mouth twice, as if hoping the action would kick-start his brain into giving an answer.

'Esme,' Andrade replied, looking a little sheepish as he did so. 'Short for Esmerelda.'

Everyone now looked at the Colombian diplomat as he shuffled uncomfortably in his chair.

'And you know this because...?' Declan started, the fun part of the conversation over, and his more serious, *detective* voice now. He really didn't want to hear the answer he expected.

Because I am a spy, of course, and I have dossiers on all of you.

'Because I met her once, and I asked her,' Andrade replied. 'She was the officer on the front desk when I first arrived at Temple Inn, the night I met Billy.'

The moment now defused, and his cynical, overactive imagination sated for the moment, Declan chuckled as he shook his head.

'A man who only met her once knows more about PC Esme Cooper than we do,' he said. 'Some detectives we are.'

'If it makes you feel better, your commanding officer,

Monroe? He said he believed I was a spy,' Andrade smiled. 'And spies know all sorts of stuff.'

'They also don't tell people they're spies,' Billy replied.

'And you know this how?'

'We know a few,' Declan said cryptically. He wasn't going to mention Whitehall's *Section D* or their connection to the Last Chance Saloon, but he couldn't help the small gloat.

Andrade simply nodded at this.

'I am impressed,' he said, looking back at Billy. 'He impresses me. Maybe I should date him instead?'

'Get in line,' Anjli growled, and Declan honestly couldn't tell whether or not she was serious, until the table erupted into laughter.

Declan *hated* these sorts of meals. And, he made a quiet prayer to St Jude, the patron Saint of policemen, for some way to get out of this.

Nothing happened.

Which wasn't surprising, as Declan wasn't sure if St Jude even was the patron Saint of police; it'd been mentioned by Sean Connery in the Kevin Costner movie *The Untouchables*, but someone had told him years later that St Michael the Archangel was the patron Saint of police, and St Jude was only the representative for Chicago.

But, Sean Connery said it in the film and that made it cooler—

Declan was brought back to the table as Billy's phone, face down on the table from where Anjli had placed it, buzzed with a message. A few seconds later, both Anjli and Declan's phones buzzed as well.

Declan pulled his phone out while looking nervously at Anjli. There was every chance this was a simple group chat, but it was incredibly well timed, considering his prayer.

Glancing at the phone's screen, he read the message. It was from Monroe.

Sorry to kill your dinner plans but you're needed. Amen Court. Now.

'Amen Court?' Anjli asked. 'You got the same message?'

Declan nodded, Billy too.

'I have a little more,' Billy replied, showing his message. 'I'm off to man the monitors at base. Looks like I'm more use there than on the ground with you guys and that miserable bloody Scot.'

'That and you like your chair more,' Declan laughed. Billy wasn't wrong, though; Monroe could be the most miserable of Scots when he wanted to be.

'I'm so sorry,' Billy said as he turned to Andrade. 'We have to cut this short.'

'It's okay, you can make it up to me,' Andrade leaned in, kissing Billy. 'We always knew this was the life.'

Billy waved for the bill, stopping Declan as he went to grab his own wallet.

'On me,' he said as he passed a solid metal credit card to the waiter. Declan didn't even want to know how much a metal card like that cost, and simply nodded a thanks in reply.

'Next time's on me,' he said, instantly regretting it.

'Amen Court,' Anjli was checking her phone's map app. 'I know that place. It's just off St Paul's, on the other side of us. I met John Gale there once, when we were investigating the murder at Greenwich.'

'Did you tell Monroe we were coming here?' Declan rose from the table, pulling his jacket on.

'Yes,' Billy was doing the same. 'We're a five-minute walk away. If we don't go, he'll probably come here.'

'Well, whatever he needs us for, let's not bring it inside,' Declan replied as, shaking Andrade's hand farewell, and with Anjli and Billy following, he went to work.

2

AMEN CAUGHT

DECLAN HAD BEEN RIGHT; THE WALK TO THE CRIME SCENE HAD been just under five minutes from exiting the restaurant. Billy had hailed down and then disappeared in a taxi, aiming for Temple Inn, a mile to the west, and Andrade had grabbed his own ride back, an Uber that had been suspiciously waiting for him around the corner.

That, or he'd ordered the car the moment the texts arrived, which was far more likely. Stop thinking he's a spy, Declan.

The single road entrance to Amen Court was closed to traffic, with crime tape across both the road and entrance through the arches, and Declan could see the reflected blue flashing lights before they even reached the turning. It wasn't a full-on circus yet, though; PC Cooper manned the tape barrier, with DCI Alex Monroe beside her, stroking his white goatee with a blue, latex-gloved hand as they talked. Usually the first on scene was a Sergeant, but the Last Chance Saloon never played by the rules.

Stopping, Monroe nodded at Declan and Anjli as they approached.

'Guv,' Declan said to him as they stopped beside the tape, now nodding at Cooper in greeting. 'Esme.'

Cooper frowned at the use of her first name.

'Sir?'

'I was just pointing out that I knew your name,' Declan, unsure why he'd named her as such, began floundering. 'You know, I didn't want you to think you were nothing more than a nameless number or rank to us. We know all about you.'

'Uh, thank you, sir?' Cooper replied uncertainly as Monroe raised the tape, allowing Declan and Anjli to pass under.

'For God's sake, laddie, stop terrifying the poor girl and come with me,' he said, leading them down the street.

'I wasn't terrifying her,' Declan protested, looking to Anjli for support. 'I wasn't, was I?'

'You quite literally did the "I know your name and where you live" speech that villains do to people they're about to kill, Or Liam Neeson uses when he's about to kill a ton of baddies,' she replied with a smile, turning to Monroe. 'You should be proud of the boy. He only learned her name tonight.'

'What, and you knew it?' Declan laughed. 'Even Billy only knew it began with an E.'

'Jesus, how many months has she been with us?' Monroe shook his head in disgust. 'How many teas has she made you both in briefings?'

'And *you* knew her name?' Declan retorted.

'Esmerelda?' Monroe smiled. 'Course I did, son. I signed her transfer papers. But I never threatened the wee bairn when I did it.'

As if realising Declan was still dressed for work at this

time of night, Monroe's smile branched into a wide, mischievous grin.

'So, how was your swanky dinner in your swanky restaurant with Billy and the swanky spy?'

'Shortened,' Declan muttered in response. 'And because of your cryptic messages, we still don't know why it was.'

'Aye, I didn't want the spy to know anything about it. Force of habit.'

'Do you really think he's a spy?' Anjli frowned. 'I mean, he's a foreign diplomat—'

'Spy,' Monroe replied with certainty, but the hint of a smile around his lips showed he wasn't too fussed about his revelation. 'Anyway, I called you here for this.'

By now they'd reached the curve in the road, and in front of them rose a giant, old-brick wall, with forensic examiners in their white PPE suits examining a gas lamp in the middle of it. On the other side of the road was a small car park, a Jaguar currently taking one of the two spaces, and a tiny, postage-stamp sized piece of grass, with a slide and children's swing on it.

Doctor Marcos, in her custom-fitting grey suit, looked up at their arrival, pulling off her hood and mask as she approached.

'Middle-aged, balding man found hanged from that lamp,' she said, pointing back at it as she did so. 'No visible signs of struggle, although we'll know better when I do the autopsy. The body's been taken down now, and I'll be joining it at Temple Inn soon.'

'So it's a suicide?' Declan frowned. 'Although if it was, I wouldn't expect so many CSI around.'

He looked at Monroe, who stared back innocently.

'Or expect to be called out from a double date.'

'Oh, you didn't,' Doctor Marcos glared at Monroe. 'You could at least have let them finish.'

'I don't make the rules,' Monroe placed an innocent hand to his chest.

'Could be a suicide, but it's unlikely,' ignoring the DCI now, Doctor Marcos motioned to a larger CSI officer in full PPE, waving him over and pointing to bring a clear evidence bag with him. As he approached, pulling off his hood to reveal his blond hair, Declan realised this was PC De'Geer, the unit's resident Viking, which should have been obvious because of his height. In his hand, held in the bag, was a narrow sheet of cardboard. And scrawled on it in marker pen was one word.

Justice

'Yeah, apart from no note, this was a bit of a giveaway,' Doctor Marcos added. 'And, before you ask why such a board would have been around the man's neck, we know the identity of the victim. It's Jacob Spears.'

Declan looked back up at Doctor Marcos at this.

'The *Essex Ripper*?' he said, surprised. 'He's in prison.'

'He was, until two months back,' Monroe took the baggie in his latex gloves and peered down at it. 'He was charged with the murders of three missing girls, which gained him the nickname by the press, but he could only be connected to one of them, and as such, he was only convicted for the murder of Anna Callahan. He got twenty years for it, did fifteen, came out in late June.'

Declan looked around the courtyard area. He was

surrounded on three sides by red-brick residential buildings, the courtyard interspersed with tall trees, and behind the old brick wall where the lamp post was attached, he could see the tall, white walls of the Old Bailey.

'So this is a vigilante killing,' he mused. 'But why here?'

'Because that's Newgate,' Anjli pointed at the wall. 'Or, rather, it's the only surviving wall of it. John Gale pointed at this street when I met him during the Greenwich case, and said "*you follow that around, and you walk beside one of the few remaining walls of Newgate Prison*".'

'I thought Newgate was torn down and the Old Bailey replaced it?' Declan walked over and touched the brickwork. He didn't know why he did this; he almost expected to gain some kind of psychic connection to the onetime prison.

'DS Kapoor's right,' De'Geer, in full professional mode, added. 'When they demolished the prison, they kept this wall up, as it was once a Roman wall, as shown by the difference in brickwork from lower to upper wall, and it was actually the boundary of the Newgate graveyard. In fact, on the other side of this was a passage known as "Dead Man's Walk", where the condemned would be taken to be hanged.'

He leant in closer.

'This is also where the *black dog of Newgate* is seen,' he whispered.

'Black dog of what?' Anjli, ever the skeptic, laughed.

De'Geer, not realising he was being mocked, continued.

'Well, during a famine in the reign of King Henry the Third, a scholar was incarcerated in Newgate,' he began. 'Now, there's debate if he was a scholar, or if he was a prisoner called Schoiler—'

'Keep to the dog bit please, or we'll be here all night,' Doctor Marcos interrupted, although her eyes sparkled with interest.

Declan knew Doctor Marcos liked a good ghost story, and Billy had once returned to the office white faced, after she'd told him a rather gruesome one while performing an autopsy.

'Yes, of course,' De'Geer nodded. 'Anyway, there was a famine, as I said, and the prisoners were starving and resorted to cannibalism. Basically, they *ate* the new arrival. But the guilt at this started to build, and eventually manifested into appearances of a fierce black dog patrolling this very wall, which they believed was the spirit of the prisoner, looking for revenge. It reportedly killed and ate those responsible one by one, until the last survivors, driven mad by fear, broke out and escaped. But, wherever they went, or tried to hide, it followed them, and killed them all.'

He pointed at the wall.

'Even now, a mysterious black shape is often seen creeping along the high wall,' he finished. 'Sightings of this shape have never been clear enough for its physical form to be identified, though.'

'So it could be a cat,' Anjli replied.

'Well, yes.'

'Bit of a rubbish ghost dog, if it can be mistaken as a cat,' Anjli continued, deliberately needling De'Geer, who, deflated, stepped back.

'So, dodgy ghost stories aside, this is the closest you can get to the original gallows, without actually going into the Old Bailey, right?' Declan interjected. 'I can see why you'd hang a criminal here, or whatever Spears was classed as.'

'True, although Spears wasn't hanged here,' Doctor Marcos, no longer enthralled by the ghost story, added.

At the confused expressions now facing her, she sighed.

'I said he was *found* hanged from that lamp, not that he

was hanged,' she explained. 'You really need to listen when I show my genius. We found no oblique or partial ligature marks above the thyroid cartilage, and there were no petechial haemorrhages in the conjunctiva of the eyes and eyelids. These would be usual in such a death.'

'So he was brought here after he died, and strung up?' Anjli whistled. 'That's not passion killing or spur of the moment. That's pre-meditated.'

Declan nodded at this. For someone to kill Jacob Spears and bring him here, to the place where murderers were executed was a definite statement.

'Do we know the cause of death, then?'

'Not as yet, but give me the night and I'll have something more tangible in the morning,' Doctor Marcos replied, and Declan could tell she was irritated at not being able to give a solid answer.

'I don't see any CCTV,' he muttered, looking around once more. Monroe shook his head at this.

'Aye, the trees don't really help, and they aimed the cameras at the car parking spaces and the houses rather than a tatty old wall at the back,' he replied. 'That's why I sent the boy back to Temple Inn to see if he can pick up anything on the surrounding streets.'

Declan made an approving *hmm* as he watched the forensics testing the ground around the lamp.

'I thought DC Davey would have jumped at the chance of being here,' he said matter-of-factly. 'Has she gone back with the body?'

'Joanne's not involved on this case,' Doctor Marcos explained softly. 'She recused herself before we could bring her in.'

Declan stopped. That Doctor Marcos had used Davey's first name was not wasted on him.

'What don't I know?' he asked.

'What don't *we* know,' Anjli added. 'Why can't she work the case? Is this to do with the therapy she's having?'

Doctor Marcos looked over at De'Geer, and nodded slightly, as if giving him permission to speak.

'The second victim of Jacob Spears, one of the two they couldn't pin on him, was Lorraine Davey,' De'Geer explained. 'Joanne Davey's older sister. It's what made her go into forensics in the first place; she wanted to prove he was the killer.'

'Christ,' Anjli groaned. 'I didn't know.'

'None of us did,' Monroe replied.

'I did,' Doctor Marcos added.

'None of us, except for Doctor Marcos, and probably bloody De'Geer, did,' Monroe quickly adapted his statement. 'Apparently, she's been in private therapy, on and off, for years because of it, which is probably what you're talking about. But that aside, it was felt that in the interests of the case, having Davey investigate the death of her sister's alleged killer wasn't in good taste.'

'We've done it before, though,' Declan replied. 'I hunted my parent's killers, and you hunted down your brother's—'

'Aye, and I almost lost my job for it,' Monroe snapped. 'And as for you, we were investigating a *new* murder when you had Whitehall spooks tell you the Red Reaper killed your parents.'

Declan paused, taking a long breath.

Monroe was right.

'So we're shorthanded on the forensics side,' he replied. 'This team—'

'Are borrowed,' Doctor Marcos waved at them. 'As is

De'Geer. He's been doing classes, and his on-the-job experience is second to none, mainly as he's been following me, so he'll be able to do most of what Davey does tonight.'

Nodding agreement at this, Declan stretched out his back, looking around at the windows that peered over the court.

'Who called it in?' he eventually asked.

'A young woman named Helen Crome,' Monroe read from his notebook.

'Resident?'

'No, passing through,' Monroe looked back at Declan. 'Apparently, there was some kind of confusion involving someone following her, and she took the path down here to confirm her suspicions.'

'And was she correct?' now it was Anjli's turn to ask.

'Yes and no,' Monroe shrugged. 'The man was identified as Taylor Lowell, and he had apparently believed Helen was a friend of his sister's named Roisin.'

'So he followed her?'

'He thought she was playing a game.'

'That's still not a cool thing to do,' Anjli muttered.

'Aye, I think he's realising that now, especially when the uniforms heard about it,' Monroe chuckled. 'We were quite insistent he called his sister so we could have a wee chat to her about this, and confirm his story. She was most unimpressed. Apparently he and this Roisin had a one-night stand a year back, she told him it was a mistake, and they never saw each other again.'

'Unrequited love,' Anjli almost shuddered as she spoke. 'Did they see any vehicles?'

'No, just the body,' Monroe looked back at the gaslight.

'And from what they said, Helen hadn't even realised it was a body.'

'So we have a body placed here before what, nine-thirty?' Anjli asked.

'The call came in at nine-fifteen, and apparently there was nothing there at seven, as one resident parked up just over there,' Monroe pointed at the expensive-looking Jaguar. 'He would have been staring directly at it.'

'One resident said she saw a white van near the wall, but couldn't remember the time,' De'Geer added. 'Said it was only around a couple of minutes, and she assumed it was a delivery. They get a few around here.'

'So a white van arrives, someone gets out, hangs up Spears and leaves,' Declan was visualising the scene as he walked back to the lamp. 'That's difficult for one man to do. It has to be a team effort.'

'There's a CCTV camera up there,' Anjli was looking up the street she'd walked down, working out an invisible line from the camera lens as she too now paced the courtyard. 'If the van pulled up against the wall, we might have a partial from when it left the area. We might even have a windscreen view.'

'Aye, that'd be nice,' Monroe followed her gaze. 'We noted it earlier on, though, and the details were sent to Bullman, who's back at base. Hopefully, Billy can get something from that.'

'Maybe we can find out where Spears was over the last couple of days, Sarge?' De'Geer said to Anjli, while mainly asking the group. 'Perhaps if we can find his last moments, we can work out where he could have ended up.'

He looked at the remnants of rope hanging from the lamppost.

'I mean, before he ended up here,' he added sheepishly.

'We'll know more once we get the autopsy results,' Monroe looked at Doctor Marcos. 'With luck, we'll be able to access his phone records too, not that his phone was on him.'

'Is it still on?' Anjli pulled her own phone out.

'Already tried,' Doctor Marcos shook her head. 'Turned off, goes straight to voicemail. Billy's working out when it was last on, and where it was pinging, too.'

'Right then,' Monroe decided. 'Until we know what happened to Spears, we can't move on to anything there. I'll get Cooper—that's *Esme*, Declan—and the uniforms to finish up with the locals, see if anyone saw something. Once Billy has something more on this white van, we might be able to follow up there, too.'

'What do you need us to do?' Declan asked, now wondering whether the whole angle of bringing him and Anjli to the crime scene had actually been purely to spoil their date night.

At this, Monroe grimaced.

'Aye, I've got a shite job for you,' he muttered. 'And if it makes you feel better, I'm doing it too.'

He pointed up the street where cameramen were already setting up.

'Within a couple of hours, the press will work out who's been left here,' he said. 'And once that happens, Jacob Spears' name will be everywhere.'

'You need us to call the families,' Declan nodded. 'We need to give them advanced warning.'

'Not only that, but we need to arrange for them to find some time to have wee chats with us,' Monroe replied. 'Because currently, we have a dead man who was accused of killing three bairns, and only went to prison for one. Which means two families never got their pound of flesh, and one family might not think they got *enough*.'

'You think it could be the families who did this?' De'Geer sounded surprised.

Monroe looked back at De'Geer.

'You know Davey well,' he said. 'She ever talk about this?'

'Never,' De'Geer replied. 'I didn't even know until about a month or so back, when she met her therapist at the Unit. I asked her what was going on, she explained about the recent therapy with Doctor Penhaligon, and why it was happening.'

'She hadn't been doing therapy before that?'

'No, Guv. She did back when—well, it happened, but she'd been triggered, just after Vauxhall and that whole thing with Johnny Lucas, I think, and decided to seek help.'

'I wonder what triggered her?' Anjli was curious as to this.

De'Geer shrugged, uncomfortable at being the centre of attention.

'I think she was approached, Sarge,' he explained. 'A book, or a show, or something's being made and Spear's part of it. I believe they came to her asking for the family's permission to take part. You know, a talking head.'

'That's incredibly convenient,' Declan added. 'To be doing something on Spears right when he dies. We should look into that, too.'

'You can ask Davey about it when you interview her tomorrow,' Monroe suggested.

At this, Declan raised his eyebrows in surprise.

'You think she's a suspect?'

Monroe leant in, lowering his voice, as if worried the press at the entrance had some kind of super microphone, to catch his voice.

'Laddie, currently I think they're all suspects,' he said. 'Because I know what I'd do in their place, and so do you.'

Declan nodded at this, considering the words. When he'd caught his parents' killer, he'd not arrested them or placed handcuffs upon their wrists. He'd had them picked up by a Security Service's special op team and placed in an unknown black-ops site, left to rot forever.

And it had taken everything he had to do that, rather than commit murder himself.

'Let's get some numbers and make some calls,' he said, looking around. 'Although perhaps we could do it at the office, rather than here? The place gives me the creeps.'

'That's the Black Dog,' De'Geer nodded wisely.

'I told you, it's nothing more than a pissed off cat,' Anjli smirked.

'A pissed off cat can still give you problems,' Declan muttered. 'Come on, let's go make some calls.'

And with that decided, Declan, Anjli and Monroe left Doctor Marcos and De'Geer to their forensics, and walked out of the court, leaving the high Roman wall that once held Newgate Prison and graveyard within, to the night.

This wasn't the time to consider stories of murder from hundreds of years ago.

There was a far more modern murder to solve.

3

DARK BEFORE THE DAWN

BILLY HADN'T GONE HOME WITH THE OTHERS AFTER THEY'D made the phone calls; instead, he'd scrolled through the footage, to see what he could find. And, while that was happening, he pulled out his phone, video calling Andrade.

Who was in bed, shirtless, when he answered.

'Shit, sorry,' Billy said. 'I forgot it was late.'

'Your hours are so strange, you forget normal people sleep when it is dark and work when it is light.'

'I thought you partied when it was dark?' Billy grinned.

Andrade returned the smile.

'Do I look like I'm partying right now?' he mock-moaned. 'I am alone, and mourning the loss of my lovely, hot—'

'Okay,' Billy blushed. 'I don't think we should carry on this conversation while I'm at work.'

'I was going to say *shower*,' Andrade laughed. 'My hot water is out and will not be fixed until tomorrow. I had to have a cold shower.'

'They're supposed to be very beneficial,' Billy offered. Andrade's face scrunched into a grimace.

'Then you have one,' he said. 'And then tell me how—beneficial—you feel.'

He paused, his face softening.

'Is it bad?' he asked.

'Why would you think that?'

Andrade shifted in the bed, sitting up.

'It is now tomorrow and you are still at your desk.'

'I enjoy working at night,' Billy replied, almost automatically. 'With nobody around, I can't be distracted.'

'And yet you call me,' Andrade grinned wolfishly. 'Perhaps you want me to distract—'

'Goodnight, Andrade,' Billy said quickly, disconnecting the call, reddening as he did so. Placing the phone at the side of his keyboard, he went to move through the footage again—

'You're very cute together, you know,' a woman's voice spoke, and Billy almost yelped as he spun around to see DC Joanne Davey, her red, curly hair loose, as she sat on the desk behind him.

'How the hell did you appear—' he started, but trailed off. 'Are you okay?'

'Why wouldn't I be?' Davey's face was emotionless.

'Well, the man who was believed to have killed your sister—'

'Is dead,' Davey finished the sentence. 'Am I sad about this? Hell no. But am I happy?

She frowned.

'Weirdly, also no,' she said. 'We never locked him up. I wanted him in prison, not dead. I wanted him to sit in a small cell for the rest of his life and never see the sun again.'

'I don't think that's how prisons work,' Billy replied, before realising he wasn't helping the situation. 'Sorry.'

'And now? Now we have to find the person who killed

him and arrest them,' Davey looked to her trainers, kicking her feet against a chair. 'Which doesn't sound fair. We should be giving them a medal.'

Billy kept quiet. He didn't know how to respond to such a comment, having never been through what Davey was currently suffering.

'Why are you here, Joanne?' he eventually asked. 'You should be with your family.'

'Mum and dad are pissed up and having a party,' Davey shook her head. 'I was there when Declan made the call. They knew because I'd told them, and a minute after I gave the news, they opened up the champagne bottles.'

She sniffed.

'I may have had a couple of glasses,' she admitted. 'But I had to get out of there before I started to see the world the same way. It's not a good way to see things. So, I thought I'd come here, see what my old mate Billy had found out.'

'If Monroe knew I was even talking to you, he'd be furious,' Billy turned to fully face her now. 'You're off the case and you know why.'

'But I shouldn't be,' Davey replied, and although her face was expressionless and her voice calm, Billy couldn't help but think she was actually boiling with rage. 'This is my case.'

'This is a personal situation—'

'Oh, come on, Billy!' Davey couldn't help herself as she exploded in anger. 'The whole bloody remit for this Unit is "personal"! We've solved cases Declan's dad screwed up, cases connected to Monroe and Declan's old colleagues, hunted Declan when he was accused of terrorism, caught the man who killed his parents, who killed his old partner in the Military Police...' her anger fading, she trailed off. 'And Monroe and Anjli haven't exactly been angels here. How come they get to do this while I don't?'

Billy couldn't answer this.

'It's Bullman's call,' he replied. 'Speak to her. She isn't an ogre. She'll decide what's best.'

'Best for who?' Davey snarked in reply. 'Best for me? Or best for the Unit?'

She looked away now.

'It's not just Spears,' she breathed. 'There will be more. This is a vigilante killing, and once they taste justice, they'll keep going.'

'You don't know that,' Billy protested. 'This could be someone connected to the original killings, this could be someone getting revenge for something Spears did in prison, there's a whole ton of reasons why someone might want him dead.'

'Exactly,' Davey climbed off the desk and straightened, stretching her back as she did so. 'And I'm the one being punished. That's bullshit, Billy, and you know it.'

'Speak to Bullman,' Billy replied again.

'Marcos won't let me.'

'Then go over her!' Billy now snapped, finally tiring of this circular conversation, It was late, he was tired, he'd left a dinner with a man he liked very much for this and the last thing he needed was to spend hours sorting out Davey's problems. 'But stop using me as a sounding board. Call your therapist for that.'

Davey seemed stricken by the comment.

'I spoke to you because we're friends,' she whispered.

'Are we?' Billy, still angry, replied. 'You barely talk to any of us. You spend more time with Marcos than anyone else, poor De'Geer—'

'What, so I'm the bad guy because I won't shack up with the Viking?' Davey laughed bitterly. 'I don't hang out with you guys much because you never invite me. Or I'm at the main labs in Lambeth while you're having your pub "working lunch" sessions. And De'Geer is nice, a great and a wonderful person, but we went for a drink or two, it didn't feel right and I decided we should just stay friends.'

She deflated, tears coming to her eyes.

'I shouldn't be punished just because Declan, Anjli, Monroe and Rosanna are all happy together,' she muttered. 'And I shouldn't be punished because the case involves someone who affected my life when I was nine.'

And with that, before Billy could reply, she spun on her heels and walked out of the office.

'Where are you going?' Billy called out.

'To do what you suggested and call my therapist,' she said as she passed through the doors. 'Maybe he'll give a shit about my feelings.'

Billy wanted to rise up, run after her, tell her she was wrong, and that they did care, but it was too late.

Davey was gone.

'Bugger,' he muttered to himself before checking his watch and turning back to the computer screens.

It was going to be a *very* long night.

It was close to dawn when the two scared-looking men arrived at the Minories lockup, down a small, side alley around half-a-mile north of Tower Bridge. One, the braver of the two was white, middle-aged and portly, the product of too many beers and curries, his thinning brown hair cut into a faded "level two" buzz cut, while the other one, a younger black man who obviously took more care of himself, and with a baseball cap on his head, was as stocky as his companion, but more made from muscle than cholesterol-building fat.

Neither of them wanted to be here.

'This is a mistake,' Buzz-cut said, as he looked around. 'We shouldn't have agreed to this. I shouldn't have agreed to this.'

'Come on,' Baseball Cap replied with a definite false bravado over his trembling voice. 'He probably hasn't done what he said he would.'

'You don't know that,' Buzz-cut moaned, wringing his hands now as he glanced around the street again. 'Why hasn't he opened the door? He said he'd open the door.'

'Probably because you haven't bloody knocked,' Baseball Cap muttered. Jumping at the accusation, Buzz-cut steeled himself and rapped on the metal shutters. The sound of the hammering echoed around the street, and Baseball Cap stared at him in anger.

'Do you want to try a little louder?' he hissed. I don't think they heard you in bloody *Wapping*.'

'Sorry,' Buzz-cut yelped again as the metal shutter rose slowly with a monotonous clattering noise, and they now faced a new entrant into the meeting.

He was tall and slim, a jacket with the collar up shadowing his jawline, tinted glasses hiding his eyes and a flat cap doing the same to his face as Baseball Cap's cap did to his.

'Gentlemen,' he breathed. 'You are on time. That's good.'

'Are you Mister Pravda?' Buzz-cut asked nervously.

'For tonight, yes,' Mister Pravda replied, stepping back, allowing them to enter.

'So it's not your real name?' Buzz-cut continued on.

'Of course it's not,' Baseball Cap hissed. 'Why the hell would he use a real name?'

'Because he knows us!'

'Dude, we were sent to *him*,' Baseball Cap was getting irritated now. 'It wasn't the other way around.'

By now they'd entered a garage, a double door shuttered, and a single vehicle lit by a standard lamp parked up in the room's corner. It was a white van of some kind, with a side door and double doors on the back.

'So, what do you need us to do?' Baseball Cap asked. 'I didn't think we were needed until tomorrow.'

'It is tomorrow,' Mister Pravda replied happily, whistling a tune as he walked over to four black, heavy duty carry cases. 'And I intend to start early today. So, I need you to put these into the van in a minute.'

'What are they?' Buzz-cut asked, picking up one end of the closest box. 'Hey, these aren't heavy at all.'

'They're not filled yet,' Mister Pravda said as he walked to one of the shadowed corners of the garage. In it was some kind of gas bottle, a large one, attached to a trolley. On it was a tube that led to what looked like an air gun, like the types you'd find in petrol stations, where you'd fill your tyre pressure to the correct level.

'What's that?' Buzz-cut couldn't help himself.

'It's an oscillating saw,' Mister Pravda was now taking a disposable waterproof poncho and hood, pulling it over his jacket and cap.

'And why do you need one of those?'

Mister Pravda looked back at the two men, and even through the shadows, they could see the glint of a smile on his lips.

'Because we're going to saw someone up,' he replied, as if it was the most normal thing in the world.

Baseball Cap swallowed.

'I didn't sign up for that,' he whispered.

'Ah, but I'm afraid you did,' Mister Pravda attached a blade to the saw and hefted the trolley back, so he could wheel it. 'But don't worry. You're not a part of that. We'll do this, all you need to do is fix the van.'

He pointed to a table where, scattered carelessly upon it were licence plates and a rather official looking orange light.

'Oh, and you have clothes on the driver's seat,' Mister Pravda walked into the back of the garage, towards a door, half open. Listening, Buzz-cut almost believed he could hear whimpering through it. 'I suggest you try them on for size. We won't have another chance to alter them.'

As Mister Pravda left the two men alone now, Baseball Cap walked over to the van, opening the driver's side up.

'It's gloves, a high vis jacket and a hard hat each,' he said, holding up one hat. 'What the hell are we supposed to do with this—'

He didn't finish his comment, as at that moment, through the door, the sound of an oscillating saw echoed through the garage, followed immediately by the gurgling, terrified scream of a grown man.

Buzz-cut turned and almost ran for the metal shutters, but something stopped him. Mister Pravda had been right; he *had* agreed to do this. They both had. They wouldn't get their hands bloody, so to speak, but they were as much a part of this as everyone else was. And to do what was asked meant they'd gain closure too.

As the second, gurgling scream echoed, the saw having stopped, Buzz-cut ran to the corner anyway, retching, vomiting up his dinner onto the floor as the room started to spin.

He wasn't a killer. They were killers.

This was revenge.

Rising, he wiped his lips.

'This was revenge,' he whispered.

'What did you say?' Baseball Cap asked, still holding the hard hat, and wrinkling his nose at the smell of sick on the floor.

'I said let's get to work,' Buzz-cut straightened, walking over to the table and grabbing a metal plate. 'Quicker we get this done, the quicker we can get it all done.'

4

FAKED PLATES

It was the following morning when everyone could finally congregate in the briefing room.

Declan and Anjli had spent another hour in Temple Inn the previous night, calling up the immediate families of Anna Callahan and Holly Bruce, letting them know what had happened, and asking for them to not only pass the message around their own immediate families but also arrange for either face-to-face or video call meetings the following day. DC Davey, although not part of the case, was still in the building, and had already called up her parents to give them an update, and when Declan had called the number, he was convinced he could hear the sound of more popping corks.

Which was completely understandable, he considered. *I would have done the same.*

After this had been done, Declan and Anjli had finished for the night, and had returned home to Hurley, spending another hour discussing the case before going to bed. Declan had been initially surprised by how *happy* the families had been when hearing about the murder, but at the same time, he could understand completely why this would be. And, early the next day, Declan and Anjli had once more returned to Temple Inn, this time in separate cars; not because they didn't want to talk to each other, but because they'd decided during a hastily grabbed breakfast that they were likely to both be doing a lot of driving that day, and both cars were going to be required.

By the time they arrived in the office, though, pretty much everyone was in the glass-windowed briefing room; even Detective Superintendent Bullman had emerged from her office and had taken her usual spot of hanging around the door.

Billy was, as ever, manning the laptop connected to the large plasma screen behind Monroe and Doctor Marcos, as they faced the team. He looked tired, and Declan knew he would have been staring at monitors until the early hours of the morning. De'Geer and Cooper were at the back, and so Anjli and Declan settled into their usual seats. The only one visibly absent was Davey, for obvious reasons.

'Jacob Spears,' Monroe said, once Declan and Anjli had sat down, nodding at Billy to begin. Behind Monroe, the police photos of a younger Jacob Spears taken at the time of his arrest appeared on the plasma screen.

'Arrested for the murders of three teenage girls in the Essex area,' Monroe said, tapping on the screen and revealing three more images; photos of three separate girls, taken from school gatherings, family photos and passport booth pictures. All three were young, smiling, and brunette. 'Anna Callahan, Holly Bruce, and Lorraine Davey.'

'Christ, she looks like her sister,' Anjli exclaimed aloud. 'Sorry, Guv.'

'No, you're right,' Monroe nodded as he looked back at

the third image. 'Take away the darkened hair shade and it's a dead ringer. And it's a reminder that this case is close to us, through poor Joanne. Who, currently, sits in the canteen room, waiting for us to finish.'

'She can't do any other work?' De'Geer was surprised at this. 'I mean, I'm sure she shouldn't, this is a traumatic time for her—'

'She can't work on the case because of her connection, and Spears—that is, his body—is in the Temple Inn morgue until we move it, so she can't really work downstairs,' Doctor Marcos explained. 'I thought it best to simply keep her out of everything. And trust me, she's unhappy about that. She reckons she's perfectly fine.'

She turned and glared at Billy.

'Apparently someone last night suggested she go over my head and speak directly to the chief.'

Billy blushed.

'I thought I was helping,' he mumbled.

'Stop helping,' Doctor Marcos replied icily.

This exchange now finished, Monroe turned back to the group.

'Almost twenty years ago, these three girls disappeared over a four-month time period,' he carried on. 'They eventually found the bodies in shallow graves, dotted over north Essex, in Hainault Forest, Weald Country Park and Epping Forest, not far in fact from where we discovered the body of Angela Martin last year.'

He tapped the screen again, and now autopsy pictures appeared of the three girls. Declan looked away for a moment, swallowing.

'You okay?' Monroe, catching this, asked.

'Yes, sorry,' Declan nodded. 'It's just... they were the same age as Jess is right now. And I can't—'

'None of us can,' Bullman stated from the door. 'You're not the only one. My niece is the same age. And to think that someone like Spears could...'

She trailed off.

'Let's just say I understand why someone would want revenge,' she finished.

There was a long second of silence at this; everyone in the room could relate to that.

Eventually, Monroe cleared his throat.

'Spears was eventually picked up after witnesses identified his work van at one of the abduction scenes, that of Anna Callahan.'

Tap. On the screen, an image of a white van appeared, the registration R687 WLF.

'Scraps of her clothing were found in the van when he was pulled over,' Doctor Marcos now spoke. 'After he was arrested, he admitted to taking and killing Anna, the only one they could link him to, but didn't—*wouldn't* confess to the others.'

She pointed at the autopsy images again.

'All three victims had been strangled, but before this had been attacked with an electroshock stun gun device,' she said. 'It was believed that Spears would walk up behind his victim, electroshock them, and then load the unconscious victim into the van before leaving.'

'Do you mean a taser, Ma'am?' Cooper, confused, looked up.

'No,' Doctor Marcos shook her head. 'And it's *Doctor*, not bloody *Ma'am*, I've told you before. Electroshock stun guns and tasers refer to two completely different devices. Stun guns administer an electric shock through direct contact, while a taser device, such as the X26 stun guns the police use, administers shock through thin, flexible wires connected to two probes, which fire into the target once a trigger is pressed.'

She double-tapped the plasma screen and a file folder window revealed itself. She tapped a file in it, and an image of what looked to be a short cattle prod now appeared.

'This was found in Jacob Spear's possessions at the time of his arrest,' she said. 'Although it was matched to burn marks found on all three victims, only one held up in court.'

'Anna Callahan,' Declan nodded. 'And he was in prison for how long again?'

'He was sentenced to twenty years, but was released after fifteen,' Monroe spoke now. 'He'd requested a new identity upon release, but they ignored it. Instead, he went to live in Kent, using his middle name, Dexter, as his "known" name.'

'Bit on the nose for a serial killer,' Billy muttered. 'Although I suppose you can't change a middle name.'

'So, Jacob Spears goes to Kent, and pretends to be someone else,' Declan stroked at his chin. 'How does he then turn up hanging from a lamppost?'

Monroe looked at Billy now.

'I can tell you how he got there,' Billy tapped on his keyboard, and the plasma screen cleared, replaced now by CCTV footage of the wall at the back of Amen Court. It was slightly pixilated, obviously zoomed in, but in the middle of the screen was a white van parked beside the wall and obstructing the lamppost.

'This is what the resident that witnessed it claimed was a delivery van,' Billy explained. 'And I can see why she'd think so, because many companies use a similar colour. But, as you can see, there's no logo on the side here.'

'Can you enhance that?' Declan asked before stopping himself. 'No, sorry, I forgot. No need for the "we're not in a movie" talk.'

'Actually, we're trialling an AI upscale app at the moment,' Billy smiled. 'It examines the image and uses artificial intelligence and mathematics to clean the image up. It can't be used in court yet, as it's using algorithms to create what it *thinks* is real, but it helps a little in cases like this.'

He tapped on the laptop and after a moment, the video on the screen altered, clearing up ever so slightly.

'I didn't say it was great,' Billy added.

Declan pointed at the van.

'It's good enough for what I wanted,' he said. 'Look at the reg.'

'R687 WLF,' Anjli leant in, squinting. 'The same registration as Spears had.'

'It can't be,' Monroe shook his head now, unsure of what he was looking at. 'The van was destroyed over a decade ago.'

'No, the van's a newer model,' Billy was zooming in, but again, the image was blurring as he did so. 'These aren't the real plates.'

'So, someone went to the detail of faking the same van and plates for him,' Anjli nodded. 'This was definitely planned out. Do we have a time of death?'

Doctor Marcos nodded.

'Around two in the afternoon,' she said. 'Around seven hours before the body was found.'

'Cause of death?' Declan asked. 'I'm guessing it wasn't the hanging.'

Doctor Marcos shook her head as she picked up an iPad, reading from it.

'His heart gave out after prolonged torture,' she replied. 'Someone tied him up, as shown by rope marks on his wrists and ankles, likely to a chair, and then used some kind of electroshock device on him, repeatedly, until he suffered a ventricular fibrillation, which is an erratic, disorganised firing of impulses from the ventricles—'

'The what?' Monroe interrupted. 'I mean, *I* know what the ventri-whatsis are, but the younger ones might not.'

'I'm talking about the heart's lower chambers,' Doctor Marcos sighed. 'When ventricular fibrillation occurs, the heart can't pump blood and death occurs within minutes, if left untreated.'

'So, a heart attack?' Billy asked.

'No, not a heart attack, more sudden cardiac arrest,' Doctor Marcos corrected. 'Far quicker, far more fatal. And, this caused him to soil himself, which we previously believed was the hanging.'

'This is even more personal than we thought,' Monroe mused. 'Someone using the same weapon Spears used to capture his victims to kill him, and then the same van to drop his body off? Complete with registration?'

'He didn't just capture them with the prod,' Doctor Marcos added. 'Marks on the bodies showed he'd attacked them with it after. Not in the same way this had, but he... had fun with them, shall we say... before killing them.'

'I can't be the only person happy he's dead,' Anjli muttered, Nobody replied, but it was obvious everyone was considering the same question.

'Can we see how many people dumped the body?' Declan pointed back at the footage.

Nodding at this, Billy scrolled through.

'It's not great, and they're wearing hoodies, but it looks like two people,' he said, pausing the footage as two people walked around the van. 'They block visibility of the lamp while parked, so we can't see them string up the body, but there's only two seen; one stocky, one slim, perhaps female. And, unless someone else hides inside the van...'

'Spears was heavy,' De'Geer added. 'I had to get PC Mastakin from the front desk to help me and the Doctor get the body onto the table last night. But not heavy enough to need more than two people. After all, once the rope was around the lamp, they just winched the body up like a rope on a pulley, and secured it.'

'Can we use automatic number plate recognition here?' Anjli asked. *ANPR*, as it was better known, was a series of cameras that picked up registration plates of cars, allowing police an advantage when it came to hunting suspects in vehicles.

'I've been looking through them, but it's a needle in a haystack,' Billy replied as he pulled up a map of the City of London on the plasma screen. On it, in a variety of locations, were pins. 'We can see here we have cameras on the A40, north of Amen Court, and on Ludgate Hill itself. And, with thousands of ANPR cameras in London, we should be able to follow a van.'

'But?'

'But the van's using fake number plates,' Billy replied. 'So, even if we found the van, they could stop down a side road and click them off. They're probably magnetic, come off easily. Hell, they might even have taken them off the moment they left the court. And, with no guaranteed time of body disposal, I'm working through several hours of footage.'

Declan leaned back in his chair at this.

'The CCTV doesn't give a time?'

'No,' Billy replied. 'At best, I have the Jaguar arriving, and I've worked out a rough estimation there. But even then, I'm raising this on a vague time, as it wasn't marked down on any clocks when it arrived. I've got it nailed down to a half-hour period around eightish. Still not fun.'

Declan nodded.

'There was only one camera down there,' he said. 'They parked there specifically, so the camera picked it up. They wanted to be found.'

'Well, they could have made it bloody easier for me,' Billy growled. 'The problem we have is half the cameras around here are down for recalibration, anyway. So if they drive out, stop, change number plates and carry on, it could be another mile before they get pinged. And then, they're one of hundreds of vans in London, with a different plate, and nowhere near the crime scene.'

'Do what you can,' Monroe replied. 'If anyone can do it, it's you. Or the people in Scotland Yard. Actually, they're probably better than you. Can you get their number, see what they can find out?'

Billy knew Monroe was joking, pushing his buttons to make him work harder, and so he gave a faint smile in response.

'My house,' he said. 'I'll be the one to get it sorted, Guv.'

'Good man,' Monroe looked at Declan and Anjli. 'How were the phone calls last night?'

'Honestly, not great,' Anjli admitted. 'There was a kind of glee in their voices when we told them Jacob Spears was dead. They wanted to know how he died.'

'The mother of Holly Bruce actually wanted to know if he

was in pain when he did so, and actively screamed at me when I wouldn't tell her,' Declan added. 'If you want prime suspects, they're all there. But both families had alibis for yesterday we're looking into. Even Davey's parents had proof they weren't anywhere near London.'

'All three having alibis on the same day makes me suspicious,' Monroe muttered.

'Why?' the voice at the doorway was new, and everyone turned to see DC Davey standing there behind Bullman, who now spun to face her. 'People have alibis every day of their life, unless they're alone. Nine times out of ten when we enquire, we're told the person in question was somewhere else, or was with someone else. And we immediately place them out of the scenario. So, why is this different?'

'DC Davey, you shouldn't be here,' Monroe replied carefully. 'I know you're angry—'

'With respect, sir, you know nothing,' Davey snapped. 'I'm not angry he's gone. I'm happy. Happy that someone did what the courts and his fellow prisoners wouldn't do.'

She looked apologetically at Doctor Marcos.

'I know you told me to stay in the canteen, but there was a call,' she said. 'Front desk passed it along to us, and I picked it up, as you were all in a briefing.'

'What sort of call?' Doctor Marcos asked suspiciously.

'DCI Cohen at Paddington nick,' Davey replied, checking her notes. 'There's been another serial killer murdered, and he thought we'd want to know.'

5

GET OUT OF JAIL CARD

For the last couple of months, Jennifer Farnham-Ewing had been in the doghouse.

At the start of the year, her future had looked golden; brought into Charles Baker's team under his right-hand man, Will Harrison, Jennifer was the perfect, 'television-friendly' spokesperson; barely in her twenties, slim and tall, her long blonde hair pulled into a ponytail and her makeup minimal whenever she spoke to the cameras, giving the impression of a woman who didn't care about looks, and was more invested in the country's state.

Which was bollocks, really.

Jennifer didn't wear makeup because she knew she was a *hot ten* even without it. Just watching the male MPs ogling her pencil skirt as she walked through the Houses of Parliament showed her this daily. And, when Will's role became open once more because of tragedy, even though her age was classed as a hindrance by many in the office, Charles pulled her into his inner circle, giving her the role of his "Girl

Friday", a role she attacked with relish. And, no matter what people said, she was damned good at it.

At the time, Baker was on track to be the new Prime Minister. And right beside him, in the shadows, Jennifer Farnham-Ewing was going to be his most trusted advisor, joining the hallowed ranks of world changers such as Dominic Cummings, Sir Humphrey Appleby or Alistair Campbell. Unelected by the people, but controlling their lives in the process, this was a role she relished. She would be a Kingmaker, in a world where the monarchy was pretty much just wheeled out for pageants and foreign tours, a world where the head of Parliament was the true power.

Jennifer had even considered moving into politics herself, perhaps even demanding a safe Conservative seat to take in the next election, but soon into her new role, she realised it would take her a good decade to get to the levels of power she would already have, as soon as Baker was chosen by the party and the 1922 Committee (a committee of backbench Conservative MPs that had considerable influence within the party) to be the next Conservative Leader, which was pretty much a given at that point.

And then came bloody Detective Inspector Declan Walsh, and the infamous State Dinner.

She'd seen the internal reports; how he'd been both an ally and thorn in the side of Charles Baker, and when problems appeared in an upcoming State Dinner, one which Baker was organising, problems that brought DI Walsh back into Baker's, and therefore his department's orbit, she decided he was nothing more than a distraction, or a *hindrance*. And, after a particular meeting, one where she'd been sent to get Walsh a sandwich like a simple errand girl, she'd missed a vital part of the conversation Walsh and Baker had. When she asked Walsh what was said, as Baker's trusted advisor, he was arrogant, insulting almost, telling her to ask Baker herself, believing himself better—and this had riled her.

In fact, the moment he was escorted out, she instructed the front gate to revoke any credentials he had to enter Parliament. She even remembered her last words to him.

'No more free sandwiches from Westminster, Detective Sergeant,' she'd said, deliberately demoting him. She'd felt good doing this. Powerful.

And then it'd all gone to hell when DI Walsh uncovered intelligence about an assassination attempt at the dinner but couldn't enter and act on this *because* of her order.

An order that nearly killed the Prime Minister, the entire Cabinet, and the bloody *Queen*.

The fact it didn't happen was irrelevant; the moment it came out that Jennifer had told security to bar the very officer that saved the day was effectively the moment her political career died, along with Charles Baker's hopes of the Prime Ministership.

But Charles Baker hadn't let her go completely; she had her family's influence and their sizeable donations to the party to thank for that, and so they sent her to Siberia or, rather, the lower levels of Whitehall, the basement floor; windowless offices, still part of Baker's retinue, occasionally performing tasks for him, and in the process, still finding herself tied to Walsh and his bloody police unit, as if this were some kind of divine penance given to her from up high. In fact, it was on one such assignment that removed her boss's main rival for the Premiership and allowed Charles Baker to re-enter Number Ten, Downing Street.

She'd entered with him, but only as part of his staff. She

still hadn't earned enough points to get even close to the level she was once at. And Nigella Waterstone, the insipid bitch that had taken *her* role, wasn't going to ever let her get close again.

However, this time, she had something important.

The Prime Minister's office was actually two floors above where Jennifer now worked and, placing the receiver down onto the phone handset, having just taken a call that could change her life for the better, Jennifer took a moment to consider whether this was the one she wanted to risk everything on.

It was.

Making her way quickly up the stairs, Jennifer walked determinedly to the *Office of the Prime Minister of the United Kingdom.* Standing behind the desk in front of the door, however, was a junior aide, only an intern, likely manning the phones while Baker and his advisors worked out that day's answers for the *Prime Minister's Questions,* occurring at noon.

'No,' he squeaked, moving to intercept her. 'I was told you're not allowed to see him.'

Jennifer took the aide in, staring up and down coldly, lengthening the moment, making him squirm for daring to state such an order at her.

'Tell the Prime Minister I have important news,' she eventually replied after a long, uncomfortable pause. And, when he didn't reply, she darted to the side of him, trying to pass.

The aide sidestepped to block her once more.

'It can wait until tomorrow,' he said, a little more forcefully, growing a spine in the moments since she arrived, and Jennifer stopped, glaring at him. She had a good foot in height, especially in these shoes, and the force of her gaze made the aide step back slightly.

'He needs to hear this *now*,' she hissed. 'Tell his secretary I'm coming in.'

'This is improper—' the aide whined, but Jennifer, tired of this, flung his weakly held arm to the side as she walked past him, knocked on the door and opened it before a reply could be heard.

She didn't recognise everyone in the room; she'd not been around since Charles Baker had become Prime Minister, and it was understandable there would be more people needed here than before, so a larger inner circle than in the old days. She did, however, recognise Nigella, who rose from her chair, furious, waving her arms like some plus-size banshee.

'Get out—' she started, but Jennifer held up a hand to silence her.

'Wait,' she said commandingly, and even though there was a good ten years between them in age, the older woman stopped in her tracks, as she paused for a moment. 'I just need to tell the Prime Minister one thing.'

'You'd better let her speak,' Charles Baker said from his desk with a chuckle. He was wearing a modern navy blue suit with a blue striped tie, different from his usual traditional pin-striped look, but on-brand for the television cameras during the upcoming PMQs. His white hair was groomed perfectly, still lustrous and flowing despite his age, which, thanks to his tanned complexion and secret Botox regime, looked somewhere in his late forties, even though he was mid-to-late fifties. 'She might delay us if we don't. And the last time she did that, I almost died.'

The room burst out into laughter, and Jennifer bit her tongue, giving a sickly smile in return.

'I've heard something,' she said simply. 'Something you need to know, and something connected to discussions we had, back in the days when I was once in the room.'

'Go on then,' Charles waved a hand for her to speak. Jennifer, however, shook her head.

'Alone,' she said. 'I've seen the leaks this place has, and I don't trust any of these people.'

She made a point of glaring at Nigella as she said this.

After a moment of consideration, and checking his watch to work out how long he had before he appeared on TV, Charles sighed.

'Look, we have to be in the Commons in less than an hour, and we need—'

'You *need* to know this,' Jennifer replied. 'Because when you do, it might change what happens in the Commons.'

At this, Charles nodded. He might not rate Jennifer as highly as he once did, but Jennifer knew very well the relevant point here was *once* did. He knew that apart from one mistake, no matter the size of it, she was capable, and he knew that, apart from one catastrophic error, she'd worked hard over the time she'd been in his employ.

'Everyone out,' he said, waving the advisers out of the room. 'Including you, Nigella.'

'Prime Minister?' Nigella looked appalled, but Charles waved her on.

'This'll take seconds, nothing more,' he soothed. 'Then we can go back to winning the populace over.'

Irritably, Nigella Waterstone stomped loudly out of the office behind the other advisors, slamming the door behind her.

Now alone with Jennifer, Charles Baker rose.

'Good to see you, Jennifer,' he said conversationally. 'And

good to see you still reaching for greatness. Other people would have slunk out the back door, never to return after such a catastrophic issue, but you've hung on like a Rottweiler. So, what's got you into such a state?'

'I think I've found an opportunity,' ignoring the *Rottweiler* line, Jennifer moved closer to the desk. 'I had a call from a contact about the police.'

'God, is this about Walsh again?' Charles raised his eyes in frustration, looking at the ceiling. 'And there I was, thinking you were past all that—'

'In fairness, the last time I dealt with Walsh's Unit, it was on your orders, and it resulted in you becoming Prime Minister,' Jennifer replied. 'I'd be happy never dealing with them again. But as you can understand, I have been, shall we say, *interested* in how DI Walsh and his department have been since they—'

'Saved all of Parliament and then gave me this job?' Charles smiled.

'Yes sir,' Jennifer admitted. There was no point in sugar-coating it. And besides, Charles knew she had her part in this too. 'Anyway, they were given a fresh case last night. A hanging in the City of London.'

'Suicide?'

'Looks more like retribution,' Jennifer shook her head. 'They hung him outside the remnants of Newgate Prison. The contacts I have said it looked like he was executed. And he had a note reading "Justice" around his neck. They gave me a name, too. Jacob Spears, the *Essex Ripper*.'

'I remember that case,' Charles nodded. 'He's out already? That's terrible. But it was only just before we came into power under David Cameron. I don't know—'

'That's not all,' Jennifer interrupted excitedly. 'I just heard there's another body. Appeared this morning, during rush hour. Near Paddington.'

'Another serial killer?' Charles Baker had now focused solely on Jennifer. 'Can you confirm this?'

'No, but I do know the DCI in charge there has brought the Temple Inn Unit onto the murder site. It's the pedestrian crossing at the junction of Edgware Road and Marble Arch. Whole place was closed, and we even had the bomb squad there.'

She leant in conspiratorially.

'And the person I'm talking to is saying it's another serial killer, but one that might have *got away with it.*'

Charles sat in his chair, considering this.

'Vigilante killings,' he muttered, his eyes vacant as he considered the implications of such executions. 'Angered by how the police are dealing with things, the people are taking the law into their own hands.'

'Exactly, sir,' Jennifer now sat opposite Charles, nodding as she did so. 'And it reminded me of one of your plans from earlier this year.'

Charles was nodding as well now. He knew what plan she was considering.

'Capital punishment,' he said.

'Exactly,' Jennifer was excited as she continued. 'Look, sir, we both know you weren't the popular choice for PM.'

Charles pursed his lips, but shrugged in agreement at this.

'The bloody right-wingers hate me,' he said. 'They remember my early days, remember me starting as Labour, one of Blair's golden boys, accusing me of being way more Centrist than I claimed to be when I came across. All the crap I went through with Frankie Pearce, and then with Malcolm

Gladwell and Rattlestone? It tainted me. If I hadn't had the *Star Chamber* on my side, I'd have been kicked out early on any Leadership votes.'

'But you did have it, and you did get through.'

'I didn't bloody win, though, did I?' Charles snapped. 'Michelle Rose pipped me at the post. And why was that again? Oh yes. *You*.'

Jennifer paled slightly at the accusation, and worrying the conversation was about to become circular now, but Charles carried on, past that.

'But then *she* managed to righteously shit the bed too, and here I am, *best of the worst,* hanging on by my fingernails but currently in the role. And also very aware that currently I'm an unelected Prime Minister, two years before an election, and with a party unsure if they even want me leading them into it.'

He leant forward on the desk.

'But this, yes, *this* might warm the right-wingers to me,' he said. 'We can test the waters, see what the British public think about returning Capital Punishment to the table. Only for the worst cases, of course, but with the press and the far-right claiming we're too weak on criminals, we can show we're willing to listen, willing to change. Yes, I do think this could work.'

He shifted back now, returning to the moment, and Jennifer, sitting in front of him.

'But we have to be careful,' he said. 'If it's shown we're doing this for the wrong reasons, we'll get burned alive.'

'*We'll*, Prime Minister?' Jennifer forced herself to keep her voice level.

'Of course,' Charles smiled. 'If I get destroyed by this, you're coming with me.'

'And if it succeeds?'

Charles Baker watched the woman in front of him for a long moment. He knew why she'd come now. He could tease something during PMQs, maybe comment on how the previous regime was weak on criminals, maybe even pin this on the opposition somehow. Allow the press to argue at this, push at him to do something about the problem, *say* something about the problem, even.

Maybe a candid comment that could be taken either way. He could then, as if considering their words and acting on them, offer a referendum to the masses; whether Capital Punishment should return for the worst cases. Sure, it could blow up in his face, like it had for Cameron and *Brexit*, but this was a slam dunk, to coin a basketball metaphor. If the public didn't want it, he could go with that, and the right-wing backbenchers would have to accept that he could make the tough choices, and had listened to the will of the British people. And if the vote went the other way—

Well, it wasn't as if he *hadn't* made life or death decisions before. And it wouldn't be Charles Baker who decided.

It would be the people.

The people, who would now see him as a genuine leader, and who'd vote for him in the election. This was his *Falklands War,* his moment to shine, and to finally be seen as a bloody leader of a country.

As long as Declan bloody Walsh and his bag of misfit toys didn't kill this before it started.

And, for all her problems, Jennifer Farnham-Ewing had made the right decision and brought this to him, when she could have decided not to bother trying to regain her role, and instead gone to one of the more right-wing darlings of the party like Tamara Banks, and used it as collateral on a high-ranking role within a *new* regime change.

'If it succeeds, Miss Farnham-Ewing,' he smiled warmly, 'then you'll be back in the room where it all happens, rather than in, well—actually, I have no idea where the hell they dumped you.'

'Thank you, Prime Minister,' Jennifer said as she rose. 'It's a pleasure and an honour to be working with you again.'

And this time, she thought, *Declan bloody Walsh and his friends weren't going to screw it up.*

6

TYBURN TREE

Over the last year, Declan had found himself at a high number of murder sites. Usually, however, they had the good grace to stay hidden, out of the way of normal people. Apart from the more public ones, that was—a shooting in a small nightclub, an electrocution in a City wine bar—most of the deaths had been found in houses, apartments, restaurants, and even hidden in shallow graves, far from any passersby. Even the one the previous night had been placed on a private road, where only a few people at best would have seen it.

This, however, was possibly one of the most public murder sites Declan had ever been to.

The junction where the body had been found was an incredibly busy tourist destination, even first thing on a weekday morning. To the south you had the Marble Arch itself, a 19th-century white marble-faced triumphal arch that was once created for Buckingham Palace, before being moved to the north-east corner of Hyde Park. Declan knew about the arch because from 1851 until at least 1968, three small rooms inside the rebuilt arch were used as a police station, at one point housing the royal constables of the Park, and later the Metropolitan Police.

It wasn't a police station anymore, though, and currently it was a witness to a gruesome act.

To the north was Edgware Road, heading northwards towards Hampstead; to the east were Park Lane and Oxford Street, and to the west was the Bayswater Road, heading towards Shepherd's Bush and Heathrow. The junction itself was a triangle, allowing people to cross both Edgware Road and south to Marble Arch, but today it was closed off in all directions, a dozen officers holding back crowds, and tape pulled across the lanes, while the sounds of frustrated drivers shouting and expressing anger with their horns, echoing around the high buildings that surrounded them on two sides was painfully audible.

Declan had journeyed here in his Audi with Monroe and Doctor Marcos, and upon arriving, Doctor Marcos had immediately met with the local CSI on the scene while Monroe and Declan walked over to DCI Cohen, a slim, stick of a man with closely cropped grey hair and a pair of chunky black glasses that looked too big for his head.

'Alex,' Cohen said as he shook Monroe's hand. 'Thanks for coming.'

'Neil,' Monroe smiled, showing Declan. 'This is DI Walsh. You know Doctor Marcos, who's already wandered off.'

Cohen shook Declan's offered hand before turning back to the junction.

'We're being pressured to open the road up, so the blasted cases are gone,' he apologised. 'I'm sure Rosanna would prefer doing the autopsy off site, anyway. It's a bit...'

He stopped, shuddering.

'Sorry to stop you there, but can you explain what you

mean by the *cases?*' Monroe asked, watching the police cleaning up the scene. 'We were told there was a body here, but you seem to be opening up before anyone has a right proper look around.'

Cohen's eyes bulged out behind the glasses.

'You weren't told?' he replied.

'Told what?' Monroe was getting irritable now. 'Your office called ours, said there was a body here. Neil, just tell us what the bloody hell's going on, aye?'

Cohen nodded, pointing out at the junction.

'So about two hours back, middle of rush hour, a white van pulls up, hazard lights on, orange flashing light on top,' he explained. 'Proper workman's van. Two men get out, one white, one black, both in hard hats and high vis jackets. They open the back doors and pull out four boxes. Cases, I mean. Those ridged, black hard cases film or touring crews have, yeah? The protective ones with foam inside that you see in movies holding rocket launchers and all that.'

'I get the type,' Monroe waved for Cohen to continue.

'So, they pull these four boxes out, and although people see them, they think nothing of it. Hard hats, jackets, officious-looking cases, it's probably work related. You know how people are. Anyway, the two men then place the four cases around that,' Cohen pointed across the junction at a round manhole about twenty feet away, 'and then, once it's done, they get in the van and piss off.'

'Just like that?'

'Just like that,' Cohen agreed. 'Anyway, a minute later, someone gets suspicious. Four boxes left in the street near a major landmark...'

'Terrorism,' Declan finished the unspoken thought.

'That's what people think, so the police get called,' Cohen

nodded, looking at him. 'Paddington's closest, so we get the nod. And when we arrive and see the boxes, we immediately call the bomb squad in.'

Declan looked around the street now, realising now why the tape had been placed.

'You closed everything down,' he said as a statement.

'Damn right we did,' Cohen replied. 'Better safe than sorry. Anyway, bomb squad turn up around thirty minutes later, send a little robot thing in, have a squiz around the cases and then they piss off too.'

'They left?'

'Yeah. "It's not a bomb," they said. No need for them. Clue's in the name. So now, we go and have a proper look. And I'll be honest, Alex, I wish I hadn't.'

Cohen waved to an officer, standing to the south of them, an iPad in her hand.

'Pass me that, will you?' he asked as the officer offered it over to them. Now, with the gained iPad held in his hands, Cohen opened the images folder.

'All they did was drop the boxes, so there's nothing much to scoop around for, forensics wise,' he explained as he wiped through a series of crime scene photos. 'All we did was take some shots before we had the cases moved.'

The first image was of the four large cases, each the size of a small suitcase, lying on the ground around the circular manhole. As Cohen had described, they were black hard cases, and ridged.

'Is that writing on them?' Declan peered closer; on the closest, he could see two spray-painted letters.

'I.C?' Monroe pondered this. 'I see?'

'This will help better,' Cohen swiped, and now a second image, taken from after the boxes had been examined, showed the cases in a row, each with letters sprayed on the tops in white paint.

JU ST IC E.

'Justice,' Declan nodded. 'Exactly the same as Jacob Spears. I'm guessing the body was in one of these? Tough squeeze.'

'Not quite,' Cohen wiped his brow. 'One dead body, four containers. Do the math.'

'He was in bits?' Monroe didn't seem shocked by this. 'Or was he in *quarters?*'

'Quarters?' Declan glanced at his boss. 'As in—'

'Aye, cut into four equal pieces,' Monroe looked over at Doctor Marcos, still talking to one of the forensics.

'*Rosanna!* Was he quartered?'

Doctor Marcos, her eyes tight, looked up at him and nodded before returning to the conversation.

'You seem to have a better idea of what the bloody hell this is than I do,' Cohen replied.

At this, Monroe sucked air in through his teeth.

'Aye, based on our other victim, I think I do,' he said. 'Do we have the identity of the victim yet?'

'Darryl Marr,' Cohen scanned through the photos, looking for a particular one. 'And yes, it's *that* Darryl Marr. We know this because—'

He stopped at an image; a close up of the dead Darryl Marr's forehead, inside a case, a driving licence stapled to it.

'Bloody hell!' Monroe exclaimed. 'They wanted us to know alright!'

'I don't know Darryl Marr,' Declan said, looking away from the image. 'Should I?'

'Possibly before your time in the force,' Monroe nodded. 'Did you ever hear of the *Durham Ripper?*'

Declan nodded at this. 'Dad mentioned it a couple of times. I think I saw it on the news, too. Never caught, right?'

'He was caught, but he was never convicted,' Cohen muttered. 'The police screwed up the chain of evidence and Darryl walked.'

'And if he killed again, he was clever enough to not do it in Durham,' Monroe examined the photo of the ID. 'He kept a low profile. Until now, that is.'

He winced.

'That looks like a proper staple there, too. Not the through-paper ones, either, more of a staple gun job. Do you think he was alive when they did it?'

Once more, he looked up at Doctor Marcos. This time, however, she saw his gaze before he spoke and walked over.

'What do you need?' she asked, all professionalism.

'What can you give us so far?' Monroe asked. 'I know you've not examined the body—*bodies*—*bits* of body yet...'

'I'll perform the autopsy later, but I'm pretty sure what the cause of death is,' Doctor Marcos replied. 'The SOCOs took some solid photos. Good close-ups, as ghoulish as that sounds.'

'He was hanged, drawn and quartered, wasn't he?' Monroe shuddered as he spoke.

Doctor Marcos nodded.

'There's bruising on the neck, possibly from a noose, created before death, but I'll need to check,' she explained. 'Also, one wrist has what looks like rope burns on it.'

'Does the other wrist?'

'I don't know,' Doctor Marcos admitted. 'It's in a different case. But if he was pulled by his hands, the rope burns would be accurate.'

'Hanged, drawn and quartered,' Declan shook his head. 'That's torture, not execution!'

'No, it's execution, just of a different type,' Monroe pursed his lips as he considered this. 'It was held for the most serious of crimes, including treason. The victim would be dragged to the place of execution by their hands, and then hanged by the neck, until almost dead. They'd then be cut down before being emasculated, disembowelled, both while conscious, and then finally beheaded, before being cut into four pieces. Sometimes they'd die when their heart was removed and held up in front of them, but either way, that was the moment of death.'

'You seem to know a lot about this,' Declan almost took a step back. Monroe gave a grim smile.

'Aye, I do,' he said. 'I was taught it as a bairn. You ever see the film *Braveheart?*'

'Mel Gibson? Sure,' Declan nodded, suddenly understanding. 'Of course. William Wallace was hanged, drawn and quartered at the end.'

'Aye, in 1305,' Monroe replied. 'And all that Hollywood bullshit aside, it was a turning point for Scottish independence.'

'If you paint your face and shout "Freedom", we're having words,' Doctor Marcos interjected at him. 'I won't know for sure until I see the body, but just from the photos, I can see he was beheaded, strangled in some way, dragged by the hands and quartered.'

She shivered.

'It only makes sense to assume the other things were

done, too. And yes, to your first question, I think they used some kind of staple gun to his forehead before they cut it off.'

Declan felt a cool wind travel down his spine.

'So why leave the bodies—*body* here?'

At this, Monroe took him by the arm, leading him to where the manhole cover was.

'Because of this, laddie,' he said, pointing down at it.

Now closer to the spot, Declan could see it wasn't a manhole, but a circular plaque embedded into the pavement. In the middle was a stylised cross, and written around it in a circle were five words.

THE SITE OF TYBURN TREE

'This was a gallows,' Declan was catching up now.

'It was more than that, laddie,' Monroe looked around. 'Tyburn Tree was hanging people here from the eleven hundreds. Back then this was a small hamlet with a little river, the Tyburn, passing through.'

He pointed up Oxford Street.

'A few miles that way was the City of London,' he continued. 'Our remit now, but back then, that was the entire ball game here. And, for hundreds of years, they brought people from Newgate to the "Tyburn tree" to be hanged. They even built a special gallows here, with three vertical pillars holding three beams, set into a triangle that could hang over twenty people at a time.'

He pointed off down the street.

'Several of our sayings are supposed to come from this, too,' he said, now getting into the flow. '*One for the road* is from when the cart, taking the prisoner from Newgate, would stop at a tavern for them to have their final drink before they carried on along the road. And even *hangover* is reckoned to be from this, where people got so drunk at a hanging that the following day, when the hanging was over, they felt rough.'

'I bet you're a joy at parties, with all this trivia in your head, Guv,' Declan muttered, pulling away from the plaque. 'But wasn't this high treason? Spears was electrocuted to death and hung. Why do all this to Marr?'

'He was accused of killing the King sisters,' Monroe suggested, stroking at his beard as he did so. 'And if I recall, I think when they found the King sisters, they were...'

'In pieces?'

His eyes narrowed, Monroe nodded.

'Aye, but not in equal parts, more a frenzied attack.'

'So, like Spears being electrocuted to death, they executed him in the manner he killed his victims, rather than just executing him. That just sounds like someone wanting an excuse to kill,' Declan muttered. 'And someone like that is more dangerous than the people they're killing most of the time.'

'Aye, you might be right there,' Monroe was watching Doctor Marcos, now climbing into a squad car, going off to examine the body as he spoke. 'If Rosanna finds something we can use, that might explain more what was going on. But the case is too similar to our own to not be connected.'

'White van, body already dead, sign saying "Justice"?' Declan nodded. 'Yeah, this has to be connected.'

He stopped.

'This was a *message*,' he said. 'They could have put the body anywhere. They wanted people to see this. Rush hour on a Wednesday, bomb squad bringing the press, they wanted views. This isn't some kind of revenge spree, or even vigilante justice, this is someone with an agenda.'

'Then why hide Mister Spears?' Monroe asked as they walked back to their car. 'That was a wall in the middle of nowhere.'

'It was Newgate, and it was definitely targeted, and they made sure the CCTV could pick up the licence plate,' Declan argued. 'Whoever this is doing these murders, these executions, so to speak, are using London execution spots to reveal their handiwork. Besides that, they're killing serial killers who, so far, were labelled "Ripper" by the press. How many execution spots are there, and how many "Ripper" murderers are out there? On one hand, I can name the Tower of London, Tower Hill, Smithfields, and we already have here and Newgate. How many bloody places do we now have to monitor? And when do they appear outside of London?'

'Too many,' Monroe admitted. 'To both questions.'

And, with a last nod to DCI Cohen, now commanding his officers to reopen the roads before the motorists started their own lynchings, Monroe and Declan left the onetime site of Tyburn Gallows, and headed back to Temple Inn.

7

MULTI-TASK

Billy was returning to his desk when Declan and Monroe arrived back in the main office.

'Are you allowed to be away from your little temple of cyber power?' Monroe asked, as Billy settled into his chair once more.

'Even Gods need to wee some times,' Billy smiled back.

'Probably more information than I needed,' Monroe said as he looked around. 'Where is everyone?'

'De'Geer's downstairs with Davey, Anjli's in with Bullman, and Cooper's grabbing us all some sandwiches,' Billy replied. 'And before you kick off about Davey being involved, she's not. Bullman asked if she was okay working on the Marr murder, as that's nothing to do with her family.'

He checked they were alone before continuing.

'She came here last night, talked to me,' he said. 'She reckons she's fine, and that our history of personal cases should give her a mulligan here—'

'A what?' Declan asked.

'Mulligan,' Monroe replied on Billy's behalf. 'A second

chance. Comes from golf, when you lose a ball.'

'Anyway, she thinks that with our history she should be allowed to investigate the case, but I'm not sure,' Billy continued. 'I saw her eyes. She wasn't happy, and she wasn't excited. There was nothing there.'

'Makes sense, considering what happened,' Monroe nodded. 'And I don't think she should be anywhere near that case, so Marr is a suitable alternative.'

He thought for a moment.

'Although I'd rather she wasn't down there with Spears' body.'

'It's been moved,' Anjli replied as she walked from Bullman's office and into the main bullpen area. 'Doctor Marcos had it sent to the main labs in Lambeth half an hour back. It's where the—'

She paused, unsure what to say.

'—the *bits* of Darryl Marr were taken to. She can work on them both at the same time.'

'If they have enough slabs for him,' Declan commented.

'That aside, what do we have so far?' Monroe spoke to the room, but he was really talking to Billy, who pulled up an image of Jacob Spears.

'I think I have a connection between the two,' he said.

'Apart from the fact they were murdering bastards?' Monroe politely enquired.

'Yes sir,' Billy held back a grimace as he continued. 'They were in Belmarsh together.'

'That cannae be right,' Monroe walked over to the monitors now as Billy started bringing images up on them. 'Spears was convicted, but Marr walked free.'

'Of the crimes of murdering the King sisters and Ethan Roe, yes,' Billy nodded. 'But ten years later, he was sent to

Belmarsh for two years, after he was involved in a vicious fight outside a pub in Rotherham in 2015.'

He pulled up two prison files; one for Jacob Spears, the other for Darryl Marr.

'As this shows, there was a seven-month period where Marr and Spears were in the same House Block.'

'Can we find out if they knew each other?' Declan rubbed at his chin. 'Maybe there's more here than we thought? Perhaps this is revenge, but for something in prison?'

'I can ask the warden, get them to speak to the guards, but it'd be something that's unlikely to be documented, unless they were worried about anything being said between the prisoners,' Billy interjected. 'And apparently Spears was an exemplary prisoner while he was there, so they'd have given him leeway.'

'I might know someone who could tell us,' Monroe muttered. 'Derek Sutton would have been in Belmarsh during that time, and I think he was on the same block.'

Declan watched Monroe as he said this; Derek Sutton was an old acquaintance of Monroe's from his childhood in Glasgow, a mountain of a man who enforced for a local family, and who'd helped Monroe hunt down the men who killed his brother, Kenny, decades earlier. He'd been set up for another murder in the nineties, came back into the remit of the *Last Chance Saloon* when their investigation into the *Magpies* proved his innocence and freed him, and, travelling back to Glasgow, he'd only returned once, a few months earlier, dragging Monroe and De'Geer up to Edinburgh to help him with a family issue.

Declan didn't know if Monroe and Sutton still spoke. He knew, however, that getting Sutton involved was always going to be messy.

'Are you sure?' he whispered. 'We can find out in other ways.'

'Aye, it's okay,' Monroe smiled. 'He's gone straight. I have a fellow in Drumchapel keeping an eye on him. Thought it best, just in case.'

'Your history with him almost had you removed from the force, Guv.'

'I *am* aware, Declan. I also had a full pardon from the Prime Minister, so I think I'm good for a few more skeletons to fall out.'

'Michelle Rose isn't PM any more—' Declan protested, and Monroe raised a hand to stop him.

'And if there's any problems, I'll call your best mate Charles Baker and *he'll* bloody fix it,' he replied irritably. '*Mary, mother of God*, laddie. It's just a phone call.'

Now angry, he looked back at Billy.

'Tell me you have something on the van,' he said.

'Not really,' Billy tapped on his keyboard. 'Although I have a few questions.'

'Aye, don't we all?'

'I'm serious, boss,' Billy lowered his voice as he continued, and Anjli, Declan and Monroe were forced to lean closer to hear him.

'Are you scared we're bugged?' Monroe mocked. 'Has your wee boyfriend been by?'

'Wouldn't be the first time we were bugged,' Billy replied solemnly. 'Wouldn't be the second time, either. And no, *not* by my boyfriend.'

He pulled up photos of white vans, taken from CCTV cameras.

'The problem with white vans is they're so prevalent these days,' he explained. 'It's why "white van man" is such a cliché.

On an average day, the City of London has thousands of them driving around.'

'But not at nine in the evening?' Monroe countered.

'No, but even then, we're still talking dozens.'

Several ANPR images of white vans, all different makes but similar to the one in Amen Court, appeared on the screen to make Billy's point. After a moment, Billy pulled up some CCTV the detectives had seen before, footage of the white van in Amen Court.

'This was taken from security cameras, at around eight to eight-fifteen in the evening,' he explained. 'Now, moving on, we can see on the ANPR camera on Ludgate Hill—'

Click. Another image appeared on the screen.

'At eight-ten in the evening, the same van headed west, towards central London,' Billy pointed at the number plates. 'It's definitely the right van, and should hit another camera at the crossroads with Farringdon Street, but nothing appears. In fact, we don't see it anywhere.'

'Vans can't just disappear,' Declan frowned.

'Here, they can,' Billy pulled up a map of the area, pointing to a street to the south of Ludgate Hill. 'This is Pilgrim Street. There's no camera there, and it effectively leads nowhere for the van. But it's quiet, and more importantly, there's no security, so the van could park up, lose the plates and then, after ten, maybe fifteen minutes waiting time, it could return out into Ludgate, a completely different white van.'

'Okay, so can we check the local cameras?'

'I did,' Billy nodded. 'And the problem I have is that in the next fifteen minutes, at least eight white vans travel through the Farringdon Street crossroads. Sixteen if I push it to half an hour. And another five head east. I can follow them, but each one takes a ton of paperwork, and if they've changed the plates, we don't know what one it is. Especially as we don't keep the data.'

'How do you mean?' Anjli asked.

'When a car or van goes through an ANPR camera, we don't record full number plates,' Billy explained. 'They're converted into a tag through a non-reversible encryption process. The same plate will produce the same tag when the vehicle pops up on other ANPR cameras, and this enables journey times to be judged and anonymity to be maintained. But until we have the tag, we have to do all of it manually.'

Declan nodded. 'So why the low voice?'

'Because nobody outside the police knows where the ANPR cameras are,' Billy replied cautiously. 'Even freedom of information acts only give the answer that there's fifteen hundred or so cameras, not the actual locations. Nobody knows the crossroads, the streets, the lights. And for this van to drop down a side road, far enough from any of them to make things harder...'

'Could be a coincidence,' Monroe rubbed at his beard.

'I thought that, until today,' Billy pulled up another feed, the CCTV from outside a building on the south end of Edgware Road. On it, they could see the triangular junction where, earlier that day, Darryl Marr had been found. 'This is the best security feed for the van, and it turns up around now.'

On the screen, they watched as another white van pulled up to the left of the island, its hazard lights blinking, and what looked to be an orange flashing light on the top.

'Different plates, but it's the same van,' Billy pointed at a dent in the back door. 'The one in Amen Court had that too.'

'The one in Amen Court didn't have a light on the roof,

though,' Monroe tapped the screen. 'Or is it fake?'

'It's likely one that secures magnetically to the roof,' Billy pointed to the edge of the window on the passenger side. 'A wire could feed in there and connect either to the cigarette lighter or a USB slot, but I think this is self powered. You can buy them online with batteries in for twenty-five quid.'

'Amazing how one flashing light makes you look official,' Monroe muttered as, on the screen, two men in hard hats and high viz jackets walked to the van's back doors and, after opening them, started carrying boxes onto the traffic island. 'Nobody gives them a second glance. Can we get a better view of them?'

'Not really, Guv,' Billy shook his head. 'This is the only camera I can find angled on it. And the social media images all started once the men were gone. I'd say they're both stocky, one's black, one's Caucasian and dark-haired, although it's super short. And that's about it.'

On the screen, the two men, having placed the boxes down, closed the van doors and, after getting back into the van, drove off.

'And where does this one go?' Monroe leant in.

'Again, nowhere,' Billy replied. 'The plates are fake, this time a grey Mercedes Sprinter van from Wapping. They head off left, towards Park Lane and Oxford Street, but then cut left into Great Cumberland Street. Then it's right into Bryanston Street, by the *Hard Rock Cafe*. They should appear in Portman Street, but they don't.'

'Let me guess, but another van does?'

'Several,' Billy nodded. 'And here's the thing. The way they seem to know where to stop? Makes me think they're being helped.'

Now it was Declan's turn to whisper.

'You think someone in the police is *guiding* them?' he said incredulously. 'That's conspiracy talk right there.'

'I know,' Billy turned to face Declan, Monroe and Anjli. 'But these guys seem to know way too much.'

'Are you telling me that the *police* are providing details for killers to hide their vans?' Anjli looked horrified at this.

'Well, think of it more this way,' Billy replied, his voice still low. 'How many times have you heard stories of child molesters falling down stairs or having accidents while they've been in police custody? Vicious monsters found hanging in cells, or wife beaters beaten by police officers?'

Anjli winced a little at the last one; it was well known in the Unit that beating a domestic abuser badly was what caused her to be transferred to the Last Chance Saloon.

'It's not that much of a leap to consider that police officers would actively assist murderers,' Billy continued. 'They might actually think it's classed as vigilantism, that they're getting justice for things that weren't done—'

'Bloody Punishers,' Declan muttered. 'I've met a few in my time. People who don't want to wait for the courts to let the villains off.'

He looked at Anjli.

'I didn't mean you,' he said.

'No, you can, you're right,' Anjli replied. 'I did vigilantism. I beat a deadbeat abuser and would do it again. Just like you'd throw the Red Reaper back into a black ops site.'

Trying not to catch Anjli's eye again, Declan looked back to the screen, knowing she was right on every point.

'Okay, so going on the basis they're getting help somehow, and they know how to avoid the cameras, how much more of a nightmare is this going to be for you?' he asked Billy.

'There's a dent in the back of the van, so that should help

as long as I can see it on the camera,' Billy suggested, already returned to the screen. 'And it's a Mercedes Sprinter, and they have a particular shape.'

'What do we know about Kent?' Declan asked.

At this, Monroe frowned.

'Flat, rainy, not known for its mountain ranges?' he replied.

Declan paused, realised what Monroe meant, and shook his head.

'I meant Spears in Kent,' he said. 'Do we know where he went?'

'Broadstairs,' Anjli looked at her notebook. 'I picked it up when we were checking into things last night. He moved in with a...'

She looked at the notebook, scanning the page.

'...a Kym Newfield,' she said. 'With a "Y" apparently.'

'Newfield?' Monroe frowned. 'How do I know that name?'

He shook away the question.

'Unimportant,' he continued. 'So Jacob Spears moves in with Miss Newfield in Broadstairs. Let's speak to her, see when she last saw him, or whether she has anything that could help us. Declan, take DS Kapoor and climb those thirty-nine steps.'

'Sir?'

Monroe grimaced.

'Gods, man, how do you not know the *Thirty-Nine Steps?* John Buchan?'

'I saw the movie.'

'Well, the steps that inspired it are from Broadstairs.'

Declan frowned.

'And you want me to go look at them?'

'Sometimes, laddie, I don't know if you're joking, or truly

broken in the head,' Monroe muttered, already tiring of this game.

Declan grinned.

'We'll head to Broadstairs,' he said, glancing at Anjli. 'Do you want to drive, or shall I?'

'Good, good,' Monroe, not caring about the answer, looked around the office. 'Billy works on the van, Declan and Anjli visit the—well, whatever Kym Newfield was to Jacob Spears, and I'll see if I can find out anything more about the connection between Spears and Marr.'

He looked back to the office doors as De'Geer walked through.

'Ah, good,' he said. 'Davey okay?'

'Yes Guv, she's agreed to go help Doctor Marcos on the Marr autopsy,' De'Geer replied. 'I'd picked something up though, that I thought you should know.'

'Aye? And what's that?'

'I spoke to two family members this morning, follow-up calls,' De'Geer continued. 'And Gillian King, the mother of the King Sisters, she said a year back, a production company approached her. Said they were doing a series on serial killings in the UK and wanted to get interviews.'

'On the Marr case?'

'That, and also Spears,' De'Geer replied. 'She gave me the details of the man who called, so I was going to call it up, unless one of you wanted to do it?'

Monroe stroked his beard.

'Both Marr and Spears are connected in a show? That can't be a coincidence.'

'It could be, Guv, I mean, there's not many serial killers in the UK,' De'Geer replied. 'Gillian said she told them where to go, and she never heard from them again. But I know Joanne

—DC Davey—had also been approached by a film crew about talking to them. It's what triggered the recent sessions of therapy, bringing it all back to the surface and that. She said no, too.'

'Declan, when you speak to Newfield, ask if she had the same people call her,' Monroe ordered. 'Maybe this is the link we're looking for.'

Declan went to acknowledge this, but stopped as Bullman leant out of her office, pointing at De'Geer.

'PC De'Geer, my office,' she commanded, before ducking back in.

Concerned, De'Geer glanced at Declan.

'Don't want to keep her waiting,' Declan smiled. 'She gets really ratty when you do that.'

Nodding nervously, De'Geer headed towards the office as Declan looked back at Anjli.

'Toss a coin for driving?' he suggested.

'Christ no, you can drive,' Anjli was already grabbing her coat. 'I prefer having a chauffeur.'

And, his role in the partnership now adjusted, Declan followed Anjli out of the office, doffing his imaginary cap.

'Yes, Mi'lady,' he replied as, grinning, Billy returned to the monitors.

Watching De'Geer enter Bullman's office, Monroe frowned. Even though she was his immediate superior, D Supt Bullman would usually keep him informed on any departmental issues. And De'Geer being pulled into an office out of the blue felt very much like that.

'Stay safe, laddie,' he muttered, half to himself as he picked up his own jacket and left the office.

8

CHOICES

'Am I in trouble, Ma'am?' De'Geer knew this wasn't the best start to a conversation with a superior, but at the same time, he wasn't often waved into his superior's office, and the sudden way this had occurred now worried him.

'Sit down, Morten,' Bullman was already returning to her chair on the other side of her desk, running a hand through her short, currently spiked white hair with an unreadable expression.

De'Geer, noting the use of his first name, didn't move.

'I'd prefer to stand, Ma'am,' he said. 'Whatever I've done—'

'You've done nothing,' Bullman waved a hand. 'Sit.'

'Is it my family—'

'Ah,' Bullman chuckled. 'I'm sorry, PC De'Geer, I think your imagination has created a situation far worse than you would care to imagine.'

Leaning back in her chair, allowing it to rock back slightly, she smiled.

'This isn't a conversation about your family, or any kind of issue concerning your policing. Well, in a way it is, I suppose.'

'Ma'am?'

Bullman irritably waved De'Geer to sit, and this time he did so.

'I'm talking to you about your future,' she said.

'My—oh,' De'Geer visibly relaxed when he realised he wasn't about to receive a bollocking. 'Ma'am.'

'And stop parroting bloody "Ma'am",' Bullman snapped. 'Look, De'Geer. People like you and me, we're different.'

'We are?'

'Yes,' Bullman shifted in her chair, rocking it back and forth like a rocking chair. 'Monroe created this unit of misfit toys, not only to solve major crimes, but to make sure officers and detectives that were too good to be fired after what *dumb-assery* they'd done could continue to work usefully in the force.'

'Ma—I mean, yes, boss.'

'But me and you? We're different,' Bullman continued. 'We were brought in due to our connections to the Unit. Or, in your case, because Monroe saw something in you, and brought you with us when we returned from our little holiday in Hurley.'

De'Geer didn't answer, still wondering where this was going.

'You're probably wondering where this is going,' Bullman continued, as if reading his mind. 'I know you're doing night classes, and that you have an interest in joining forensics with Doctor Marcos, who speaks highly of you, by the way.'

'I do,' De'Geer nodded vigorously now. 'I mean, honestly, I love my job, and I know that policing is a vocation—'

'About that,' Bullman interrupted. 'I want to speak about your police career, too.'

'Sorry, but I thought we *were* talking about my police career,' De'Geer was frowning, confused by the conversation now.

'Yes,' Bullman clicked her tongue against the top of her mouth. 'So let me explain better. I've been talking to your superiors, and I know Sergeant Mantel downstairs is moving on in a couple of months. He'd only come here to make sure the transition to an actual police Command Unit, rather than a broom cupboard in a Barrister's office was seamless, and now that's done he's on the move again, and I'd like to put you forward for your Sergeant's exam, so you can replace him.'

'Sergeant De'Geer,' the words sounded strange, but strangely comforting on De'Geer's lips, as he spoke them aloud. 'Ma'am, thank you. I—'

'Hold on,' Bullman raised a hand. 'That's not all, as I also had a chat with DCI Freeman over at Maidenhead nick.'

De'Geer knew his old boss, DCI Freeman well; back when DI Walsh had taken on the Red Reaper case, De'Geer had been part of Maidenhead's Command Unit, working as a motorcycle unit police officer, and had been brought on to DI Walsh's case as a liaison.

'I hope he was complimentary?' De'Geer offered.

'More than that,' Bullman replied, watching De'Geer as she spoke. 'It seems that Berkshire and Thames Valley in general are building up their SOCO and CSI units, and have a couple of vacancies coming up. One's for an experienced applicant, but there's a role opening for a Crime Scene Investigator. It asks for a two or three-year probationary period as a general police constable, and I know you've only just reached that, but the level of work you've done during that time, added to the variety of roles you've taken, the work you've done with Rosanna Marcos and the forensic degree you've been taking night classes in, all give you enough brownie points to be considered. And, after chatting to Freeman, I think you could fit that bill nicely.'

De'Geer stared open mouthed for a moment.

'I could actually *work* in forensics?' he whispered. 'I could do what...'

He trailed off, frowning.

'Ma'am, to be a Sergeant is a dream, and definitely on my career checklist,' he said carefully. 'And working in forensics is what I've looked to do since arriving in the force. And I'll admit, as much as I love the Unit, there is comfort knowing I'd be close to my family. But this feels like a *one or the other* situation.'

Bullman nodded.

'If you take the Maidenhead job, you'll need to resign from the force,' she said, checking a piece of paper. 'CSIs aren't police officers as such, they're now classed as support staff, civilians employed by police forces. And you would be required to be a civilian to be accepted into the role.'

'But DC Davey—'

'Yes, Joanne Davey,' Bullman leant back in her chair. 'Technically, she's not forensics. She moved into the police from forensics, and therefore went the opposite way, from civilian to officer. When she joined the police, she worked alongside Doctor Marcos, and because of her prior knowledge was brought into Doctor Marcos' old team to assist when they were shorthanded and was damned by association when Doctor Marcos was banned from crime scenes a year back. Because of this, she ended up staying with her, because the alternative was to start all over again on the career ladder. On paper, she's a DC in this Unit. In actuality, we both know she's more CSI.'

'Could I not do that?' De'Geer seemed put out that he had to leave the force, while Davey had been allowed to keep the rank; but at the same time, he understood how her own route had worked.

'Rosanna asked the same,' Bullman smiled. 'She was trying to expand her own department, but we don't have the funds. Scotland Yard already keeps telling me Davey is one officer too many in her department.'

'But Joanne is the only officer in her department,' De'Geer replied.

'Exactly,' Bullman leant forward once more, the leather in the chair squeaking as she moved in it.

'Look, Morten,' she said softly. 'I don't need an answer now, so go out, take a day or two by yourself to mull it over. If you want to go for the Sergeant's exam, I'll happily put you forward, even give you some pointers to get yourself through it. You're a hell of an asset, and I'd prefer to keep you, especially at a higher rank. But, if you want to follow a forensics career, I can definitely get you into Maidenhead, once you hand in your notice. It's up to you.'

De'Geer sat in the chair opposite, wide-eyed and silent.

'Thank you, Ma'am,' he eventually said, rising from his seated position and standing to attention. 'Whatever the answer I give, I won't let you down.'

'I know,' Bullman waved De'Geer off. 'Now go catch a killer.'

As De'Geer left the office, Bullman rubbed at her temples and watched the Viking through the windows. While she had multiple uniforms at her disposal, De'Geer had become an integral part of the Unit, and the thought of losing him to DCI Freeman was galling. However, no matter how hard she'd tried, she simply couldn't make the numbers work to keep him. And, during the fallow periods between intense cases, a heavy forensics department simply wasn't needed.

'Bollocks,' she muttered to herself as she returned to her paperwork. 'Bollocks, bollocks, bollocks.'

THE ROUTE TO BROADSTAIRS WAS EASIER THAN DECLAN HAD expected; most of it was down the M2 motorway and it was only the last section, running south of Herne Bay and Margate where the roads became more winding and complicated.

Although Broadstairs was often linked to Margate along the coast and to the north, it was actually a small residential street off the Ramsgate Road where Kym Newfield lived. Declan had wanted to find the thirty-nine steps Monroe had talked about, but had learned there were around a hundred concrete steps instead, eroding away after time, the location now a bush-covered abandoned entrance, secured with a metal gate at the back of a private residential estate.

'Should have called it the hundred-and-ten steps,' Declan muttered as he glared out of the window. Even though Anjli had suggested he drive, they'd ended up going in Anjli's car, and as such, Declan had been designated as the navigator, as Anjli still didn't trust her car's navigation system, and hadn't wanted to use her own phone in CarPlay mode.

'The concrete ones weren't there when Buchan was here convalescing and writing his novel,' Anjli replied knowledgeably, beeping her horn at a compact car that had undertaken her. 'They were put there in the forties. Back in his time, they were wooden steps that broke over the years.'

'So *they* were the thirty-nine steps?' Declan asked, interested once more.

'Well, more the seventy-eight steps,' Anjli smiled, enjoying the growing irritation on Declan's face as she spoke. 'So, yeah, even they weren't right. But that's the way with authors and inspiration. Look at Temple Inn. We work there every day and we don't see half the things named in books like the *Da Vinci Code*.'

Declan shrugged at this.

'That's because we're barely there,' he replied. 'If we're not in Birmingham or Hurley... the City of London's a rarity for us these days. I mean, look at that incident in Middle Temple Hall, where that con man guy was being hunted for murder? We were all in the bloody Peak District, and there it was, happening on our doorstep.'

'You mean Damian Lewis?' Anjli frowned.

'Lucas,' Declan corrected. 'Damian Lewis is an actor.'

'Well, whatever his name was, he was innocent in the end, wasn't he?'

'Still didn't stop half of Bishopsgate turning up,' Declan commented.

'We had our officers there too,' Anjli grinned. 'PC Cooper was one of the first on scene, as she wasn't with us up north.'

Declan leant back in the passenger seat.

'Can't believe I never knew her first name,' he muttered.

'In fairness, how many of the uniforms do you know?' Anjli kept her eyes on the road as she spoke, but Declan could feel the gaze mentally burrowing into his head. 'You're never talking with them downstairs.'

'It's because I still get the look,' Declan said softly. 'They remember DCI Ford and DC Hart, and how I sold them out.'

He went to speak, stopped, and then continued, emboldened.

'A lot of the officers—no, scratch that, all of them—are good people,' he said. 'They do well, they're efficient and they're honest. And some of them understand what I had to do over a year back. But then you have the other types, the career officers who've been there for absolute ages, who got dumped with us when the Government upped our budget after the Red Reaper affair, and many of them came from Mile End, Whitechapel, places where they'd learnt the ropes from people who instilled the belief in them that *what happens in the station stays in the station.*'

'Those people are long gone,' Anjli shook her head. 'And I worked under Ford briefly, before you did, and I never realised what she was doing. Your instincts weren't wrong. And you shouldn't be ashamed of them.'

Declan shifted.

'I still get a lot of "no smoke without fire" comments, though,' he growled. 'From punching Father Corden—'

'Who told you your daughter was going to Hell, right before you did it,'

'—to being accused of terrorism—'

'Which you overturned, after proving your innocence,'

'—to the death of Francine Pearce,'

'Who faked her own death, after you found where she was,' Anjli was getting irritated now. 'Come on, Declan. Any police officer worth anything knows you've been targeted. And many of them said they'd do the same if they were in your shoes. Especially when you stopped the Red Reaper.'

'Yeah, that,' Declan looked from his phone now. 'I still get winks from them when it's mentioned. Little nods, as if they're saying *I know you found him and the fact he was never arrested only convinces me you offed him and buried him somewhere in a wood near Maidenhead.*'

'Well, they're not *that* wrong there,' Anjli smiled. 'You did dump him in a secret Government black site.'

'Exactly!' Declan jumped up in his seat and, surprised, Anjli swerved the car instinctively. Declan held a hand up in silent apology.

'Exactly,' he repeated, this time quieter. 'I didn't follow the rule of law like I should have. I fed my anger and performed vigilantism, just like these people in the white van are doing.'

'No.'

Anjli slammed on the brakes, the car veering sharply onto a lay-by at the side of the road as it screeched to a halt.

Anjli threw the car into neutral and glared at her partner.

'You called in that favour because we all knew the moment he was taken, the US Government would pull him out,' she said. 'It was justice, yes, but because you had no other option.'

'And the victims of Jacob Spears and Darryl Marr had options?' Declan asked. 'Because from where I'm looking from, they had their chances of justice lost. With Spears it was through a mistrial, and with Marr—'

'I didn't say it was a flawless world,' Anjli, placing her car into drive once more clicked the indicator on and pulled out into the road. 'But I won't have you comparing yourself to—well, *those* people.'

Declan smiled weakly.

'It's still why I have trouble with getting to know coppers,' he said. 'Going back to the original conversation, that is.'

'Save the cat by proxy, that's what you need,' Anjli nodded.

'What bloody cat?' Declan frowned. 'And why does it need saving?'

'It's a movie term,' Anjli smiled now as she spoke, knowing that this would confuse Declan enough to pull him away from whatever melancholy he was aiming for. 'Back in the day, movies would spend ages building up the anti-heroes, showing the audience why they needed to root for them. But nowadays, you need to get it in there fast. So, "save the cat". This guy's on the edge, and he's just killed some bad guys, but look, he's stopped to pull a kitten out of a tree and pass it to a little kid. He's not that bad after all.'

'I still don't get how this affects me.'

'Save the cat by proxy is different,' Anjli continued. 'That's when a character the audience already like vouches for someone. Then, you kinda like that person by default, because you trust the first character's instincts.'

'How do you know this?'

'Read it during the *Magpie* case,' Anjli shrugged, turning left down a small residential street. 'Anyway, we can use it here. You tell me who doesn't like you, and if they like me, I'll be super nice about you, and they'll like you by proxy.'

Declan smiled.

'PC Deval doesn't like me.'

'There you go!' Anjli nodded as she pulled the car into a parking space on the side of the street. 'Jimmy Deval likes me. So I can help you there. Why doesn't he like you?'

'Because he fancies you, and I'm currently dating you.'

Anjli went to reply, and then decided better, laughing.

'Okay, so that one might be unsalvageable.'

'Anj,' Declan was removing his seatbelt. 'We do enough, right?'

'How do you mean?'

'Well, Billy and Andrade, they're always out on dates,' Declan felt uncomfortable bringing this up, but the cork was already out of the bottle. 'And we never really did that. We went from friends to—'

'To cohabiting?' Anjli opened the door, stepping out onto the street. 'We did that long before we started sleeping together.'

She laughed as Declan flushed at the comment.

'Dates are nice, but they're mainly for people who don't live together,' she said. 'Billy and the spy can only really see each other when they're on dates. And, remember, Billy's richer than God and doesn't remember how an oven works, so he's always eating out when his butler's off for the night.'

'Billy has a butler?'

'I dunno,' Anjli shrugged. 'He always strikes me as someone who should, though.'

Considering the rabbit hole they were now about to fall into, Declan decided the best thing was to steer the conversation back onto track.

'Would you like us to go on more dates?' he asked.

'What I'd like is for you to stop asking silly bloody questions while we're outside a murder victim's house,' Anjli gave Declan a little squeeze on the arm. 'And stop worrying about things like this, or I'll dump your arse and go shack up with Jimmy Deval. He has a velvet smoking jacket. It's red. I saw photos.'

'Well, then in that case I can't compete,' smiling back, Declan led Anjli up the path towards the front door of Kym Newfield's house. Standing in front of it, he began knocking forcefully on the door in the way that police officers all seemed to know, a knock that was both commanding and, at the same time, respectful. Pulling out his warrant card, he looked up from it as the door opened, and a middle-aged woman, no taller than five feet and with frizzy blonde hair that looked more permed than natural, stared out at them.

'Miss Newfield?' he asked, raising his card to show. 'I'm—'

'Detective Inspector Declan Walsh,' a male voice spoke, and Declan looked above Kym Newfield's curly hair to see a large black television camera aimed at his face, the owner of which was half hidden by the eyepiece, but with a visible and excited smile on his lips.

'We're big fans of you,' the cameraman said, stepping back, partly to allow Declan and Anjli in, but also to get a better shot. 'And we've been waiting for a while for you to turn up.'

9

MANKY BAMPOT

'So explain to me again why exactly you seem to be swanning around London, at the same time two serial killers get offed?'

Monroe picked up his glass of whisky and sipped at it as he looked across the table at Derek Sutton, currently drinking a pint of bitter ale with a smile on his face.

'What's the matter, Ali?' Sutton drawled comfortably, his Scottish accent broader since his return home. 'Did your wee birdies forget to mention I wasn't in Drumchapel at the moment?'

'I don't know what *wee birdies* you mean,' Monroe kept his poker face calm as he replied. 'If you're insinuating I've been keeping tabs on you—'

'Aye, that's what I'm insinuating, fella.'

'—I can tell you without fear that you're mistaken,' Monroe didn't even skip a syllable as he lied, deciding quietly to get better spies in Scotland, while speaking over Sutton as he continued. 'I have no earthly interest in whatever shenanigans you've got yourself into. Especially since the last time we met, you convinced me I had a grandniece that turned out to be yours.'

'Hmm. Sorry for playing you like a dobber,' Sutton placed the pint down, fixing Monroe with his eyes. 'I do owe you for that. You sorted a problem I couldn't fix, and I appreciate it more than you know. So, whatever you need, aye?'

He looked around.

'Why are we meeting here again?'

'It's the Clachan Pub,' Monroe was writing in his notebook as he spoke. 'Gaelic for "Meeting Place". I thought it'd remind you of home.'

'Aye, thanks for reminding me of what Clachan means, you eejit,' Sutton growled sarcastically. 'And thanks for bringing me to what Walt Disney obviously decided was a Scottish bar.'

Monroe watched Sutton carefully. He'd arrived in a suit, which was the first red flag to Monroe; usually Derek Sutton wore clothing that allowed more movement, with bulkier jackets tailored to hold weapons.

But right now, Sutton looked like a solicitor.

'Christ,' Monroe muttered in revelation. 'You're in court, aren't you? That's why you're here. What did you bloody do this time?'

'I am in court, but not the way you think,' Sutton smiled darkly. 'It's my court case. Against the Government.'

Monroe raised his eyebrows.

'Already?'

'Aye, Ministry of Justice want it gone fast,' Sutton was talking about his incarceration in Belmarsh for almost thirty years, a sentence given to him after he was set up in a Government-sponsored scheme, one which had been blown open and exposed by the Last Chance Saloon a few months earlier, while investigating the death of a prominent author. With the case now public, and Sutton playing the *innocent man jailed for decades of his life* card with wild abandon since, Monroe knew that case or not, he'd be receiving a rather hefty windfall soon.

'I'm glad for you, Derek,' he said. 'Truly. They screwed you over something rotten.'

Sutton didn't reply; instead he took his pint and took a deep draught of it.

'What do you need, Ali?' he eventually asked, wiping the froth off his lips with the back of his hand.

'Actually, it's about Belmarsh,' Monroe replied. 'In particular, two men who were there at the same time you were.'

'And you want me to grass on them?' Sutton was surprised at this, but relaxed when Monroe shook his head.

'They're both dead.'

'Oh, aye? Did each other in?'

'That remains to be seen, but from the manner of death, I'd think not,' Monroe shuddered. 'One was electrocuted, one was hanged, drawn and quartered.'

'Bad way to go,' Sutton nodded. 'Saw a man done that way once. Stays with you.'

'You saw a man hanged, drawn and—'

'No, you *manky bampot!*' Sutton exclaimed. 'Electrocution! Blew him across the room, but not before he found himself stuck to the socket. It was like he was welded to it. You could hear the skin bubbling, smell the burning.'

Now it was Sutton's turn to grimace.

'Bloody nasty way to go. Who'd it happen to?'

'Jacob Spears.'

Sutton grinned.

'Oh, aye, well then, it was perfectly fine.'

'You weren't a fan?'

Derek Sutton took a long moment to consider this, leaning back on his stool as he sipped once more at his pint.

'So, I knew Spears,' he said. 'You probably already know we were on the same block. They stuck all us dangerous ones there. And he was a winky innocent.'

'I don't know that term,' Monroe frowned.

'So, I was innocent, aye?' Sutton explained. 'All my time there I tried to prove this, constantly told the guards, wrote letters, shouted from the rooftops, all that. *I was framed, I'd been set up.* Nobody believed me, but I kept to it, because it was the God's own truth.'

His face darkened.

'Jacob Spears would do the same,' he snarled. 'He was done for those wee girlies, and the courts had him dead to rights, so I hear, but one of the police in the case buggered it up royally, and the evidence wasn't admissible. They could only do him for one murder, and even then his briefs screamed bloody murder at this. And, when he turned up in Belmarsh, he was very much "I didn't kill those girls, guard", but then he'd punctuate it with a bloody wink. As if you were part of this sick little secret the little scroat had in there. Cost him a few teeth over the years. I'm stunned the little prick stayed alive until he was released.'

'How did he stay alive?'

'Kept with his own,' Sutton shrugged. 'There were a few "wrong in the heads" there. They had a little gang. And they all claimed they were innocent, of course. Even tried to start a therapy club. Asked me if I wanted to sodding join.'

'What did you say?'

'Nothing, but I broke the wee bastard who asked me's wrist when I tossed him out 'ma cell.'

Sutton chuckled at this.

'He was still in there when I got out, I think,' he continued. 'You lose track in there. I know they were saying he was likely to be out by summer, though. We couldn't work out how he'd managed it, but he was a sneaky, arse licking little bastard, so he probably wormed his way to a parole.'

He shifted forward in his seat.

'So how did he die? I mean, he didn't ram a fork into a socket, did he?'

Monroe shook his head and, as Sutton sipped at his pint, he told the tall, bald Scot what had happened in Amen Court the previous night.

'Bloody righteous,' Sutton chuckled again once he'd heard all the acts. 'Couldn't happen to a bigger and more deserving bastard.'

'And you weren't in the area last night, or wandering around with a taser yesterday?'

'If I had, and if I'd seen it? Damn, I have to say, Ali, I'd bloody well *help them* string him up,' Sutton smiled before stopping. 'Wait. Who was the other one? The hanged, drawn and quartered one?'

Quickly, and while Sutton finished his pint, Monroe brought the Glaswegian up to speed on the various discovered pieces of Darryl Marr.

'Bloody hellfire,' Sutton placed the empty pint glass on the table. 'Well, that makes sense.'

He motioned to Monroe to hold any thought he had, wandered off to the bar and came back with a replenished pint glass. Sitting back down and taking a mouthful, he smacked his lips, smiled, and sighed.

'Now then,' he began. 'Darryl Marr was a bastard too. But he was a whiny little runt. You see, most of us in there? We were bad buggers. We claimed we were innocent, and lord knows, some of us were, but we were always destined to be there. Marr? They cut him from a different cloth.'

'How so?'

'He wasn't in prison for the crimes he was known for,' Sutton shrugged, pursing his lips. 'He was known in the papers as the prime suspect for the King sisters' killings, Monica and Penny, and also for the abduction of Ethan Roe, the young laddie who also went missing around that time. But the police couldn't pin either on him, so he never paid the price. Few years later, he glasses someone outside a Rotherham pub, The Marksman. Vicious fight, more an attempted murder. He gets sent down for that, and the judge, remembering ol' Marr as the onetime *Durham Ripper* candidate, isn't shy on putting him in with the big boys for a couple of years.'

'But that says he *is* cut from the same cloth,' Monroe commented.

'No, Ali, that's the point I'm getting to, if you'd let me finish,' Sutton shook his head. 'So your man Marr there, he turns up in Belmarsh. And he calls himself the *Durham Ripper,* like he's taking credit for it. He tells people, quiet like, that he did it, did *them*, and the police screwed up the evidence chain and couldn't find the corpse of wee Ethan. And here's where it gets real; he said to a few of us, while trying to look tough, that they'd never find the bairn, because like the King sisters, he'd cut Ethan Roe up, but unlike them, he'd cut him up and buried him all over the place.'

'He cut up the body, like the King sisters.'

'Aye. But with the bairn, it was apparently into *quarters*.'

Monroe felt a whooshing noise in his ears at this, as if the room was sliding out of focus for a moment.

'That's not in the records,' he whispered. 'Nowhere in any public record does it state he dismembered Ethan's body into equal quarters...'

'Of course not,' Sutton replied. 'How can you know he's been cut up if you canna find the bloody pieces?'

'No,' Monroe leant forwards, his elbows resting on the table now. 'I mean, nobody knew this, except for Marr, the people he said this to—and the person who killed him.'

'Oh, aye,' Sutton nodded in realisation. 'You think the killer's someone from Belmarsh?'

'I think they're someone Marr definitely told,' Monroe was writing notes down as he spoke. 'And from what you said, he was trying to build a rep in there, so was very talkative. Who else did Marr talk to? Did he talk to Spears?'

'Aye, he had this love-hate relationship with Spears,' Sutton muttered. 'He felt he was better than him, that he'd got away with it, but at the same time he saw the other nonces sucking up to Spears, treating him like a sodding messiah, and when he started doing his whole "I'm the Ripper" thing, everyone laughed at him. You're only as hard as your crime states, you know? Your rep is everything, and his serial killer rep wasn't visible. Christ, Ali, even I was a serial killer by the law—'

'I hope to God you're not telling me something the courts don't know,' Monroe raised his eyebrows at the words.

'A serial killer is most commonly defined as a person who kills three or more people for psychological gratification,' Sutton replied. 'When I avenged your brother, I killed three men in a club. Sure, I only went to fight, they started it, and I killed them in self-defence, but I avenged your brother, my honour and a dozen other things that night. I gained psychological gratification from the closure. Ergo, I am a serial killer.'

He made a sucking in sound from the lips, mimicking Hannibal Lecter from *Silence of the Lambs.*

'I just don't dress like a nun while I do it, or sit in a corner having a cry-wank when it's done, you know?'

Monroe didn't want to envision either of these scenarios and cleared his throat.

'So, Marr,' he said, trying to return the conversation to the correct topic. 'He came to blows with Spears?'

'Aye and nay,' Sutton smiled. 'Marr hated Spears, mainly through jealousy. But, he knew he needed Spears and his buddies to protect him from us dark bastards. He may have been cleared in the courts, but if you're walking around a prison claiming to butcher bairns, then you're gonna get a shiv in the side. And so he joined the little therapy session Spears had helped start.'

'The serial killer's club,' Monroe shook his head as he spoke the words. 'Bloody hell. Who else was in it?'

'It was on and off over the years, but I remember seeing Eric Coble in the room with them, Lee Mellor, too. Oh, and that Yank, Kendal Rushby, but they moved him to another lockup soon after he arrived. Man was a nutter.'

Monroe stared at the names in his notebook. Amateur rock climber Lee Mellor had killed four nurses in a Welsh hospital as a teenager, three women and one man, literally climbing the side of the hospital to gain entry before they caught him. He'd claimed they'd let his brother, Kevin, die but in the trial it came out Mellor himself had accidentally bumped into him while free climbing on a nearby cliff face, and after Kevin Mellor's vicious fall, had transferred the blame onto the hospital and nurses who treated him for his injuries.

Eric Coble was a killer of at least three gay males in the late nineties, cutting them open before dousing them in petrol and setting fire to them, giving him the nickname *The Soho Ripper* before he was caught, claiming that his attraction to them had been because of spells laid upon him, and that as witches, they had to burn.

And they had caught Kendal Rushby after he murdered three whole families on Christmas Day in 2006. The police had found Rushby at the last crime scene, stuffed with pudding and turkey, a Christmas cracker crown on his head, sitting beside the tree, his shotgun in his hand, the barrels empty and exposed, waiting for them. He laughed at the police as they took him in, saying they were toothless. And in a way they were, as if Kendal had killed the families while in his home state of Texas, he would have received death by lethal injection, rather than life in a mental institution.

'They're all rippers,' he whispered. '*The Christmas Ripper. The Soho Ripper. The Angel Ripper.*'

'As I said, Spears had his club,' Sutton nodded.

'And are they all still there?'

'When I left, Coble had made his deal, and Mellor was gone to the psych ward,' Sutton thought about this. 'No idea about Rushby. He kept to himself.'

'Why wasn't Rushby in a psych ward?'

'No idea, I ain't a shrink,' Sutton drained the rest of his second pint. 'But I can tell you for free that they all said they were innocent. Even Rushby, wearing the bloodstained paper crown, reckoned they set him up.'

'Go back a bit, what do you mean, Coble made his deal?' Monroe pursed his lips. 'What sort of deal?'

'Coble was next door to a gangland boss,' Sutton explained. 'We were all clever enough to keep out his way, but Coble was a snitch. He got me in a lot of trouble for that, too.'

'How come?'

'Bugger looked like me,' Sutton shrugged. 'I mean, not as attractive, obviously, but he was my height and build, and shaved his head like many of us did.'

'Why shave your head?'

'So you can't be grabbed by your hair in a fight, of course,' Sutton explained like it was the most obvious thing in the world. 'I was almost knifed three times in the dinner line because of that prick.'

'So the deal was against the gangland boss?'

'Aye, and it got him out of Belmarsh, that much I know,' Sutton nodded. 'I heard they gave him a new identity in a faraway prison. Never heard from him again.'

Sutton placed the glass down onto the table, frowning as he did so.

'Those places you mentioned have to be linked,' he said. 'The location of the death is as important as the way they're murdered.'

'How so?' Monroe sipped at his whisky. He'd guessed this also, but wondered where Sutton's thoughts were going here.

'Remember wee Bertie MacIntyre?' Sutton enquired, not waiting for a reply as he continued. 'Got caught sleeping with one of Lennie Wright's cousins up in Glasgow. His male cousin. They castrated him and left him to bleed out in the docks, where the cruisers and doggers would meet.'

Monroe nodded at this.

'I remember,' he said. 'Nobody knew Bertie was gay. The

murder didn't out him, but the location did. It was a message.'

'Aye, and that's the same here,' Sutton glanced around the bar as he spoke. 'Spears would shock his victims, so the killer shocked him back. Marr reckoned he cut Ethan Roe up into quarters, and the killer did that back to him. They're going biblical here. Eye for an Eye and all that.'

'Could it be someone from the prison?'

'Nah, we'd have done him there,' Sutton considered the thought. 'Why wait until now? We could have got just as creative. Even the guards wouldn't have told.'

'What about the guards?' Monroe asked. 'Could any of them be involved?'

Sutton shook his head at this, but then stopped.

'Oh, wait, aye there might be,' he said. 'There was a guard. Mister Ames. Miserable old bugger, they let him go while Marr was in with us. I think he had some kind of twitch for serial killers. Spears was clever enough to keep out of his way, but Marr was an eejit, and mouthed off at him. Ames fair took his head off before he was pulled away. Was moved the following week, I dunno where he went after that.'

'Would he have known about Marr's claims?'

'About cutting up the kiddies? Aye, he would have,' Sutton whistled. 'Christ, Ali. All this talk about prisoners, and it's a screw that does him in, eh?'

'We don't know that yet,' Monroe finished his drink and rose. 'I should head off. You around long?'

'Til the end of the week, most likely,' Sutton rose to meet the detective. 'I'll know better in a couple of days.'

'Well, let's try to catch up when I don't need you to answer questions,' Monroe's face broke into a smile. 'Apart from ones about your new family.'

'That'd be nice,' Sutton shook Monroe's offered hand, and, with a loud cough, sniff and a straightening of his tie, he left the bar, en route for the court.

Monroe stared down at his notebook for a moment. Not only did Marr know Spears, but he also claimed to have killed his victims in the same way he was eventually murdered.

Now, Monroe had to create a list of people who not only knew this, but had the resources to repeat it.

Shivering as an icy wind slipped down his collar, Monroe headed outside to the now-busy street, walking back to the office.

10

LIKENESS RIGHTS

'So, if you could wait a second, I'll run in and film you both walking into the room, yeah?' the man with the camera said as Declan entered the hallway of Kym Newfield's house. He was young, in his late twenties, with curly black hair, a neatly trimmed black beard and a pair of chunky glasses on; they were in the Ray Bans *Wayfarer* style, but likely cheaper knock offs, holding clear prescription lenses within them.

'Yeah, that's not happening,' Declan held a hand up, quickly grabbing the camera before the man could reply and pulling it downwards, aiming it at the ground. 'This is a police enquiry. Not bloody *Inspector Morse*.'

The cameraman looked perturbed at this.

'It's not going out live or anything,' he whined, as if this made everything alright.

'*No*.'

The word was commanding, solid, and spoken by Anjli. 'Unless you want us to take that camera, get a warrant for your footage and confiscate it? We could do that quite easily.

It'd help our case, but it could take years until you got it back.'

The man reluctantly lowered the camera further, sliding it off his shoulder, patting at his beard, as if to make sure nothing had got stuck in it as he did so.

'Fine,' he said. 'Can I at least record audio?'

'What you can *at least do* is get your arse out of here until we've finished speaking with Miss Newfield,' Declan snarled. 'We have important and sensitive questions to ask, and I'm not happy with having ghouls like you in the room as it happens.'

'I'm not a ghoul!' the man exploded. 'I'm a serious investigative—'

'Are you making money from people's misery?' Declan interrupted. 'Filming victims, getting them to relive moments on the camera?'

He waited a moment.

The man didn't reply.

'As I thought,' Declan finished. 'Ghoul.'

'It's okay,' Kym replied as she moved in now, patting the man on the shoulder, 'I want Ian to stay. This isn't an interview, right? I mean, I'm not being arrested, detective...?'

'Walsh,' Declan added. 'I thought your man there said you were fans?'

'No, I meant *we* as in me and my boss,' Ian flushed with embarrassment. 'We knew you'd turn up. I only told Kym the police would be here.'

'Ah,' Declan nodded. 'So, in that case, Miss Newfield, I'm DI Walsh, and this is DS Kapoor.'

Kym nodded at this.

'And in relation to your question, this is mainly to collect a statement,' Anjli confirmed.

'Then he stays.'

Holding back an explosive breath of anger, Declan turned it into a sigh of irritation.

'Your prerogative,' he replied. 'Living room? Without the theatrics?'

Kym led the way into the house's living room with a wave, and, with Ian and Anjli following, the former still grumbling about the ban on filming, Declan took up the rear of the procession, pausing as he glanced at the photos to the right of him, secured in frames on the wall of the hallway. One of them showed Kym and Jacob, relaxed, another couple showed Kym, alone in group gatherings. In one, she had the haircut she had now. In another, she had a peroxide blonde hairdo.

Before he could be checked on, Declan pulled out his phone, snapped a couple of photos of the frames and slipped it back into his pocket as he entered the living room after the others. He didn't know if they'd be relevant, but with Ian around, he didn't know if he'd get another chance. And once out, he'd email them to Billy.

It was a cluttered, busy room; a bay window at one end gave light to a red-wallpapered, narrow space with a TV on the wall, black IKEA bookshelves either side, and filled to the top with an assorted and haphazardly placed collection of books and DVD box sets. There wasn't a single space visible, and Declan wondered whether pulling out a book from the shelf became the literary equivalent of *Jenga*.

Against the wall was a wide, leather sofa, well used and, from the current positions of Anjli and Ian, now sitting beside each other on a sofa created from cushions that had no support. There were two armchairs that seemed sturdier on either side of it; Kym sat in one, and so Declan took the other, settling in as Anjli, clambering out of the folds of the sofa, eventually perched on the edge of the cushion with her notebook out.

'We're here about Jacob Spears,' Declan said. 'I'm aware you've been told now about the investigation.'

'What can you tell us?' Ian interrupted. 'Do you have a suspect yet? Can I at least—'

'Are you family?' Declan asked.

'No,' Ian sullenly replied, realising this was likely to lead to another rejection.

'Then shut up,' Declan shuffled back around to face Kym.

'Ian speaks for me,' she said in response, before Declan could continue.

'And that's fine, Miss Newfield, but we have questions only you might be able to answer, and for the help of the investigation, we need *you* to give the answers, so the answers don't seem coerced.'

'*Coerced?*' Ian sat up now. 'How the hell does that come out? She's the victim here! She's grieving here! You should be doing your jobs!'

'Look at it this way, Ian,' Declan said, looking back at the cameraman. He was young, stick thin and in a black sweater. His beard was neat, and the visible part of his neck under it was acne-ridden, perhaps some form of skin condition. 'I can call you Ian, right?'

'Yes.'

'And the surname is?'

'Oh, it's Connery. Ian Connery. As in the actor.'

'Sean Connery?'

'Oh, yeah, I suppose. I was talking about Jason Connery.'

Anjli went to reply to this, but stopped when she noted Declan's frustrated expression.

'Thank you, Mister *Connery*,' Declan made a point of slowly writing the name into the notebook. 'The fact of the matter is that Mister Spears was murdered yesterday. And horrific as it is, look at it from our point of view. We've come here to what we believe was his partner's address to ask some sensitive questions, only to find her alone, with a young man who's not only filming her but also claims to speak for her.'

Ian paused, glancing open mouthed at Kym.

'No, wait—' he started, cut off by Anjli, as she, also irritated by him, continued.

'Now, we're not *saying* anything, Miss Newfield, but if this young man is in any way controlling your responses to the police, so soon after the vicious murder of whom we believe was your partner, we have to consider the young man as a potential suspect in the murder as well—'

'I didn't murder nobody!' Ian exclaimed. 'I'm just the cameraman! The producer said this was all right, that you'd be okay with this!'

'And why would the producer think that?' Declan leant in, doing his best to look more intimidating.

'Because of what the Prime Minister said!' Ian's head was swivelling around now, as if trying to keep everyone within his line of view at the same time.

'What Prime Minister?' Declan asked, a growing feeling of uncertainty building up in his gut. 'The British Prime Minister? Charles Baker?'

'Yes!' Ian nodded eagerly. 'He spoke at Prime Minister's Questions! You must have heard it!'

Declan glanced at a clock on the wall. It read the time as one-fifteen in the afternoon.

'PMQs is at twelve, right?' he asked, gaining an affirmative nod from Ian. 'We were on our way here around then. So, why don't you save us all the hassle and tell me *what our esteemed bloody PM said?*'

Ian nodded quickly, swallowing as he did so.

'He did a speech before the questions,' he explained. 'Mentioned the investigation, said there were two different murder enquiries, but that the victims were also criminals.'

Declan glanced at Anjli.

Bloody Charles Baker.

'And?'

'He talked about how the public shouldn't take violence into their own hands, and how vigilantism is wrong, but at the same time stated how he understood the frustration of victims, especially those without closure, and was going to put forward a referendum to the public, deciding whether we should bring back capital punishment for the worst cases.'

Declan almost snapped his tactical pen in half as he heard this, which would have been impressive, considering the durability of the item.

'He said what?' he growled. 'No, don't repeat it. I heard you. Bloody hell.'

Declan looked back at Kym, remembering why they were there in the first place. Nodding and catching her eye, he quickly pointed at Ian.

'Changed my mind,' he said. 'Out.'

'But she said—'

'I don't give a damn what she said about you,' Declan hissed. 'I don't know if you're a suspect or not, and by being here, you're obstructing my enquiries. So if you don't want to be arrested, I suggest—'

'Why don't we go make some teas?' Anjli patted the now concerned Ian on the shoulder. 'Miss Newfield could probably use one.'

'Yes, sure, I'll show you where the things are,' Ian nodded dumbly, rising as Anjli did. As the two of them left the living room, Declan looked back at Kym. He wanted to ask her how in God's name she could live with a monster like Jacob Spears, but he needed to step back and do the job he'd come to do.

'Sorry for your loss, as I said before,' he started. 'But I hope you understand, I have to ask these questions.'

'If you really have to,' Kym nodded.

'How did you meet Jacob Spears?'

'I wrote to him,' Kym replied simply, no emotion on her face.

'Why?'

'He looked sad. On the TV screen.'

'So you decided to become a pen pal?' this surprised Declan, but he tried to hold it back. 'When did you begin the correspondence?'

'A few months before he was released,' Kym looked up as she considered this. 'I didn't see the trial live, it was years ago. But there was a documentary on Channel 5. Not the one Ian's doing, but a different one. Anyway, this documentary haunted me. I wanted Jacob to know there were people out there on his side who believed in him.'

Declan watched Kym as she spoke. With her permed hair and bright red lipstick, she seemed vivacious, while also giving the impression of a church mouse, explaining a very rehearsed speech. Which was probably likely, as this couldn't be the first time she'd had to explain her strange attraction to an alleged serial killer.

'The evidence was quite damning, back then,' he said carefully. 'How could you know he wasn't guilty of the murders?'

'Murder,' Kym corrected. 'Singular. That's all the trial was for. And it wasn't him back then. It was the—I suppose you could call it his demon—that did it.'

Demon. Declan wrote this down.

'When did you meet for the first time?'

'About four months back,' Kym smiled. 'Jacob didn't want to at first, he replied to my letters but kept telling me I shouldn't be writing them. He said I should live my life, not wait for some nobody in a cell. But I told him I didn't have anyone else around me except my parents, you see. I'd recently divorced, a year back, and I wasn't in the mood for another normal, boring partner. I wanted exciting.'

'And a serial killer's exciting?' Declan didn't mean to say it, but the words fell out. And, as he spoke them, Kym's eyes darkened.

'He wasn't convicted of being a serial killer,' she said. 'He killed Anna Callahan, and he regretted it. He had addiction issues. The prison put him in a treatment program. He got clean. Found God.'

'Sorry, of course, please go on,' Declan replied, admonished.

'Anyway, he *was* exciting,' Kym continued. 'Through his faith, he found a vitality for life he didn't have before. And I could see it was partly because of me. I was proud. And, as time went on, we talked more. Belmarsh is only an hour and a half from here.'

She stopped, frowning.

'You know that, you've just driven from the City of London, so you know the distance,' she carried on. 'It's not like he was in Northumberland or something.'

'And when he was released?'

'I was waiting,' Kym smiled. 'I was outside the gates.

Drove him here, said he was staying with me. He changed his name to Dexter, as he wanted a brand new start, using his middle name, and he joined the church. I'd asked Craig, my cousin, to see if he could help with the name, but he wasn't able to.'

'And Craig is—'

'Craig Morris. He's my cousin. Works in Cheltenham. Always gave the big one, making out he was linked to Whitehall and did all that fake passport nonsense for spies, but he's all mouth, no trousers.'

Realising they were veering off topic, Declan went to speak, but Kym held up a finger.

'And before you ask, me and Jacob weren't sleeping together,' she said sternly. 'We were in separate rooms. Jacob still had night terrors and wanted to be alone when he was in the dark until he could conquer them with the power of prayer. We talked about being more intimate, but neither of us were teenagers, detective, and we didn't need to rush things.'

Declan nodded.

'Did Jacob ever speak of anyone wanting to kill him? Maybe hurt him?' he asked.

'What, apart from the national press?' Kym barked out a harsh, mirthless laugh at this. 'Jacob had people who wanted him dead, he'd had the letters all the time he was in prison. But at the same time, he wasn't Jacob anymore, now he was out. The demon was exorcised. I don't think half the people in this street knew my Dexter was "Jacob Spears"—until this morning.'

'Any problems from the neighbours?'

'Not yet, they're still in shock,' Kym shifted back into the chair, as if hoping it would protect her. 'But in time, I'll get the spray paint, or the burning shit on the doorstep, I'm sure of it. To be honest, I'll probably leave. There's too many memories here.'

Declan looked around the room, and saw that besides the photos outside, there were a couple more on the walls in here.

One of which was Jacob Spears, and a very familiar man.

'When did Darryl Marr come here?' He asked, pointing at the image.

'Darryl? Recently, actually. We'd only just put those up,' Kym sniffed. 'Jacob said he was a troubled man and that he wanted the warmth of Jesus to flow through him. But it never did. They had a falling out about four weeks ago, but Jacob still left voice messages on his phone, telling him not to give up.'

She stopped, her eyes widening.

'Is he the second body?' she asked quietly. 'They haven't announced the name yet.'

'I can't answer that, I'm afraid,' Declan replied. 'Did anyone else from his past ever turn up?'

'A couple of people from Belmarsh, but he always met them in Ramsgate or Margate,' Kym said, looking up as from the kitchen Anjli and Ian now entered, both holding two mugs of steaming tea each. 'He never wanted them coming here. I was his secret, I was special to him. He always said he didn't want his past to poison his future.'

'So you never met anyone?'

'There was one,' Kym took a mug of tea from Ian. 'A guard from the prison. Turned up, sat across the road in a car. Three days, he was there. In the end, Jacob had to walk over and speak to him. I never really saw him, he went as soon as Jacob went over. Had a history with Marr, I think.'

'And what happened?'

'They spoke, he left,' Kym shrugged. 'And I never saw him again.'

'His name was Ames, if it helps,' Ian offered. 'When we—well, when the company I work for started working on the documentary, he got wind of it and phoned my boss up. Offered to be a talking head, you know, interviews and that, but when they checked into him, they learned he was a right nutter.'

'How so?' It was Anjli who asked.

'Tried to kill Darryl Marr in a canteen food line,' Ian said, as if it was the most natural thing he could say. 'Didn't go down well. He was moved from Broadmoor in the nineties, too. No idea why. I guess working with bastards every day just does something to you.'

Declan noted this in his notebook.

'I'm sorry, but I have to ask a few more questions about the last time you saw Jacob,' he said. 'Can you remember when that was?'

'Yesterday morning,' Kym held the mug of tea in both hands now, cupping it as she held it to her mouth. 'He would always leave at nine in the morning and take a walk along the seafront, down to Ramsgate. It's three miles, so maybe an hour or so's walk from Viking Bay, along the West Cliff Promenade, you see. Takes you all the way to Ramsgate Harbour. He liked it because it was outside. I suppose after years of being locked up, you needed all the sun and fresh air you could get.'

She sniffed and wiped a small tear from her eye with the back of her finger.

'He'd spend a couple of hours there and then walk back. He'd usually get here by lunch.'

'What did he do in Ramsgate?' Anjli asked.

'Sometimes he'd see friends, ones he didn't want to introduce me to, but mainly he'd sit in a coffee shop and write his book,' Kym smiled proudly. 'He was writing a memoir, showing his route to Jesus.'

'And sometimes we'd meet him there,' Ian added. 'Do some interviews in the function room of the Oak Hotel.'

Declan noted this down, too.

'Just you?'

'No, there was a sound engineer too, and maybe the director, but it was only a head shot, so it was simple.'

'Did you meet yesterday?' Anjli asked.

'No,' Ian replied. 'We were done here.'

'So why are you...'

He trailed off. He knew why they'd come back.

Ghouls.

'Had anything out of the ordinary happened yesterday, before he went for his walk?' Declan asked, changing the subject.

'No, not at all,' Kym replied, shaking her head. 'In fact, he was in good spirits. But by lunchtime, I was a little concerned. Usually, if he was running late, he'd drop me a text. But he didn't. And the phone went straight to voicemail. I got really worried, even went down to Ramsgate in the afternoon, looking for him, but he wasn't there. And then, around eleven last night...'

Kym stopped, staring down into her mug of tea.

'He'd paid for his crime,' she whispered.

Declan rose, closing his notebook.

'If it's okay, Miss Newfield, could we look at the room Jacob was sleeping in?' he asked. 'We might find something that could help us.'

'I'll go with them,' Ian said, patting Kym tenderly on the shoulder. 'You stay here.'

Rising also, he nodded to the door of the living room.

'Up the stairs and on the right,' he said as he picked up his camera, and then thought better of it as he glanced up at the scowling Declan. 'I'll come back for this later.'

11

BEDDED ROOMS

As expected, Jacob Spears had lived a minimal existence in the bedroom; there were a couple of newspaper clippings, mainly of Arsenal Football Club blue-tacked onto the wall, and a canvas duffle had been placed on top of the small desk beside the window.

'I suppose he never got back into owning things after prison,' Ian suggested as Declan looked around, almost as if to remind Declan he was there. 'You literally have some changes of clothes, a couple of books and a radio. Hand held. Brought from the prison. After a few years, it becomes the norm for you. You're constantly moving cells, sometimes prisons, so you end up taking what you can carry. Kinda like a backpacking existence.'

Declan nodded at this, as he knew several prisoners who, after having the confines of the cells they'd spent years in, found it hard to readjust to life outside.

Only those with a loving and supportive network of friends and family seemed to do well, in his experience. Not that others didn't, he was sure there were people out there who did perfectly fine once they walked out, but either way, Declan couldn't envision being without certain comforts.

It reminded him of when he first moved out of his family house in Tottenham, when he separated from Liz and Jess. Liz had kept the house, Declan had been adamant on that, and he'd found a small apartment nearby, something to tread water in until he could work out his next step.

In the end, the next step had been the death of his father, and the inheritance of his house in Hurley where he now lived, but at the time, and not expecting this, Declan would sit in a camp chair in the unfurnished apartment and watch TV on a small monitor borrowed from Tottenham nick, trying to work out how he could assist with child support, pay the rent and gather enough to furnish the place.

And Declan had come from a world of plenty; Jacob would have come from a small, ten feet by seven feet, white-walled cell with nothing more than a shelving unit, a bed, toilet and a small TV.

And that was if he wasn't in a shared cell, with the various pecking orders and politics that such places gave. And he'd have stayed in that cell for fourteen hours a day, from six in the evening until eight in the morning.

The most Declan had ever suffered was a night or two in the brig while working as a Military Policeman, and usually that was because of someone else's screw up. Even when he was arrested for terrorism, he'd avoided prison.

Mainly, by escaping and running across rooftops, but why worry about schematics.

Opening the duffel, Declan found a small wash bag filled with toiletries, eye cream and moisturiser, and a Gillette razor, which he assumed had also been used by Jacob to shave his own head, causing the slight cuts to his scalp.

There was no toothbrush; Declan assumed this would be in the bathroom.

The clothes were basic and mostly thrift store bought, and the books were likely to have been picked up in the same places, as they were dog-eared and well used, with one showing a hand written "£1" in pencil on the first page.

There was nothing here, however, that gave any clue to the man that lived in the room, apart from the fact he liked thrillers and moisturised his face.

As Anjli wandered out to the bathroom to check on the toothbrush status, Ian sidled up next to Declan.

'I wanted to have a quick word,' he whispered. 'You know, while we're alone.'

'A word about what?' Declan stopped examining the bag, looking back at Ian.

'I know,' Ian nodded, his eyes not leaving Declan, as if this was some kind of super-secret code Declan would understand. 'That you're one of them.'

'Them?' Declan frowned.

'Victims,' Ian added. 'Who took the law into their own hands.'

Declan now turned to fully face the stick-thin cameraman.

'Explain *exactly* what you think you know about me,' he hissed.

'I know you had a Ripper kill your parents,' Ian said sympathetically. 'I know—'

'It was a Reaper, not a Ripper,' Declan corrected.

Ian blinked twice.

'What's the difference?'

Declan went to reply to this, but then stopped.

In all honesty, he wasn't sure if there was one, really. Perhaps the brutality of the murder? But then forcing someone to kill themselves was as brutal, mentally as anything else.

Maybe the kid was right.

'Go on,' he simply said.

'I know you took on the case, and I know you never caught him,' Ian said. 'The papers talked about it, when you saved the Queen and all that.'

'And they're right,' Declan lied. He knew very well where the Reaper was, and he knew he'd never get to him.

'I don't think they are,' Ian made a slight, cunning smile, and Declan knew without a doubt that, had he thought it appropriate, Ian would even have punctuated it with a cheeky wink. 'Come on, DI Walsh. You're telling me you found the killer of your parents, lost him and then moved on? You're not that type. You've solved half a dozen cases since then, when everyone knows you'd really be spending your every waking minute hunting down clues.'

'Who said I'm not?'

Ian paused, considered and then nodded at this, giving Declan the benefit of the doubt, before smiling again.

'I am,' he replied. 'I've interviewed tons of victims, and I've seen how they act. You're calculated. You believe in justice. And I personally believe you didn't lose him. I believe the Red Reaper is buried in a shallow grave somewhere in Berkshire.'

Declan couldn't help himself and laughed at this.

'Well, I believe you've read too many *Punisher* comics,' he replied. 'And I can honestly tell you, hand on my heart, that to my knowledge, the Red Reaper isn't dead.'

'But you wish he was, right?'

Declan took a deep breath, letting it out slowly.

He could deny this, shut down this line of questioning, but deep down, in the very pit of his soul, he knew he couldn't.

Not this time.

'Yes,' he replied, feeling a weight slide off his shoulders as he spoke. 'For what he did, I wish he paid for every murder. But what I wish and what I enforce are two separate entities.'

He leant in now, deciding to cut to the chase.

'What exactly is this conversation?' he asked. 'Where is it going, and what did you want from it? For a simple cameraman, you seem very well versed in the ways of the serial killer.'

Ian squirmed under Declan's gaze for a moment.

'I was hoping you'd agree to an interview,' he eventually muttered, nervously patting at his beard, most likely now sweating. 'As a victim of a serial killer.'

There was a very long, very oppressive moment of awkward silence as Declan's gaze never wavered, pinning Ian against the wall with his intensity.

'You know what, Ian, I've had a long think about it, and I very much believe you should leave now,' Declan hissed. 'Unless you have anything else?'

As Ian went to speak, Anjli walked back into the bedroom, pausing and frowning as she took in the scene.

'Did I miss something?' she asked.

'Only Ian here, deciding he'd be more use downstairs,' Declan snarled, still staring at the terrified cameraman. 'Wasn't that right, Ian?'

'Well, before he goes, I'd like to ask him a couple of questions first,' Anjli was still in the doorway, effectively blocking Ian's escape. 'Like why exactly he's interviewing Kym Newfield.'

'I don't know what you mean,' Ian replied, his voice now low and nervous. 'We're doing a documentary—'

'On serial killers, I know,' Anjli interrupted. 'But Kym talked a lot downstairs about how she's been hidden by Jacob, kept from the media. She even said that only now people are realising who Jacob really was. So I don't see her agreeing to interviews about being a serial killer's girlfriend.'

Ian didn't reply, unless his blinking eyes were giving morse code. However, before he could phrase a response, Anjli continued.

'But she could be interviewed as a relative of a victim, couldn't she, Ian? Is that why you're really here? Not for Jacob at all?'

'What?' Declan frowned now. 'Am I missing something?'

'Text from Monroe,' Anjli nodded. 'I'm guessing you haven't checked your phone yet. He spoke to his source and learned Jacob Spears hung out with a lot of serial killers in Belmarsh. We know about Darryl Marr, but Monroe said he also knew Lee Mellor.'

'The *Angel Ripper*,' Ian nodded. 'Killed four nurses—'

'I know what he bloody well did,' Declan hissed. 'How is this relevant?'

'Billy checked the names,' Anjli pulled out her phone, showing Declan a message. 'He found something.'

Declan stared at the message on the screen.

Lee Mellor killed nurse Andrew Holmes

Holmes was Kym Newfield's brother in law

'Bloody hell,' Declan whispered. 'So what, Kym sees what Mellor did to her family, and goes and befriends a serial killer?'

'She's already told you, she believes he's innocent,' Ian interjected. 'We think Kym started talking to Spears a while after her brother-in-law died—'

'You *knew* this?' Declan almost exploded. 'You knew this, and you *didn't tell us?*'

'I assumed you knew!' Ian snapped back. 'You're the police!'

'We're on the back foot, it seems,' Declan grumbled as he looked back at Anjli. 'This could mean nothing, though. Just coincidence. They might not even be that close.'

'They're not,' Ian, still hoping to be useful, chirped. 'Not spoken to each other for years.'

Declan looked up at the ceiling.

'Bloody hellfire.'

He pulled out his phone, tapping on the glass to wake it up.

'I think we need to find out where Mellor is right now,' he said, reading the text written on the screen.

'I can tell you that,' Ian spoke quickly. 'We did a piece on him for the show.'

Declan turned back to the smiling cameraman.

'He's dead,' Ian replied proudly, as if winning some kind of contest. 'Died in prison. Heart attack.'

'When?' Declan asked, already tapping out a message.

'About six months back,' Ian shrugged. 'I think so, anyway. Completely natural, so the doc said.'

'He was what, twenty?'

'Twenty-six.'

'Do you get heart attacks at twenty-six?'

Ian shrugged.

'You'd have to ask the doctor who signed the death certificate,' he finished. 'Maybe he can give you the details better.'

After considering this for a moment, Declan turned, walked past Ian and Anjli, and made his way down the stairs.

At the bottom, standing in the hallway, was Kym Newfield.

'I heard shouting,' she said softly. 'Is everything alright?'

'Did your sister, or any of your family know you were seeing Jacob Spears?' Declan asked.

At this, Kym's face fell.

'Oh.'

'Oh,' Declan repeated. 'Oh, indeed.'

'I'm allowed to see who I want,' Kym crossed her arms, obviously expecting a fight, her expression changing. 'And you, or—'

'I'm not judging you,' Declan held up a hand quickly. 'But you have to understand this gives me a new thread of investigation. From what I hear, you and your sister haven't spoken for years, possibly more recently because of your choice of partner. A man who's now been murdered.'

'You think my sister did this?' Kym started laughing. 'We stopped talking because I had an affair with Andrew! If he hadn't been killed by that maniac, we'd have run away together! As it is, we've not been in the same room since then!'

Declan froze, uncertain in which direction to go here. Something about Kym's words struck a nerve, a thread he needed to pull on, but couldn't quite see yet.

'Does she know about Jacob?' he continued.

'If she didn't, she'll know real soon on TV,' Kym spat. 'Look, Mister Walsh, or DI, or whatever you want to call yourself. I think I've had enough of you traipsing around my house. I'm grieving my true love's murder and all you're doing is pulling up gossip. Perhaps it's time for you to go speak to Marr's family, see what they know about his violent and bloody death, rather than hassling me and a cameraman just doing his job.'

Declan nodded.

'I apologise,' he said, looking up the stairs to see Anjli watching him. 'Come on, DS Kapoor, I think we should leave.'

He stopped, though, at the door.

'When did you change your hair, by the way?' He asked. 'You have an old style, peroxide blonde in some photos on the wall.'

'When Jacob came out of prison,' Kym spoke icily. 'New life, new me.'

'Well, it looks better now,' Declan forced a smile, and, nodding to Kym as he exited the property, Declan walked stiffly and quietly to Anjli's car.

Unlocking it with the remote, Anjli climbed into the driver's seat, looking across at Declan as he sat down beside her, noting the slightest hint of a triumphant smile on his face.

'You're not usually that clumsy or callous,' she said. 'What's the actual plan here?'

'Kym Newfield knows more than she's saying, so I wanted to push some buttons,' Declan mused, looking back at the house, the front door now closed. 'Earlier, when we arrived, she talked about travelling to Belmarsh.'

'Did she?' Anjli frowned.

'Oh, yeah, sorry—it was while you made the tea. Basically, while explaining it, she said it took an hour and a half,'

Declan replied. 'Which is fine, but she also mentioned I'd know it was that long, as I'd just come from the City of London. Not London, but specifically the City.'

'Maybe Ian told her?' Anjli shrugged. 'He was the fan, after all.'

'He was in the kitchen with you,' Declan shook his head. 'And if she knew we were City police, then all that confusion as to our identities was for the cheap seats, because she had to know who we were.'

'Or she recognised your name when you eventually gave it.'

Declan leant back in the seat as Anjli turned the engine on.

'Possibly,' he said. 'But then, when we mentioned Marr, she instantly asked if he was the second body.'

'She also said we hadn't named him yet, so maybe—'

'I checked the news sites,' Declan held up his phone to show Anjli. 'Before we arrived, just to make sure. The reports say a body was found, but not in what state. And as we left, she dropped her guard, snapped at me, said we should *speak to Marr's family about his violent and bloody death.*'

Anjli stopped at this.

'Jacob was hanged, so not bloody,' she said. 'And in a way, not what I would class as violent. We won't have given out the true cause of death for Darryl Marr yet. There's no way she'd know anything like that.'

Declan was tapping on the phone.

'And there's one last thing,' he said, pulling up a previously cached news piece on the screen. 'When Ian mentioned Andrew Holmes' death, I wanted to check something. See this photo? That's Andrew and his wife, Sheila. It's the image all the papers had when he was murdered.'

It was a simple image; a young couple in a summer wedding photo, their whole lives ahead of them.

'Okay, and?' Anjli waited, knowing something more was coming here.

Declan scrolled through the photo app.

'I took this photo of Kym's wall.'

'Looking for interior design hacks?' Anjli took the phone from Declan, pinch zooming on the image, blowing it up so she could see the frames on the wall better. 'Which one am I looking at?'

'The group gathering one, bottom right,' Declan replied. 'Kym, with what looks like family around her. Look at the woman, two people to the left of Kym.'

Anjli focused on the brunette woman Declan had pointed out.

'That's Sheila Holmes,' she said. 'Older than the wedding photo, but obviously her.'

'Kym said she'd stopped talking to her sister after the affair,' Declan took the phone back. 'She said "we've not been in the same room since then". But her hair is the same as she has now, which she claims she changed when Jacob came out two months ago.'

He counted off the points on his fingers.

'Lee was convicted of the murder of Andrew Holmes. He goes to Belmarsh, meets Jacob, and then, in his mid-twenties, dies mysteriously of a heart attack. Then, some point later on, Jacob is released and moves in with Kym. Only after *that* does this photo get taken.'

'With Mellor being captured, sentenced and sent to Belmarsh before dying, this photo has to be a good year and a half since Andrew's death,' Anjli nodded. 'It destroys Kym's statement about not seeing her since the affair. So, should we take her in?'

'No,' Declan looked up at the house one final time. 'But I want CCTV of that bloody cliff walk she reckoned Jacob was taking as right now, I don't trust a damn thing she's saying.'

12

RE-BRIEF

It was gone four in the afternoon by the time Declan and Anjli returned to Temple Inn and the other members of the Unit; they'd made the error of travelling back along the A2 and through the Blackwall Tunnel, and shortly after hitting Greenwich, as the traffic hit a standstill in front of them, they realised with the incredible hindsight that all motorists have when it's *just too late,* they should have gone the other route.

Monroe didn't particularly care about the minuscule details of the journey, but Declan continued to berate him with them for around ten minutes while he stood in the canteen, waiting for the kettle to boil—before realising he hadn't even turned it on.

Monroe had patted him on the shoulder then, looked at him as if he was a lost cause and left the room quickly.

Declan didn't blame him, if he was brutally honest. He would have likely done the same thing, probably with a little more mocking, if it was Billy who'd done it.

'So, what do we have?' he finally asked as he walked into

the office, passing Anjli a mug of tea. After one sip, she grimaced.

'Tea?' she moaned. 'Why didn't you use the machine?'

'Machine's broken,' Declan lied. He'd actually been so distracted as he made the drinks, he'd forgotten there even was a coffee machine, made worse by the fact it was literally beside the kettle. 'I think I might have fixed it, but I'd already boiled the kettle by then.'

'How did you fix it?' Monroe, having been with Declan and aware this was a blatant untruth, raised an eyebrow.

'I did a thing to the whatsit,' Declan gave Monroe a look.

'And how did you know what to do? With the whatsit, and all that?' Monroe, enjoying this, smiled.

'I don't know,' Declan glared at his boss. 'Just lucky, I suppose.'

Anjli, also aware Declan was likely lying to cover his own arse, grinned as she turned back to Billy, sitting in front of his monitors.

'Tell DI Walsh what you just told us,' she said, and Declan realised that rather than waiting for him to arrive, the others had just got on with things.

'Cliff notes,' he offered, as a way of saving Billy the hassle of repeating everything he'd likely just explained.

Billy turned back to his keyboard, typing on it.

'So, we're waiting on Ramsgate to send us CCTV, but they promised to transfer it to us, or send us some kind of FTP link to their cloud servers by the end of the day,' he said. 'This should help us not only work out Jacob's last hours on this planet but also show us what his regular haunts were.'

'Might even show us his abduction,' Monroe suggested. 'Well, okay, that's a little unlikely, but it can't help to dream.'

'Anything on the van that dropped him off, and then went to Edgware Road with Marr in boxes?' Declan asked.

'We found the white van in Marylebone,' Billy tapped on his keyboard as he spoke. 'Parked on a double line off Manchester Square. There's so much construction going on in the area, people didn't pay it a second glance. Still had the light on top, which was, as we suspected, battery powered and magnetic.'

'Plates?'

'The same ones we saw on the CCTV earlier today,' Billy pulled up the earlier footage of the van at the Edgware Road junction. 'I think they dumped the van shortly after they did this.'

'Any CCTV of the square in question?' It was Anjli who asked, wincing as she took a last sip of the tea, before dumping it on the side desk, glaring at Declan as she did so.

'There is, but...' Billy smiled, allowing Anjli to finish.

'Somehow, they avoided all the bloody cameras.'

'Five points to Gryffindor,' Billy nodded. 'The annoying thing, and the part that concerns me, is that we see them cut into Great Cumberland Street, then right into Bryanston Street, and just before the next ANPR camera, they disappear into thin air. Now, they could have changed their plates, maybe thrown the algorithm and the tag system, but we can see here—'

He tapped the screen, showing the image of the van.

'—that when they parked up, they hadn't. They'd have had to travel down Portman Street to get there, which we know they didn't as they didn't trigger the ANPR, so I think they mounted the pavement instead, bypassed a bollard and travelled up North Quebec Street, turned right onto Seymour Street, missing the camera they'd hit if they'd legally turned left, then up Berkeley Mews, and then zig-zagged along Berkeley Street, Gloucester Place, Portman Close and Robert Adam Street, all to get there without hitting a single ANPR camera.'

As he stated the names, he pointed at streets on a map.

'In fact, if they did do this, they've added way more distance to their journey, but bypassed half a dozen cameras. There's no way they did this without help from in the force, or from someone who knows the ANPR camera map.'

'Why park on the square?' Declan asked. 'Why not a side road?'

'ANPR cameras are usually built into speeding cameras,' Monroe replied. 'Manchester Square is where the Wallace Collection is. Roads are short, often turning at right angles. You can't really speed around there.'

'So your concerns were right,' Declan pursed his lips. 'They most likely got information from someone. But who?'

'Could be anyone, laddie,' Monroe shifted as he spoke, and Declan could see he was uncomfortable with the question. 'We've had a few people in the higher levels of Scotland Yard let us know, in subtle, roundabout ways, that they agree with Charles Baker's statement in Parliament today.'

'I heard he went off on one,' Anjli looked around. 'We missed it. Did he really tell everyone he was looking into capital punishment?'

'He kept his words safe and vague, as he's not that stupid,' Monroe stroked his beard as he spoke. 'But aye, he let it be known that although he condemned the acts, he understood the acts. It was almost a tacit way of saying "keep doing it".'

'Are we sure it's not him?' Declan enquired, almost a little too innocently. 'I recall he has his own private black bag organisation and all that. What if he's offing these guys to forward his agenda?'

'No, not now he's PM,' Monroe's lips narrowed as he considered this. 'He's only just hanging on by a thread, he wouldn't do something like this until he was completely secure.'

Declan nodded at this, accepting the answer.

'Derek Sutton?'

'He knew Spears, but not as golfing partners or anything,' Monroe replied. 'Said they had little get togethers, Spears and the other serial killers, some sort of therapy group in the prison. Darryl Marr was part of it. Also Lee Mellor, who our cyber-man here discovered had killed Kym Newfield's brother-in-law.'

'Which, if she had any emotions about it, she hid really well,' Declan replied sarcastically. 'But still, her entire story sounds suss.'

'Declan thinks she knows something she isn't telling,' Anjli translated. 'That she knew who we were, like she'd been expecting us, and she already knew about Marr's gruesome death.'

'Do we need to bring her in?' Monroe asked, his eyes narrowing in suspicion.

'We couldn't do it while the bloody cameraman was there, but it's a possibility,' Declan nodded. 'Let's see where we are tomorrow. At the same time, I'd like to look into this Ames guard they talked about.'

'Aye, Sutton mentioned him too,' Monroe replied as Billy started tapping on his trackpad to bring up a variety of screens.

'Jeffrey Ames,' Billy eventually pulled up a picture of a prison guard. It was a standard ID shot of a large man, thinning and slightly curly blond hair, fat in the cheeks and with the jowls of his neck slightly spilling over the collar of his uniformed shirt. 'Fifty-seven years old, although this photo was taken a few years back. Joined the prison service in 1996, after a stint as a social worker.'

'That's a jump,' Declan commented.

'I suppose they wanted people who knew how to talk to the prisoners?' Billy suggested. 'Anyway, he was at Broadmoor for about a year or two in the nineties, but was transferred in 1998 to Strangeways. Then, around ten years back, he was transferred to Belmarsh.'

'Where he attacked Marr.'

'Nothing on the record about that,' Billy read the screen. 'Left the prison service at fifty-six, taking early retirement as a form of redundancy.'

He frowned.

'The file is glitchy,' he eventually said. 'That's civil service for you.'

'What do you mean, glitchy?'

'I can't put a finger on it,' Billy frowned. 'But the page is playing up. I'll get there, eventually.'

'So he left the service a year ago,' Monroe stroked his beard. 'Find him. Let's see what Mister Ames has been doing now he's gainfully unemployed.'

'Do we have anything else on Darryl Marr?' Declan asked.

'Living in a bedsit in the middle of nowhere,' Billy replied. 'Cooper's there now, interviewing neighbours, but nobody seems to know anything.'

'Anything come from the Amen Court witnesses?'

'Only that there's a yellow barrier that comes down, blocking cars from coming through unless they have reason to,' With a swipe of his mouse, Billy now removed Ames' image and brought up one of the crime scene photos, that of a yellow parking barrier, currently raised up. 'The barrier had been left up after the Jaguar had entered, but the owner claims he'd lowered it after he passed through. Which means someone had to do that, but deliberately left it up.'

'Maybe there's fingerprints,' Anjli suggested.

'Already being checked, but unlikely.'

'Any news from Doctor Marcos?'

'Nothing as yet, but she did call in an hour back saying both bodies died in the way Spears and Marr, when alive, murdered their victims,' Monroe added. 'Spears was electrocuted and gagged, and Marr was sliced apart with a sharp weapon, with something heavy or powered, cutting through the bone. She thinks it could be an angle grinder, or something similar with a circular blade.'

'That's messy,' Declan considered.

'Anything involving Marr's death is messy,' Monroe corrected.

'I also checked into your production company,' Billy looked back from the screen. 'The lad you saw, Ian? He's Ian Connery, and his bio on IMDB Pro, that's the Internet Movie Database for industry professionals, shows he works for *Them Is Productions,* a London based film company. They're new, apparently, only have one documentary on the page, in pre-production. Working title of "Serial Killer documentary", apparently.'

'Catchy name,' Declan smiled darkly.

'Usually, if a project is early, they'll give it a title explaining what it is, but nothing more,' Billy shrugged. 'There's only one other name on the company register, a

Florence Dorey. I'm guessing she's the producer or director, and Ian's the cameraman.'

'Only two?' Declan was surprised at this. Ian had given the impression of multiple people involved. 'I thought production companies had loads of employees?'

'Not usually, believe it or not,' Billy leant back in his gamer's chair as he considered this. 'My family's invested in small budget movies before—'

'Of course they have,' Anjli interrupted sardonically, ignoring the blown kiss in response. 'Because what else does a little Fitzwarren need than a film studio?'

'We're not talking studios,' Billy smiled. 'A production company can make a movie with some basic equipment and Final Cut Pro these days. All that matters is the impression it gets. Them Is Productions has an office in Mayfair, so has the right postcode, but doesn't have a receptionist. In fact, when I called, I got an answerphone message saying *they couldn't come to the phone now as they're likely on set.*'

'Two-person crew makes sense,' Declan sipped at his mug, forcing himself not to grimace at the taste, as he knew without looking that Anjli was watching him. 'Although I'd like to know if they outsource. Ian mentioned others, and maybe one of them has links to the killers, too. We should get them in, see if they know anything. Also, I want to know why they were there today.'

'If they're doing a documentary, they'd want the best story,' Bullman spoke, now in her doorway and listening. 'They can sell it better if the primary focus of the documentary is murdered, so they're probably re-writing the whole damned thing on the fly.'

She looked directly at Declan.

'You mentioned in your notes they interviewed Jacob

Spears at the Oak Hotel,' she said. 'Check into that, see if the staff remembers anything strange going on.'

'On it already,' Declan nodded. 'And by that, I mean I asked Billy to have a check before we got in.'

'Because I have nothing else to do, boss,' Billy gave a quick smile. 'The manager's on break until six, so I'll call back then.'

'Get Cooper to do it when she gets back,' Bullman shook her head. 'You're at capacity already.'

'Ma'am,' Monroe looked over at Bullman. 'Are you joining us?'

'Actually, I only came by to see if you'd seen the video that just went up, connected to the case,' Bullman nodded at Billy. 'I emailed Spanky there, but as I said, he's probably missed it because he's at capacity, thanks to all of you using him as Google for things you could do yourself.'

She said the last part at Declan, and he flushed. Billy *had* become the catch-all for the jobs none of them wanted to do.

'Charles Baker? We saw the footage,' Monroe replied, but stopped as Billy pulled the link from Bullman's email onto a screen, and a YouTube video opened up.

It was a CGI woman, a very good render in fact, dressed as *Lady Justice*, the symbol of law and order in the UK, the traditional scales she usually held up left on the table beside her, as she spoke to the camera, staring at the audience from behind her blindfold.

'That's not Charles Baker,' Declan muttered.

'People of Britain,' the CGI woman spoke, her voice strangely off somehow. 'I am Justice. I am hope for the downtrodden, and righteous revenge for those left helpless by the authorities.'

'That's a computer voice,' Billy spoke as he typed, his

fingers flying across the keys before pausing the video for a moment. 'I can't get anything from it.'

Bullman had walked over by now and was standing at the back of the group.

'It hit YouTube twenty minutes ago without any fanfare,' she said. 'An account called "LadyJusticeUK", opened last week. The video was picked up immediately on social media, went viral, and looks like it's already on thirty thousand views.'

Billy restarted the video, and the CGI woman lurched back into life.

'I have been ignored,' she said. 'But no more.'

Two images appeared on the screen; images of Jacob Spears and Darryl Marr.

'Shit,' muttered Monroe, realising where this was going. 'She's outing our investigation before we can get anywhere.'

'She's not real—' Declan started, but stopped, realising he was arguing technicalities.

Lady Justice continued.

'Today, two predators, murderers, serial killing monsters are dead, killed in the name of justice,' the voice continued as the images changed to those of the victims; the King sisters and Ethan Roe, all believed killed by Marr, and the three women murdered by Spears. 'The courts failed to convict them, to punish them for the enormity of their crimes. They boasted of them. They laughed at us. At you. But they laugh no longer. Both men have been executed by the people, by *you*, the *helpless*, finally holding the sword of righteousness in your hands. They paid for their sins, and they will not be the last.'

'Oh bloody hellfire,' Monroe added by way of colour commentary.

'We are here to gain closure, but not just in the way you might expect,' the CGI image of Lady Justice now returned to the screen. 'For years, the family of Ethan Roe waited nightly for news of their missing son. A child known to have been abducted and murdered by Darryl Marr, but never found. Until now.'

On the screen, four lines of what looked to be numbers and code appeared.

54.783890143176556, -1.5169388490351035
54.81403390073841, -1.5595863588291887
54.779517759526854, -1.4768142031469158
54.77663788419051, -1.5567001387001294

'Christ,' Monroe muttered, leaning in as he looked at the list. 'That's GPS coordinates.'

He looked back at Bullman, who nodded.

'I'm guessing the local police are already cordoning them off as we speak,' she said, as Billy started typing the numbers into a map application. 'If they haven't, there's going to be a lot of amateur armchair detectives digging up land.'

'Oh, damn,' Billy muttered as the pins on the map application, each mapping one of the coordinates started to flash up on the screen. 'One of these is literally in the woods outside Ethan Roe's Durham school.'

Declan stared at the YouTube video still, as the lines of coordinates faded away, replaced by the CGI face of Lady Justice once more.

Four lines of code. Four parts of a body. Hanged, drawn and quartered. No wonder Marr died so.

'Before he died, Darryl Marr confessed to the murders, and gave us the details of where to find Ethan Roe as his last act of confession. This information has now been passed to the authorities,' she said in her robotic computer voice.

'Aye, by bloody YouTube,' Monroe hissed. 'Get me someone on the ground in Durham. I need to know what's happening here.'

Anjli was already moving to the phones as the CGI Lady Justice finished her video.

'We killed him,' she explained, her computer voice emotionless. 'We tortured him. We have no remorse for this, as he was an animal and needed putting down. And we have solved a missing persons case, left open by the ineffective police force for years. He died as he murdered; brutally, painfully, and screaming in fear.'

The CGI Lady Justice now reached up, pulling off her blindfold. Behind them, her eyes were glowing red orbs.

'And we will not stop,' she ended. 'We are Justice. And we will make sure no killer will ever feel safe again.'

And, with that, the video stopped abruptly.

'Bloody Nora,' Monroe hissed. 'Well, if we wanted it kept under wraps, we can't now. And with sodding Charles Baker making it his personal crusade to screw us—'

'Look at the comments,' Billy was scrolling through the feed. 'In the time we've spent watching, the views have gone up past a hundred thousand. We have messages of support from all over the world. People are happy about this. People *want* this.'

'Well, we're going to have to ruin their bloody days then,' Monroe looked at Anjli. 'Anything?'

Anjli shook her head, phone to her ear, still trying. As she did this, Declan's phone rang.

Reaching over, he picked it up.

'Walsh,' he said, listening for a moment before placing the receiver down.

'Well?' Monroe asked. 'Tell me that was Durham, and they decided to call you personally?'

'No,' Declan pulled on his jacket reluctantly. 'That was the front desk. There's a car waiting for me out front. A black, Government one. Apparently, the Prime Minister requests my attendance.'

Monroe looked at the phone on Declan's desk, as if it was about to attack.

'Marvellous, we're hunting a killer the public want to see win, the Prime Minister wants a wee chat about it before offering the keys to the damned city to them, and someone in the police is assisting them in their murder spree,' he muttered before stomping angrily back to his office. '*Find me someone in sodding Durham!*'

'See you at home,' Declan said to Anjli. 'I think this might be a late one.'

'Rather you than me.'

Nodding at Anjli, now returning to the phones in her quest to find someone in Durham who could answer their questions, Declan smiled reassuringly at Billy, finished the frankly hideous cup of builder's tea and placed the mug back on the desk with an audible groan, ignoring the vicious smile from Anjli, phone to her ear.

It was a necessary sacrifice.

Because he had a feeling he was going to *need* the caffeine.

13

CLANDESTINE MEETINGS

DECLAN HADN'T EXPECTED TO BE BROUGHT TO THE FRONT DOOR of Downing Street; he assumed he was still *persona non grata* to the Conservative party, especially as he'd not only shown up Baker through the actions of his staff, primarily in blocking him from Parliament, but also that the last time a member of the Last Chance Saloon had been in the building, D Supt Bullman had effectively blackmailed the then Prime Minister to reinstate DCI Monroe while agreeing to solve a problem for her; one that also ended the Prime Minister's brief career as such, which probably wasn't the best way to guarantee a future promotion of any kind.

He'd expected to meet Charles in some dank, dark members' club in the heart of Whitehall, with Charles Baker wearing some kind of fake moustache or something, a hat hiding his eyes, maybe, a far cry from the first, or even the last time they publicly met, on the Members Terrace of the Houses of Parliament. The only other time they really met, outside of a brief meeting in Temple Inn, was in the court-yard of Portcullis House, during the *Magpies* case, and Declan had soon realised this was because Charles Baker wanted to use him and his public sway as a line of political credit.

However, the car did head towards Downing Street, but instead of stopping on Whitehall and allowing Declan to enter through the wrought-iron gates that many Ministers were often seen walking through as they went for their own meetings there, the car continued, up to Trafalgar Square and down the Mall through Admiralty Arch, turning left on Horse Guard's Road.

'We seeing a parade, lads?' Declan asked the two burly special branch officers in the front seats; rather than answering his rather light-hearted question, they instead kept their attention on the road.

Sighing, Declan settled back in his seat. He knew there was a pub used nearby for meetings; he'd even been there in connection to a fatal poisoning recently, but instead of continuing southwards, the car turned sharply into a side road beside a statue of the Earl of Mountbatten, stopping at a set of black, wrought-iron gates that were similar, if not identical to the ones on the Whitehall side, a gatehouse to the left of them, and armed police officers watching intently, fingers on their rifle triggers.

Well, this is fun, Declan thought to himself. *Haven't had this many armed police watching me since I was a believed terrorist.*

After the driver passed his ID through to the gatehouse, there was a brief pause as the ID was scrutinised, and then the gates opened, and, after taking back his ID, the driver carried on through. Watching out of the window, Declan knew this was the *other* entrance to Downing Street, the one the crowds rarely hung around, as there was no clear view to Number 10 from it. That said, on a day-to-day basis, it was more likely to be the more used of the two entrances, mainly as it was a quick and simple way in for the lower-level workers and civil servants who worked in the buildings on Downing Street.

Directly ahead was a red-bricked house, known publicly as Number Eleven Downing Street, or as the Chancellor of the Exchequer's house. In fairness, the entire side of the street was all one massive building, with hundreds of rooms and around a thousand staff within the walls, so the idea of this building being there for two people was a little ludicrous.

Now through the gates and pulled up beside the building, out of sight of the cameramen further down the street, their lenses all aimed at the wonky ***o*** on the door of Number Ten, the driver nodded at a small doorway to the left.

'They're waiting for you there,' he said.

Declan nodded, leant forward and patted the man on the shoulder. He'd had his fill of special branch over the years, and recent conflicts had given him a bit of an attitude when faced with them.

'You know, some working coppers often say that you special branch guys are unfriendly, personality-vacant knobs,' he smiled patronisingly. 'But that's simply not the case.'

Leaving the car, and the two officers scratching their heads as to whether Declan had just insulted them or not, Declan walked to the door, which magically opened, like one of those shopping centre motion-detected entrances.

On the other side of it, with an expression of disdain, an expression Declan had once heard Bullman describe as "a bulldog that had eaten a thistle", was the reanimated corpse of Jennifer Farnham-Ewing. That is, Declan thought she had to be a reanimated corpse, as after the screwups she'd performed, he could see Charles Baker repeatedly running her over in his Prime Ministerial car.

'DI Walsh,' she waved Declan into the courtyard on the other side. 'Please, before anyone sees you.'

Declan smiled as he walked past.

'Look at you, actively allowing me into a building,' he said lightly. 'Will wonders never cease?'

Jennifer glowered at him as she closed the door.

'No, really, I'm proud of you,' he continued. 'This is genuine progress. Maybe next time you'll actually allow me to enter of my own free will.'

Jennifer clicked her tongue against the roof of her mouth in genuine annoyance at the man opposite her.

'The Prime Minister will meet with you in one of the smaller, lesser used rooms,' she explained coldly, as if by stating this she was scoring a point. 'Afterwards, you'll be taken back to your office by the same car that brought you here.'

Declan mentally groaned at this. He should have mocked special branch *after* they brought him home.

'It's a nice day,' he replied. 'I'll walk, thanks.'

'Your choice,' Jennifer replied with no care to his answer, as she led Declan through the corridors of power. Or, rather, some back corridors of low-level civil servants offices, many of whom probably never saw the light of day after they arrived.

'I'm guessing this is because of Spears and Marr?' he asked as they walked along the narrow corridors.

'I couldn't possibly guess what the Prime Minister wants to speak to someone like you about,' Jennifer replied coldly as they turned right at a T-junction, pausing beside a small, unobtrusive wooden door. 'He's in here.'

Declan smiled. 'So, be real with me for a moment. Is this about the video?'

'What video?' Jennifer frowned.

'The YouTube one, with Lady Justice and her weird eyes,' Declan said. 'The one that appeared tonight and gave four sets of coordinates.'

Jennifer shrugged.

'I have no idea what you're talking about,' she said. 'As for you, perhaps you should stop focusing on CGI people and look for the real ones?'

Declan considered this. Jennifer looked like she didn't have a clue what he was talking about, but there was something off with her reply.

'Must really bite you to know you can't come in with me,' he said, changing the subject. He had no love for Jennifer, and the only time he'd really met her, she'd expressed, in great detail, her utter disdain for him.

Well, turnaround's fair play, it seems, he thought to himself.

'Actually, Mister Walsh, I know what he's going to say, because I *told* him what to say,' Jennifer couldn't help herself, eyes widening as she realised she'd opened her mouth a little too much.

'Thought as much,' Declan grinned as he opened the door. 'So much for couldn't possibly guess, eh? And it's Detective Inspector, not Mister.'

Walking into the room, Jennifer now stopping at the doorway, Declan found it was designed as a sitting room, or reading room; the walls were lined with old books, shelves of them on every wall, giving the impression of a rather compact library. Beside the window were two ornate leather chairs, a small table between them.

In the one to Declan's left was a familiar figure.

His white hair was a little tousled, his tie loose, his shirt's top button open. Declan felt, however, that this was all for him, a charade to let Declan feel more at ease.

A man relaxing, having a relaxed conversation with friends.

Far easier to sell your soul to the Devil when it doesn't look like a sales meeting.

Charles didn't rise from the chair, instead waving to the one facing him.

'Declan, thank you for coming,' he drawled, currently at ease and comfortable in his place here, both physically and metaphorically. 'Please, sit down. Jennifer, please get us some drinks?'

'I'm fine,' Declan waved a hand as he sat down in the chair. Jennifer, however, ignored his reply, nodding curtly to Charles and leaving the room, the door closing behind her.

'She'll probably poison yours,' Charles smiled. 'She really hates you, you know.'

'That's her prerogative, and she can join the queue,' Declan settled into the seat, finding the leather both squeaky and uncomfortable. Again, he wondered whether this was a deliberate action on Charles Baker's part. 'I have so many on the list now, they should all have social days out and get some badges made. And you don't need to thank me for coming. I didn't really have a choice.'

'No, I suppose you didn't,' Charles nodded. 'When the Prime Minister summons, and all that.'

He leant forward.

'How are you, Declan?' he asked, and for a brief moment Declan wondered if Charles Baker was actually interested in his wellbeing.

'What is this?' he scoffed in response. 'Come on, Charles, what's the gameplay here?'

'Is it so unreasonable I could worry about your wellbeing?' Charles seemed a little miffed at Declan's outburst. 'After all you've done for me?'

'I seem to remember you forgetting what I did for you once you started pushing for power,' Declan observed Charles as he spoke, looking for any kind of tell on the politician's face.

'I had allies—that is, I *have* allies, who prefer me not to be associated with you,' Charles raised his hands in a *what can I do* gesture. 'And unfortunately, I needed their help to keep myself in this role. You may have moved Michelle Rose out of the chair I now sit in, but I wasn't the *shoo-in* you seem to think I was.'

Declan shrugged.

'I didn't vote for you, so I don't care,' he replied. 'And I think we've done enough for you over the last year not to be dragged into your political games, time after time.'

'Oh you do, do you?' Charles' face darkened. 'And how do you see that?'

'Well, for a start, I saved your career and life when Susan Devonshire tried to kill you,' Declan counted off points on his fingers. 'I removed Malcolm Gladwell and saved your reputation when Rattlestone fell. I saved your life—even when your own people didn't help—when a maniac wanted to poison you, and my team removed Michelle Rose, which opened up the chair you so like to mention.'

'You also left me in a car, and then on a roof, both times believing I was about to be shot by a lunatic,' Charles retaliated. 'You made sure everyone knew of my past indiscretions with rival MPs years ago, and also during the more recent Rattlestone situation—'

'MPs should be transparent. If you don't believe that, you shouldn't be one.'

'—you revealed my mole in the army research base, and you failed, Declan, you *failed* to stop our poisoning, allowing a *chef* to work it out.'

'Because of *your woman!*'

Charles folded his arms.

'I could have died. Right there. Badly. Slowly. All because you couldn't talk your way past a gate guard. In fact, the way I see it, you owe me.'

Declan sighed, staring up at the ceiling.

'So, go on then, what's this all about?' he said, eventually. 'Why all the cloak and dagger? And is it to do with your statement on Prime Minister's Questions?'

'Oh, you saw that, did you?' Charles smiled slightly as he leant back into his chair.

'No, I was given the crib sheet later,' Declan replied. 'Actually, while we're here, could you answer me a question? I can't find anyone who can tell me why is it called Prime Minister's Questions, when you never answer a single bloody one of them. None of you do. It's always deflections and attacking the opposition.'

Charles Baker continued to smile, and Declan knew it was fixed on while Charles tried to find a way to finish this obviously inconvenient meeting quickly.

'I suppose they just have to ask better questions,' he said. 'Anyway, the reason you're here is I need your opinion. A man of the people, so to speak.'

'You want me to go on record saying your bill for capital punishment is a good idea,' Declan leant forward now. He'd known why he was summoned from the moment the car appeared, and he was angry to be used in such a way. 'You want me to risk my career for your ambition.'

'Well, when you put it like that, it sounds terrible,' Charles grimaced. 'I'd never expect such a thing.'

His expression flattened out, emotionless.

'But yes, that's pretty much what I'm asking,' he finished.

Declan shifted in the seat.

'Why?' he asked.

'Why what?'

'Why do this now?' Declan repeated. 'Is it because of the murders? Is it because you've had this in your pocket for a while? I'll admit, you've placed a rocket under our arses, but also a spotlight shining on us with your speech. We hoped to get at least another day under the radar before the press came sniffing.'

'Sorry about that,' Charles apologised, but Declan was utterly convinced it wasn't sincere. 'It's all about the timing, you see.'

'Was it her?' Declan continued. 'Farnham-Ewing?'

Charles nodded.

'She has a remarkably unhealthy fixation on you, I'm afraid,' he said. 'She was given information from a source about the Spears murder, and this morning learnt of Marr.'

Declan forced himself to stay calm, to not rise from his chair, walk out of the office, find Jennifer Farnham-Ewing and strangle her, while wondering at the same time whether the source that told her was the same unnamed police officer who'd been over-sharing some traffic camera data recently.

Charles, seeing the barely restrained anger, sighed and moved closer.

'Look,' he said simply. 'I'm in a bind here, Declan. I'm

Prime Minister, but we both know I wasn't the first choice. The only reason I got the job was because Michelle Rose couldn't stay in it. And I'm fifty-odd letters of no confidence to the 1922 Committee away from another leadership vote attempt, which would likely lead to another bid, probably from Tamara Banks, the bastard child of Cruella De Vil and Heinrich Himmler, taking all this from me.'

Charles sighed audibly, and Declan could see the faint stress lines at the sides of his eyes. In the last few months, Charles had aged five years.

'She's a toxic bloody Thatcherite and a darling of the far-right-wing Tories,' he continued. 'I'm a Centrist who defected from Labour. And even though that was twenty years or so back, to some of them it might have been last week. And if I'm going to keep in power, I have to appease them all.'

'This whole bill, it's a way to keep the right-wing from kicking you out,' Declan nodded as realisation kicked in. 'This isn't about justice, or righteousness, or recompense for victims, it's purely about saving your own hide and staying in power as long as you can.'

Declan rose now, furious.

'You want me to risk my own career to keep you in a role you'll likely lose in the next election? To state how I'd rather side with vigilantism than with the law? Even with your little black bag organisations in your pocket—'

'It's those little black bag organisations that link us!' Charles rose now. 'I know about Karl Schnitter, remember? I know how you didn't arrest him, and instead used my Section D officers to stick him in one of *my* black sites; anonymous, and forgotten, left to rot forever. So don't start preaching your righteous lawman act at me, Walsh. We both know you would have done the same as whomever is killing these monsters. You just had a secret unit to do it for you instead, and kept your conscience clean in the process, leaving others to drag him off to hell while you washed your hands like Pilate.'

Declan stopped, unable to reply.

Charles Baker was right.

He had done the same, maybe even worse; he'd left the Red Reaper alive to regret the things he did, hunted down his parents' killer, and although it turned out to be rather complicated, and involving other people, he'd still let others make the tough decisions for him.

No.

'That's not entirely correct,' Declan shook his head. 'You're wrong. My dad wasn't killed by Karl, and *his* murderer is still in prison, awaiting trial. And Karl himself? The moment he hit a jail cell, we both know the CIA would have swooped in and taken him, given him a new identity. They owed him. Tom Marlowe took the favour on purely to ensure he *did* pay for his sins.'

'And how did that work out for you?' Charles almost sneered at he spoke, the fake bonhomie now missing. 'Tom Marlowe in hospital, now on indefinite medical leave, three or four agents of the Crown dead, Schnitter turning himself into the American Embassy, and the same CIA agents you wanted gone picking him up and jetting him out for a new life somewhere warm and fuzzy.'

'There was a mole in your organisation,' Declan replied. 'Your Rattlestone rejects did that. Not me.'

Accepting the reprimand, Charles slumped a little.

'I need this,' he said finally, returning to the topic at hand. 'And I need you and your department to ease off the pedal a little here.'

'You want us to *not* capture this killer?'

'Of course not, no,' Charles shook his head. 'I just think he's got one more in him, so let's allow him to do it. That way I can use it to build my base, and then you can find and arrest him.'

He placed a hand on Declan's shoulder.

'Whomever he kills would be a monster, Declan, we both know it. Someone who deserves to die. Someone who killed, who murdered—'

'For years, you believed you murdered someone,' Declan hissed. 'And on that roof, I stopped you from being killed for it. Are you saying I shouldn't have? Or are you saying only the *right* kind of murderers should be punished?'

Charles didn't reply.

'And how soon, before we decide what the right kind is?' Declan pulled away from the hand. 'How soon before it becomes based on colour, on class, on political advantage? You already tried to create a secret police, Charles. Don't start making death squads, or I'll be bringing you in.'

He leant close.

'You won't be the *first* Prime Minister we've pulled from grace.'

'Oh, I think this meeting is over now,' Charles replied icily.

'Damn right it is,' Declan snarled as he walked to the door. 'I don't work for you. My boss's boss's boss might, but there's a chain of command there. Next time, use it.'

Declan didn't allow Charles to reply, and swung the door open to find Jennifer standing there, embarrassed, having obviously been listening.

'Another great idea from you,' he snarked as he stormed past. 'I'll find my own way out. And don't worry, it'll be the back entrance. I don't want anyone out there knowing I've been talking to you today.'

As Declan carried on down the corridor, turning left at the end and moving out of both sight and audio range, Jennifer looked at Charles, standing in the office.

'It didn't go well?' she whispered, as if worried the leaving Declan might hear, return, and start all over again.

'On the contrary,' Charles Baker smiled. 'It went exactly as we planned.'

14

THREE-WAY FIGHT

PC Cooper turned back to the table with three pint glasses held precariously within her grasp. She rarely drank pints, but the pub had some sweet perry ciders on tap, and to be honest, she felt a little awkward sipping spirits while her fellow officers drank from the larger glasses.

Her fellow officers this evening in The Cockpit, a small, out of the way pub near St Paul's, and around a five-minute walk from the Inns of Court were Morten De'Geer and Joanne Davey, the former trying desperately to keep the latter's spirits up, even though the latter didn't seem to need this in any way whatsoever.

'I've told you all day, Morten, I'm fine,' Davey muttered as De'Geer, seeing Cooper arrive with the pints balanced together, leant back in his chair, moving off the small, rectangular table in the corner of the rather small bar to give her space to place them down. As Cooper did so, passing each officer their own beverage, she sat on a padded stool opposite them, raising the glass.

'What shall we toast to?' she asked.

'We don't usually toast,' Davey grumbled as she picked up and drank from her own pint, ignoring the offered toast. 'We usually just drink.'

'To friendship,' De'Geer clinked glasses with the grateful Cooper, before glancing back at Davey. 'And helping friends out, even when they think they don't need it.'

Davey pushed herself back onto the cushioned bench she currently sat on, folding her arms as she glared at De'Geer.

'I'm fine,' she repeated. 'Stop clucking around me like a bloody mother hen. It's bad enough when Marcos does it, and she's my boss.'

Hurt by the accusation, De'Geer's body language subtly altered. Davey seemed oblivious to this, but Cooper noticed it.

Cooper noticed everything.

'It's all right to be angry,' she said, placing the glass onto the table. 'It's a very traumatic moment for you.'

'Oh, is it?' Davey snarked back. 'Thanks for explaining that to me, *PC* Cooper.'

However, as soon as she spoke the words, Davey's expression softened.

'Shit, I'm sorry,' she blurted. 'I'm being a right old bitch today and it's not your fault. I shouldn't take my frustrations out on you.'

'So tell us your frustrations instead,' Cooper offered. 'Maybe we can help?'

Davey took another mouthful, swallowing as she took a deep breath.

'I'm benched from the case I should be on, and dumped into effectively an admin role with Marr,' she bemoaned. 'I'm not traumatised, I'm not angry. I mean, hell, I want to stand over the body of Jacob Spears and spit on his dead face, but I've got it together enough to know that's unprofessional.'

'You think?' De'Geer asked, and for the first time that night, Davey's face broke into a grin.

'Maybe it's a little excessive,' she said, holding up a thumb and index finger, holding them slightly apart. 'A tiny little bit.'

'Look Joanne, Spears killed your sister,' De'Geer sipped at his own pint between sentences. 'You joined the police because of this. Now he's dead, and you weren't able to nail him for the murder before it happened, so of course it's going to affect you.'

'I don't care about—'

'Do you want his killer convicted?'

Davey looked confused at De'Geer's sudden change of topic.

'What?'

'A simple question,' De'Geer turned to face her now. 'Do you want us to find and convict the killer of Jacob Spears, or do you class this as justice, and as far as you're concerned, "job done"?'

Davey looked away, glancing up above the bar where a small balcony stood, a couple of fake cockerels behind it. At one point the land this pub now stood on had been one of the few places in London that William Shakespeare had owned, and one of the six surviving Shakespeare signatures had been on the deeds. After the building was demolished, centuries later, the pub built on its spot had become a haven for cockfighting, a popular sport at the time.

Now, nothing more than another memory, a sealed-off balcony was the only reminder of what this place had once been.

'They used to stand up there and watch cocks fight,' she

whispered. 'Poor bloody cockerels, sent to their death. And that makes me angry.'

'Cockerels?' Cooper was confused where this conversation was going.

'Cockfighting. It's barbaric. Or, rather, it was. Back in the day. And the thought of people standing up there watching innocent creatures fighting each other, sometimes to the death, for their amusement, even though it was hundreds of years ago, and they're all dead as well? It makes me furious.'

Davey looked back at Cooper.

'But when I think of Jacob Spears, dead and his body now lying in a Lambeth morgue as people cut into it? I feel *nothing*.'

Her face darkened as she continued, her voice lowering in pitch.

'I don't feel anger, I don't feel happiness,' she continued. 'Spears was a rabid dog, and he needed to be put down before he bit someone else. And he would bite again, believe me. Because once a dog tastes blood—'

'Listen to yourself!' De'Geer interrupted now, the concern clear on his face. 'Rabid dogs that need to be put down?'

'I might think that, but I wouldn't do that,' Davey insisted. 'I'm explaining my emotions, not my desires. And that's why I should be on the case, because at the core of my being, there aren't any emotions. They all burned away when I gained closure. Not by an inability to arrest him for my sister's murder, but because his soul now burns in hell.'

As if realising she'd become carried away with her explanation, Davey stopped, taking a breath and calming herself.

'And now, I look at Darryl Marr, and I feel the same way,' she finished.

'Apart from the spitting on Jacob's face part.'

Davey made a little shrug with her shoulders.

'I'd wipe it off afterwards.'

'You don't need closure, you need therapy,' De'Geer shook his head.

At this, Davey actually laughed, but it was a bitter, callous noise.

'I already have that,' she said. 'It's how I'm the well-balanced officer you all know and adore.'

There was a moment of silence, interrupted by some cheers at the bar nearby, as a group of city workers downed some shots.

'Anyway, why do you care?' Davey moved back to her pint now. 'You're leaving us, anyway.'

'What's that?' Cooper felt a slight *butterfly* sensation in her gut as she looked over at De'Geer now. 'You're leaving?'

'I don't know,' De'Geer stared into his own pint as he replied. 'Bullman said I have an opportunity to become Sergeant.'

'That's great news, isn't it?' Cooper smiled. 'Although I'm not sure I could take to calling you "Sarge" and all that.'

'Well, you don't need to worry right now, as that's not all,' De'Geer added. 'There's an opening in Maidenhead for a forensics investigator.'

'But that's good, isn't it?' Cooper frowned, looking at Davey. 'It's good, right? Why's he look so miserable when it's what he's wanted?'

'Because he'll have to quit being a copper,' Davey replied sadly. 'Forensics aren't technically police officers. If I transferred anywhere else in it, I'd have to do the same. I only keep my Detective Constable rank because Doctor Marcos wanted me with it, to save her having to deal with other police on crime scenes.'

Cooper looked back at De'Geer, understanding now. All his life, he'd wanted to be a police officer; he'd told her so when they were out on calls together. But, at the same time, he'd recently found this love of forensics, and to have to choose between them was a horrid situation to now be in.

'You should take it,' she whispered. 'It's the best option for you.'

'But becoming Sergeant would place me on the career ladder,' De'Geer looked up at Cooper now. 'Forensics would be a dream, but at best my career ladder is crime scene manager, crime scene coordinator, and then *senior* crime scene investigator.'

'But you'd still be examining crimes,' Cooper insisted.

De'Geer smiled.

'Or I could ignore it and stay here.'

'Yeah, I don't think that's likely to happen,' Cooper replied sadly, and was surprised at how gut-punched she felt by the news. Morten De'Geer had become a good friend over the time she was at Temple Inn, and there was a solidarity between uniforms that the civilian-suited brigade sometimes didn't get.

'I can hope,' De'Geer glanced at Davey, and for a moment Cooper wondered whether the *hope* part of the statement was about his career, or rather the people he worked with.

'For Christ's sake, Morten, I'm not gonna shag you,' Davey muttered, seeing the look, and Cooper couldn't tell if it was a joke or not until the next line was spoken. 'So if you're waiting like bloody Greyfriars' Bobby for a shack up that's not gonna happen, I suggest you move on to Maidenhead, because I won't be here forever either.'

De'Geer's head snapped back at the first line, his face stricken with shock at the accusation.

'I didn't—I never—' he stammered until Davey held a hand up.

'Sorry, bitchy mood right now. Ignore it.'

'Why won't you be here forever?' De'Geer continued, narrowing his eyes. 'What don't we know?'

'Jesus, De'Geer, give it a rest!' Davey slammed her now empty pint glass onto the table, the noise momentarily silencing the small bar. 'Just get on with your life and stop trying to control mine.'

De'Geer took the suggestion in silently, before eventually nodding and rising from his seat.

'I need the loo,' he said, as if it was the most momentous decision in the world and, without another word, he left the two remaining officers at the table, walking past the bar to the men's toilets.

Davey, alone with her thoughts for a moment, scowled at the table and, after a few, uncomfortably quiet seconds, Cooper cleared her throat.

'DC Davey, I know we don't know each other well, but can I make a candid comment?' she asked carefully.

Surprised at the formality of the statement, Davey nodded.

'DCs and PCs are the same rank, technically, so I couldn't stop you if you wanted,' she replied.

Cooper cleared her throat again, obviously nervous about the question she was about to ask.

'Why are you being such a goddamn bitch to Morten?' she eventually blurted out.

Davey actually smiled at this.

'Wow,' she said. 'Way to sugarcoat the question.'

'I'm not joking,' Cooper was gaining courage now. 'You treat him like shit, pardon my language. You know he likes you, and you have to like him back, because you dated him.'

'I went on one, maybe two dates,' Davey corrected. 'That's not the same as "dated". And I do like him. He's fun to be with. But it's not in the way he likes me.'

'Then maybe you should tell him that again, in a better way than how you're doing it right now, because I don't think he's getting the memo.'

Davey breathed out an audible sigh at this.

'I know, believe me,' she said by explanation. 'Look, he's great and I really do like him, but not in the way he feels in return. Esme, I'm broken. I'm not good to be with, and even with the closure Spears gives me, it's not changing any time soon. I'm in therapy again, three times a week, and even then I might be upping to more, maybe also starting medication. De'Geer's got decisions to make that will shape the rest of his life. He needs to be with someone stable right now, who can give him what he needs. Someone like you, for example.'

Cooper blushed at the comment.

'So what, you're deliberately being a bitch?' she asked.

'Partly,' Davey admitted. 'I've always found it's easier to have them hate you, or at least dislike you when you break up with them, as in a weird, twisted way, it's easier on them. And, as I said, I'm not around for much longer, so—'

'And why is that again?' Cooper didn't mean to interrupt, but she was getting angry now. Davey had no right to play with De'Geer's emotions in such a way, especially if it was just to give her an easy way out of the non-relationship.

'I joined to prove Spears killed my sister,' Davey said softly, lowering her voice so the others in the pub couldn't hear. 'With him dead, there's no point carrying on now.'

'So what, you just leave the police? Move on?'

Davey smiled sadly.

'I don't think I'll be given a choice,' she said. 'The universe will probably decide for me.'

'Well, I still think what you're doing to Morten is a little crappy,' Cooper muttered 'He deserves better. He—'

'Deserves someone like you?' Davey finished the sentence with a wry smile. 'Come on, Esme. I see how you look at him. It's the exact same way he looks at me. It's very recognisable.'

Cooper flushed at this.

'He's not interested in me,' she replied.

'Are you sure?' Davey leant in close now. 'I've seen how he looks at you when you're not paying attention. He's attracted to you, it's definitely there. And he should be—you're a fox.'

'This isn't about me,' Cooper, uncomfortable with the way the conversation was now going, backed away on her stool.

'Of course it is,' Davey carried on. She had a smile on her face, but the words she spoke didn't seem to match the mood. 'I've seen you watch him. I recognise the expression. *Thirst.* You're hungry for him, and he's an *all you can eat* buffet.'

Cooper didn't want to continue this conversation, partly because she didn't want to consider De'Geer as any kind of buffet, but also because, in her heart, she knew Joanne Davey was right.

She was attracted to De'Geer.

She hadn't been at the start, they'd just been friends, but there was a moment in the last case, where De'Geer had jumped off a boat like a Viking warrior, wielding a boat hook like a spear, that had made her heart flutter. A definite *oh my* moment. And from that point onwards, whenever she'd seen Morten De'Geer, she'd flushed, remembering that moment.

But he still liked someone else.

'You should *want* me to be like this,' Davey continued. '*Want* me to hurt him. Because then he'd be all yours.'

'Well, from the sounds of things, he'll be neither,' Cooper said sadly. 'When he quits and moves to Berkshire.'

Davey went to reply but stopped as, from the back of the pub, De'Geer returned.

Sitting back in his seat, he looked at both women.

'What did I miss?' he eventually asked, his eyes narrowing with suspicion.

'Cooper told me off for being a pissy bitch,' Davey said with a slight smile. 'For how I act to you. And she's right to do so, as I'm pretty toxic right now.'

Rising, she tapped on the empty pint.

'I'm off,' she said, nodding to both officers. 'I'm going to check in with Doctor Marcos and then head home.'

'Need me to—' De'Geer half rose, but Davey held out a hand to halt him.

'Stay, boy,' she smiled. 'Keep Cooper company while she struggles with that pint. Who knows, you might even get lucky.'

And, before either officer could reply, DC Davey grabbed her bag and left the pub.

'Well, that was abrupt,' De'Geer said, almost mournfully. 'What did you say to her?'

'Not enough,' Cooper lied, sipping at her cider. 'Look, do you mind if I get something else? I absolutely bloody hate this drink.'

'Get me a pint of coke while you're up there,' De'Geer smiled. 'And then you can tell me what's been on your mind. You've had a face like thunder all day.'

And, faking a smile and walking to the bar, Cooper wondered what lie she could tell the man she fancied to stop him enquiring more, while glancing at the door to the bar.

Davey was hiding something, she knew it.

She just didn't know how to find it out without destroying everything.

15

NIGHT MOVES

DECLAN ARRIVED BACK IN HURLEY JUST BEFORE NINE IN THE evening, having made good time after leaving Whitehall.

When he entered the living room, he saw Anjli had left a note on the coffee table, saying she'd gone for a late dinner at The Olde Bell, and so even though he'd likely missed last food orders, Declan grabbed his jacket and headed over there.

He hadn't expected date night or anything, but at the same time, he hadn't expected any kind of *intervention*.

'About time you turned up,' Monroe said, pushing his finished dinner plate away as he placed the napkin on top. 'Thought you'd left us for a life in politics.'

'Guv,' Declan replied, frowning. 'You're a bit out of your patch, aren't you?'

'Had a craving for the pie they do here,' Monroe tapped with a fingernail on the plate. 'You should try it. Very good.'

Declan glanced at his watch; it was past nine, and the kitchen was closed.

'You knew the answer to that before you said it,' he muttered. 'This is why we don't invite you to parties.'

'You don't invite me to parties, because you hate parties,' Monroe picked a piece of food out of his tooth as he replied. 'You're miserable, Declan. I fear for the bonnie lass here. She'll waste away, stuck in your basement.'

'I don't have a basement.'

'Aye, and you didn't have a secret crime room either, until you had to show us it,' Monroe patted his stomach approvingly. 'I look forward to the basement visit.'

'I had looked forward to food, but now I'll just have crisps, I suppose,' Declan turned to the bar, ignoring the rumbling in his stomach.

'Don't worry, I asked Dave to hold off closing the kitchen for you,' Anjli grinned. 'I knew that cheapskate Baker wouldn't cover dinner, and I guessed you'd get out as quick as you could.'

'I wasn't in there long enough for food,' Declan said, walking over to the bar, where Dave, the portly, smiling barman nodded to him.

'Round for the table, yours being a Guinness?' he asked, pouring the moment Declan nodded.

'And a chicken and mushroom pie,' Declan replied. 'As long as it's a pie, and not a—'

'A casserole in a dish with some puff pastry on top,' Dave the barman finished. 'I know. I'll pass them over. Your man there's started a tab and said this all goes on it.'

Nodding, Declan walked back to the table.

'Thanks for buying dinner,' he said to Monroe as he sat down on one of the two spare chairs, with Monroe now to his right and Anjli to his left. 'I'm trying the pie. Apparently, some people around here speak quite highly of it.'

'Who said I'm buying dinner?' Monroe raised an eyebrow. 'I only set up a tab.'

Declan said nothing, deciding not to reply. Monroe was just baiting him; which meant that he was either in a mischievous mood, had information, or was waiting for some, the latter with the patience of a small child.

'So what did you learn from Baker?' The banter over and now back to business, Monroe leant back, stretching.

Ah, option three, Declan smiled to himself.

'Charles thinks he's played me, but he was quite blatant,' Declan replied. 'He made a big thing about getting me to join his capital punishment club, but I think he really wanted me to tell him to piss off, so he can keep his right-wing buddies happy.'

'How does pissing Baker off help his MPs?' Anjli was confused at this.

'They don't like Declan,' Monroe said, as Dave brought the drinks over. 'Nobody does. Hey, David, do you like Declan?'

'Of course not,' Dave smiled. 'Nobody does.'

As Dave walked off, Declan sipped his Guinness.

'We've talked before about you believing you're funny when you're not,' he said to Monroe, his lips now foamy. 'Anyway, Baker didn't want me seen there, but I also got the impression he wanted me to feel slighted, like I was being pressured by him. He knew this would make me work harder to solve the case. It's like reverse psychology from someone who uses crayons when writing.'

'I thought he liked the whole vigilantism angle?'

'I think publicly he's all about it, but when he's on his own, I don't think he does,' Declan considered this, placing the pint back down. 'I genuinely think he's relying on us to bring in the murderer, and show them to be something so bad, so absolutely abhorrent to what a normal person would consider, that Baker has to drop the bill, or back down off it. That way, he plays both sides, I look like the villain for going against him, the police save the day and he gets a rub from that, and by showing he was even interested in doing this, he placates his bloodthirsty fox-hunting friends.'

He smiled.

'Oh, and Jennifer Whatsit-Whatsherface was there, too,' he said. 'I got the impression this was all her idea.'

'It's a good idea, loathe as I am to admit it,' Monroe sighed. 'But it's also backfired on Prime Minister's before. David Cameron and the *Brexit* referendum comes to mind.'

Declan sipped at his drink, mulling the conversation over again in his head.

'He made a lot of noise about Karl,' he eventually explained. 'Said I should be on his side because he knows what I did to hide him away.'

'You think he was threatening you?' Anjli's face darkened as she spoke, the anger behind her eyes building. 'Suggesting if you don't stand with him, he'll tell everyone you became your own judge and jury? That would do more than just kill your career. You could do time.'

'Nah, I don't think so,' Declan shook his head. 'He knows the moment he does that, I bring out all the things I still have on him. For the moment, in that respect, I'm bulletproof. I think he was trying to get a read on me.'

'And what did you say?'

'The same thing I'd say to anyone who asks whether I'm on the side of murderous vigilantes,' Declan replied, pulling out his warrant card and placing it on the table. 'My loyalty is to this. Not personal gratification.'

'Although there's an argument to be made that—'

'*Schnitter would have been taken by the CIA,*' Declan hissed, cutting Monroe off and instantly regretting it, as the dour Scot watched him carefully and silently for a moment.

'Sorry,' Declan continued, sheepishly. 'Triggered a nerve.'

'Maybe we should swap Davey with you on this case?' Monroe suggested. 'She seems to have things locked down mentally better than you do.'

Declan smiled weakly.

'You might be right with that,' he admitted. 'Sorry again.'

He glanced around the pub as a thought, resting in the back of his mind since he arrived, poked its head up again.

'Why are you here again?' he asked. 'And don't give me that rubbish about pies.'

'Aye, that's a fine way to speak to a friend and colleague!' Monroe exclaimed mockingly.

'I'm serious, Guv,' Declan frowned. 'You could have taken us to the pub across the road from the Unit. You could have chatted with us in the office. But instead you came here. Why?'

He snapped his fingers as the revelation hit him.

'It's not bugged.'

At Declan's suggestion, Monroe looked at Anjli for a moment.

'You told him?'

'He's a good detective,' Anjli smiled. 'I didn't need to.'

'And it's not like we haven't been bugged before,' Declan automatically lowered his voice as he spoke, and fought to stop himself. Monroe pulled a box of matches out of his pocket, and, opening it, revealed two small microphone bugs.

'I've been reliably informed they're dead now,' he said. 'A cyber friend in Whitehall had a look.'

'Trix?' Declan asked. Trix Preston had once worked for the Unit until she was revealed to be placed there undercover. Now she worked for one of Whitehall's less known about agencies and helped the Last Chance Saloon now and then as a form of self-governed penance.

'Aye, I thought it best to let someone knowledgeable at planting bugs to have a look at these,' Monroe replied, passing the box over.

Declan picked one bug up, looking at it.

'Who planted them?' he asked.

'No idea, but the first was found in the office, under one of the spare desks,' Monroe pointed at the larger of the two. 'The second was found in the canteen, behind the coffee tin. You dislodged it when you took out the tea bags. If you hadn't had your coffee meltdown, I wouldn't have seen it later that day.'

Declan shook his head in disbelief.

'We should gain commissions from bug salesmen, the amount of times we've found them.'

'The Guv thinks it's Andrade, or as he calls him, "the spy",' Anjli added. 'He's been in both locations.'

'And I've heard in the past that embassies have a lot of assets in bars and cafés in London, eavesdropping on particular targets,' Monroe added. 'So currently, as far as I'm concerned, most of our usual haunts are closed for business, if we want to talk business.'

Declan went to reply, but paused as Dave the barman placed his late dinner in front of him. Thanking him, Declan tucked in for a moment, savouring the food before coming back up for air.

'It might not be Andrade,' he said, his mouth half full. 'It could be half a dozen people. And if Baker is pushing for this bill, he might want an inside track on what we're doing.'

'These aren't British government,' Monroe said, picking one up, examining it. 'Apparently you can buy them from specialised stores. There's one on Holborn, and Trix reckons these could have come from there. Tomorrow you'll send De'Geer and Cooper to check it out, but give them the order outside the building, aye?'

Declan nodded, swallowing another mouthful before replying.

'Let's not tell Billy until we know conclusively, though, right?' He suggested. 'He's twitchy enough that people think his boyfriend might be using him. Until we know for certain, Andrade is still innocent.'

'Aye, that's the plan,' Monroe placed the bugs into the matchbox and passed it over to Anjli. 'I don't want to end the poor wee bugger's dreams until we absolutely have to.'

THE WATFORD GAP MOTORWAY SERVICES ON THE M1 HAVE been classed many times as one of the oldest motorway services in Britain, having opened the same day as the M1 itself, back in 1959.

Between junctions fifteen and sixteen of the motorway, regardless of the name, the services were primarily based in Northamptonshire, almost eighty miles north-west from London, seven miles south of Rugby and almost seventy from the town of Watford, where people usually assumed the name came from.

In fact, the name came from the narrowest and lowest point in the limestone ridge that crossed England diagonally from the Cotswolds to Lincoln Edge, a ridge named the *Watford Gap* due to its proximity to the village of Watford, not to be confused with its bigger brother down south.

It wasn't the first time the two would be confused, either; for centuries, the Watford Gap had been classed as the middle of England, a dividing line that separated the north and the south of the country, and the term "north of the Watford gap" had been used in this manner. But then, with the more southern Watford gaining greater notoriety and fame over the years, the phrase had shortened to "north of Watford", and now meant more of a cultural split than a geographical one.

The man on the bridge liked that.

He liked stories, factual snippets of information that gave a place life. To many this was just a service station, a place to stop and grab a drink, two separate stations either side of the M1 and joined by a connecting bridge, the one he currently stood on, watching the traffic below him as it travelled southwards towards London, unaware of the scrutiny they were receiving from the man in the flat cap, his overcoat's collar pulled up around his cheeks.

Pink Floyd, The Beatles and *The Rolling Stones* had all stopped here while travelling the country for gigs. Jimi Hendrix claimed he'd heard so much about the place when it was known as "The Blue Boar" services that he thought it was a nightclub they all played at.

The man liked this, too.

He liked the idea of double names. Secret, confused identities. This was good for multiple purposes. Even seventies soul-rocker Roy Harper wrote a song named *Watford Gap*, about the services. The man didn't like Roy Harper's music, but he respected his beliefs. To musicians in the sixties, before all the other motorways were opened, this was the British Route 66. This was their temple, their church, their safe place.

And right now, it was *his* safe place.

He smiled to himself, a small, private smile as he considered the services. He too had double names. Currently, he was Mister Pravda, and that suited him fine.

Once more, he was fascinated with locations and events that happened in them. Not the big places, not the known locations, oh no, but the smaller ones, the places people had forgotten. Nobody here right now considered that *musical gods* had walked the same steps, stared out of the same glass windows at the tarmac lanes below, over the years; just as they didn't really consider that a three-sided gallows had once been the medieval equivalent of the London Eye in Tyburn, or that Amen Court now held back the ghosts of Newgate's worst. And even places like West Smithfield, where the witches and heretics had been burned, were now nothing more than—

'Are you Mister Pravda?' a soft, nervous voice spoke, and Mister Pravda pushed his shaded glasses up his nose and looked around at the questioner.

A woman in her mid-sixties, a long, grey coat over black tights, her auburn hair pulled back into a bun, stared at him, trying to make out his facial features.

Good luck, he thought. The whole reason he stood here was the light above him was broken, and the lights from the cars flashed shadows constantly, making both their faces morph and shimmer in the corridor bridge.

'I am,' he said softly, disguising his voice. The woman made to walk towards him, but Mister Pravda held up a leather-gloved hand.

'No closer,' he said.

'You said to come here,' the woman continued, wringing her hands together. 'I don't know why…'

'You know very well why you came,' Mister Pravda hissed. 'I did what you asked. And now in return *you* do as *I* ask.'

'But they'll find out,' the woman shook her head. 'Please.'

Mister Pravda cursed silently to himself as he reached into his inner coat pockets. The woman was a simpering fool, and he didn't know whether he could trust her at all, but he knew with Spears and Marr now dead and being investigated, the others would all be under scrutiny. It was only a matter of time until someone realised who was in the room during those therapy sessions. And, with two more to go, he couldn't be in two places at the same time.

Quietly and carefully, he pulled a saline bag, the type that hospital IV stands would have hanging from them, and held it out for the woman to take.

'All you need to do is swap this in,' he said. 'Nothing more. And, if you keep your latex gloves on, you won't leave a print—'

He snatched it back as the woman nervously went to take it.

'Gloves!' he hissed. 'Where are your gloves?'

'Oh, yes, sorry,' the woman mumbled, pulling on a pair of leather gloves. 'Fingerprints. Of course.'

Again, Mister Pravda passed the bag across. This time, the woman took the bag, placing it gingerly into her oversized handbag.

'What's in it?' she asked.

'Justice,' Mister Pravda replied. 'That's all you need to know.'

'Will it… will it hurt?'

Mister Pravda forced himself from smiling.

'Yes,' he said, rather matter-of-factly. 'But do you really have a problem with that? You didn't with the other one, with what he did to your granddaughter.'

At this, the woman straightened.

'This isn't my fight.'

'No, you're right,' Mister Pravda looked back out across the motorway. 'But then your fight has been finished, hasn't it? Your closure gained, your journey complete. Did I ask for payment, for what I did?'

'No,' the woman admitted.

'*This* is the payment,' Mister Pravda said, still watching the cars. 'Do it when he arrives tomorrow.'

'And if it fails?'

'The only way it fails is if you fail,' Mister Pravda looked back at the woman now. 'I'd suggest you don't. And make sure it doesn't come back onto you, because I don't want it to come back onto me.'

The woman nodded, swallowed, and then, without saying goodbye, turned and walked back to her side of the motorway. She was heading back north, while Mister Pravda would head south, ready to finish one more task before feeling the sweet release of ending.

He breathed onto the window, steaming it up with the condensation. Then, with a gloved finger, he wrote seven letters in it.

Justice

Now turning the other way from the woman, Mister Pravda started towards his own side of the motorway and his car ride home. He wondered idly whether the Watford gap, either in its various uses as a Roman road, a stagecoach route, or simply as a Norman village, ever held executions within its boundaries, but he didn't expect this to be the case.

That said, it was always the small, innocuous places that held the greatest secrets.

16

FLY ON THE WALL

MONROE HAD STAYED THE NIGHT AT DECLAN'S, PREFERRING TO sleep on the couch than crash in what was Jess' room when she visited, even though Declan had promised it would be perfectly okay to do so. And, as they'd arrived at Temple Inn, Anjli once more driving her own car while Declan brought Monroe, the Guv had disappeared into his office for his wash kit and spare clothing—something pretty much all members of the Last Chance Saloon had at the offices, because of the long nights and potential full weeks spent in the office during the busiest of cases, crashing on the upstairs cot when needed, or even in an empty cell when everyone else was using the cot—and disappeared to the showers downstairs for a freshen up.

Billy arrived half an hour later, which surprised Declan, as usually Billy was the first to arrive. Declan had once suggested that Billy actually lived in the office like some unquiet spirit, but for this morning at least, the spirit had been quiet.

'Sorry I'm tardy, I had a late night,' Billy yawned. 'Or early morning, rather.'

'Playing with your boyfriend?' Anjli, already at her desk, smiled. Only Billy would use "tardy" to explain his lateness. It was as quaint as his three-piece suits.

'Working,' Billy replied with a mock groan. 'I was sent a ton of CCTV footage of Broadstairs by Kent County Council —two months worth to be accurate. I had to go through it all.'

'Couldn't you, I don't know, write some kind of app or algorithm for that?' Declan asked.

At this, Billy stared at him like he was the stupidest man he'd ever met.

'You remember when we had that talk a while back, about how enhancing images in the movies isn't like real life?' he asked.

'Right... I'm guessing in this case, neither's creating algorithms and apps out of thin air?' Declan nodded. 'Got it.'

'Good boy,' Billy smiled. 'Now, who wants to know what I found?'

'We all do,' Monroe said as he emerged from his office, his hair damp and slicked back. 'Amaze us with your incredible skills.'

'Now I feel you're just mocking me,' Billy muttered as he opened up a video footage screen on the monitor.

'Heaven forbid, laddie,' Monroe smiled. 'So, were you able to follow our man Spears from the house to Ramsgate?'

'No,' Billy smiled, scrolling through the feed on the monitor; it was a street, a suburban one, and from the architecture, Declan felt it was only a hundred yards from Kym Newfield's house. 'Because he never went to Ramsgate. Or, at least, never went in the last month.'

'What do you mean?' it was Anjli asking this time,

moving around to get a better look. 'I can see him on the screen, right there.'

'That's Jacob Spears, but he's not going to Ramsgate,' Billy sped though the CCTV footage, and the team watched as, on the screen, Jacob Spears waited for a bus, eventually climbing onto one. 'That's the Margate Loop, it's a bus that runs every fifteen minutes, and it goes from Bairds Hill, where we are here, a five-minute walk from Kym's house, to Margate, where he gets off at the Cecil Street Council offices, here.'

Now the CCTV was a street camera, and the team could see Jacob exit the bus, glance quickly around, and then head off to the left, away from the bus and street.

'He then turns down Union Row, where he stops at a coffee shop. We managed to get the footage from them before they closed last night, too.'

'How did you manage that?' Anjli was impressed. 'Coffee shops don't usually stay open late.'

'Owner's home address was on record, so I called up and got access to their cloud server,' Billy shrugged. 'Just needed to log in, download, log out.'

'Careful laddie, we might not believe you're a miracle worker if you keep playing down the things you do,' Monroe mock-chided.

Ignoring this, Billy swapped screens, and now the CCTV of a small, modern looking coffee shop appeared. It was in black and white, but Declan could tell that the walls were white, maybe cream, with what looked like pine wood, Ikea-style furniture and pale grey slabs on the floor. Behind the counter was a young woman, no more than eighteen, with black hair pulled into a bun, serving someone at the counter, with some kind of cake being bought.

In the corner, sitting at a table and reading a book, a coffee beside him, was Jacob Spears.

'So, once I worked out his pattern, I was able to check through three weeks' worth of footage quickly,' Billy half-boasted. 'Every day he comes in here first thing, sits at the table, drinks two, maybe three coffees and then leaves around twelve.'

'Which matches what Kym told us,' Declan nodded. 'But surely they only keep their footage a couple of days?'

'Apparently they upload to a cloud and it stays for a few weeks,' Billy shrugged. 'There are, however, three days in the last two weeks where he changes this.'

Billy now pulled up three screens.

'Two weeks ago, there were two days in succession where he arrived, bought a coffee to-go and left. And, last week, on Friday, he did the same. Look.'

Billy set all three days' footage off at the same time; in unison, all three showed Jacob come in, talk to the man behind the counter, pick up a coffee in a to-go cup and leave.

'The girl,' Monroe muttered. 'She's not there on any of these occasions.'

'Exactly,' Billy paused the footage. 'Rebecca Shultz. College student, her schedule seems to be all afternoon classes, so she works the weekday morning shifts at the coffee shop. Finishes at lunchtime, goes to classes after that.'

'Dear God,' Monroe breathed. 'Put up the photos of Callahan, Davey, and Bruce.'

Billy did so, and the whole Unit took in a collective gasp of breath.

'He definitely has a type,' Billy muttered as they stared at the four young brunette girls, each with their hair pulled back into a ponytail.

'He was stalking his next victim,' Anjli whispered. 'He'd watch her while she worked, and when she wasn't there, he'd find something else to do.'

'All while telling Kym he was taking a morning constitutional in the other direction,' Monroe nodded. 'Looks like the lassie got a lucky break.'

'Should we contact her? Tell her?' Billy looked at Monroe, who shook his head.

'No, I think she doesn't need to spend the rest of her life playing through the *what ifs*,' he replied. 'But you should keep on with the checking of these. I want to know what he did on the three days he didn't see her.'

'One of those was the last day,' Billy started typing. 'I'm already going through it.'

As Billy spoke, Doctor Marcos entered the office through the main door. She looked exhausted, and was still wearing the clothes she'd worn the previous day.

'Have you been to bed yet?' Monroe asked, concerned.

'I'm going to grab an hour or two upstairs,' Doctor Marcos nodded towards the stairs at the back of the office. 'Thought I'd stop in with what I have so far.'

'Briefing room?' Monroe offered, but Doctor Marcos shook her head.

'Not worth it,' she said. 'By the time we'd all get in there and settle down, I'd be done.'

'Waste of a night?' Declan asked, looking around at her now.

'Well, I mean it was a case study in surgical techniques, so that was nice,' Doctor Marcos forced a smile. 'Whomever killed Darryl Marr, they knew exactly where to cut, and how deep to go when they quartered him. I thought it was an angle grinder when I first looked, but I now think it was some kind of oscillating saw, usually used in joint surgery, with smaller blades used in removing casts and suchlike.'

'Is there a way to find out which saw it was?' Declan asked, already regretting the question.

'A ouija board might be a good start,' Doctor Marcos smiled. 'Seriously though, not really. Once I work out the blade, though, we might have a better idea. Especially as these things aren't cheap. Even a hand piece of a good one, say the Microaire 7200-200, is five hundred quid alone. I have one downstairs, but that's because the budget covered it. If someone wanted to cut up Marr with one, they're spending a good grand's worth of cash on it. Far easier to steal it from a hospital or veterinary clinic; I mean, if you're going to murder someone, you might as well do two crimes for the price of one.'

Declan looked over at Billy.

'Already on it,' Billy said without even looking at him. 'I'll check through HOLMES 2, see if we have any records of stolen...'

'Oscillating saws.'

'Yes, that.'

Declan wrote this down in his notebook before looking back at Doctor Marcos.

'Anything else on the body?'

'Actually, yes,' Doctor Marcos nodded. 'A partial print on the driving licence they stapled to his head. I'm having the bods go through it now, see if they can get something. But it'll take a while, I'm afraid, and it won't be a solid match to work on. Although, if it links someone already connected, that might help.'

She finally noticed the CCTV screen.

'Who's the girl?'

'Jacob Spears' next victim,' Anjli muttered. 'He was stalking her.'

Doctor Marcos sucked in air through her teeth.

'What a shame he's dead,' she said with no emotion whatsoever. 'I also heard from Durham police, after they checked those four sets of coordinates the YouTube video gave us. They found four pieces of a very decomposed young male's body. They're checking now to see if it matches Ethan Roe.'

'Well, at least there's some closure from this,' Monroe muttered.

Doctor Marcos stretched her back as the room went silent, each member considering the body now rediscovered. The anonymous killer had not only killed two alleged serial killers, but had also found a missing body.

The press was going to have a field day, Declan thought to himself. *They might even give him a medal.*

'I've got something else on the van,' Doctor Marcos continued. 'As we expected, they wiped it down clean before they left, but there's some residue on the dashboard. Magnesium carbonate. They did a good job, but this little bugger is hard to wipe away.'

'What's it used for?' Declan asked, resisting the urge to Google the answer. He knew Doctor Marcos would mock him incessantly if he did so.

'Many things,' Doctor Marcos clicked her tongue against her teeth. 'Anything from fertiliser to heartburn medications.'

'That's a hell of a range,' Billy muttered, looking over at the two of them. 'How do we narrow that down?'

'Forensics,' Doctor Marcos smiled faintly. 'It's what we do best. There's traces of chalk there, too. We'll work it out.'

She stretched her back once more, wincing at the audible clicks in her spine.

'I'm hitting the sack,' she eventually stated. 'I'll be in a cell, the cot's not good for my back. If you need me, knock. I've told the day shift to send anything they find to me, care of Billy.'

As Doctor Marcos walked off, Billy made some kind of yelping noise; looking over at him, Declan saw a look of utter triumph on his face as he spun around.

'Go on,' he said.

'So there's three days where his target isn't in the coffee shop, yeah?' Billy began. 'We saw that on the CCTV. But going back into the fourth week, there's also two days where he doesn't even go there. He heads onto the seafront and a different, more basic café near the amusement arcades. Like a trucker's one.'

'Okay,' Monroe leaned back against the desk. 'And why does this make you yelp like a chihuahua?'

'Sorry, I was surprised I found him,' Billy reddened. 'Look.'

On the screen they watched footage from a CCTV camera, as Jacob Spears walked down Margate's "golden mile" promenade. Passing an amusement arcade, he ducked into a café next to it.

'I don't have footage of the place yet, but this is ten in the morning,' Billy pointed at the time code. 'And then, fifteen minutes later...'

He scrolled through the footage, pausing as another man arrived.

'Darryl Marr,' Anjli nodded. 'Makes sense, Kym said he appeared in Broadstairs at one point.'

Declan checked his notebook.

'Kym Newfield said Jacob and Darryl had a falling out

about four weeks ago, and didn't speak again,' he said. 'I'm wondering now whether the falling out was for her benefit.'

'Or they're having some kind of truce meeting here,' Billy suggested. 'Neutral ground and all that.'

Declan went to reply, but then stopped. The CCTV had been playing in the background as they'd been talking, and now, on the screen, Jacob Spears and Darryl Marr emerged out into the Margate sunshine.

'Quick meeting,' Anjli said. 'I'm guessing there's no sound?'

'And it's not defined enough for lip reading,' Billy tried zooming in, to no avail. 'Whatever they're talking about, we won't know.'

The two men faced each other for a good minute, finishing their conversation. Then, Jacob patted Darryl on the shoulder, and pointed back up the street. A moment later, they both walked off in different directions, Jacob towards Dreamland, the other end of the promenade, and Darryl back towards Margate's High Street.

'Can you follow them?' Declan asked.

'It's not live, so no,' Billy frowned as he ran a hand through his stylish blond hair. 'Although... no, it wouldn't...'

He tapped on his keyboard.

'I have some footage of that day,' he explained. 'The coffee shop Jacob went to. I'd already checked it to see he wasn't there, so I'd discarded it. But it's the same direction Marr's going.'

'That would be a massive coincidence,' Monroe replied, but his expression showed uncertainty.

'Spears pointed back that way,' Declan ran through the options in his mind. 'He was sending him somewhere, or giving directions. It could well be—'

He stopped.

On the screen was the coffee shop, the brunette behind the counter.

'This is the feed from the same day,' Billy said quietly, scrolling through the footage. 'Let's give Marr ten minutes to get from the meeting place from here. That would mean—'

He stopped, pausing the CCTV footage.

'Looks like he did it in six.'

Everyone stared at Billy's monitors; on the middle one, caught in a frozen CCTV moment, Darryl Marr was seen buying a coffee from the brunette server.

'They're working together,' Declan realised aloud. 'They're hunting in a pack.'

'Aye, but how big is the bloody pack,' Monroe muttered. 'We need to find this woman, make sure nobody else is part of the game Jacob was playing.'

He stopped as the phone beside him rang. Answering it, he placed it onto speakerphone.

'Monroe,' he said.

'Boss, we have a visitor,' PC Mastakin said through the speaker. 'A Doctor Bruce Penhaligon. Says he needs to speak to you urgently.'

'Send him up,' Monroe looked at Declan, mouthing *who?*

'Isn't that Davey's therapist?' Declan shrugged.

Monroe frowned, looking back at the phone.

'Davey's not here, so tell him—'

'He's already on his way,' Mastakin continued. 'DC Davey's bringing him up—'

'Aye,' Monroe interrupted as through the main doors, Davey and a bookish man in his fifties entered. 'Cheers.'

Disconnecting the call, Monroe rose to face the

newcomer as Davey, her task now complete, looked over at Monroe.

'Sir, this is my therapist,' she said.

'Aye, so we heard,' Monroe looked at Declan briefly. 'I didn't realise it was "bring your shrink to work day" or anything, but perhaps we should talk in my office?'

'Oh, I'm not here as her therapist,' Doctor Penhaligon said, moving forwards and shaking Monroe's hand. He was tall, slim, and seemingly made of arms and legs. His nose was long and hawkish, and he had a pair of round *Prada* glasses perched on it. His peppered hair was combed back, and he wore a tweed jacket with leather patches on the elbows. If Declan hadn't already been told he was a doctor, he would have assumed "Oxford Don" from the uniform.

'Well, in that case, I don't exactly know why I'm seeing you,' Monroe replied calmly. 'Perhaps you or DC Davey could enlighten us all?'

Doctor Penhaligon looked across at Billy's monitor, seeing the images of Jacob Spears and Darryl Marr on it.

'I'm here because of that,' he said. 'I'm a psychoanalyst and practicing therapist, focusing on serial killers and their victims. That's why I've been working with Joanne recently. However, I've primarily worked with prisoners and patients in Belmarsh. And, for six months, I ran a group there that involved Jacob Spears, Darryl Marr, Eric Coble, Kendal Rushby and Lee Mellor.'

There was a silence in the office as Monroe looked at Davey, who nodded slightly at him, a tacit agreement to the Doctor's worth.

'Well then, Doctor Penhaligon, you're just the person we wanted to speak to,' Monroe smiled, before looking at the group in the office. 'Walsh, get the uniforms to chat with that shop. Then come into my office with us as we have a wee chat. Kapoor? Get me anything on stolen saws. Billy—'

'I'll check for prints on that ID, see if I can find anything else, and I'll chase down the Oak Hotel,' Billy said.

'Aye, and get uniforms to bring in Kym Newfield, too,' Monroe showed his office, leading Doctor Penhaligon away from the others. 'And that bloody documentary team, too. I want every interview room and cell packed to the rafters.'

'Doctor Marcos isn't going to like that,' Anjli muttered softly, only loud enough for Billy to catch.

'Why?'

'Because if we're dumping people in cells, we're about to ruin her beauty sleep,' she said, picking up the phone and dialing.

17

THERAPY

WHEN DECLAN FINISHED HIS QUIET CONVERSATION OUTSIDE with PC Cooper by phone, he returned to Monroe's office, sitting with Doctor Penhaligon in the two chairs facing Monroe as he watched from behind his desk.

'You can sit there, or relax on the sofa, Doctor Penhaligon, if you'd prefer,' Monroe attempted a smile. 'That's a little psychiatrist's humour to make you feel at home.'

'Your need to ease the situation is quite interesting,' Doctor Penhaligon replied blankly. 'Maybe *you* could lie on the sofa and we could talk about that?'

At Monroe's stricken expression, Doctor Penhaligon grinned.

'That was my own little bit of psychiatrist humour,' he replied. 'And please, call me Bruce.'

'We'll keep with Doctor Penhaligon for the moment,' Monroe nodded as Declan pulled out his notepad and tactical pen, opening it up and jotting things down inside it. 'This currently feels like a conversation you'll be having at some point in an official manner. How about you tell us what brings you here today, and what exactly you bring to the table?'

Doctor Penhaligon nodded slowly, glancing at Declan.

'Interesting pen,' he said. 'Not a fan of biros?'

'It's from when I was in the military police.'

Doctor Penhaligon smiled.

'Yes, but it's also for breaking car windows,' he said. 'The pointy end.'

Declan paused, nodding.

'I know.'

'Are you scared of being in a position where you can't get out—'

Doctor Penhaligon suddenly paled, looking back at Monroe.

'I'm so sorry. I can't help myself sometimes. Why I'm here. Yes.'

Declan quietly breathed out a sigh of relief; Doctor Penhaligon had been pretty close to the mark in his assessment.

Doctor Penhaligon, now back to the main point of his visit, shifted in his seat.

'I've been the therapist at Belmarsh for about ten years now,' he explained. 'Was full time there until around two years back, when I reduced my hours.'

'Why?' Monroe asked.

Doctor Penhaligon shrugged.

'It's a miserable place, and I felt it getting to me,' he replied. 'I wanted to help people. And half the time I was there, it was dealing with prisoners trying to use me to give them easier sentences.'

'How does that work?' Monroe frowned.

In response, Doctor Penhaligon waved his finger around his ear in a circular motion, mimicking madness.

'If they're crazy, they get to go to the psych ward, where all the tasty meds are,' he explained, almost mockingly. 'There they can drug themselves up into blissful unawareness and float away the years. So they think, anyway. They don't really plan that far ahead, in my experience.'

'So you reduced your hours?'

'And set up a practice in Wapping. Mainly corporate, some civil servants, as the Belmarsh gig gave me some good contacts in Government.'

'I'll bet,' Monroe nodded, before stopping, an idea flickering across his face. 'Did you ever deal with Derek Sutton in Belmarsh?'

'Oh yes,' Doctor Penhaligon replied. 'Fascinating man. Claimed he was innocent, but then they all do that. Imagine my surprise when I heard he actually was! I had to completely reevaluate my opinion of him. Do you know him?'

'Aye, we know each other.'

'Well please, say hello from me,' Doctor Penhaligon practically beamed with delight now.

'How did you come to deal with Joanne Davey?' Declan asked. 'She's not a civil servant.'

'No, but I said earlier, I deal with victims of serial killers, and I'd received a referral from a friend,' Doctor Penhaligon explained. 'She'd been triggered by that blasted production company, brought back a lot of old thoughts. I agreed to help her. And, as she worked long hours here, I often did the sessions in one of your interview rooms.'

Declan nodded, writing this down. So far, the story was

matching what he'd heard. But then, Doctor Penhaligon had no reason to lie.

'Anyway, while I was full time at Belmarsh, I also ran group therapy sessions with the prisoners. Nothing major, there were a few going on. Alcoholics Anonymous, one for sex addiction—'

'Sex addiction in prison?' Declan raised his eyebrows. 'Actually, don't elucidate on that one.'

'Probably for the best,' Doctor Penhaligon nodded. 'I was approached by one of the guards at some point in my tenure, it seemed that Mister Spears had found God while in prison, and wanted to help his fellow man. And by that, I mean he wanted to examine the soul of a serial killer, and see how he could stop the urges they had.'

'He wanted to set up a serial killer club,' Monroe shook his head. 'And you bloody well let him?'

'He was guilty of murder, but not of serial murder,' Doctor Penhaligon replied haughtily. 'And they accused Darryl Marr of murder, but was in prison for violent attacks. Only the other two, Eric Coble and Lee Mellor were bona fide serial killers, so to speak. Kendal Rushby gained the title by scatter-gunning multiple victims—'

Again, he stopped.

'Sorry, I don't really have a filter,' he apologised. 'Where was I?'

'You were saying they were all serial killers,' Monroe hissed.

'Ah. Well. You may know that, and I may *suspect* that, but on paper, this wasn't the case,' Doctor Penhaligon argued.

'So you started what, a self-help group for killers? "Hello, my name is Jacob and I like hunting and killing young women" and all that?' Monroe continued.

Doctor Penhaligon's face darkened at the jibe.

'If you're going to mock my work—' he started, but Monroe interrupted him by holding up a hand.

'Two of your patients might be dead now,' he breathed, his voice ice cold as he spoke, 'but we have CCTV footage of them both planning their next victim.'

'You have proof?'

'I have them independently stalking a café, and watching the same young woman.'

'So no, then,' Doctor Penhaligon nodded, as if this was expected. 'They went to a coffee shop? They sat and watched a woman? That's not a crime. Did Jacob or Darryl speak to her? Outside of ordering their coffees?'

Monroe opened and shut his mouth, as he found he had no answer.

'Look, you may well be right, DCI Monroe, but this is how the mind of a serial killer works. They don't kill when they're being watched. They would have known there was CCTV in the coffee shop. They wouldn't have been foolish.'

'You seem to know them very well,' Declan said, his voice emotionless.

'I worked with them for over six months,' Doctor Penhaligon replied conversationally. 'But then I made my decision to leave.'

'So let me get this straight,' Monroe leant his elbows onto the desk. 'You were at Belmarsh for ten years, and after six months working closely with five serial killers, you lost your stomach for it? What exactly happened in those sessions?'

'Doctor patient privilege, I'm afraid,' Doctor Penhaligon looked back at Declan. 'Even though they're dead, I'm still bound.'

'I understand,' Declan nodded calmly. 'But I want you to

understand this. If we find you knew something that could help us, and someone else dies, I'll be arresting you quicker than you can say "tell me about your mother", and dumping you in a cell next to the people you work with.'

Doctor Penhaligon's expression didn't alter at this threat. If anything, Doctor Penhaligon seemed happier with the answer.

'I'm on your side,' he said, still in his irritatingly calm manner. 'I know what you went through.'

'You have no idea—' Declan started, but realised Doctor Penhaligon hadn't finished.

'I know how the Red Reaper killed your mother, and how his daughter, continuing his mission, killed your father,' Doctor Penhaligon continued. 'I know you never arrested him, even though you confronted him, in an abandoned pub car park in the middle of nowhere in the middle of the night.'

Declan lowered his notebook.

'How do you know that?' he asked. 'That was never placed in the report.'

'Prisons are prisons,' Doctor Penhaligon smiled slightly. 'Whether they're official, or perhaps one of those off-the-books, secret ones we hear so much about in cheap novels. And people talk, DI Walsh. Guards, wardens, visitors... As I said, I deal with a lot of civil servants, so perhaps one of those told me?'

'No,' Declan half rose from his chair now. 'Because you wouldn't break your bloody doctor-patient thing. *What do you know?*'

'Declan,' Monroe warned. 'Don't let the man get into your head.'

'My apologies,' Doctor Penhaligon leant back in his chair, hands held up. 'I wasn't intending to disrespect you. Your strength of will is impressive. I'm afraid I wouldn't have let him flip a coin. I would have killed him, for what he did.'

He sighed.

'But then that's why you're the policeman, and I work with criminals.'

'You sound a bit like someone who has their own demons,' Declan replied carefully. And, surprisingly, this hit home; Doctor Penhaligon pulled his glasses off with shaking fingers, cleaning them as he considered his answer.

'My sister was killed when I was a child,' he said. 'It was the late sixties. We never knew what happened to her until thirty years later, when Lynda Crawley was arrested for murder. She was young, no older than sixteen when she killed a small child, a four-year-old girl to be accurate, on the railway tracks outside of Penge.'

'I remember this,' Monroe nodded. 'It was the mid-nineties. They pulled her in and she tried to cut a deal. Said her dad made her do it and then grassed him up for half a dozen murders throughout her life. All buried in the cellar.'

He paled.

'Christ, your sister was one of those?'

Doctor Penhaligon nodded.

'I was three when she went missing, so I don't remember her,' he replied. 'And when they found the body three decades later, she was one of many. And I was already working as a psychiatrist by then. I had my closure, and for me, nothing more was needed. My parents, God rest their souls, didn't last to see justice. My mother died of cancer, my father, well, he just gave up.'

'I'm sorry,' Declan said. 'They placed Jamie Crawley in Broadmoor, didn't they?'

'For about a week,' Doctor Penhaligon nodded. 'And then

he slit his throat open with the end of a sharpened spoon he'd stolen.'

He shrugged.

'I probably need to see a therapist about that,' he replied, his tone lightening. 'But that was the past. And yes, my sister's disappearance and eventual discovery may have made me the therapist I am today, and I will admit to having a morbid fascination into what makes such a person like that tick, but after six months meeting with these murderers on a weekly basis, I couldn't bear to be in that room anymore.'

'Do you have any idea who could be doing this?'

'Actually, I think I do,' Doctor Penhaligon placed his glasses back on. 'I think it's Lee Mellor.'

'Lee Mellor's dead,' Monroe softly replied. 'You might not have heard. From what we can find out, he died of a heart attack in HMP Wakefield last year.'

'Oh, I know what the records say,' Doctor Penhaligon shifted uncomfortably in his seat, looking around the room, lowering his voice. 'But I also know what I've read in those records.'

'And what would that be?'

Doctor Penhaligon sighed, almost theatrically, and Declan wondered whether the therapist was secretly enjoying this.

'I couldn't possibly know for sure, but I do know Lee Mellor had contacts in the criminal underworld, and believed that he had several debts owed to him. He was young, healthy, and exercised regularly when I knew him, so didn't fit the usual candidacy for heart failure. And, working as a therapist in several of Her Majesty's prisons, I can tell you without any doubt that you can get anything for a price. Even a death certificate.'

'We'll look into that,' Monroe's face was stone as he spoke. 'So, how about you explain to us why you're here? So far, all you've done is psychoanalyse us and talk about your special group.'

Doctor Penhaligon stared at Monroe for a long, silent moment, and Declan wondered whether he was about to leave.

'I came to speak to you, because of conversations we had in group,' he replied cautiously. 'I said to you that what I spoke to them about, dead or alive, is covered in patient-doctor confidentiality, however, there is a little wiggle room I can use.'

'How so?' Monroe furrowed his eyebrows at this. 'Surely it's all or nothing, white or black?'

'There can be shades of grey,' Doctor Penhaligon forced a tight smile, and Declan wondered for the first time how much the doctor was risking by being here. 'For example, I can talk to you about anything I overheard in meetings that wasn't directly concerning myself.'

'Water cooler talk,' Declan nodded now, understanding. 'The time before and after the session. I'm guessing you had to wait for them all to arrive, there was a lot of dead time?'

Doctor Penhaligon clicked his tongue against his teeth.

'In a way, yes,' he stated. 'Technically, my services only started in group once the patients, or the prisoners involved, were all there. So, technically, anything I heard spoken, both before and after my services began and ended, is fair game.'

He leant forwards at this, clasping his hands together.

'However, I do have a problem with this. I dealt with three of them, individually over time, and anything they said to me is covered, and therefore anything I hear within the context of what they may have previously told me, is also covered.'

'Sounds a bit of a minefield,' Monroe tutted. 'So take your time if it helps.'

'One of my patients was Lee Mellor,' Doctor Penhaligon continued. 'And during sessions, he...' he paused as he struggled to find the words. 'Let's just say that when the other members of his group were discussed, he became very agitated about them.'

'He didn't like them?'

'If I was to give an official assessment, I'd say he hated them with a fire I'd never seen before.'

'Now why would a serial killer hate other serial killers so much?' Monroe pondered this.

'That is something I can thankfully answer,' Doctor Penhaligon smiled. 'You see, he spoke to Kendal once about this. He said, and I'm paraphrasing, that "they were just rippers, butchers of the weak, while I was an angel of the Lord, bringing divine retribution and justice." Or something to that extent.'

At the word justice, Declan and Monroe glanced across the desk at each other.

'Were you paraphrasing "justice", or was that an actual word spoken?' Declan asked.

'Oh, that was definitely stated,' Doctor Penhaligon nodded. 'I remember it clearly. He spoke it with such venom.'

He glanced to the corner of the office, where Monroe had a small bottle of whisky and two glasses on the top of a cabinet.

'Would you mind if I...?' he left the question hanging.

Monroe, realising what he was saying, shook his head.

'I don't drink on duty,' he insisted. 'But if you'd like a tipple—'

'Thank you,' Doctor Penhaligon gratefully rose and

walked over to the cabinet, pouring a generous glass. 'All this talk of my past, it's a little... triggering.'

Monroe allowed Doctor Penhaligon a moment to gather his thoughts before continuing.

'In your professional opinion, and not using anything given to you under privilege, do you think Lee Mellor could have killed Jacob Spears or Darryl Marr?'

Taking a mouthful of whisky, Doctor Penhaligon nodded vigorously until he swallowed.

'Not only that, but I think he'll kill again,' he said. 'Either Eric Coble or Kendal Rushby. And he'll have planned this meticulously, to the day. I honestly think that Kendal could be next, because Coble, well, disappeared after informing on his fellow prisoners, and as far as I know, nobody knows where he is.'

'But Kendal's in Broadmoor,' Declan pursed his lips as he looked up. 'How's a believed dead killer getting in there?'

'He doesn't need to, as Kendal's not there anymore,' Doctor Penhaligon walked back to the chair, glass in hand. 'He was transferred to Manchester, better known as Strangeways Prison, when it was discovered he had cancer. He's undergoing chemotherapy at Kirkleys Hospital in Manchester, under escort, and they have a mobile unit he visits, under escort, once a week at the moment.'

He looked at his watch.

'And he's probably there right now. In the open, in public, and ready for an attack.'

18

INTRAVENOUS

KATIE ALTON HAD BEEN A NURSE IN MANCHESTER FOR CLOSE to a decade now, and in those years had pretty much seen everything, or so she believed. From stabbing to shootings in the middle of a busy Wednesday afternoon, often by gangs too eager to even wait until darkness to overdoses in shopping malls, all the way to strange things found up the bum, where the patient had "slipped over and fell on it", who then claimed it was a complete accident, and got real snarky when you took the piss a little about it.

But over the last couple of years, she'd changed roles a little; bored with A&E cases, she'd trained up as a cancer nurse, and moved across to Kirkleys Specialist Cancer Hospital in Manchester. First, because it was closer to her house, but also because she felt that in oncology, she could really make a difference to someone's life, rather than the usual triage she did while keeping pissed-up pub fighters conscious while they waited for someone to stitch them back together.

The Kirkleys chemotherapy day service unit was one of

the largest in the world, treating hundreds of patients a week, and Katie felt proud of this achievement, even if none of it was down to her.

However, there was one part of the job that she didn't enjoy, and that was the mobile visits. The Kirkleys Hospital had a mobile chemotherapy unit, created especially to visit the patients who were less able to get into Manchester, and this unit was effectively a fifty-foot long, fifteen-foot high, ten-wheeler lorry, fully kitted out with the very latest chemotherapy treatment equipment and decked in burgundy and white, the colours of the hospital. And, filled with the latest innovative cancer technology, it travelled to five different locations in Greater Manchester every week, serving over two thousand patients a year.

Katie liked the truck; that wasn't the problem. She wasn't part of the team that would drive it to the locations and set it up; the sides expanding out, glass doored entrances now appearing, or setting up the steps and placing the branded skirt around the base, turning it from a wheeled trailer to a mobile office, all she had to do was get a bus to the location and turn up. Or, sometimes, if she was feeling adventurous, she'd sit in the front with the driver, watching the people as she drove past.

The problem wasn't even with the patients. Katie knew what she was doing helped people, and she'd met patients, after they'd been through this, who told her their stories, and were utterly convinced that without Kirkleys help, and in part, her own activities, they wouldn't have survived long enough to explain this to her.

No. Her issues with her job, and the one part of it she didn't enjoy, focused around a particular patient.

Kendal Rushby.

Katie prided herself on never taking sides in any conflict; when you're sewing up rival gang leaders on neighbouring beds, you become very good at negotiating localised peace deals, but with Kendal Rushby, it was different. For a start, thanks to the news reports his face had been everywhere when he was caught, and through this she knew what he'd done, why he did it, and what he'd been given as a sentence for it. Personally, she believed he should burn in hell for the murders on his conscience, but she never openly stated this, especially on the days when he attended, surrounded by guards.

No, to do so would have had her removed off the lorry, and probably cast out of Kirkleys altogether, for some kind of bullshit "unprofessionalism" claim—even if he was a psycho serial killer, and she was probably right for thinking it.

And think it she would. As far as she was concerned, monsters like Kendal should be put down like vicious dogs, it was as simple as that. The cancer medication he was getting was expensive, and instead could go to someone who could make something of their life. All Kendal Rushby would do with his was eke out a year or two more until someone knifed him in the showers.

At least a girl could hope.

And so, reluctantly, every couple of weeks, she found her shift rotated her to lorry duties, or "mobile centre" nursing, on the day the lorry stopped near Strangeways. Which was the day Kendal Rushby came for his chemotherapy treatment.

There were three nurses on duty today; Charlie, a young black man in his twenties, fresh from a GP surgery in Salford after training, and still nervous he'd screw something up, and Monica, in her mid-sixties, her auburn hair pulled back into a bun. Katie had worked with Monica a few times over the last few weeks and always found her to be exceptional in her work, but today she was off; a little distant, definitely snappy when spoken to, and Katie assumed that, like her, Monica wasn't happy about having a serial killer in their midst.

Standing by the door, they watched as the van pulled up beside the lorry. They were parked in a supermarket car park, near the back wall, where the cars barely ever came, so as not to cause any parking issues, and the van, a HM Prisons one was the only vehicle that approached, as it had been made very clear from the first time he arrived, that Rushby's session had to be a solo one. Nobody else could be there, no matter how urgent it was.

Monica was already sorting out the IV when the two guards brought Kendal Rushby out of the back of the van. In prison hoodie, zipped up the middle and in pale grey joggers, he was thin, painfully so, his hair white and fading. Katie had seen photos of Kendal when he was caught, the ones the papers had put out there, and he was a shadow of the man he'd been ten years earlier. He'd lost almost half his body weight, and his once-thick black hair was almost gone. The cancer had ravaged his system, and Katie had to really fight the urge to be on cancer's side this time.

As Kendal was walked up the steps to the entrance, Charlie slipped into place beside Katie.

'Bloody hell, that's the Christmas Ripper,' he hissed, as if Katie had never realised this. Glancing back to him, she smiled tightly, her eyes emotionless.

'First time on this shift, right?' she asked dispassionately.

Charlie nodded, unable to take his eyes off Kendal as he entered the mobile unit, passing the three nurses without a word.

'Does it show?' he asked, eventually looking back.

'A little,' Katie said, seeing a way out of her role in this session. 'Hey, do you want to do this one? Monica's already sorted the IV, so all you have to do is connect it.'

'I could make a mistake,' Charlie whispered nervously. 'What if I hurt him?'

'I don't think anyone will give a damn here,' Katie replied calmly. 'The guards might even give you a medal.'

'Okay, yeah, sure,' Charlie said nervously as, now placed in one of the grey chairs by the guards, Kendal smiled across at them.

'I'm ready for my closeup now,' he growled.

'Seriously though, what if I do make a mistake?' Charlie hissed. 'What if a complication occurs? What if I kill him?'

'Then we'll all buy you a drink,' Katie winked as Monica walked over to them. She seemed more agitated than usual, and Katie noted she'd been wearing latex gloves throughout the setup.

'Are you okay?' she whispered. 'You look like you've seen a ghost.'

'This isn't my favourite part of the job,' Monica replied simply, and Katie knew exactly what she meant.

Charlie, still staring at the grinning Kendal, hadn't moved.

'It's a central line,' Katie said softly to him. 'Two tubes inserted into his chest for ease. All you have to do is connect them.'

'Why doesn't he have a cannula?' Charlie frowned at this. In response, Katie nodded to one guard who, now having handcuffed Kendal's wrists to the armrests, now unzipped the hoodie, revealing a white-haired, bare chest with two tubes coming out of Kendal's right-hand side.

'They can't secure him if his wrist is free,' she explained. 'And that guy needs to be secured, no matter how weak he looks right now.'

Feeling embarrassed, Charlie grinned nervously.

'Oh, yeah. That makes sense.'

Katie looked over at Monica, as Charlie nodded to himself, silently building his self-esteem up before walking over to Kendal.

'He'll be fine,' she whispered, assuming that Monica was concerned over Charlie, but was surprised at Monica's answer.

'I hope he dies,' she said simply, staring at the killer secured to the chair.

Charlie, meanwhile, was attaching the lines.

'You're new,' Kendal smiled, a slight Texan drawl to his voice, making it sound a little nasally. 'I'm Kendal. What's your name?'

'Charlie,' it was an automatic reply, and Charlie immediately regretted it.

'No talking to the prisoner, please,' the nearest guard added. 'It's for your own safety, mate.'

'Charlie, Charlie, Charlie...' Now with a small tidbit of information to play with, Kendal rolled the name around his mouth for a long moment. 'I knew a Charlie once. But it was short for Charlotte. Which is weird, wouldn't you say? That ain't short at all. Charlotte, Charlie, they're both two syllables. It don't shorten it at all. Did I kill her? I can't remember.'

He winced a little as the first tube was connected.

'Are you a Charles, Charlie?' he now enquired. 'Were you beaten as a child, thought that *Charlie* would make you sound more approachable, less middle class? Charles is a middle class name, after all. You're gonna have a King Charles soon. The third. They cut the head off the first one.'

Charlie ignored this, his hands shaking as he attached the second tube.

'I'd like to cut your head off, Charles,' Kendal hissed, straining against the restraints, lurching forwards and at this Charlie yelped, leaping back, dropping the tube as he did so.

Muttering under her breath, Katie walked over, placing a hand on Charlie's shoulder.

'It's okay,' she said. 'I'll finish up.'

Kendal started chuckling as Charlie backed over to Monica.

'I'll do it slow,' he continued, 'I'll use a bread knife. You'll feel every serration as I cut through to the—ow!'

He stared balefully at Katie, who smiled sweetly at him.

'Oh, did I pull too hard on the tube?' she asked innocently, her voice all sweetness and light as she nodded to the guard. 'It's all done.'

'Thanks,' the guard nodded. 'We'll monitor it here.'

As per usual, Katie led the other two nurses out into the car park. Their job was done, and all they had to do was keep an eye on Kendal intermittently over the next couple of hours as the chemotherapy being pumped into his chest ravaged the cancer cells in his system.

'Why doesn't he have a pump?' Charlie muttered, still affected by Kendal's outburst. 'One of those that gives continuous chemo, so he doesn't have to come here?'

'He had one,' Katie replied. 'Two days after they inserted it, he pulled it out and sold it to another prisoner. Almost bled to death, but said he'd do it again.'

'Why would anyone want black market chemo medication in the UK?' Charlie frowned. 'The NHS gives it for free.'

'It can be used for attacking other prisoners,' Monica replied now. 'You could put it into someone's food and it'd make them sick, attack their immunity.'

'Shit,' Charlie hadn't considered such an option before. And Katie wasn't surprised, as only monsters looked at life-saving drugs, and worked out how to kill people with them.

'Anyway, after we got it back, it was decided by the board and the NHS that in his case, this was the best option,' she finished. 'Regardless of what we thought, he still has rights.'

Charlie nodded.

'And you've been doing this every week?'

'It's a rotation,' Katie nodded. 'So I end up here every other week. He's been on this chemo session for five weeks now. It'll be over soon.'

Monica nodded at this, and her expression concerned Katie.

'Are you sure you're okay?' Katie asked, turning to face her fellow nurse. 'Usually we can't shut you up.'

'Just tired,' Monica forced a smile. 'Long night travelling.'

'Why are you even here?' Katie frowned. 'You're not due on this until next week.'

'Swapped with Meg,' Monica shrugged. 'Her son is sick or something, so I said I'd do this week and she can do two on the go.'

Katie went to say Monica was a fool to agree to that, and Meg was likely just getting out of doing this session, when a guard ran to the glass doors of the lorry, leaning out.

'There's something wrong with the psycho,' he said.

Running into the lorry, Katie could immediately see that something was indeed wrong; Kendal Rushby wasn't screaming, but his face was pulled tight, every muscle straining, as he arched up from the seat, evidently in incredible pain.

'What did you do?' Katie ran over, trying to push Kendal into the chair. 'Kendal, can you hear me? What's going on?'

'Is it a blood clot?' Charlie was now beside her, helping the guard push Kendal down. 'The line goes into an artery near the heart. Shit, did I do it wrong? I thought I placed—'

'It's not a clot,' Katie opened one of Kendal's eyes, shining a torch into it. 'It's different. New. Something's very wrong.'

She moved to the tubes inserted into his chest now, unclipping them quickly, allowing them to fall back onto Kendal's body as the now-freed IV tubes hung idly to the side, dripping liquid onto the floor.

'Kendal!' she cried out. 'Can you hear me?'

'It... burns...' Kendal hissed, his face now scrunched into one of intense pain. 'Can't... breathe...'

Katie glanced back at Monica, standing at the back dispassionately.

'You secured the IV,' she said frantically, the slow moans of Kendal now rising as the pain wracked through his body. 'Was there anything wrong with it?'

'No,' Monica replied, still not moving, still standing across the lorry from the now screaming Kendal. 'I did what I always do.'

'Get me something to sedate him!' Katie cried at Charlie, who ran over to a counter by the wall, pushing past a confused guard as he did so.

'What's going on?' the guard asked nervously. 'This hasn't happened before.'

'You're damn right it's not happened before,' Katie took a syringe from Charlie, jabbing it into Kendal's arm. 'He's having some kind of cardiac arrest, possibly an allergic reaction to the chemo. But I can't work out why—'

She staggered back as Kendal Rushby arched up, a

hideous, ear-shattering scream emerging from his throat as he stared up at the ceiling, tears running down his face.

And then, as quickly as he'd arched up, he collapsed back into the chair, his head slumping.

'Was that the injection?' the guard asked, unsure.

Katie, meanwhile, was grabbing the handcuffed wrist, checking for a pulse.

'I don't think so,' she said, now moving to the neck, pressing two fingers to the side of it. 'He's not sedated. He's dead.'

The panic and chaos in the room now stopped as Charlie and Katie stared down at the lifeless form of Kendal Rushby.

'I swear, I put it in just as I was told,' Charlie whispered, tears running down his face. 'It's not my fault.'

'I know,' Katie reached across and patted Charlie's hand. 'I checked when I put in the second one. It was all fine. And Monica's an old hand at this, I saw the drip didn't have any air bubbles.'

'So why did he die?' uncuffing the dead man's hands, the first guard looked up, concerned. 'Was it these?'

'I don't know,' Katie looked back at Monica. 'Call the hospital. Let them know what's happened.'

Monica nodded and pulled out her mobile phone to call, but as she did so, the faint sound of sirens could be heard in the distance. Walking to the glass doors, Katie watched as two Manchester Police squad cars sped into the car park, making their way directly to the lorry.

'Did one of you call this in?' she asked the guards, who both shook their heads, still stunned by the situation. Looking back out into the car park, Katie opened the door and waited for the first car to pull up. A suited Asian woman jumped out, obviously a detective of some kind rather than a uniform.

For someone like this to be appearing, they had to know something.

'You're too late,' she said. 'He's dead.'

'Dammit!' the detective turned back to the squad car. 'Call forensics. Don't let anyone in or out before they attend the murder scene.'

'Wait, what?' Charlie walked out now, gripping his trembling arm. 'You think *we* murdered him?'

'We had a call,' the detective replied. 'Said there was credible evidence that someone was going to kill Kendal Rushby today. And from the looks of things, they succeeded.'

Katie went to reply, to contest this, but something stopped her, and she looked back into the lorry, through the glass windows.

Monica hadn't left, and was still staring at the body, hidden out of sight, the guards still likely to be checking the body.

She'd been nervous all day, and Katie had been utterly positive that something was wrong.

But now, looking at Monica, Katie saw that the expression of nervousness had been replaced.

Now Monica stared at the dead body of Kendal Rushby with what could only be classed as *triumph*.

'Yeah,' Katie nodded. 'They did.'

19

PURCHASE ORDER

Detective Superintendent Sophie Bullman relaxed back on her leather office chair, looked to the ceiling, and *screamed.*

A moment later, Declan and Anjli, both concerned, ran into the office.

'Boss?' Declan asked, concerned. 'You okay?'

'Just spoke to a friend in Manchester,' Bullman straightened, 'DCI Hannah Miller. Used to work with her before I went to Birmingham Met. She just let me know Kendal Rushby died today while in chemo.'

Declan straightened. The warning from Doctor Penhaligon had been treated lightly, but they'd still sent the message up to Manchester.

'Do we know how?' he asked, glancing at Anjli. 'I thought he had guards around him, who'd stop anyone getting close enough to attack?'

'Apparently he died in the chair, with nobody around,' Bullman frowned as she read the notes she'd written during the call. 'Something to do with the medication he was taking, I believe. The forensics are checking into it, but Hannah's solid, and she'll keep me involved. I've given her Billy's details for first contact.'

Monroe now walked in, far more casually than the others.

'Heard screaming,' he said. 'You okay?'

'I am now my two best detectives came to save me,' Bullman muttered. 'Where were you?'

'I saw your two best detectives come to save you through my window, and knew you'd be okay,' Monroe deadpanned. 'What happened? Rushby?'

'Dead,' Declan confirmed.

'So Penhaligon was right,' Monroe nodded. 'I was kinda betting on him not being correct with this one.'

'I think we all were, boss,' Declan looked out of the window of Bullman's office as he spied Doctor Marcos entering, a phone to her ear.

Seeing Declan watching, she waved for him to come over.

As all four detectives now left Bullman's office and walked to Doctor Marcos, she pointed at the phone.

'On a call to a mate in Manchester,' she whispered. 'On hold at the moment. They've not started on the body yet, but they've made a discovery. The IV that was used for his chemo session was slightly discoloured.'

'Blood in the IV?'

'No, the bag itself,' Doctor Marcos shook her head. 'Chemo treatments are clear, and gravity works against blood going upwards here.'

Declan nodded at this.

'Can we find out somehow what was in it?'

'That's what I'm on the phone waiting for,' Doctor Marcos was almost mocking as she replied. Then, straightening as her call reconnected with a human, she listened for a moment, clicking her fingers for someone, *anyone* to toss her a pad of notepaper, and with one now in front of her and a pen in hand, she began scribbling some notes onto it.

'Cheers, I owe you,' she said before disconnecting the call.

'You have something?' Bullman asked.

'It's a preliminary investigation right now, so we don't know the amounts used, but I've just been told by a reliable source they found traces of pancuronium bromide and potassium chloride in it. At the moment, we don't know how much, but it was enough to kill Rushby.'

'I don't know either of those,' Anjli said. 'And, with a mum who went through chemo, I'm guessing the fact I've never heard of them means they shouldn't be in the IV bag. Do we have a usage—'

'Oh, damn right we have a usage,' Doctor Marcos' face was tight as she replied. 'Pancuronium bromide is a known paralysing substance, while potassium chloride stops cardiac activity. Usually, when these two are found together, you'd find traces of sodium thiopental, a known anaesthetic with them, because when all three are used together, it's most often found in American prisons like Death Row, when prisoners are executed by lethal injection.'

'Bloody hell,' Declan muttered.

'Kendal mocked the police, saying they were toothless,' Monroe nodded. 'He was Texan, said that in a real police state, he'd be given a lethal injection.'

'Obviously someone listened to him.'

'You mentioned the third one, the sodium something—' Declan started.

'Thiopental.'

'Yeah, that one,' he continued. 'You said that wasn't in the mixture?'

'Not that they could find,' Doctor Marcos shrugged. 'But

then I'm getting information on a phone call during the CSI investigation. Why?'

'You said it's an anaesthetic,' Declan looked around the group. 'It sends the prisoner to sleep as they die, right? So, if it's not there...'

'It would mean that the accused would suffer breathing issues while unable to move, and would be conscious while their heart literally stopped,' Doctor Marcos nodded. 'It's a terrifying and incredibly painful way to die.'

'Justice,' Monroe muttered. 'This was the third.'

He looked back at Billy, watching from his monitors.

'Penhaligon was right about this, so he may be right about other things,' he said. 'See if you can get CCTV from the area, look for someone matching Lee Mellor's description.'

'You think he did this?' Declan asked.

'At the moment, if he's alive, he's a good bloody option, wouldn't you say?'

He glanced back to the doors to the office as De'Geer and Cooper entered, both looking shifty, anxious.

'You get something from the Holborn shop Declan sent you to?' Monroe asked.

De'Geer, stone faced, nodded.

'I think we should speak to you alone first, sir,' he said.

Monroe, picking up on this, looked over at Bullman.

'Both of you, and Monroe, in with me,' she said, taking the hint, and walking into Monroe's office. Reluctantly, De'Geer and Cooper followed her in, Monroe pausing as he looked back at Declan, Anjli and Doctor Marcos.

'Find me something,' he said. 'Anything.'

Entering Monroe's office, De'Geer stood nervously beside the window, looking out onto the street below as Monroe walked behind his desk.

'Okay, so out with it,' he said. 'What's so bad that it couldn't be said out there?'

De'Geer looked imploringly at Cooper, who stepped forward.

'Sir, we went to the spy shop that sold these bugs,' she said, pulling a matchbox out of her pocket and passing it over to him. Monroe noted that now the matchbox was in a forensics baggie. 'As DI Walsh said to us when he gave us the task, we weren't to speak to anyone except you.'

Monroe nodded. He'd wanted to make sure Billy was kept far away from this.

'Did they give you what you needed?' he asked.

Cooper shook her head.

'Not in the way you might consider,' she replied. 'They're small, GSM audio transmitters.'

'GSM?'

'Global system for mobiles,' De'Geer spoke from beside the window.

'Basically, they can transmit for about four hundred yards or so,' Cooper replied. 'We reckon there's some kind of recording device that's been taking the audio and saving it.'

'Was it the spy?' Monroe muttered. 'Was it Andrade?'

'The bugs were paid for in cash, so there's no record there,' Cooper replied. 'But the man behind the counter could take the ID numbers and work out when they were sold. It was just under a week ago.'

'So a couple of months into Andrade's relationship with Billy,' Monroe nodded. 'Enough time to get comfortable, get his feet under the table.'

'Sir, it wasn't Mister Estrada,' De'Geer interrupted.

'Then who was it?' Monroe snapped. 'Stop with all this bloody cloak and dagger bullshit!'

Cooper pulled out her phone.

'The shop could tie the time down to a ten-minute period, and we could gain access to the CCTV footage,' she said uncomfortably. 'Unfortunately, there were eight people in the store purchasing items during that time, and the footage doesn't give a clear view of what each person bought.'

'Of course not,' Bullman muttered. 'Wouldn't want footage of your customers buying slightly dodgy stalking items now, would we?'

'That said, we could gain footage of all eight faces,' Cooper said. 'And one of them... well...'

She held out the phone to Monroe, a CCTV image on it.

Monroe stared at the image for a moment, looked over at De'Geer, as if for confirmation, and, after receiving a reluctant nod, stormed out into the main office, pointing at Doctor Marcos.

'Where's DC Davey?' he shouted.

'I think the magic word is—'

'*Where the bloody hell is DC Davey?*' Monroe shouted louder. '*Right now!*'

'Downstairs!' Doctor Marcos replied, confused now. 'And I don't appreciate the tone—'

She stopped as Monroe passed her the image on Cooper's phone.

'Cooper, De'Geer, bring DC Davey up here,' he said. 'In handcuffs if you have to. Billy, I have an apology to make to you.'

'You do?' Billy looked confused, turning to face his boss.

'I thought your boyfriend had bugged our office,' Monroe

tossed the baggie with the matchbox inside over to him. 'We found bugs in two locations, and I had Trix pop in to sweep the offices when you were playing with your Masonic friends.'

'You had someone else sweep the offices?' Billy was hurt.

'I wanted to give you plausible deniability,' Monroe wasn't apologising, but was explaining the reasoning nevertheless. 'As it turned out, though, it wasn't Andrade, or Charles Baker, or any of the usual suspects.'

'It was one of our own,' Doctor Marcos hissed, showing the phone image. On it, walking out of the shop, a baseball cap doing a terrible job of hiding her face, was *DC Joanne Davey*.

Declan looked at Anjli.

'Why?' he asked. 'She's been with us for years. Why would she spy on us?'

'Maybe because she was locked out of the Spears' case?' Billy suggested.

'These were bought before the murder even occurred,' Bullman shook her head. 'There's every reason to believe that not only was she aware of the murders before they happened, but she was actively keeping tabs on us.'

'There could be more,' Billy said. 'Remember how I thought we could have a mole in the office, who was passing details to the white van on how to avoid cameras? Davey could easily have done that.'

'No, I refuse to believe this,' Doctor Marcos vigorously shook her head now. 'I've worked beside her. She's a good copper. She's never had a reason to do anything like this before.'

'We never had her sister's killer under a microscope

before,' Declan added. 'We have to place her on the suspect list, Doc, beside Lee Mellor.'

De'Geer entered the office again, Cooper a step behind him.

'She's gone,' he said. 'Nobody in there.'

'She must have guessed we'd be looking for her,' Monroe pursed his lips. 'We need to put out a—'

'No,' Doctor Marcos placed a hand on his arm. 'Please, Alex. She's one of us, no matter what's happening here. We put an APB out on her, we're killing her career. Look what happened to Declan when he was falsely accused.'

'Dammit, Rosanna, we don't know if it *is* false—'

'We need to at least find out what's happening,' Doctor Marcos pleaded.

'I might have something else,' Billy leant back in his chair as a small window on one of his monitors was clicked on, zooming in on the screen. It was a CCTV camera, showing a Margate street. 'I've been trying to follow Jacob Spears on his last day, but it's been difficult to find him, as he wasn't going to his normal haunts, and he didn't go to the coffee shop. I've had to literally scrape through every camera in the area, but I've found him.'

Coffee shop. There was something about that phrase, niggling at the back of Declan's mind. *What was it?*

Returning to the screen, Declan saw Jacob Spears had walked out of an amusement arcade now, and was arguing with another man, who seemed to have been waiting for him.

'Can you scroll back?' Declan asked, watching carefully. Billy did so, and Declan could now see the second man walk up to the amusement arcade, look in through the door, and shout into the building. Then, stepping back, the man stroked, or rather patted, at his short, black beard.

'Recognise him?' Declan looked over at Anjli.

'Yeah, that's Ian Connery, the cameraman we met at Kym's,' Anjli walked over now, intently watching the screen. 'But he doesn't have his camera here.'

By now, the scene had caught up to where they had started; Jacob Spears now stood outside the arcade, arguing with Ian.

'Maybe he wasn't happy with the interview?' Monroe suggested as, on the screen, Jacob grabbed at Ian's face. The CCTV wasn't clear from the angle where Jacob reached for, but Ian immediately pulled back, patting again at his beard.

'They're not as friendly as Ian made out,' Anjli noted. 'Jacob's downright belligerent there.'

Billy paused the footage.

'I forgot,' he said, paling slightly. 'I'm sorry, I'm spinning a lot of plates.'

'Not to worry, laddie, what did you forget?' Monroe soothed.

'I spoke to the Oak Hotel in Ramsgate,' Billy rummaged through some post-it notes, looking for something. 'They never heard of Ian or Them Is Productions, and definitely never allowed interviews to be filmed there.'

'So Ian lied to us,' Declan nodded for Billy to press play again. 'What else did he lie about?'

Whatever the issue between Jacob and Ian was on the footage, it didn't last long, as a moment later a familiar white van pulled up beside them, for the moment obstructing the view of the two men.

However, the driver of the van was very visible.

Kym Newfield.

'You're bloody kidding me,' Monroe hissed as, a second later, the van drove off, with neither Jacob nor Ian left on the street. 'Jacob Spears was abducted by Ian the cameraman, and Jacob's sodding *girlfriend?*'

'We know she has connections to serial killer victims,' Declan replied. 'Maybe there's more here than we expected.'

Monroe considered this and was about to speak when Billy's computer *dinged* with an email. He closed the CCTV feed, now showing an empty street, and opened the email up with a whistle.

'It's Manchester nick,' he said. 'The DCI that Bullman put me in touch with. They have a suspect already.'

'They do? Bloody hell, that was quick,' Bullman replied. 'Puts us lot to shame. Maybe I should bring them all in and fire you.'

'Maybe an exchange scheme,' Monroe absently suggested. 'Go on then, laddie, what did she say?'

'There's a nurse, a Monica Nadal,' Billy brought up a photo of a woman, in her sixties, auburn hair pulled back. 'One of the other nurses in the chemo session felt she was acting strangely today, before Kendal was brought in. Actively swapped shifts with someone, even though she told everyone she was doing it as a favour. And she was the one that set up the IV bag, the one that was tainted with poison.'

'Can we prove she was involved?' Monroe leant closer. 'I mean, this could be an accidental poisoning on her part. The bag could have been swapped earlier, and she simply was the poor cow who picked it up.'

'I'd agree, especially as we only have one witness statement to this,' Billy nodded. 'But looking at her record, she only moved to Kirkleys a couple of months back, asking to work in the mobile chemotherapy unit.'

He clicked through some folders, scanning them.

'She wanted to be there today. There has to be a reason.'

'Keep on it,' Monroe said, looking back at Declan. 'Do me a favour. Sweep the offices again with the bug sweeper Trix left us, just to be sure.'

'I thought she got all the bugs?'

'She may have, but Davey's been in the building since, so she may have replaced them,' Monroe muttered.

Declan nodded, walking off, as Bullman looked over at Doctor Marcos.

'You okay?'

Doctor Marcos glared back at her.

'I worked with her for months, years, even,' she hissed.

'You said yourself we don't know what's going on,' Monroe replied. 'We don't have the full story here.'

Reluctantly, Doctor Marcos relented on this as Billy, still typing, made another surprised yelp.

'You're like a bloody Jack Russell, laddie,' Monroe replied. 'What do you have?'

'The medical records, Guv. Monica Nadal was married,' Billy read from the screen. 'Her maiden name was Purvor.'

'And should we know that?' Anjli flipped through her notes.

'No, sorry, it was in my own notations,' Billy clicked up another window on his screen, flicking through it. 'I was checking into Ethan Roe after the YouTube video came up about him. Ethan's mum was Lucinda Roe, but her maiden name...'

'Was Purvor,' Monroe read from the screen. 'Jesus wept. Monica was the bairn's grandmother.'

'Hold on,' Declan stepped back from the others now. 'Monica Nadal kills Kendal Rushby, even though she has no connection at all to him. She does, however, have a connection to Darryl Marr.'

'And Kym Newfield is shacking up with Jacob Spears when he dies, but was the sister of a victim of Lee Mellor,' Anjli added. 'Not to mention Davey having an alibi for the night of Jacob's murder, but now bugging the department, and possibly aiding the killers' escape.'

'It's *Throw Momma From The Train,*' Monroe muttered, noticing the confused expressions facing him. 'Or, if you're an ignorant movie philistine, it's Hitchcock's *Strangers On A Train*. Both are a story of two random people, both with a desperate need to kill someone, who offer to "trade" murders.'

'Someone kills Darryl Marr, and in return Monica Nadal kills Kendal Rushby,' Anjli said.

'We should check anyone connected to the murders,' Bullman nodded. 'On the victim's side. Many would have given prints and DNA to keep them out of the search, so check into those. See if any match the partial print on Marr's driving licence.'

'That's screwed up in so many ways,' Anjli picked up the phone, dialling. 'But something as ambitious as this would take someone to plan it all.'

'Someone with an agenda,' Monroe nodded, stroking his beard. 'Maybe Lee Mellor?'

Declan stared at Monroe as he did this, frowning.

'I used to have a beard,' he eventually said.

'Aye, I remember, and a scraggly little thing it was, too,' Monroe smiled. 'You look better with it gone. Especially as your daughter said the grey in it made you look older.'

'I'm not talking about that,' Declan shook his head. 'I'm thinking that when I had the beard, I'd often stroke it, like you just did.'

'So you're having wistful memories?' Monroe enquired with a smirk. 'Would you like me to let you stroke it?'

'Would you let me pat it?' Declan countered.

Monroe frowned.

'Now who in God's name pats a beard?' he started before pausing, realisation setting in.

'The blasted cameraman.'

'Exactly,' Declan replied. 'Ian patted at his beard when we met him, and he did it after Jacob grabbed at it. As if the beard wasn't real.'

'And Jacob knew, and wanted it removed,' Anjli nodded. 'But why?'

'Lee Mellor,' Declan said, looking at Billy. 'Can you put up a picture of him? In Photoshop or something?'

Billy looked quizzically back at Declan, but after a moment opened up an image of Lee Mellor. It was the one they'd seen before; a slightly pudgy, overweight man in his early twenties, clean shaven with peroxide blond, spiky hair.

'Can you narrow the face?' Declan asked, leaning in. 'Like reduce the jowls, as if he lost weight?'

Nodding, Billy used the software's warp function to narrow the cheeks.

'Now draw on him,' Declan pointed at the image. 'Black hair, a beard and black glasses. Ray Bans, but with clear lenses.'

As Billy did this, the office quietened to a whisper as everyone stared at the man on the screen.

Ian Connery.

'Bloody hell, Lee Mellor's been there since the start,' Bullman said from the back. 'But why would Kym Newfield work with him?'

'She doesn't know,' Declan replied. 'Lee lost weight in

prison, and the glasses and hair change his face. Add a beard, and someone claiming to be working on a documentary...'

Declan started pacing.

'He had acne on his neck, I didn't even think twice about it. But he could have an allergy to the spirit gum keeping the beard on.'

'If Kym was driving the van, then she was in on this with "Ian", possibly from the start,' Monroe moved from the desks now. 'I want her in here right now. And I want Ian or Lee or whatever he's calling himself arrested as well.'

He stopped, turned to face the team, and screamed.

'*And find me Joanne Davey!*'

'I'm right here,' a woman's voice spoke, and everyone looked to the door to the office, where DC Davey now stood.

'Arrest that woman and put her in interview one,' Monroe hissed, and De'Geer reluctantly walked over to Davey, already holding her hands up.

'I'm not resisting,' she said as he led her out of the office and to the interview rooms upstairs.

Monroe glanced at Declan.

'You, with me,' he ordered, following De'Geer and Davey.

Before moving, Declan looked at Anjli.

'Do you think she knew?' Anjli asked, still processing this.

'At the moment, I have no idea,' Declan replied slowly. 'But there's a very good chance nobody knows who he is, so she might not know he's a serial killer.'

He shook his head, unable to take this all in.

'One thing's for sure,' he said. 'If it was Mellor, he planned the whole thing, and he only has one more serial killer to execute.'

Anjli punched the desk in anger.

'We had him,' she hissed. 'We had him and we didn't know. He was even the one to tell us Lee Mellor was dead.'

Declan stared at the face on the screen, Lee Mellor looking directly at him, taunting him, even, before turning and walking towards the back doors, where moments earlier the arrested DC Joanne Davey had been taken.

Police help or not, Lee Mellor was going down—even if Declan had to destroy someone's police career to do so.

20

ROLL THE DICE

Mister Pravda pushed his shaded glasses up his nose as he stared across the road at the Temple Inn police unit.

He knew that Joanne Davey would be taken; he'd known since the bugs had been found by Monroe that eventually they'd work out she'd bought them for him.

She had to be captured, and the police needed to focus on her; only then could Mister Pravda make sure the last on his list, Eric Coble, was executed. For Eric Coble had gone into some kind of witness relocation while in Belmarsh, and even with the computer access of one of Mister Pravda's assets, he was still hidden from view.

Mister Pravda chuckled at this. Apparently, it was easier to fake an identity than *find* someone who'd faked one already.

But it was only a matter of time until they found him. And, once they did that, Mister Pravda could capture him, and allow his partner to kill him—no, *execute* him—in the manner he deserved, before leaving his partner to be captured himself, and returned to prison.

The problem was, which location should they do it in?

London had so many suitable spots; Marr and Jacob had both been executed elsewhere, their bodies brought to the locations of their deaths. Rushby had been killed in the style of a Texan, just as he'd spoke of so many times in those stupid bloody group sessions, but he hadn't been able to find the perfect spot for it, as US executions weren't performed on UK soil. However, Strangeways itself was a place for executions, and Manchester had several places used during the Middle Ages, so Mister Pravda took what joy he could from this righteous execution.

Coble, however, needed to not only be killed at the correct location but also personally. Rushby's death had been unfortunately denied to them, even if he'd created the manner of the execution and passed it on. That, to him, however, was the same as passing an executioner an axe; he hadn't performed the deed.

And Mister Pravda knew they had to perform the deed. He knew very well that his partner *wanted* to perform the deed, to find his four victims, just like the last time.

But that meant having the police looking for them. And, with the nurse now taken by the police in Manchester, the silly bitch—he'd told her to throw it onto someone else—would surely tell everyone his name, even if she only knew a pseudonym. He didn't mind the other name being out there; the police hunting Mellor meant they weren't hunting him, but now the dice had been rolled, and he had to wait, to see what happened next.

Pulling the flat cap out of his pocket, he placed it on his head, pulled up his collar and walked away from the entrance before he was spotted. He needed to find a way to get Eric Coble out into the open. Walking out of Temple Inn, Mister Pravda tipped his cap at the two guards. He'd spoken to them earlier that day, and as far as they were concerned, he was perfectly normal.

Because he *was* perfectly normal.

They nodded back at him, smiling. Carrying on, Mister Pravda turned down a side road, heading towards the embankment, and a large black London Taxicab, the type that had the sliding side doors and the wheelchair access. It wasn't his, although he was using it for the moment. And the licence plate was that of a Range Rover in Shadwell Basin, so he had no fear of the police finding it soon.

Arriving at the cab, he opened the driver's door, climbing in and looking back at his passenger.

'All good?' he asked with a smile.

'All good,' Lee Mellor nodded. 'She agreed to meet.'

'Good,' Mister Pravda started the engine, pulling out onto the street. 'Put a seatbelt on, please. It's the law. And her, too.'

Before placing his belt on, Mellor looked at the unconscious woman beside him. Kym Newfield had been out for quite a while now.

'You sure she's not dead?' he asked, looking up at the window that divided the driver from passengers. 'She doesn't look well.'

'She's not dead, because I didn't want her dead,' Mister Pravda replied. 'She'll be out for another hour or so. And after that, it's up to you.'

'You don't want to kill her?'

'We only kill the guilty ones,' Mister Pravda said, his eyes still fixed on the road as he pulled into the traffic from the right. 'You're the one who kills the others.'

Mellor smiled, looking down at the unconscious body beside him.

'Finally,' he whispered. 'Bloody finally.'

DC DAVEY SAT ON ONE SIDE OF THE TABLE, WITH DECLAN AND Monroe facing her. She was quiet, unusually so, and had stared at the surface of the table while Declan had started the recording, stating for the record the time, the date, and who was in the room.

Before he could carry on, however, there was a motion at the door, and Doctor Marcos entered.

'She needs a Federation Rep,' she stated as she walked across and sat down beside Davey, not looking her in the eyes once. 'We keep to the rules.'

'Aye, I'm okay with that,' Monroe nodded. 'For the tape, Doctor Rosanna Marcos has taken on the role of Federation Representative for PC Davey.'

He watched Davey for a long moment.

'Tell us about the bugs,' he said.

'The what?' Davey frowned, looking up at him.

'The listening devices you bought from the Holborn shop,' Monroe carried on. 'And don't tell us you didn't, as we have footage.'

Davey's frown deepened as she looked from Monroe to Declan to Doctor Marcos.

'You've been following me?' she asked incredulously.

'We found where they were bought from,' Declan said, leaning closer. 'We saw CCTV of you.'

Monroe had been about to add to this, but stopped, watching her confused expression.

'You genuinely don't know, do you,' he said as a statement

more than a question. 'So, let's change the subject. *Why* did you buy the bugs?'

'Doctor Penhaligon was being followed,' Davey replied. 'He was convinced it was a particular patient, and he asked me to help with picking up some items.'

'Penhaligon used them?' Monroe folded his arms. 'Why would he need radio transmitting bugs?'

'I don't know,' Davey shrugged, looking around as if for support. 'He couldn't go in there, because they'd see him. He gave me cash, asked me to pick them up on his behalf.'

Monroe reached into his jacket, pulling out the baggie containing the matchbox and bugs from within.

'Are these the bugs?' he asked icily.

Davey took the bag, leaning in to examine the items within. After a moment, she sat up, her eyes narrowing as she tried to work out what was going on.

Either that, Declan thought to himself, *or she's just realised she's been caught, and she's looking for a way out.*

'Where did you get these?' she asked.

'One was in the office, taped under a desk, and gathering together everything said in there,' Monroe replied, his tone cold and unemotional. 'The other one was in the canteen area, taped to the coffee tin. Which hasn't been used since we moved to the machine, apart from when Declan made bloody terrible builder's tea and revealed it without realising.'

Davey shook her head in disbelief.

'No, that can't be,' she replied.

'Aye, it can be,' Monroe snapped, slamming the palm of his hand against the table. 'You planted the bugs, so you'd know if we were onto you! You passed ANPR details to the killer! What else did you do to help Lee Mellor?'

'Wait, you think I did this?' Davey's eyes widened in horror. 'Why would you think that?'

'You started taking therapy with Penhaligon after Them Is Productions contacted you,' Declan said, checking his notes. 'We now believe Ian Connery, the cameraman for the productions is actually Lee Mellor, who faked his death in prison, paying off a doctor to label him as dead.'

'And you think I'd help a serial killer?' Davey still stared at Declan.

'If it meant the death of the man who killed your sister, possibly,' he replied. 'Did Mellor tell you to contact Penhaligon?'

Davey's eyes clouded at this, and her expression darkened.

'Do I need a solicitor here?'

'I dunno, lassie,' Monroe replied. 'Do you?'

'You know something, Guv?' Davey spat out now. 'I've found the way you keep calling us all "lassie" to be incredibly condescending. You might think it's quaint or twee, maybe a way to humanise you, but it's not. It's creepy.'

'That's enough—' Doctor Marcos started.

'No, Rosanna, it's not,' Davey interrupted, tears building. 'I thought I was in trouble because I spoke about the case to Penhaligon! That I'd talked to the other victims in my own time before the murder, and you'd found out! Not because I'd bought three of these!'

She tossed the baggie onto the table.

'You were my colleagues, and you think me capable of this?' she hissed. 'Declan was accused of terrorism and murder and not once did you think there was another answer.'

'So give us one,' Declan replied, his voice calm. 'Give us a way to clear you.'

Davey considered this.

'Fine,' she said. 'You want the truth? I'll tell you everything.'

BILLY HAD BEEN WORKING ON HIS COMPUTER AS ANJLI, ON HER own, less-tricked out PC, had been working through the HOLMES 2 files. Ever since Davey had returned, being taken upstairs by Declan, Monroe and Doctor Marcos, the air in the office had been thick with tension, and Billy desperately wanted to cut it.

'Did you really think Andrade placed the bug?' he asked. 'When Monroe told you?'

'Of course not,' Anjli replied, eyes glued to her screen. 'But, you know, all avenues had to be examined.'

'I'm guessing the avenues didn't include "one of our own" on that list,' Billy said morosely, typing on the screen, as, from the room door behind him, Bullman walked in, struggling with a Windows Desktop unit.

'What's this?' he asked, running over and helping her with it. 'I didn't ask for anything new?'

'We're short staffed right now, so I thought I'd bring it up,' Bullman said. 'It's Davey's computer from downstairs, and I thought you could do your Billy Whiz magic.'

Placing it on the desk, Billy looked at the box.

'It doesn't come with accessories?'

Bullman placed her hands on her hips indignantly.

'I'm your superior,' she hissed. 'Do you think I do monitors and keyboards?'

Annoyed now, she grabbed a transmitter from Declan's desk.

'As Walsh is busy, I'll carry on with the scan now,' she said. 'You can get the rest.'

'Hey,' Billy frowned, pulling out a USB cable from the back. 'What's this?'

'You're the computer expert,' Anjli grinned. 'Surely you can tell?'

'It looks like a USB extension cable,' Billy pulled it out, looking at it. 'Was something plugged into this?'

'Yeah, the keyboard,' Bullman said as she continued into Monroe's office.

Concerned, Billy walked back to his chair, inspecting the cable.

'What?' Anjli, leaning back from her own screen, looked over at him, recognising the expression.

'Davey's keyboard was right beside her computer,' Billy still examined the cable. 'She didn't need an extender.'

'Maybe it came with the PC?'

Billy shook his head, reaching over to his drawers, pulling the top one out and grabbing a tiny flat head screwdriver.

'They don't,' he said, prising the plastic cover off the USB connector. 'Ah, shit.'

'Well, you can't send it back now,' Anjli smiled. 'You broke the warranty.'

'This isn't police issue,' Billy threw the wire onto the desk like it was a snake. 'It's not even a cable. As such, anyway.'

He tapped on his keyboard, bringing up an image of a similar USB cable.

'It's an Air drive Keylogger,' he explained. 'You plug it into the computer and then attach the keyboard to it. Any time you write on the keyboard, this then sends every key tapped to your stalker's computer, laptop, tablet, or smartphone. Or email it to them after a set amount of data has been reached.'

'So if Davey typed in a passcode...'

'It's been found, along with her user ID, the website she searched, everything,' Billy replied. 'She might be innocent after all.'

'Well, that's good news at least,' Anjli looked back to the screen. 'All we have to do is prove it.'

'I might have something else connected to the production company,' Billy glanced over at her. '*Them Is.* It's being annoying me, as it's grammatically incorrect. But that's probably the point. However, I typed it in wrong.'

'How do you mean?'

'I mean, I missed the space, and typed it in as *Themis*,' Billy pointed at a Wikipedia page on his left monitor. 'And that opened up a rabbit hole.'

'What kind of rabbit hole?' Anjli now rose, ignoring her screen now.

'Themis is from Greek mythology,' Billy explained. 'She was the second wife of Zeus, and the personification of justice.'

'Justice.'

Billy nodded.

'Hell of a coincidence, right?' he now pointed at the other screen. 'So, I look into the other details, yeah? And the other name on the production company page. Florence Dorey.'

'Let me guess, she doesn't exist?'

'Oh, she does,' Billy nodded. 'That is, she did. A long time back. She was one of the children killed by Jamie Crawley.'

'The man who killed Doctor Penhaligon's sister,' Anjli leant closer. 'Who died in Broadmoor.'

'Yes,' Billy nodded. 'Although I've got another question

there. None of the victims were connected to anyone in the Penhaligon family, but Florence Dorey was the half-sister of Jeffrey Ames.'

On the screen, Billy pulled up the image of Jeffrey Ames once more.

'Ames? The prison guard?' Anjli's mouth hung open at this. 'There's no way they'd allow him to be working at the prison, if he's immediate family—'

'He's a half-sibling with a different surname,' Billy pointed at the screen. 'This was before the internet. They probably didn't realise until...'

'Until Crawley mysteriously sliced his own throat open with the end of a spoon,' Anjli finished the sentence. 'Then they got him out of there as quick as possible. Last thing they wanted was for him to be publicly exposed. They'd open themselves up to a ton of scrutiny.'

'Records say he was transferred a couple of months later,' Billy nodded. 'Enough time for them to gain space from the murder, and soon enough to stop him from doing worse.'

He hissed.

'That bloody glitch is back on the file,' he said. 'It's like someone went in and saved it wrong, corrupting something on it.'

He paused at this, his eyes widening.

'I've seen this before,' he whispered. 'Back when we were having issues with the Government. This feels like spook work.'

'Trix?'

'No, but she might be able to help,' Billy tapped a quick message and sent it on. 'We'll see what she comes back with. In the meantime, let's carry on with Ames.'

'Who's realised at this point he could get away with

murder,' Anjli whistled. But before she could continue, Anjli's computer beeped as the HOLMES 2 system found something relevant to her search.

Walking over, she checked it.

'The partial fingerprint has a match,' she said. 'It didn't get picked up before, as he's not technically in the system. Hold on, I'll send it across.'

After a moment of Anjli's slow, one-finger typing, Billy's own computer beeped, and he pulled up the image of a white, middle-aged and portly male, his thinning brown hair cut into a faded buzz cut.

'Mickey Fallon,' Billy leant back in his chair. 'Father of Susan Fallon, killed while at her boyfriend's house one Christmas by Kendal Rushby.'

Anjli was already walking for the back door.

'Tell De'Geer and Cooper to pick him up when they bring back Kym Newfield, and I'll let Monroe know,' she said. 'We can pause Davey's interview for a moment—'

She stopped as Bullman walked out of Monroe's office, a small transmitter bug in her hand.

'Are you going to speak to Monroe?' she asked. 'If so, I think he needs to see this, too. Stupid sod's letting everyone and their dog bug his office these days.'

'That's impossible,' Anjli looked back at Billy. 'He had that room swept by Trix.'

'Obviously Trix didn't do a good enough job,' Billy replied, and Anjli could sense a little piece of triumph in his voice. 'Go tell him. I have a lead I want to chase.'

21

PUZZLE PIECES

Davey sighed as she considered the question.

'Look, he came to me,' she said. 'I'm part of a victim outreach group, and his sister—'

'Aye, his sister,' Monroe nodded. 'We heard.'

'So, when the production company sniffs around, I have nightmares,' Davey continued. 'Doctor Penhaligon was contacting people they'd contacted, checking we were okay, and offered to help.'

'If you helped him buy bugs.'

'That was later,' Davey's face wrinkled in irritation. 'And you're just being pedantic there. Penhaligon genuinely wanted to help. And, as I worked odd hours, he made sure all his sessions were places I could make.'

'You never went to his offices?'

'I never had the time.'

'But you came here?' Declan asked.

At this, Davey stopped.

'Well, of course,' she said, but now her voice was a little

more cautious, as if she too was considering the question a little deeper. 'We held many sessions in this room, in fact.'

'Why not the briefing room?'

'Glass windows,' Davey admitted. 'I know Billy couldn't hear us, but it felt weird talking about my past with him across the room. And the bugger never sleeps.'

'Did he—Penhaligon, that is—ever talk about your work?'

'Of course,' Davey nodded. 'We talked a lot about it. He worked in the prison system, and he knew a lot of the police terminology. It was nice to be able to, you know, talk shop.'

'Did you ever talk about the ANPR?' Declan asked now.

Davey looked away.

'I didn't know,' she said. 'He told me one night he'd been flashed by a speeding camera in London, going down Lower Thames Street. It used to be thirty miles an hour, but now it's twenty. He asked if there was any way I could check if he was snapped. Not to remove it, just to check.'

'And you did,' Doctor Marcos sighed. 'You bloody fool! Did you at least hide your login details?'

'Of course.'

'Could he have seen this?'

'He wasn't in the room,' Davey shook her head. 'I did it on my PC downstairs. He was only ever in there once, and that was right at the start of our therapy. We lasted ten minutes before it freaked him out. I had to get him a water, he was having a panic attack.'

'And you didn't tell this to us after Spears was found because...?' Monroe leant in.

'Because I knew I'd logged into ANPR, so at some point someone would link that to the van avoiding the cameras, but as I said, I checked on my own, away from anyone. There's no way he could have seen it.'

'And you didn't think of telling us?'

'He couldn't have seen it!'

Monroe went to speak as once more the door to the interview room opened, and Anjli stood there, pale faced.

'Interview paused,' Declan quickly stopped the tape. 'What's up?'

'How many bugs did you find?' Anjli asked Monroe.

'Two,' Monroe frowned, looking back at Davey. 'How many did you buy?'

'Three,' Davey replied. 'Why?'

Anjli tossed the third onto the table.

'It was found in the Guv's office,' she explained, looking at Monroe. 'Near your side cabinet.'

Monroe picked up the bug, staring down at it.

'I lock my office at night, so it couldn't have been placed when the others were,' he said. 'And Trix swept the whole place.'

'Billy thinks she missed it.'

'No,' Declan, realising, shook his head. 'Someone could have planted it after the sweep. We even let them do it. When they gathered a drink.'

'Penhaligon,' Monroe hissed. 'Bloody wee fellow had a dram of my whisky and could have planted it then. He'd have known the other two were found by then.'

He looked back at Davey.

'In the times you were in here with him, was he ever alone?'

'Sure,' Davey shrugged. 'There was a time in here I needed to be sick, as the memories were a little raw, and then there was a time when he was left in the briefing room while I took a call. Billy was out with his Colombian that night, so...'

She trailed off, tears welling in her eyes.

'That bastard,' she said. 'He used me.'

'Aye, I think he did,' Monroe replied. 'And you should be grateful we trust you, because otherwise you're in a lot more trouble than you could be.'

'We can trust her,' Anjli added. 'Billy found a keylogger attached to her computer. Someone saw everything she typed.'

Davey's face crumpled at this and, with her head in her hands, she sobbed.

'I'm such a bloody fool,' she hissed.

'Okay, so Penhaligon planted the bugs, and possibly stole the ANPR details from Davey and gave them to the van drivers, but how is he connected to Lee Mellor and his revenge spree?'

Declan clicked his fingers.

'Coffee shop,' he said.

Monroe paused, staring at him funny.

'You want to go grab a coffee?' he asked.

'No, Guv, it's been niggling me since he said it, and I didn't know why,' Declan said. 'When we talked about having footage of Jacob stalking again, he replied that sitting in a coffee shop wasn't a crime.'

'Aye, I remember. And it's not.'

'But we said café,' Declan continued. 'And *café* doesn't immediately equate to *coffee shop,* in which the CCTV clearly showed it to be.'

'You think he knew about the lass—' Monroe stopped, glancing momentarily at Davey, '—at the woman behind the counter?'

'Could be,' Declan replied, nodding. 'I think there's a few warning bells there.'

'That's not all, boss,' Anjli said. 'You all need to come with us. Billy has new intelligence, and we now have a name to the fingerprint.'

'We're sticking a pin in this,' Monroe rose from his chair, looking at Davey. 'Are you involved, consciously, in any of these murders, DC Davey?'

'No sir, I swear,' Davey looked at Doctor Marcos as she replied. 'Honest, Rosanna.'

'She's under your watch,' Monroe said, looking from Davey to Rosanna. 'Use her skills to prove her innocence. The rest of you? Let's go find a fake bloody therapist.'

De'Geer and Cooper had not had the most productive of days. They'd driven all the way to Broadstairs to find nobody in at Kym Newfield's house and, after a check around the premises, they'd started back towards London in the squad car before the message arrived from Monroe, asking them to make a diversion on the way back and arrest Michael Fallon, now revealed to be the owner of the partial fingerprint on the driving licence stapled to Darryl Marr's forehead. Fallon lived in Gravesend, Kent, and so it was only a minor diversion for them to come off the A2 and pick him up.

Michael Fallon, however, had different plans on this.

Arriving outside his house, a small two-up, two-down house in a cul-de-sac to the south of Gravesend, a narrow street that'd once been a new-build, but was now looking dated, with a high-fenced open parkland opposite, De'Geer immediately knew they'd made a mistake. The squad car was obviously "police", and Fallon had been watching.

He knew this because the moment they left the car, there

was a crash from the side of the house, and down the side path De'Geer could see a portly, balding man sprinting out into his back garden.

'Head him off!' Cooper shouted, already running after the fugitive and, caught between telling her to get back or climbing in the car, De'Geer chose the latter. He could see from the map view on the sat nav that Fallon's garden backed onto Gravesend cemetery, and from there De'Geer saw a multitude of exits. Revving the engine, he decided to roll the dice and head towards Dashwood Park, an open space next to it.

COOPER WAS SHORT, ONLY JUST TALL ENOUGH TO ENTER THE police force, but she was quick. Very quick. A school and college sprint champion, she did park runs for fun, and even in a pair of police-issue work boots, she could still tear up a fair pace when she wanted.

Michael Fallon, however, had the advantage of local knowledge, and distance.

By the time she sprinted into the back garden, a dog barking frantically in the kitchen, jumping up at the window as she passed, she saw Fallon clamber up and over a six-foot high fence at the back. He was taller, so the jump would have been even easier, but he was heavier, and so struggled at the top, costing him seconds of valuable time.

'Mister Fallon!' Cooper shouted as she carried on. 'Give it up!'

And with a flop over the top, and a crash on the other side, Fallon was gone. Cooper aimed for a small compost bin to the left of the fence, leaping up onto it, using it to help her flip over the fence, finding herself in the tree line that edged the south side of the cemetery.

'Suspect is on foot, heading northeast through Gravesend cemetery,' she shouted into her radio, following Fallon as he struggled across the grass-topped graves.

'Coming up on the east side,' De'Geer's voice spoke through the speaker. 'Keep me updated.'

Cooper didn't reply, instead saving her energy for a last, frantic dash, veering to the right and ducking as she ran along the gravestones. She hoped that Fallon, unable to do more than glance back as he ran, wouldn't see her, and perhaps slow down.

Of course, her fluorescent jacket wasn't exactly helping her.

Fallon had reached the centre of the cemetery now, a roundabout with spurs leading off in five directions. He paused, only for a moment, his eyes wide as he tried to consider the best option here—and fell, as he was violently rugby tackled by PC Cooper at full speed.

'Stay down!' she screamed as she pulled out her handcuffs. 'Michael Fallon, I'm arresting you for—'

She didn't finish as, before she could secure him, Fallon flung his arm out, catching her on the side of the head, sending her stumbling back.

'I didn't do it!' he cried out desperately. 'I didn't know what they were doing! I thought we were just passing a message—*whuff!*'

The last noise made was a reaction to Cooper, charging back in and, before he could stop her, ramming a knee hard into Michael Fallon's groin. As he crumpled to the floor, Cooper placed a knee on his back as she brought his hands behind, cuffing them.

'Who are the "they" you're talking about?' she asked. 'And who was your co conspirator?'

'I want a solicitor!'

As De'Geer, now through the gates of the cemetery and driving at speed, approached them, Cooper took a breath as she sat on the now silent Michael Fallon's handcuffed back.

'You're bloody nicked, mate,' she smiled. 'Don't worry, you'll be getting your solicitor. Right before we nail you for murder.'

JENNIFER FARNHAM-EWING DIDN'T WANT TO BE A MESSENGER; for a start, she wanted to be in the room where it happened, not in the back of some sleek, modernist bar in Hatton Garden.

The Argyle was on Greville Street, a short walk from the famous jeweller's street, and caught in the middle of half a dozen spiderweb streets, some turned into one-way roads, some pedestrianised. In fact, it was an absolute nightmare to find a taxi driver who could make the journey without stopping at roadworks or road closures. If she'd had a Minister's car to use, like in the old days, this would have been way easier. But no, she couldn't do that, because she was still the lowest of the low, and the universe still hated her.

But, she was also very aware that *needs must* and all that, and today's meeting could possibly push forward Charles Baker's capital punishment initiative further and faster than any single public enquiry.

Entering the bar, she looked around to spy her informant. She'd never personally met him, but he'd been the one to tell her about Marr. He'd also been the one who gave the coordinates of the burials, who'd given her a heads up after Manchester police found Kendal Rushby dead in a cancer truck, whatever the merry hell that was, and now she'd been told, by an encrypted message, that he needed to meet.

She saw a man at the back wave to her. Playing with his black beard, Ian Connery looked nervous, watching behind her, as if expecting her to bring others with her to the meeting. Sitting down, Jennifer forced a smile. She didn't want to be here, but this one man was about to save her career.

'Mister Connery,' she whispered. 'Tell me why this is so important?'

Ian leant closer to her, lowering his voice.

'I've got something else for you,' he said.

'Another murder?' Jennifer was horrified at the thought, but at the same time, there was a deep fascination within her.

'Not yet,' Ian smiled. 'But it's happening. Tomorrow, at dawn.'

'Why dawn?' Jennifer frowned.

'Because that's the time allocated.'

'Yes, I get that, Mister Connery, but it's not exactly a time now, is it? It's autumn, and the sun rises differently every day. That's not a time. That's a—'

'Do you want the information or not?' Ian snapped. 'I'm risking a lot coming to you.'

Jennifer leant back in the seat, observing the bearded man. It was true, he'd been an incredible help here so far; Ian Connery's nameless police informant had been on the money three times so far. But, these had all been murders, *past* tense.

Now Jennifer was being given an advanced warning. She could tell the police, she could save the life of—

Of a serial killer who most likely deserved his death, just like the other three had.

'Who?' she asked.

'Eric Coble,' Ian replied. 'The Soho Ripper.'

'Where?'

Ian shook his head, patting at his beard as he did so.

'I can't tell you that.'

'Then why bring me here?' Jennifer snapped irritably. 'Apart from telling me there's going to be another death, what possible good comes from this meeting?'

'I said *I* couldn't tell you that,' Ian rose from his chair. 'That doesn't mean someone else can't.'

Without saying anything else, Ian walked across the pub, Jennifer snapping at his heels.

'What do you mean, someone else? Who else? Where are we going?'

'Come with me,' Ian opened the door to the bar, walking out into the late afternoon daylight. 'They're around the corner. Speak to them, see what you think and, if you're not sold, then you can tell the police and be a hero. Or get your boss to do it.'

Following the bearded man along Leather Lane, past the street food vendors, now preparing for the rush of evening workers returning home, Jennifer caught up with him as he passed some bollards on Beauchamp Street, heading into Brooke's Market, comprising what seemed to be an unremarkable collection of black iron benches on a bubble-gum and bird-shit spattered pavement, a few bins, recycling units and a bright green donation bank for clothes to the side.

Jennifer wrinkled her nose at this; she really didn't want to be here right now.

Ian seemed to head towards a black taxi, one of those with the sliding side doors, the back windows tinted. For a moment, Jennifer wondered whether this was there by chance, or maybe someone waiting for a customer from one of the buildings surrounded them, but as she got closer, she saw Ian wave to the driver, a thin, older man in a flat cap and tinted lenses.

'I have a meeting I need to be at,' she protested, as the driver climbed out of the vehicle, nodding to Ian. 'I'm not getting in any cab with you. The Prime Minister knows where I am.'

'The Prime Minister knows a lot of things,' the driver nodded at this. 'And listening to what he said on the TV this week, he speaks a lot of sense, too.'

At this tacit endorsement of Charles Baker, Jennifer relaxed a little as the driver gave her a brief nod.

'Don't worry, my name is Mister Pravda, Miss Farnham-Ewing.'

'Are you Ian's contact with the police?' Jennifer, hoping this was the case, asked. Mister Pravda, however, shook his head, still smiling.

'Eric Coble is in witness protection,' Mister Pravda explained, moving around the car. With Ian at the back of it, Jennifer now found herself beside the sliding door, feeling a little boxed in. 'Your boss could tell us where he is. Your boss could arrange for him to be in Spitalfields for tomorrow.'

"Why would he do that?' Jennifer asked nervously. 'Ian said that Eric Coble was being executed, not that he needed my help to be executed.'

She looked around; she could see a CCTV camera on the corner of the square, and one further down the street, but there wasn't one nearby.

'I thought he was giving me scoops about murders, not committing them.'

Mister Pravda considered this for a long moment.

'You see that church over there on the corner?' He said, pointing at an unassuming four-storey, brown brick building at the end of Dorrington Street. 'That's the church of St Alban The Martyr. You know him? He was the first British Saint.'

Jennifer shook her head, confused where the conversation was going now.

'Is this like St Albans, the city?' she replied.

At this, Mister Pravda's face broke into a wide grin.

'Exactly,' he said. 'In fact, he was living in the Roman city of Verulamium, which is what St Albans once was.'

He looked at the church as he continued, obviously speaking to Jennifer.

'Have you ever read *Bede's Ecclesiastical History of the English People*, Miss Farnham-Ewing?' he asked. 'You work with academics and scholars every day in Downing Street, I'm sure you've flicked through the pages.'

'Can't say I remember,' Jennifer replied, wondering if this idiot was serious. She didn't think anyone she knew had read the bloody thing. 'I'm more of an action thriller person.'

Mister Pravda smiled wider at this.

'Possibly not then,' he said, looking back at her. 'Let me tell you the story.'

'I really have to leave, I have a—'

'Alban met a Christian priest, who was fleeing from persecutors,' Mister Pravda continued, ignoring her. 'At the time, you see, Christians were suffering cruel persecutions by the Romans. Anyway, Alban sheltered the priest, Amphibalus, in his house for several days, and during this time the priest prayed and kept watch day and night.'

'So he was a good man. I see,' Jennifer wondered how

she'd come for a clandestine meeting and ended up at a church service. 'Can we skip to the important part?'

'This is the important part,' Mister Pravda's smile faded. 'Alban was so impressed with the priest's faith and piety that he emulated him, and because of this, converted to Christianity. However, the Roman soldiers learned of his sheltering thanks to an informer, and came to Alban's house to seize the priest. But, as they arrived, Alban put on the priest's robes and presented himself to the soldiers in place of his guest, and because of this, was taken instead of the priest, as well as tortured and executed, again, instead of the priest.'

'I don't know where this is going,' Jennifer sighed, pulling out her phone. 'But as fun as it was, we can't help you find a man to be murdered.'

'The point of this is simple,' Ian spoke now, bringing her attention back to him. 'Alban knew, the moment he put on the priest's clothing, that he would surely die. He literally became another person to do God's will, knowing it would end badly.'

Jennifer looked from Ian to Mister Pravda.

'Are you saying you're not who you say you are?' Jennifer whispered. 'Who are you?'

'That's fair,' Mister Pravda nodded. 'You should know our real names. Ian, beside you, is actually Lee Mellor. You may know him as the *Angel Ripper*.'

Jennifer looked at Lee, her phone still in her hand, yet unable to move as Lee Mellor grasped her wrist, leaning in as he smiled.

'Pleasure to meet you,' he said. 'Please don't think of screaming.'

Jennifer pulled at her arm, trying to wrench it free from Mellor's grasp—but then arched back, as a sharp stab of electricity slammed into her spine, causing her to spasm uncontrollably, the phone falling to the gutter as she collapsed against the bearded man. Who, with a nod to Mister Pravda, held her upright while the taller, skinnier man opened the side door. Then, with a quick and well-practised movement, Mellor bundled the unconscious body of Jennifer Farnham-Ewing into the taxi, seating her beside the still unconscious Kym Newfield, and closing the door behind him.

Now alone in the street, Mister Pravda took one last look around and, leaving Jennifer's phone where it landed, he walked back to the driver's seat of the car, started the engine, and drove off westwards.

22

THE GANG'S ALL HERE

DECLAN HAD BEEN SURPRISED BY MONROE'S INTERVIEWER suggestion, but, as he sat in the interview room, facing Michael Fallon, he realised that, in a way, it was probably the only way to get him to talk.

'Look, Michael, can I call you Michael?'

'Mickey,' Fallon sniffled. 'My friends call me Mickey.'

'Okay then, Mickey,' DC Davey replied with a warm smile. 'I know what happened here. I've had the same thing happen to me.'

Fallon looked up at her, suspicion on his pudgy face.

'How?'

'My sister was killed by Jacob Spears,' Davey leant back in her chair, giving the impression of distance, as if she was giving Fallon his space. 'Penhaligon came to me after the film crew tried to get me to talk. It was only today when I realised they were working together to catch me out.'

Fallon looked at the table.

'I'm not ashamed of what I did,' he whispered. 'I did what anyone would have done.'

'Are you sure?' Declan asked, frowning. 'I can get you'd want your daughter's killer dead, but Susan was murdered by Kendal Rushby. And you killed Darryl Marr.'

'I didn't kill him,' Fallon looked up angrily. 'Neither did Dean.'

'Dean Hastings, whose family was killed one Christmas, also by Kendal Rushby, while he was abroad?' Davey looked at her sheet of notes. 'That Dean?'

'Yeah,' Fallon nodded. 'He was there too.'

Declan noted this down.

'So, both of you what, agreed to move the body?'

'Yeah.'

'Why?'

'Because they promised to kill the people we wanted,' Fallon hissed. 'We both wanted Rushby dead, so we helped kill Marr. You must have got the same offer.'

'I did,' Davey nodded. 'So, let me ask you. Did the man, Ian Connery, speak with you? Black hair and beard, glasses?'

'Yeah. But I said I wasn't interested in his documentary.'

'And then the doctor came by, Penhaligon?'

'Yeah. He said they disgusted him, but offered to talk it over in session. There were a few of us there. That's where I met Dean.'

'So it was what, a survivor's group?'

'In a way, yeah,' Fallon looked at Davey. 'Didn't see you there.'

'I had a more one-on-one session, because of my job,' Davey replied. 'I also wasn't recruited to help in some sick execution campaign.'

'We didn't realise it was real,' Fallon whined. 'We thought it was about making a splash, yeah? Like those fathers who dress up like superheroes to get press attention.'

'Penhaligon came to me four months ago,' Davey leant closer. 'When did he come to you?'

'Almost two years ago,' Fallon replied. 'That's when the sessions started.'

'Do you remember anyone else from those sessions?' Declan spoke before Davey could continue. He knew she'd now be questioning why she was left over a year before being groomed, and the answer was simple; Penhaligon didn't need her until then.

She was controlled from the very start.

'Dean was there,' Fallon considered this. 'There were a couple of older women, I can't remember the names—'

'Monica? Kym?'

'Yeah, that's two of them, although the younger one only turned up once. And there was a Lucy, too. Short woman, sister of someone killed by Eric Coble, I think. One of those gay guys burned up.'

Declan noted this down. Kym Newfield and Monica Nadal had both helped, in their own ways, to capture and kill Kendal Rushby and Jacob Spears, but neither of them had been attached to the actual death of the killer connected to their own lives.

'*Throw Mama from the Train*,' he muttered.

'Sorry?' Fallon strained to listen.

'How did you get the van?'

'We were told to arrive at a lockup near Tower Hill before dawn,' Fallon replied. 'There was a van in there. We saw Pravda—'

'Who?'

'Mister Pravda,' Fallon repeated. 'He contacted us when Penhaligon stopped.'

'Stopped the sessions?'

Fallon nodded.

'Stopped about six months ago, out the blue,' he said, playing with the cuffs of his shirt. 'And then we had, well, at least me and Dean had, messages from Mister Pravda turn up a couple of weeks later, offering to gain us closure. Said he was connected to Penhaligon, that we needed more than just therapy could give. And we agreed.'

'And what did Mister Pravda look like?'

'I only saw him the once, and it was dark,' Fallon scrunched his face as he tried to remember. 'He was tall and slim, a jacket with the collar up, tinted glasses over his eyes and a flat cap. Until he put the poncho on.'

'Poncho?' Davey looked up from writing.

'Waterproof thing. It's what he used when they...'

He gulped, paling a little.

'When they cut him up in the back room.'

'*They*.'

Declan spoke the word slowly, rolling it around on his tongue.

'Tell me who the other one was. Was it Penhaligon? Was it Lee Mellor?'

'Lee Mellor?' Fallon looked confused. 'Why would he be there?'

'Lee Mellor was Ian Connery, the cameraman that originally contacted you,' Declan said as he pulled a photo printout from a folder. 'What about this guy?'

Fallon examined it.

'I don't recognise him,' he said. 'Who is he?'

'Jeffrey Ames,' Declan said, taking the photo back. 'You never heard his name mentioned?'

Fallon shook his head.

'I told you, we were given Pravda's details, we emailed

him. I mean, I did, and so did Dean, separately, like, but he contacted us in a group message on WhatsApp. Told us to turn up. We did, we waited until...'

He *urped* at this point, and Declan worried whether he was about to be sick. But after a moment, Fallon calmed himself down.

'Until the boxes were finished, and then we placed them in the van,' he said. 'We then put on the hats and vests, attached the light to the roof and drove to Edgware Road.'

'How did you know to avoid the ANPR cameras?' Declan asked, and, on receiving a blank look from Fallon, carried on. 'The journey you took, it was random, all over the place. Why?'

'We had notes,' Fallon whimpered, the seriousness of the situation finally hammering down on him. 'Pravda gave them to us. We had to follow them to the yard.'

Declan leant back on his chair, considering the man in front of him.

'So let me get this right,' Declan said. 'A man you'd never met before, calling himself Mister Pravda, brings you into a lockup where you wait for him to cut up Marr's body—'

He stopped as Fallon started to cry, shaking his head.

'He wasn't a body by the time we got him,' he sobbed. 'We —we heard the gurgles as they did it next door...'

He *urped* again, but this time couldn't stop himself. Declan only just kicked a metal waste bin over to him before he vomited into it.

'So they executed Darryl Marr in the room next to you, and you didn't stop it.'

A shake of the head, more an agreement to the not stopping than as a rejection of the premises.

'For the tape?'

'Sorry. No. We didn't stop it.'

'And then you placed the four boxes, of which you knew were parts of Darryl Marr, into a van.'

'I had to staple the driving licence to him,' Fallon still held his face over the bin. 'It was a staple gun. He was... he looked at me.'

Declan didn't have any sympathy for Michael Fallon. And, from the looks of her expression, Davey had even less.

'You drove to the junction, left the cases and fled the scene,' she said. 'You followed the route, parked in Manchester Square... then what?'

'Then we left,' Fallon replied. 'The plan was to never speak of this again.'

'Were you in the van the previous night?'

Fallon shook his head.

'I was at a gig,' he said. 'I was told to make sure I had an alibi.'

Declan stared at Fallon, and then looked to Davey.

'Fallon. Hastings. Newfield. Nadal. You. All people linked to the killers, but not gaining revenge on the one who performed the act.'

'And some more willing than others,' Davey replied, her face set as stone. 'We need to work out who this Mister Pravda is. Maybe Manchester has some more information?'

Declan nodded. By now, Bullman's contact up there would be dealing with Monica Nadal.

'We'll pause this for the moment,' he said, glancing back at Fallon. 'I'd suggest you call your solicitor.'

Fallon didn't say anything, simply sobbing into his waste bin.

To be honest, Declan hadn't expected anything more.

'WELL, THIS IS A FINE BLOODY MESS YOU'VE BROUGHT ME IN TO, Ali,' Sutton was not happy, and his voice didn't hide it as he entered the Temple Inn upper office, De'Geer walking beside him. 'If you hadn't sent your man from Edinburgh here, who I have a lot of respect for, I'd have told them to go do one.'

'Sorry about that, Derek,' Monroe said with the tone of a man who wasn't apologetic whatsoever. 'I hope we didn't pull you from anything important?'

'Nah, your man waited until the session was done,' Sutton pulled off his tie and dumped it on the back of Declan's chair. 'So, what did you break this time?'

'Nothing, but we could do with your insight,' Monroe replied. 'We've got serial killers and what looks to be therapists killing each other and it's becoming a right royal pain in the behind.'

'Therapists?' Sutton was surprised. 'You're talking about Penhaligon?'

'Aye, it's looking like he's been running the whole bloody thing,' he said. 'You haven't even heard anyone call themselves Pravda, have you?'

Sutton stared at Monroe for a long moment, before laughing.

'You're not serious, are you?' he asked, looking around. 'You've translated it, I bet?'

'Yes, it means "truth" in Russian,' Billy frowned. 'Why?'

'Because it also means "justice" in Croatian,' Sutton smiled. 'We had those poor buggers crying out for it in their language for hours back then.'

'Billy, I'm about to replace you with Derek here,' Monroe said flatly. 'Just so you know when I fire you.'

'Ach, you couldn't afford me, Ali,' Sutton smiled as he looked at Billy's screen, noticing the photo of Jeffrey Ames.

'Aye, why's yer man on the screen?' he asked. 'You hunting screws now?'

'Ames? He's a suspect,' Monroe replied, frowning. 'Unless you know something else?'

'I know that's not Ames,' Sutton pointed. 'That's Mister Henderson.'

Billy tapped on the screen. The file for Jeffrey Ames refreshed, the photo still showing.

'Not according to this,' he said.

'Can you bring up Henderson?' Monroe asked. 'I'm guessing he was a guard too?'

'Aye,' Sutton nodded. 'Right vicious bugger, too.'

On the screen, the image stayed the same as the surrounding file altered.

'Shit,' Billy muttered. 'Sorry, Guv.'

'You're okay, laddie,' Monroe stared at the image of Wesley Henderson, a guard at Belmarsh. He was also the spitting image of Jeffery Ames. 'Just tell us what's going on here.'

'And tell us all,' Sutton nodded. 'Because I'm in the bloody dark here.'

'Someone's cloned the image and stuck it over Ames' record,' Billy muttered. 'I told Anjli there was a glitch here.'

Monroe considered this change in events for a moment.

'Pull up Doctor Penhaligon,' he said.

As Billy typed on the keyboard, Monroe looked back at Sutton.

'Describe Ames to me, without looking at the screen,' he said.

'Tall, lanky streak of piss, stupid wee glasses on his head, balding and a massive hooter,' he replied, emphasising this by tapping at his nose.

'And now describe Doctor Penhaligon.'

'Short, black, bushy beard—'

'Aye, you can stop there,' Monroe nodded. 'I think I know where we stand.'

Looking back at Billy, they saw the image of Doctor Penhaligon on the screen. It was the same man they'd seen earlier on that day, who'd been talking to DC Davey for weeks. His nose was long, with glasses perched on it. His peppered hair was combed back, and the same tweed jacket he'd been in that day was in the image.

'I'm guessing that's Ames?' Monroe asked.

'Aye, that's the bastard,' Sutton looked at Billy. 'He moonlighting as a shrink now? That'd be about right. Prick always had delusions of grandeur.'

'So tell me your theory,' Monroe looked at Billy. 'How did this happen?'

Billy turned to reply, only to see Declan and Davey entering the office.

'What have we missed?' Declan asked, looking at the faces.

'Let's have your news first,' Monroe replied, glancing at his watch. 'Unless the wee scroat made a full confession pretty immediate, like, there's no way you're done this fast.'

'You're actually bang on the mark there,' Declan nodded. 'He admitted to everything and said it was himself and Dean Hastings who drove the van.'

'And killed Marr?'

'No, boss,' Davey shook her head. 'He said that Mister Pravda and another man, most likely Lee Mellor, did that elsewhere.'

'He didn't recognise Ames,' Declan started, but paused as Monroe shook his head.

'He wouldn't have, as it wasn't Ames,' the Scot replied, looking back at Davey. 'Go back, show Fallon a picture of Penhaligon. Billy will print it out now.'

'Why, sir?' Davey asked. 'He's already told us he knew Penhaligon, as he had therapy sessions with him.'

'Humour me,' Monroe said as Billy handed her the sheet. Nodding, confused but knowing better than to argue with her superior, Davey left the office, heading back to the interview room.

'Fill me in?' Declan asked.

'Ames isn't Ames,' De'Geer explained badly. 'That is, he is Ames, but the picture's not Ames. The picture of Penhaligon is Ames. Which means Ames is Penhaligon. Now, that is. Not then.'

There was a moment of confused silence.

'It's amazing you're being considered for promotion,' Monroe sighed, looking back at Declan. 'Did you get that?'

'Actually, boss, I did,' Declan nodded. 'And once Anjli and Cooper get Penhaligon, I think I'll understand everything.'

'Can you let me in on it too?' Billy muttered. 'Because I don't know how a spook-level ID change is done by a serial killer.'

'It wasn't done by a serial killer,' Declan replied with a slight smile. 'You're right, though. It was done by a spook.'

Declan thought back to the conversation he'd had in that Broadstairs house.

"Always gave the big one, making out he was linked to Whitehall and did all that fake passport nonsense for spies, but he's all mouth, no trousers."

'Kym Newfield's cousin worked in Cheltenham and had

connections to Whitehall. He has to be GCHQ. Kym told me this, as she'd asked him to change Jacob's name when he was released, but he wouldn't do it.'

Billy nodded at this.

'That'd work,' he said. 'Do you have a name?'

'No,' Declan smiled. 'I didn't want to do all your work for you—'

He stopped as the doors to the office crashed open, and two suited men stood there. Declan recognised one of them as the special branch officer who'd driven him to Baker.

'Hello, lads,' he smiled. 'Come for some lessons in real policing?'

'Everyone out,' the recognisable officer said, waving his warrant card.

At this, Monroe stepped forward.

'You might be Johnny Big-Balls in Whitehall, but this is City property, laddie,' he said. 'And you have no right to ask us anything, let alone demand it.'

'I wasn't asking,' the officer said as he stormed towards Monroe. 'Everyone out except you and Walsh.'

'Not happening.'

'I'm serious.'

'Learn to live with losing.'

'For God's sake,' Declan snapped, boring of this. 'Is Baker downstairs? Get him up here. We're in the middle of a murder inquiry, and we don't need any more Government hassling, asking us to slow down so he can push a bill through.'

'It's not like that at all,' Charles Baker said as he entered the room now, an armed SCO 19 officer beside him. 'I need your help, Declan. All of you, in fact—'

He looked confused at Sutton, still in his suit.

'I don't think we've met, detective...'

'Dalgleish,' Sutton grinned.

'He's with me, and he's a source to this case,' Monroe said, as, from her office, Bullman now appeared.

'And he stays, no matter what your issue is,' she ordered. 'Get your men to stand down and tell the bloke beside you to stop waving his rifle or I'll remind people how I removed your predecessor.'

'Fine, fine,' Charles Baker nodded, waving his men down. 'I wasn't joking. I need your help. It's to do with Jennifer Farnham-Ewing.'

'What's she done this time?' Declan half mocked, but paused as he saw Charles' stricken expression.

'She's been abducted,' he replied. 'And we think it was by the killer.'

23

NOSY NEIGHBOURS

ANJLI AND COOPER HAD AGREED TO PICK UP DOCTOR Penhaligon, and, after the issues with picking up Mickey Fallon, had decided that discretion was the better part of valour. And as such, they'd travelled to Richmond in Anjli's less "police-centric" car, to use Cooper's own words.

According to the records, Penhaligon lived in a semi-detached house near the Thames, which as far as Anjli was concerned, was proof being a therapist was a licence to print money. However, when they arrived and knocked on the door, there was no answer.

'Another runner?' Cooper asked as she stepped back, looking up at the upper windows. 'I can't see any movement.'

'You looking for Brucie?' a middle-aged woman in a towelling robe leaned out of the next door bathroom window, looking down at them as she spoke. 'He okay?'

'Bruce Penhaligon, yes,' Anjli flashed her warrant card. 'Do you know where he is?'

'He's at a friend's house,' the woman replied. 'He's not able to live alone anymore. Not since the accident.'

'Accident?' Cooper frowned. 'He was fine when we last saw him.'

'Then that must have been a while back,' the woman waved a hand. 'Hold on, I'll be right down.'

She shut the window and, after a few moments, the front door to the neighbouring house opened, the woman, now minus the towelling robe and in a pair of comfy joggers and a hoodie leant out.

'He fell off the roof,' she pointed up at the slated roof of Penhaligon's house. 'Lost a couple of tiles in the storm, and the stupid sod thought it'd be quicker and cheaper to do it himself. Landed in the rosemary bush over there.'

Anjli looked across at a rather battered-looking bush.

'I don't know if the stroke caused the fall, or whether the fall caused the stroke, but he was in hospital for ages,' the neighbour continued. 'Still, it could be worse. Look at Rod Hull, eh?'

Anjli saw Cooper's confused expression and turned back to the neighbour.

'Do you have a key to the place?' she asked. 'Just so we can have a check of something?'

The neighbour's eyes narrowed.

'Do you have a warrant?' she asked.

'Do I need one?' Anjli raised an eyebrow, leaning in closer. 'Look, between us, I think there's someone out there pretending to be Bruce. But, until I check inside, I can't be sure.'

'This person,' the neighbour began, looking around. 'They good or bad?'

'Well, they're murdering people, so not great,' Anjli shrugged. 'I just need to see the living room. Confirm a theory.'

The neighbour nodded at this.

'Give me a moment to find the keys,' she said, darting back into her house.

'What theory?' Cooper asked.

'The theory that, if I ask nicely, I get the house opened,' Anjli gave a small smile. 'And what do you know, it looks like it works.'

The neighbour emerged from her house once more, a key in her hand.

'I'm Marcie,' she said as she opened the door. 'In case there's a reward or anything.'

Anjli noted the name down in her notebook, nodding soberly.

'Of course,' she said. 'And I'm more than happy for you to come with us as we look about.'

Marcie fought against her urges for a moment, but then pursed her lips and nodded consent.

'I should,' she replied. 'I mean, just to make sure.'

Anjli knew Marcie only wanted to have a nose around the house as well, so smiled and led the way into the living room, through a door to the right of the hall as they entered.

The room was white-walled, and minimalist. One shelf of DVDs, a TV on the wall, and some speakers were all that faced a black leather sofa and coffee table. There was one frame on the wall; an artistic print of the movie *Psycho*.

On the mantel, above an electric fire, were three photo frames. One was of a short, black man in his forties, laughing with a woman, and the other two were of the same man with a tall, slender and incredibly recognisable man beside him. There were an easy two decades between the images.

'That's Connie,' Marcie explained. 'Died a few years back. Cancer.'

'And the man?'

'That's Jeff, the friend who's looking after him.'

'Jeffrey Ames?' Anjli picked up one photo, looking down and the tall man with the hawkish nose. 'They worked together, right?'

'Yeah, at Belmarsh,' Marcie smiled now, eager to give what limited help she could. 'Jeff was an angel. Brucie helped him with some kind of past problem, and in return he helped Brucie though the cancer, and the, well, her passing, and then when he had the stroke, he wouldn't let anyone else deal with the support. Jeff was retired, I think, and spent a ton of time here as a carer. Him and the lad.'

'Lad?'

'Nice guy, short blond hair. Like bleached blond.'

Anjli pulled out her phone, opening up a photo of Lee Mellor.

'This guy?'

'Yeah, but he's lost weight since then,' Marcie replied.

'Thank you,' Anjli looked around the room one last time. 'I've got all I need.'

'You sure you don't need to check the bedroom?' Marcie asked. 'They made the downstairs office into one after the stroke.'

'No, we're good,' Anjli forced a smile. 'Say, you don't know where Jeff took Brucie, do you?'

'He never told me,' Marcie furrowed her brows as she thought. 'But I heard them talking once. Said something about being close to his office. He'd kept the lease on it, as he hoped to go back.'

She shook her head sadly.

'We all knew he wouldn't, but he needed something to look forward to, you see? Something he could fight for.'

'And do you know the address of the office?'

'Sorry, no,' Marcie shrugged. 'All I know is it was in London, because most of his people were there. Clients and that. And it had a view of the Thames, which helped when he wrote his book.'

'Book?'

'Oh yes, he'd been writing a book on serial killers,' Marcie smiled. 'Based on focus groups and stuff. Does that help?'

'More than you can imagine,' Anjli smiled.

BILLY PULLED UP THE FOOTAGE ONTO THE SCREEN, SCROLLING through it as Charles looked at the others in the room.

'She was speaking to her source,' he explained. 'I didn't tell her to do this, it was all off her own bat, on her own initiative.'

'Of course it was,' Monroe muttered. 'Never your fault, eh, Charlie?'

'Don't speak to the Prime Minister like that—' one of the special branch officers snapped, but Charles held up a hand.

'When you save my life and career as many times as these guys have, then you earn the right,' he said. 'I don't know who she met or where. All I know is that after an hour or two, someone checked on her, and through that, found her phone in the gutter.'

'She could have dropped it,' Declan replied.

'She lives on the bloody thing,' Charles shook his head. 'We all do. And the last thing she said was she had a lead to a potential new murder.'

'Wait a moment,' Monroe moved closer at this. 'She was

talking to someone who could actively predict murders? And at what point were you going to bring us in?'

'I didn't think it was real!' Charles exclaimed.

'I think I have something,' interrupting the conversation, Billy looked back from his monitor. 'Her phone is on automatic Wi-Fi search, and attempted to connect to the Wi-Fi of The Argyle pub. She then pings the Wi-Fi of a Japanese restaurant on Beauchamp Street, probably passing, and then the phone is dropped on Dorrington Street, about fifty yards on.'

'How does that help?' Charles asked. 'There's two CCTV cameras where the phone was dropped, but they're too distant.'

'True, but there's one on Leather Lane,' Billy pulled up more footage. 'And, knowing the time her phone hit the Wi-Fi spot, I can estimate she passed by...'

On the screen Jennifer Farnham-Ewing appeared, following a bearded man.

'She's with Lee Mellor,' Declan whispered.

'The killer?' This turn of events confused Charles. 'He's dead, isn't he?'

'Apparently not,' Declan looked back at the Prime Minister. 'He's been pretending to be a cameraman named Ian Connery, and I reckon he's the source she's been using.'

'Oh, shit,' Charles paled, and Declan knew exactly why. If it came out that his radical new capital punishment referendum was created on the word of a convicted serial killer, this could not only derail the whole thing but also make him the second shortest serving Prime Minister in recent history.

'Here's the CCTV from the end of Brooke's Market,' Billy zoomed in on the right-hand corner. 'It's not in the line of sight, but you can see she walks with Mellor to this black cab.'

On the screen, slightly out of focus, a tall, slim man climbed out of the driver's seat.

'Ames,' Sutton muttered. 'I'd know that bastard anywhere.'

They watched silently as, on the screen, the distant figures of Jennifer, Mellor and Ames could be seen talking before she arched back, caught by Mellor and placed in the cab. A moment later, the two men climbed into the cab and it drove off eastwards.

'We need to follow that cab,' Charles exploded. 'I don't care what it takes!'

'Two problems,' Billy replied calmly. 'First, we don't have the licence. Second, we already know Ames and Mellor have inside knowledge where the ANPR cameras are.'

'So what, we have to wait?' Charles shook his head. 'This is on you if she dies. You seem to be a lot further along than you've told us.'

Declan's phone buzzed, and he answered it, listening for a moment before grunting a response and disconnecting.

'That was DS Kapoor,' he said. 'They found Penhaligon, but it's as we thought. He's being looked after by Ames, after he suffered a stroke about a year back.'

Monroe considered this.

'Around the same time Ames got his GCHQ buddy to fix the IDs, so he became the therapist, and Mellor became, well, dead,' he finished.

'I think someone needs to bring me up to speed,' Charles muttered. And, as De'Geer explained everything they'd found so far, Declan moved over to Davey.

'Where were Penhaligon's offices?' he asked.

'I never went there,' she said. 'He always came to me.'

'Yeah, but you must have looked him up at some point.'

'I did,' she replied morosely. 'I used the HOLMES 2 system, as I thought that would be better than web searches.'

'And of course that would link to the prison file, which was altered,' Billy nodded.

Davey clicked her tongue against her teeth as she tried to recall an answer for Declan's question.

'Wapping, I think,' she said. 'On the north bank of the Thames.'

'Billy, look into Wapping and Penhaligon,' Declan said. 'I think they may be using his offices as a base, or maybe nearby.'

Billy started pulling up browser windows, but then stopped.

'Boss, there's got to be something wrong here,' he said. 'We've dealt with people using other identities before, and they go to great lengths to hide themselves.'

'Go on,' Declan walked over, lowering his voice. 'What's your thoughts?'

'This isn't that at all,' Billy leant back in the chair. 'Mellor's death was faked, but a simple search could prove there's no body. Ames is being Penhaligon, but that's falling apart too. The production company, everything seems half-arsed. Like they don't care about keeping up the appearance.'

'They don't,' Declan realised. 'It's all temporary. All they need is to finish this. After that, they don't care what happens. They probably expect to be arrested, or worse.'

'But in that case, why take prisoners?' Billy shook his head. 'This feels like a kidnapping where the victim's seen the faces.'

'Yeah,' Declan looked across the room at Monroe and

Charles. *What was he missing here?* They'd used victims from every other killer, all being led along by Ames, pretending to be Penhaligon. So far, they'd killed three of the four—

Three of the four.

'Tell me about Coble,' he blurted. Billy, half jumping at the urgent command, spun in his chair.

'Arrested for the—'

'Not the arrest, more what happened to him after,' he said. 'Sutton told Monroe he was taken out after informing on a gang boss.'

'Aye, that's right,' Sutton walked over now, making furtive glances at the two special branch officers. 'Is there any way we can get those eejits to wait downstairs?'

Declan grinned. He wasn't a fan either.

'He gave evidence against Sacha Davari,' Billy pulled up a file. 'Disappeared the next day. Probably changed his name, put him in the system as a different prisoner.'

'He's still in prison,' Declan considered this. 'Which means they can't get to him. And they want him. Maybe this is all a bargaining tool to get Coble out and in the open?'

'That'd be difficult,' Charles Baker, having been brought up to speed and hearing this last question, replied. 'I know about Coble. He was moved up to the West Midlands, but he died seven months back.'

'How?'

Charles made a half-shrug.

'I don't know,' he said. 'I just know he died. Not foul play, just, I suppose, gave up.'

'Okay, so we now know Coble's dead, but they don't,' Declan looked back to the screen. 'How does that help us? And how do they not know?'

'Declan, even we didn't know,' Monroe said.

'Yeah, but they have this amazing GCHQ guy,' Declan replied. 'He should have been able to get in there.'

'Maybe he couldn't get into past changes?' Billy shrugged. 'The entire infrastructure is a nightmare. That's probably how he got in to fix the records in the first place, using a key logger like with Davey. Maybe he wasn't told to find Coble until it was too late?'

'Then that could be a problem,' Monroe sighed. 'Especially if Mellor's kidnapped Jennifer for a bargaining chip.'

Jennifer Farnham-Ewing's phone stopped him, suddenly blaring out a Celine Dion song as a ringtone. Picking it up, Monroe showed the screen.

No Caller ID

'Worth a punt,' he said, answering it, placing it onto speakerphone. 'Hello?'

'Who am I speaking to?' A familiar voice.

'Hello, Mister Ames,' Monroe smiled. 'Or is it Penhaligon? I get confused. This is DCI Monroe. We talked before.'

There was a momentary pause, but not enough to hint to someone surprised their identity had been exposed. Declan realised Billy was right; they didn't expect to be stopped before something terrible happened. They were Thelma and Louise, and they'd already driven off the cliff.

'DCI Monroe,' the voice of Ames carried on, calm and steady. 'Is DI Walsh there? Is, dare I ask, our esteemed Prime Minister there?'

'Just us Temple Inn coppers, I'm afraid,' Declan held up a hand to stop anyone else from speaking. 'Someone from

Whitehall dropped this off, asked if we could look into it. I take it Jennifer's with you?'

'For the moment,' Ames replied. 'Such a shame, to have to tell her they didn't even bother getting their own people to look into this. I'd hoped by now to have the head of MI5 listening in. Or MI6, whichever the local one is.'

'What do you want, Ames?' Monroe leant closer to the phone now. 'How can we help you and free your captive?'

'Which one?' Ames said with a laugh. 'Oh, you thought I only had the simpering secretary? No, I also have Miss Newfield too.'

'She's part of your gang,' Declan added. 'Why should we believe you on that?'

'She fulfilled her purpose,' Ames said. 'Now she fulfils another.'

'Hostage.'

'You say it like it's a bad thing,' Ames chuckled. 'But we can end this all, nice and quick. Eric Coble is the last on the list. He needs to pay for what he did.'

'What happened to you?' Monroe asked. 'I've seen your record. You were exemplary, apart from the Crawley death, and that was never laid at your feet. And beating seven shades of shit out of Marr, but let's face it, he deserved that.'

'Nobody believed me,' Ames continued. 'I knew they'd kill again. I knew they'd find a way to work together. Bruce Penhaligon thought they could be reasoned with, but I knew they had to be put down.'

'Is Bruce with you now?' Monroe glanced at Declan. 'I'd really like to talk to him.'

'He's with the others,' Ames was getting angry now, his voice deepening as he replied. 'Lee has them. And if you don't do what I want, he'll kill all three of them.'

'Sounds to me like your quest for justice has made you as bad as the people you hunt,' Declan added.

'Sounds to me like you need to be put down too,' Davey snapped, unable to help herself.

'Is that Joanne?' Ames was delighted. 'You lied to me! You said it was just you!'

'I said just Temple Inn coppers,' Declan hastily responded. 'Me, Monroe, Davey and DC Fitzwarren.'

'Joanne, if it means anything, I'm sorry,' Ames seemed to soften as he spoke. 'I didn't want you involved, but I needed what you offered.'

'I hope you burn in hell.'

'Oh, that's most likely to happen, and soon,' Ames was cheerful as he spoke. 'But not before we execute Coble.'

'And how do you intend to do that?' Declan grabbed a notebook from the table, scribbling on a page, showing it to Monroe, who nodded. 'Last we heard, he was in witness relocation.'

'Get your man to find him.'

'Why not get *your* man to find him?' Declan asked. 'Or would he need to know his cousin's alright?'

'Oh, you know way more than I expected of you,' Ames' voice was tight, frustrated, even though he tried to keep it light and relaxed. 'Let's just say he no longer helps the cause.'

'Realised you were insane, eh?' Monroe spoke quickly. 'Shame.'

'To want justice is not insanity!' Ames' voice cried out through the phone.

'Is that how you convince yourself this is a good thing?' Declan asked. 'Is this how you'd convince your sister?'

'Don't talk about my sister again,' Ames replied icily. 'I thought you, of all people would understand me.'

'So, say we find Coble, then what?' Declan waved down Charles, who once more was about to speak.

'I'll send you information on where to meet later,' Ames replied. 'We'll have ourselves a nice little witch burning.'

'We're meeting, are we?' Monroe jibed. 'That'd be nice.'

'No, just Walsh,' Ames hissed. 'He understands, even if he can't admit it. I'll give a location, and a time. Either you bring Coble or Mellor kills our hostages. You bring any other police, and Mellor kills our hostages. You fail to bring him, or try anything—'

'And Mellor kills the hostages. Yeah, we get it,' Declan leant closer to the phone. 'Although I have one question. We wouldn't even have considered Mellor until you outed him as alive. Why do that?'

'Because he still needs to pay for what he's done,' Ames explained. 'And by the time you'd get to him, I won't be around.'

'Oh no?' Why's that?'

'Because I'll be dead, like the others.'

'Oh, that'll be a shame,' Declan said sarcastically. 'Great chat. Talk later.'

With that, he disconnected the call.

'What the bloody hell are you doing?' Charles Baker hissed. 'We can't give him Coble! He's dead! He'll kill Jennifer and probably go to the press!'

'Which is the part you're worried about?' Monroe asked sardonically. 'That your aide will die, or you'll be outed for what you did?'

Charles stood in silent fury.

'We've got time,' Declan replied, already writing notes. 'They won't expect us to get anywhere for a few hours. We're probably looking at a dawn murder.'

'Great, so we have the time, but what about the location?' Charles whined.

'Coble burned his so-called witches, so they'll likely execute him the same way, going on the past three,' Declan mused. 'Billy, find anywhere witches or heretics were burned at the stake in London. And start trying to work out how to find this cab, or where they could be holding the hostages.'

'And what do we do about Coble?' Sutton asked.

'Actually, Derek, you remember when you told me you owed me?' Monroe asked, pulling out his notebook and flipping through the pages. 'Actually, hold on, I wrote the line down. It was worth remembering. Here. "I do owe you for that. You sorted a problem I couldn't fix, and I appreciate it more than you know. So, whatever you need, aye?" You remember saying that?'

'Aye,' Sutton growled. 'So what?'

'So you also said you were attacked in prison because you looked like Coble.'

'He had a passing resemblance to me, not the other way round.'

'Either way, they don't know Coble's dead, and expect us to bring him,' Monroe nodded to Declan, who held up the page he'd written on and shown Monroe during the call.

USE SUTTON AS COBLE. GET CLOSE. ARREST.

'You're bloody kidding me,' Sutton shook his head. 'I'll never convince them I'm Coble!'

'You convinced me I had a grandniece,' Monroe replied coldly. 'And besides, all we need is you with Declan when it all goes down.'

'Bloody hell,' Sutton chuckled. 'It's never dull around here, is it?'

'He doesn't expect to live through this,' Billy considered the call. 'He gave up Mellor out of what, some kind of damaged honour?'

'You'd better return to work,' Declan said to Charles. 'The last thing you want is someone picking up on this before we can stop it.'

Nervously, Charles Baker nodded to his two security officers, turning and following them out of the office.

As he reached the door, however, he stopped, looking back at Declan.

'Save her.'

'We always do, Prime Minister,' Declan forced a smile, even though he wasn't sure if he believed the line he was giving. 'We always do.'

24

PYTHONS

It was another hour or two before Anjli and Cooper returned to the office, and by then Monroe had also called in Doctor Marcos, who'd been finishing up the autopsy of Darryl Marr, while speaking to the Manchester crime scene investigators over Kendal Rushby's death that morning.

Bullman was also in the briefing room; she'd spent the last hour on a video call with her Manchester contact, who'd in turn spent the afternoon interviewing Monica Nadal, and had come back with almost the same story Mickey Fallon had.

'So,' Monroe said as he faced the room. 'Full house.'

It was indeed a full house, as Declan now sat next to Anjli, Billy was at the laptop, connecting to the plasma screen, Cooper, Davey and De'Geer were at the back, and Bullman and Doctor Marcos stood beside Monroe. It was as if everyone had settled into their usual positions, although tonight there were two more people in the briefing room. Derek Sutton was sitting in the corner and glowering at everyone, and Trix Preston, who'd been called in by Billy to help, publicly because she was a link to Whitehall, but privately because of her longstanding connection to the Last Chance Saloon, even if that connection had its difficulties.

More importantly, she was the only person in the room who could get through the GCHQ red tape and firewall systems, and had held this over Billy's head.

Monroe, motioning for silence, checked his watch.

'Right, it's almost nine pm, and we have until dawn to solve this case,' he said. 'We don't know when the call's coming in for Eric Coble, but when it does, We need to be ready.'

'Or catch the buggers before they make the call,' Sutton suggested. 'That way, I don't have to risk being burned at the stake.'

'Good point,' Monroe nodded. 'So, let's make sure we're on the same page. Do we have a timeline yet?'

'Two years ago, Doctor Penhaligon, the real one, starts a therapy group in Belmarsh,' Anjli read from her notes. 'He brings in Coble, Rushby, Mellor, Spears and Marr at various points, but there's a definite overlap where they're all in the same room.'

'The guard watching over this is Jeffrey Ames,' Declan added. 'He had a history too though, unknown to the prison, that of his half-sister being murdered by a serial killer. One that, when he faced Jamie Crawley in Broadmoor, he either killed him, or arranged for him to be killed with the end of a sharpened spoon, cutting his throat open.'

'Broadmoor threw a fit but couldn't prove it was him, so they transferred him,' Anjli took over. 'They hadn't picked up on the Crawley connection because his half-sister had a different surname. And, now, years later and in Belmarsh, he's involved in these talks.'

'How so?' Monroe asked.

'Penhaligon's house gave the impression Ames and Penhaligon were good friends over the years,' Cooper now read from her notes. 'Old photos of them together showed there was a history. Neighbour mentioned Doctor Penhaligon had helped Ames with a trauma, and in return he helped with Penhaligon's grieving, after Connie Penhaligon's death, to cancer.'

'So old friends,' Bullman's eyes were intense as she looked around. 'And Penhaligon knew what Ames had done. Or, allegedly done.'

'Perhaps,' Doctor Marcos considered this. 'Until we ask, we won't know for sure. Carry on.'

She aimed this last part at Declan, who reopened his notebook.

'At some point the sessions end, likely around a year to six months before Spears and Marr both get released,' he continued. 'Penhaligon, the original, starts a similar group, but for people connected to victims.'

'How do we know it was the original?' Monroe asked.

'Monica Nadal didn't recognise Ames when he met her at a motorway service station,' Bullman stepped in. 'Which she would have if he'd been playing Penhaligon during these sessions. And her description of the Doctor matches the one Kapoor saw in his house photos.'

'The people at this therapy session are all there because of a documentary company contacting them,' Anjli spoke now. 'Apart from the Daveys, who told them to sod off.'

'This is the company that Ames started with Mellor?' Bullman asked.

'Apparently, according to records, at the start it was just Ames, creating the company under his half-sister's name,

Florence Dorey,' Billy looked up from his laptop. 'I think he did it to spook them, so Penhaligon could then bring them into his therapy group.'

'Seems long winded,' Bullman pursed her lips. 'What would they get out of it?'

'Some therapy?' Monroe suggested, a little too innocently.

'A book deal,' Anjli said, bringing their attention back to her. 'The neighbour mentioned Penhaligon was writing a book on victims of serial killers, or something like that, said he was basing it on information he gained from focus groups.'

'So what, he triggers the victims, then sweeps in as a white knight?' Monroe tutted. 'Whether or not he's also a victim of Ames here, Penhaligon isn't exactly showering himself in glory.'

'And, we see here he's working with Ames,' Declan tapped his fingers on the table as he worked through his thoughts. 'We know he fell from a roof around eight months back, so could it have been deliberate?'

'From what the neighbour said, it was a complete accident,' Doctor Marcos spoke now. 'And, looking at the reports, I'd concur. Looks like he had a stroke while on the roof and fell from it. He's lucky he's alive.'

'And at that point, everything changes,' Declan replied as he flicked through his notebook pages. 'The victims aren't a focus group any more. They're weaponised.'

'Monica Nadal said that it was around then that "Penhaligon" phoned her, saying he had an opportunity for closure,' Bullman added. 'Put her in touch with a friend of his named *Mister Pravda*.'

'It's also the same time Kym Newfield started writing to Jacob,' Declan noted.

'And it's the same time Craig Morris, her cousin hacked into Whitehall,' Trix spoke for the first time. 'It's the same code he put into the cable.'

'The one in Davey's PC?' Monroe was surprised at this.

'Yeah,' Trix nodded at Billy, who tapped on his laptop. A page of unintelligible code appeared.

'This is python, a coding language,' she explained. 'These few lines of code are enough to garner all keystrokes. I'll guarantee there're computers in Belmarsh with this in them, and that's how he got into the system to change the photos. It's not a major change, and wouldn't bring up alarm bells.'

'So that's how Ames swapped his image for Penhaligon's, and duplicated Henderson's,' Monroe nodded. 'Penhaligon wouldn't be back any time soon, so he was free to act. But how did he get Mellor out?'

'Same way,' Trix was looking at her nails now as she spoke. 'Someone else died that day, they swapped the details. I'll work out who if I have enough time.'

'I can do it,' Billy protested.

At this, Trix blew him a kiss.

'Of course you can,' she smiled. 'You can do whatever you want, little soldier.'

'Remind me again why we fired her?' Billy looked over at Monroe.

'Don't bring me into this,' Monroe backed away. 'You're the one who called her in.'

'Anyway,' Bullman said commandingly, bringing the attention back to her. 'So Mellor gets out, knows Ames and works with him under the identity of Ian Connery.'

'An ID given by Morris through his actual GCHQ role, it seems.'

'And now they put the pieces together,' Declan

scratched at the back of his neck, feeling like someone was watching him. 'And over the next few months, they recruit victims to assist them with their plans. Kym's already helping, as is Craig Morris. They bring in Fallon and Hastings to drive the van, and two unknown others for the night before.'

'One might be Lucy Savy,' Cooper spoke up now. 'She fits the size of the woman seen on the CCTV.'

'Get her in,' Monroe nodded. 'We know Mellor and Ames are performing the executions, but they can't get into the police network. So Morris makes a cable to be placed into Davey's computer. Mellor, as Connery triggers her, and "Penhaligon" arrives, to help her out. In the process attaching the keystroke logger, and getting into our system, while planting bugs in the office.'

'Sorry,' Davey mumbled.

'Now Ames has our ANPR cameras, he can avoid us and he starts to kill the four men in the Belmarsh meetings,' Bullman frowned. 'But why? We know he had priors with Crawley, but what makes a man do this?'

'He was in the meetings as well,' Declan suggested. 'He was the guard there, so he would have heard everything. Perhaps he hit his limit?'

'Aye, we can understand that,' Monroe nodded. 'Some of the shite that must have come out of those sessions…'

'Mellor also contacted Jennifer Farnham-Ewing,' De'Geer looked up. 'He could have gained this from our conversations in the office, or from his Whitehall connection, but knowing he had a chance to whisper in the Prime Minister's ear was probably too much to not risk trying.'

'So Mellor, as Ian Connery feeds her information,' Monroe nodded. 'And in the process sets her up to be a hostage, alongside Kym Newfield and potentially the real Bruce Penhaligon.'

'He has to know this is a Butch and Sundance situation,' Billy leant back on his chair. 'There's no way he gets out of this. He'll either be arrested, or worse.'

'He knows,' Declan replied. 'I think he's always known. And that makes him even more dangerous. Also, I get the impression Ames wants Mellor stopped, but not until he's finished. Even when he was Penhaligon, he was aiming us at him.'

'That could have been to save his own skin,' Bullman suggested.

'Risky,' Monroe mused. 'We could have stopped the murder, we could have learned who he was through Mellor.'

'I think he liked the risk,' Bullman suggested. 'It was some extra illicit thrill he got from this. He knew we'd be cautious. He timed it so he told us too late to stop anything. And, I think he did it to distract us while he dumped another audio bug on us.'

'True,' Declan nodded. 'Do we have anything on the YouTube video yet?'

'YouTube took it down, but not before it was shared everywhere,' Billy replied. 'We're still looking into it.'

'Good. And now we're up to date,' Monroe leant against the edge of the table. 'So, let's look at our current problems. We have nothing to help where Lee Mellor is holding his hostages, and it's about six or seven hours before dawn.'

'Fallon spoke about a lockup in Minories,' Anjli suggested. 'Maybe there's something there?'

'At the moment, that's our best option,' Monroe looked over to Billy. 'Unless you have anything?'

'I might,' Billy pulled up images of the white van. 'The

van they used, and the second set of plates they placed on it? Both came from Wapping.'

'Where Penhaligon's office is,' Monroe nodded. 'We've got uniforms checking that out.'

'I don't think they'd be so blatant,' Doctor Marcos started scrolling through the iPad in her hand. 'Although there was something when we examined the van. We found traces of magnesium carbonate in the cabin.'

'You said it was used in heartburn tablets and fertiliser,' Declan replied.

'It is,' Doctor Marcos read from the iPad. 'But we also found chalk in the mix, and the two of them together create a white, chalky powder.'

'Could it be climbing chalk?' Cooper suggested. 'Rock climbers use it on their hands to get grip, but it can get everywhere.'

Doctor Marcos nodded.

'That's what we think right now.'

'Mellor was a keen climber before he was arrested, it's how his brother died,' Monroe looked at Doctor Marcos. 'How can we use this to work out—'

'There's an activity centre in Shadwell Basin,' Billy pulled up a map. 'It's half-a-mile tops from Penhaligon's office. Mellor would have wanted to get back into climbing, and if they were nearby, he could have used it.'

'See if he left a forwarding address there,' Monroe ordered. 'I don't care what it takes. Now, where are we on the execution sites?'

'I think there's only one option,' Billy replied, pulling up a woodcutting of a woman burning at the stake. 'The Elms, Smithfield. It's best known now for Smithfield Market, and—
'

'And where William Wallace was executed,' Sutton growled.

'Yes, that too,' Billy nodded. 'It's where the memorial to him is. And, during the Marian Persecution, where hundreds of Catholics were burned for heresy, many of them died here.'

'True, but Coble didn't kill Catholics,' Bullman pointed out. 'He killed what he believed were witches.'

'Yes,' Billy pointed at the screen. 'Not many witches were burned at the stake in England, as they were mainly hanged, but in 1441 Margery Jourdemayne, known as the "Witch of Eye" was burned at Smithfield for heresy.'

'We should let Whitehall know,' Declan half rose at this. 'They'll need to set up some kind of support base if we're going there.'

'We have to consider Ames has planned for that,' Bullman replied cautiously. 'And if he sees any police, even snipers on rooftops, he could make sure the hostages die.'

'Then let's not give him the opportunity,' Monroe replied. 'I'm sorry, but did I stutter, earlier? *Find me where Lee Mellor is hiding!*'

JENNIFER FARNHAM-EWING WAS GOING TO *DIE*.

As she wiped a tear from her face, she knew with a certainty this was the likely and probable outcome for her. Unless someone came to her rescue at the last minute, she was dead. And she was annoyed that she found herself wishing for *Declan bloody Walsh* to come and save her.

She looked across at the woman sitting beside her; Kym

Newfield, her makeup smudged from crying had slumped forward, head almost touching the ground.

'How did you not recognise him?' Jennifer hissed. 'He's the guy who murdered—'

'They said he was *dead!*' Kym snapped back. 'It was official! Why the hell would I think Ian was Lee, if I was told Lee was dead?'

'And you didn't question this?'

'Do you question everything you're told?' Kym asked, before chuckling morosely. 'Oh, wait, you work for Charles Baker. You believe all the lies, don't you?'

'You really want to discuss politics right now?' Jennifer looked around. 'We have to find a way out.'

'Good luck with that,' Kym slumped again. 'I'm staying. I deserve everything I get.'

Jennifer wanted to scream, but settled instead for slamming the back of her head against the metal support she was tied to a couple of times.

She was going to die, nobody was helping her here, and for the first time in her life, Jennifer Farnham-Ewing finally realised that being a bitch to everyone, whilst helping her career progression, might have actually been a *really bad* idea.

IT WAS ALMOST MIDNIGHT WHEN MISTER PRAVDA ARRIVED IN West Smithfield.

It wasn't his real name; he'd been using so many identities now that even being Jeffrey Ames was difficult. Ames was boring, and one-dimensional. A lifetime of guarding others, of listening to their secrets, of hearing the murders, the crimes never sentenced, the victims never receiving justice. Only in the last year or so had he felt alive, after deciding to no longer step back from this, and to make something happen.

He knew the moment he started that he'd made the right decision, but at the same time he knew he'd damned his soul, as the devil he'd made his deal with would demand his sacrifice, and that would be on him.

He hadn't wanted to be involved in the killings at the start; that had been Lee Mellor. He believed he was a tool of the angels, had issues with the other serial killers in his groups, and had altercations with several of them. This was good, because it meant he would be a willing associate in this plan, even if he'd have to be put down eventually as well.

That was why this was going to be so public, why the Government woman had been taken. Once Coble was dead, they'd take him down. And when they did so, he'd give up Mellor. They'd not be able to reach Mellor before he killed the hostages, but that was an acceptable loss. Kym understood the risks, and knew she'd be in prison for what she did, Bruce was different since the stroke, lesser somehow, and this was a mercy for him, and the woman, Baker's ambitious bitch deserved everything she got, for wanting to profit off misery.

Yes, they would die, but so would Mellor, cut down in a hail of SCO 19 bullets.

It would be a neat bow to all of this.

'You can't park there,' a security guard banged on the door of the truck. 'You need to move on.'

Mister Pravda looked down from the cabin of his flat-bed truck at the small, officious looking guard.

'I'm part of a cleaning team,' he explained, nodding over at the rotunda gardens to his left. 'We're cleaning up the statue tonight.'

'I wasn't told,' the guard checked his notes.

'No surprise there,' Mister Pravda smiled. 'My boss should be here soon, he'll have the paperwork. I'm just gonna start setting up, if that's okay?'

The guard looked at the van and the driver in his high vis jacket and sighed.

'Sure, but if nobody turns up soon, you'll have to chase them,' he said.

Mister Pravda tapped his flat cap at this.

'Understood,' he nodded. 'We'll be out of here by dawn, I swear.'

And, with the security guard now off on his patrol once more, Mister Pravda clambered out of his truck and walked around to the back, checking the cans of petrol, the bundles of firewood and the length of chain for securing Eric Coble.

Because tomorrow morning, a heretic was going to burn once more at The Elms.

25

DARK BEFORE THE MORN

'This has to be the biggest Hail Mary we've ever done,' Anjli muttered as she drove her car along the Wapping street. 'Searching for a black cab at two in the bloody morning.'

The last few hours had been hectic, with everyone trying to find a way to locate the cab seen on the security footage, but if finding a white van had been difficult, finding a single black cab in a city that boasted over twenty thousand was practically impossible.

De'Geer, currently sitting beside Anjli, peering out of the passenger window, had contacted the manager of the Outdoor Activity Centre, sending across an altered photo of Lee Mellor with his now black hair, adjusting for his weight loss, and they'd confirmed that this man, known on their records as Ian Connery, and had come to the centre almost every day, keeping to himself.

He was an adequate climber, and had brought his own equipment, his harness, shoes and chalk bag with him each time.

What the manager also remembered was that "Ian" never

drove there, and would always walk to the centre and back, which gave Anjli the answer she wanted; that Ian Connery, aka Lee Mellor, was living within walking distance.

Going on the belief they'd stay near Penhaligon's office, off Wapping High Street, they looked for anything they could use, and it was Cooper who found the smoking gun, while checking the land registries for companies in the area.

A small mailbox address opposite the Prospect of Whitby pub, only a five-minute walk from the climbing wall, and less than ten from Penhaligon's office, had been rented on a six-month lease by Them Is Productions.

Ian Connery had signed the paperwork, and every day, Connery would check for any post, often items purchased on the internet.

They have to be hiding nearby, Anjli had decided.

And, now, early in the morning, with Cooper and De'Geer in the back of the vehicle, Anjli was heading towards the area near Wapping Power Station known as Wapping Wall, hoping to see a familiar black cab parked there.

Slowing down as they approached the wall, Anjli pulled the car to a stop, turning off the lights and staring across the narrow street at an old, ivy-covered brick wall, with a massive metal-sheeted double gate beside it.

'That's the only place we haven't looked, but we can't drive in,' she said. 'That said, there's several entrances by foot. We can go over the wall opposite the pub, we can do the same but down a side alley a hundred yards to the left. Or, finally we go back to Monza Street and come in the back route.'

'We're exposed here,' De'Geer looked up at the long residential block facing them. 'He could be looking down at us right now.'

'Monza Street it is, then,' Anjli restarted the car and

performed a three-point turn, heading back the way they came, before turning right into a grey-bricked, residential area.

'Go check for the cab,' Anjli said as De'Geer, wearing the dark tactical gear of an SCO 19 officer nodded, leaving the car. It was far less noticeable than a fluorescent stab vest, but his height and blond Viking beard didn't exactly help him blend in.

'And what do we do?' Cooper leant forward from the back seat.

At this, Anjli shrugged.

'Now? We wait.'

DECLAN AND SUTTON WERE ALSO WAITING, ALTHOUGH Declan's Audi was nowhere near Wapping. In fact, it was parked beside the Smithfield Ambulance Station, facing the centre roundabout and rotunda garden.

'Can you see anything?' Davey, sitting in the back seat, asked.

Declan had argued against bringing her with them, but Davey had pointed out that not only was she the one person who knew Ames the best, regardless of being conned by him, and not only was she likely to be fired once this was over anyway, she was the only person to be able to talk her way into the execution, considering her past with Pravda / Penhaligon / Ames.

And so they sat, silent, waiting for a call on Jennifer Farnham-Ewing's phone.

'No,' Declan replied to Davey's question, shifting in his seat. 'I think they're doing something to the statue, but I can't see what. There're some roadworks cones out, so I'm guessing it's planned cleaning works.'

'Didn't we tell everyone to get out of the area?' Davey raised an eyebrow.

'No, not until we get the call,' Declan replied softly. 'We don't want to raise suspicion.'

As if hearing this, Jennifer's phone buzzed. Declan had placed it onto vibrate, partly to make sure it wasn't heard by anyone nearby, but also because he didn't want the song to blare out in such a confined space.

Picking it up, and nodding at the NO CALLER ID screen, he placed it on speakerphone.

'DI Walsh,' he said.

'Declan,' the familiar voice of Ames echoed through the car. 'Have you found him?'

Declan glanced at Sutton as he spoke.

'Yeah.'

'Good,' Ames replied. 'Are you willing to give him to me for punishment?'

'No, but I don't seem to have a choice,' Declan muttered. Behind him, Davey tapped Declan on the shoulder and pointed at the rotunda gardens.

There, standing outside the gate, and with a high vis jacket on, was a man with a phone to his ear. He was too far to make out, but Declan nodded.

This had to be Ames.

'No, I suppose not,' Ames said genially. 'I want you to come to—'

'No,' Declan interrupted. 'I want proof of life first.'

There was a long pause. Across the street, Declan could see the man in the vest lower the phone briefly before bringing it up.

'I can't do that right now.'

'Then I can't bring you Coble right now.'

The phone went dead.

Declan looked back at the man to see him typing on his phone.

'Messaging his serial killer buddy,' Sutton muttered. 'Asking for a pic. Should have had this ready, bloody amateur.'

Declan resisted the urge to reply as, having finished the text, Ames looked back up, scanning the area.

And, glancing towards the car, he paused.

'Nobody move,' Declan hissed. At that distance, and with the streetlights around, there was no way Ames could see into the car, but a movement could be picked up.

Ames went to step closer, still staring at the car.

And then there was the ever so faint beep of a message. Ames looked back at his phone, tapping on it.

A second later, an image appeared on Jennifer's phone; a hastily taken photo of Jennifer and Kym, tied up and crying, their mouths gagged.

'Look at the windows,' Declan said. 'They're arched. Tell Anjli.'

As Davey typed, the phone rang again.

'I don't see Penhaligon,' Declan said by answering.

'Bruce isn't up for photos,' Ames replied, audibly tiring of the conversation. 'So stop trying to delay things. 'You've only got about three hours until dawn, and we have a lot to do.'

'Fine, where do you want to meet?' Declan was watching Ames as he spoke.

'You know where to meet,' Ames said, and in the distance, he turned to face Declan's car. 'I'm right here.'

Shit.

At the rotunda, Ames looked around.

'Do we have anyone else here?' he asked. 'Do I kill the hostages now?'

'It's me, Coble and Davey,' Declan replied. 'No more.'

'I didn't ask for Davey,' Ames said gently.

'I don't care, you wanker!' Davey couldn't help herself, now outed and shouting into the phone's microphone. 'You destroyed my career! I have a right to be here!'

'Yeah, bring her here as well,' Ames said with a small sigh. 'We'll just burn the witch a little earlier.'

'Coble isn't a witch,' Declan wasn't moving.

'No, but he believes in them, and I can make a very good case he's a heretic,' Ames replied. 'Look, DI Walsh, as much as I enjoy our talks, why don't you bring Coble and Davey over here and we can talk?'

And with that, the line went dead.

'Dammit,' Declan muttered. 'I thought we could gain another hour here.'

'Let's just hope your friends find the hostages before you get me burned,' Sutton smiled darkly. 'Come on, let's get this on the road. Quicker done, quicker drinking.'

THERE WAS A DOG BARKING IN THE DISTANCE AS DE'GEER climbed over the wall, dropping quietly down into the back of a car park.

To his left, a black shadow in the moonlight, was the Power Station, and to the right was the back of the onetime warehouses, now studio spaces and apartments of Wapping Wall, one of which had a mailbox rented by Mellor.

Finding a place to hide down behind, De'Geer peered

around the side. In the corner of the car park, barely in the moonlight and hidden by the building's shadows, he could see the front of a London cab.

'Bingo,' he whispered into his radio. 'It's this one.'

'Check the windows,' Anjli's voice spoke into his earpiece. 'Any of them arched?'

'No,' De'Geer shook his head as he looked at the warehouse. 'Wait, there's arched windows in the Power Station.'

'Great,' Anjli's voice wasn't happy about that. 'They can't be in there. The workers would see them.'

'I don't think it's a working station,' De'Geer replied, staring up. 'There's no noise. No lights.'

There was a long pause down the radio.

'Cooper's found it,' Anjli's voice eventually spoke. 'Apparently it was closed decades ago, and is now a venue hire and art space.'

'So short-term events,' De'Geer nodded, even though there was nobody around to see this.

'Apparently it was sold to a real estate firm a year back, and since then it's been empty,' Cooper's voice spoke now.

'Perfect for a serial killer to hide in,' De'Geer shifted slightly, taking a long look at the Power Station. It was split into two buildings, the left-hand one showing arched windows. 'What's inside?'

'Nothing, it's just a large, empty warehouse,' Anjli said. 'Hold on, we're coming over.'

After a couple of seconds, there was a scrabble on the brickwork of the wall, and both Anjli and Cooper, with muffled grunts, landed on the side De'Geer was on.

'Where?' Anjli asked.

'There,' De'Geer pointed at the building.

Anjli leant in close, making sure the light of her phone screen didn't show towards the Power Station.

'Here's some images taken from Google,' she said, flicking through photos of the venue. 'One main entrance at the front, no arched windows until you get around the back, and they match the ones in Declan's photo with a second door, probably a fire door, there. Another door to the far right, and that looks about it.'

She turned off the phone, watching the building.

'De'Geer, take the back entrance. Cooper, the far right. I'll go through the front door.'

'Risky, Sarge,' Cooper said. 'What if he spooks?'

'Then it's up to you to get in and secure the prisoners,' Anjli smiled. 'I've met him before, and I'm hoping that'll give me a moment or two before he loses it.'

De'Geer and Cooper nodded curtly before running off into the night, and Anjli breathed a sigh of relief. The fact they believed in her, whether or not her plan worked, meant the world.

Now you just have to make sure you don't screw up, she thought to herself as, rising to her feet, she walked across the car park to the main entrance, trying the door.

No joy.

Taking a deep breath, she hammered on the door, shouting loudly.

'Little pigs! Little pigs! Let me in!'

There was a faint noise from inside, and Anjli felt her extendable baton, now up her sleeve and ready to be used. She didn't know what weapon Lee Mellor would have, but this wasn't the first serial killer she'd gone up against.

And she was damned if it would be the last.

WITH SUTTON BESIDE HIM, BUFF SCARF OVER HIS MOUTH AND nose and head down, Declan walked towards Ames, now in the middle of the rotunda.

Declan could see that Ames had been busy; around the statue in the middle, ironically named "Peace", Ames had placed bundles of wood, a small ladder resting against the edge to allow access to the plinth. And around the statue itself was a length of chain, presumably to hold the victim.

'Eric Coble,' Ames smiled. 'Why's he masked?'

'To hide the gag,' Declan said, pulling down the buff and revealing a bulky cloth tied around the face, gagging the mouth. 'You might find it okay to walk around with gagged victims, but it's a little harder for me.'

'Take it off,' Ames replied. 'I want to hear him beg.'

'If you want to wake everyone up and get the police on us, sure,' Declan shook his head. 'I want the hostages released.'

'Not until he burns.'

'That wasn't the deal.'

'I'm changing the deal.'

To emphasise this, Ames pulled out an automatic pistol, aiming it at Declan.

'You can't burn him until dawn,' Declan insisted. 'It's not time yet.'

Ames considered this.

'Well, it's your fault you're early,' he said, looking around. 'I don't have any red dots on me, but I'm reckoning I'm surrounded by snipers?'

'You said no police, so it's just us,' Declan glanced at Davey, who stepped forward.

'Before you get anything, you can tell me why,' she hissed. 'Why do all this?'

'Justice,' Ames replied simply. 'People need to pay.'

'Why these?'

Ames' face darkened.

'You want the truth?' he asked coldly. 'Fine. I was guarding them when they did their little group hug sessions. Standing in the corner, wishing I wasn't there, but making sure if Bruce needed me, I'd be ready.'

He looked up at the statue as he continued.

'They talked about a lot of things,' he whispered. 'Such is the way of group sessions and all that. Marr, Spears, Coble, Rushby, how they laughed at the things they did.'

'You didn't mention Mellor.'

'He was different,' Ames shrugged, looking back at Davey. 'What he did, he believed he did for vengeance. His brother died, and as far as he was concerned, he killed those who caused this. Yes, he's mad, but he had a kind of moral compass. And he hated these men, men who would take innocents including children and do such horrible things... he hated them as much as I did.'

'So what changed everything?'

'I made the mistake of talking one session, mentioning my connection to Crawley,' Ames spat to the side. 'It got them talking. Started saying how they looked up to him, how he got away with it for so long. Said when they got out, they'd be smart like him. And I couldn't have that.'

'Because of your connection with Crawley?'

'The only connection I had with him was slitting his throat in recess,' Ames hissed. 'Bastard deserved everything. But I'd given them something to consider. If they killed again, it could be because of me.'

'And so you decided to kill them first.'

It was a statement, not a question, that Declan spoke.

'Damn right,' Ames nodded. 'Spears and Marr were getting out in a matter of months, so I had to work fast. I knew Bruce was doing these victim meetings for his book—'

'Because you'd helped him trigger them,' Davey moved closer. 'You and your fake documentary.'

'It was Bruce's idea, but it was only to draw them into the groups,' Ames replied. 'I saw how we could do better. How they could be an army of vigilantes. But Bruce didn't want that. But then God showed me *he* wanted it.'

'Penhaligon's stroke.'

'Yeah. Suddenly he's in hospital, and I've got access to his group,' Ames nodded. 'I knew I couldn't do it alone. Mellor was inside, Spears and Marr were about to be released. So I recruited Kym and her cousin. Kym hated Mellor because of what he did, so I knew Mellor couldn't show his face to her. Now Morris, he didn't care, all he wanted was cash, so I sorted him a large payment to give me new IDs and a faked death for Mellor. This done, I convinced Kym to help me honey trap Jacob, on the condition that someone else would end Lee Mellor.'

'And then you sent Mellor in to work with her, you sick bastard,' Davey hissed.

'No, I sent Ian Connery in to work with her,' Ames smiled as he shook his head. 'Names have power. You add *detective* or *doctor* or *judge* in front of a name and it's powerful. Add *ripper* or *reaper* or *slasher* and it generates fear.'

He paced around the statue.

'Spears was our test subject,' he explained. 'He reckoned he'd found God, so I allowed God to decide. If Spears was honestly trying to change, then I'd consider what I intended to do. But he immediately went on the hunt. He even brought Marr in to help him. And at that point, I knew he had to die.'

He looked at Declan now, his face softening.

'I thought you'd understand,' he almost whined.

'I do,' Declan admitted. 'But you still can't do this.'

'You don't know what I've done,' Ames went to move closer, but Declan matched him, Sutton now blocked, standing behind him.

'Then let me tell you what I know,' Declan said. 'You convinced DC Davey to take one-on-one therapy with you, and in the process used a keylogger to gain access to our ANPR camera network, and placed audio microphones in places we'd talk. And, when we found them, you came in personally and left another.'

Ames nodded without replying.

'You also convinced victims to help you, on the basis you'd kill the serial killer they wanted dead, too,' Davey now spoke. 'Michael Fallon and Dean Hastings drove Marr's body parts. Monica Nadal poisoned Kendal Rushby. Lucy Savy and someone else drove Spears to Newgate's wall.'

'You have been doing well,' Ames smiled.

'And Mellor, as "Ian" groomed Jennifer Farnham-Ewing, desperate for something to get her back into the Whitehall rooms of power, giving her information as a "trusted source" that was purely aimed at getting the public behind you.'

'I felt it couldn't hurt. And to be honest, she went above and beyond with what she did.'

'What I can't get, though, is why this,' Declan waved around. 'You know this is the end. You can't escape. And Mellor will be caught. All I want are the three hostages released.'

'Three?' Ames frowned at this, and for the first time in the conversation, Declan worried he'd made a terrible oversight.

'Kim Newfield, Jennifer Farnham-Ewing and Bruce Penhaligon.'

Ames grinned, and it was a look Declan didn't like, as he reached into his pocket with his spare hand and pulled out a smartphone.

'Who in the world thought Bruce was a *hostage*?' he asked.

It had taken a while, but PC Cooper had gained entrance to the building through the side door, mainly through the judicious usage of some lengths of pipe and some well-positioned pressure against the frame of the door, and now in the warehouse, she slowly stalked her way into the main space in the centre of the left-hand side building.

The power plant she was in was an antique, used only for school visits and events, but with everything being metal, the last thing she wanted to do was trip in the darkness and smack into something that was effectively a large bell, and so she moved slowly and carefully, checking every step she made.

That said, the noise from Anjli hammering on the door and yelling out, currently echoing around the wide open space would muffle most things.

There was a movement to the side, and Cooper ducked back, as Lee Mellor, now without his fake beard on, made his way determinedly to the door, a gun in his hand.

Cooper knew that her priority was to make her way quietly to the hostages and get them out, but she also wanted to make sure Anjli wasn't about to be shot in the face.

She decided to help Anjli the moment the barrel of an automatic pistol rested against the back of her neck.

'Hello,' a slurring voice spoke, and Cooper slowly turned to face a smiling black man in his late fifties, half of his face paralysed by a stroke, his gun aimed directly at her.

'And what do we have here?' the *real* Doctor Bruce Penhaligon asked.

26

FIGHT KNIGHT

MONROE AND BULLMAN WEREN'T IN THE OFFICE; IN THE darkness of the early morning, they currently stood in a car park in Farringdon, only a couple of minutes' drive from Smithfields.

And they weren't alone.

'This could become a bloodbath if we don't contain it,' Specialist Firearms Officer Andrews of SCO 19 said morosely, looking down at a map. 'We don't know what weapons this guy has, and if you're right, and he is looking to go out in a blaze of glory, then we need to stop him now.'

'It's not this guy we should worry about,' Monroe looked up. 'It's the maniac in Wapping.'

'And we're looking at him too,' Andrews replied calmly. 'Look at it like this, Alex. At least this time we're on the same page from the start.'

Monroe couldn't help but smile at this. One of the last times they'd met officially, Andrews' armed police had been about to storm Devonshire House, and Billy had waved them down, standing in the way of their vehicles, trying to give Declan time. In recompense for this, the Last Chance Saloon had then played the roles of terrorist insurgents for the team's practice sessions, being repeatedly shot by gung ho officers with simunition rounds.

Rosanna Marcos had stolen one of the Glock 19s from the exercise, for "forensic reasons". She'd never given it back, and it was now in her bedside drawer.

'We have people going to Wapping, too,' Andrews tapped the location on the map. 'Good people. I trust them.'

'Sir,' one of Andrews' men listened to a radio, looking up. 'Walsh has moved in.'

'Already?' Monroe frowned at Bullman. 'This is way too soon.'

'Looks like things are going pear-shaped,' Bullman replied cynically. 'What else did we expect?'

DECLAN STARED AT THE GUN IN AMES' HAND.

'It's not too late to turn this around,' he said. 'We could say Mellor made you do this. That he made the video.'

'The video?' Ames looked confused for a moment, and then he laughed. 'Oh, you are so out of the loop here, Walsh.'

'Then explain it to me.'

'I think you should talk to someone in Whitehall about that,' Ames chuckled. 'Just toss me Coble and get on the ground.'

'What about the hostages?' Davey asked.

'Casualties of war,' Ames waved the gun, showing his phone in his other hand. 'And don't think about any funny ideas, Walsh. I have a text just waiting to be sent here, and if Mellor gets it, he kills everyone anyway. Think of it as a smartphone *dead man's trigger*. Coble. Now.'

'Fine, but don't say we didn't try to stop you,' Declan said, pushing Sutton forward so hard that the larger man stumbled into Ames.

'You bloody fool!' Ames snapped, pulling up Sutton's jaw, looking at his face properly for the first time. 'I didn't say—wait, you're not—'

'Hello Mister Ames,' Sutton said, pulling off his gag with his uncuffed hands. 'Nice to see you again.'

And with that, Sutton slammed his head into Ames' forehead, breaking his nose and drawing blood as the ex-guard staggered back, raising his gun.

'You'll pay for that!' he cried out, firing blindly as the blood from the gash low in his forehead flowed into his eyes. But by that point Sutton had moved, and now Declan was charging in at speed, baton extended. He knew he needed to end this quick, because if Ames *did* text Mellor, everything was over.

Ames had remembered he had the phone in his hand, as he now squinted down at it, trying to wipe the blood from the screen so he could see where to press—but with a *whuff* of expressed air, he went down as Declan connected solidly; the phone clattering across the floor.

Declan rose, but then dived to the side, for although Ames had dropped the phone, he hadn't dropped the gun, and he fired blindly again, two more shots before Davey kicked it out of his hand, sending him scrambling across the pavement to retrieve it.

Grabbing it, he spun, fired, and screamed in rage as the gun jammed.

'I've got the phone!' Sutton shouted, meanwhile, looking at the screen. 'Ah shite, he sent the kill text—'

Now it was Sutton's turn to make a broken sound, as the now weaponless Ames slammed into him, and Declan remembered that Ames had spent years as a prison guard; this was unlikely to be his first full-on scrap.

'End this now!' he shouted to Sutton. 'Davey! Call Anjli and warn her!'

Ames, however, had reached the statue, and climbed up onto it, kicking at Declan, stopping him from getting too close.

'You failed, Walsh!' Ames cried out. 'Lee and Bruce will clean everything up! And if your people are with them, they'll be killed too!'

Grabbing one of the petrol cans, he splattered it around the wood. Declan jumped back to make sure he didn't get caught by it, but Ames didn't seem to care, soaking himself as he created a pyre for the burning.

Then, throwing it aside, he pulled out a zippo lighter.

'I won't stop them,' he said. 'And you won't stop me—'

Before Declan could shout anything, Davey slammed into the side of him, knocking him backwards and to the floor as Jeffrey Ames dropped the lit zippo lighter into his funeral pyre, the petrol and accelerants placed around the bottom igniting in a massive and violent ball of flame, exploding out of the base of the statue, replaced by the crackling of burning wood and the screams of the now engulfed in flame Ames.

He didn't scream for long, though, as a gunshot echoed through the night, and Ames, the side of his burning head now missing, collapsed into the burning pyre.

Declan looked around to see SFO Andrews, lowering his automatic rifle.

'Mercy shot,' he said. 'You okay?'

'Call DS Kapoor!' Declan shouted. 'Get your men there now!'

DOCTOR PENHALIGON HAD INDEED SUFFERED A STROKE, BUT IT wasn't the debilitating one they'd believed; his left arm was hanging down and his face was lopsided because of the facial paralysis, but the gun in his hand was very real—for about two seconds.

Cooper may have been female, she may have been new to the team, she may even have been short for the role, but she was a trained City of London police officer, and currently, she was *majorly* pissed. If Penhaligon had been expecting a conversation, he was sadly mistaken as Cooper grabbed the gun, twisting it to the side as it went off, the gunshot echoing through the power plant, and then wrenched it, double handedly from Penhaligon's hand. Tossing it to the side, she gave the therapist a swift and violent kick between the legs, spinning around, ready to defend herself as another shadow entered the room—

'Christ, Cooper, don't kill him,' De'Geer whispered.

'Mellor! Now!' Cooper pointed off to the front of the building with one hand as she pulled out her handcuffs with the other. 'I've got this.'

De'Geer nodded, running off into the darkness as Cooper stared down at the crying Penhaligon, now in a foetal position, and clutching between his legs.

'Shouldn't have aimed a gun at me,' she said.

Anjli had almost given up shouting, wondering if she was actually in the wrong place after all, but as she was about to stop, a slight movement behind the glass door gave her strength for one more bang on the window. She hoped by now at least one of the other two had got into the building, but when she saw Lee Mellor, she froze.

He held a shotgun, and it was aimed directly at her.

'Stop that noise,' he said, opening the door and waving her back. 'I hate noise.'

'Lee, it's over,' Anjli started, wincing as Mellor's face darkened and he brought the shotgun up. 'We know where Ames is. Coble's already dead. He died at the start of the year in Wolverhampton. His arteries just gave up the ghost.'

'Lies,' Mellor hissed, and Anjli went to run, to charge him before he could get a round off—as deep in the building, another gunshot echoed around the walls.

'You set me up!' Mellor cried out, leaving the door open as he ran back into the building. Releasing the pent up breath she hadn't realised she was holding, Anjli leant against the doorframe and took a new one.

'I need to work in cyber with Billy,' she muttered. 'Nobody ever shoots at Billy.'

Lee Mellor knew the end was coming before he even reached the hostages. His phone had buzzed after the gunshot, and the message had been from Ames.

It's over. We lost. Clean up.

Ames had been defeated, Coble was already dead if the copper was to be believed, and this had all been for nothing. That Spears, Marr and Rushby would never kill again was irrelevant; he hadn't gained his fourth kill. He *needed* his fourth kill.

So now, he would *have* his fourth. *And* his fifth.

And then, Lee Mellor would slit his own throat and take his life, and join his brother with the angels.

What Mellor hadn't expected was the seven-foot tall Viking that charged into the side of him as he entered the warehouse; tumbling to the floor in a collection of arms and legs, Mellor only just kept his hands on the shotgun, slamming back with the butt at the Viking's head, sending him staggering.

He wanted to kill the Viking, but that would take a cartridge. He needed both for the hostages, as Penhaligon had taken the gun, and from the looks of things, he was gone, too.

Bringing up the shotgun, he aimed it at the Whitehall bitch first. She'd been so desperate to get him to give her the information she needed, the answers she wanted and use it for her own advantage, she hadn't even cared where they came from. Nobody would miss her.

'Put the gun down, Mellor,' another voice, a third voice, now spoke. It was another officer, Penhaligon's gun in her hand, aiming at Mellor. He quickly spun around now aiming the shotgun back at her.

'Put yours down,' he hissed. He could see out of the corner of his eye the Viking run to the hostages, but there was nothing he could do about that. If he moved, the bitch with the gun would shoot him. If he shot her, the Viking would have a fighting chance to take him down.

You need to fight clever.

Nodding, he placed the shotgun on the floor, stepping away from it, his hands in the air.

She was the police. She'd work by the rules. The system could be used to his advantage.

'I want my solicitor,' he said. 'I've been used by people who didn't have my best interest at heart. I don't even know who I am anymore.'

He lowered his arms as the officer walked towards him. The DS, Kapoor, walked over to her first, though, taking the gun.

'I've got this,' she said, turning the weapon back on Mellor as she approached.

Mellor shook his arm slightly, letting the blade he had secreted up his jacket sleeve slide down into his palm. He'd only have a moment, but if he could, he'd cut her, make her drop the gun, and then he'd grab it and kill them all.

'Mellor, get down on the floor,' Kapoor said, motioning for him to do so. Mellor stood still, defiant.

'I'll die on my feet, he said. 'You'll have to shoot me.'

'I don't want to do that, Mellor,' Kapoor said, but then she stopped, holding a hand up to someone else. 'No!'

Mellor spun around to see Kym Newfield standing behind him, the discarded shotgun in her hands.

'You lied to me,' she whispered through her tears. 'I thought you understood me, but you were playing me, the monster who killed the man I loved.'

'Kym, don't,' Anjli whispered.

'I'm going to prison for helping kill Jacob Spears, aren't I?' Kym didn't waver from Mellor's gaze. 'I might as well go down for *two* monsters.'

'Kym! Don't do it!'

'This is for Andrew, you murdering bastard,' Kym Newfield said through clenched teeth, pulling the trigger and firing both barrels, close range into Lee Mellor's chest.

As he fell to the ground, Lee's last mortal thought was one of utter surprise at his situation, but it didn't last long.

THE FIRE BRIGADE WAS ON THE SCENE ALMOST AS FAST AS THE armed police were, as Declan, Sutton and Davey were escorted away from the blaze by SCO 19 officers, walking over to Bullman and Monroe, the former standing to the side, listening to a voice on the other end of her phone.

'We just heard from Anjli,' Monroe said. 'Mellor's dead, Penhaligon's in cuffs. Kym and Jennifer are safe and sound, if a little mentally scarred and all that.'

Declan nodded, looking back at the smouldering body now to the side of the Peace statue.

'He genuinely thought he was doing the right thing,' he said.

'Killing monsters?' Monroe shook his head. 'That's fodder for fantasy novels, laddie.'

He looked over to Sutton, rubbing at a nasty bruise to his forehead from when he head-butted Ames.

'You okay?' he asked.

Sutton, in response, laughed.

'I've wanted to nut that wee bastard for years,' he said. 'Thanks for letting me scratch it off my bucket list, Ali.'

'You should take me in, sir,' Davey said now, looking at Monroe. 'I need to give statements, and more importantly, pay for what I did.'

'Aye, and you will, most likely,' Monroe replied sadly. 'But I won't be the one that does that to a member of my own team. Go home, get some rest. The both of you. Nothing more's happening tonight.'

'I'll go back to the Unit, wait for Anjli,' Declan said. 'Davey, if you want, I can give you a lift.'

DC Joanne Davey stared back at the body of Jeffrey Ames.

'I think it's best if I'm on my own right now, Guv,' she said, forcing a smile. 'Thanks.'

As she walked off, Bullman disconnected her call with a few well-placed expletives and looked over at Declan.

'Your Prime Minister mate is being a dick,' she said. 'Reckons with Ames and Mellor dead, there's no way it can land on his lap. He'll likely get away with it too, give Jennifer a cushy role in Number Ten for her sacrifices, and nobody will know he was being scammed by a serial killer all the while.'

'Yeah, they will,' Declan smiled. 'I'm guessing you neglected to mention Penhaligon?'

'Oh, you know, I think I might have,' Bullman smiled. 'I might go over to the tape line and loudly think to myself near some of those tabloid buggers. Could be career ending, but what a way to do it.'

'I think we've had enough career endings tonight,' Monroe said softly, watching Davey leave. 'She doesn't know the shit that's going to hit her.'

'Then we shield her from it,' Declan said. 'Like you did for me. And we did for you.'

'Aye, we look after our own,' Monroe nodded, glancing up at the sky. 'Look, it's almost dawn.'

And, leaving the forensics teams, armed police and

special branch to deal with the mess they'd left, Monroe, Bullman, Sutton and Declan left Smithfields before anyone could stop them, heading for Temple Inn, Monroe's office and a well-deserved drink.

EPILOGUE

Monroe was sitting outside Temple Church when Declan found him.

He was on a stone bench that enclosed a circular plinth, the top of which had a statue of two knights riding on one horse, the symbol of the Knights Templar, as Monroe sat facing the entrance of the church, his eyes vacant, his thoughts taking him miles away from the current moment.

'You're a hard man to find, Guv,' Declan said as he sat down beside Monroe. 'Any reason why you're here, apart from the fact it's a nice day?'

'I find it's easier for me to think out here these days,' Monroe came back to the present, looking at Declan. 'I'm paranoid now someone's bugging my office. Even though I know it's not, I'm still cautious. Too cautious.'

'I get that,' Declan said, leaning against the pillar and feeling the cool September sun against his head. 'And you don't get hassled for all the little things.'

Monroe grinned.

'Didn't stop you finding and hassling me,' he said. 'What's the problem now?'

'You missed the morning briefing,' Declan replied. 'I thought I'd bring you up to speed.'

Monroe nodded, leaning forward, staring at the ground.

'Did they fire her?'

'No,' Declan replied. 'She's suspended until they decide what to do, but the fact she was misled and not acting on her own cognisance helped her a lot.'

'Still not going to end well,' Monroe mused. 'She won't be able to continue. She'll have to leave the force.'

Declan sighed, releasing the pent-up breath he'd been holding for too long. It'd been over a week since Ames and Mellor had died, and the press still had a field day with it. Half the country believed they were heroes, while the other half didn't seem to be too sure what they wanted. The bloody CGI Justice video was still being shared around the forums and Charles Baker, ever the opportunist, had made a point of welcoming Jennifer back to his Number Ten staff; not the role she'd had before, but at least in a room near his own offices, and one with a window.

Everyone knew this had been an effective bribe for her silence, and currently, she seemed to be okay with that. It also placed his referendum plans on hold, partly because he didn't want to rock the boat, but mainly because Charles Baker knew the moment he did so, someone, probably in a small Temple Inn police unit, would leak the news that his own team had been working with the killers from the start.

They had charged Kym Newfield with the murder of Lee Mellor, but Declan knew she'd get off, mainly because of the situation she'd been in at the time. Self defence, being in fear for her life, all these things would go in her favour. The only thing they could charge her with was assisting in the murder of Jacob Spears, but with both Mellor and Ames dead, her personal statements couldn't be contradicted.

Michael Fallon, Dean Hastings and the others had all been arrested and charged as accessories too, but again, Declan didn't know how the courts would sway. Penhaligon had done a good job of convincing them they were doing the right thing, and there was enough leeway in every case for a not guilty verdict. Even Davey had this option, although that was a unique situation.

Doctor Bruce Penhaligon was a different matter. With no accomplices alive to state he was lying, he could have claimed the victim card as much as any other, but his one moment of clarity with Cooper, holding a gun at her head, was enough to damn him. And, unfortunately, the fact there was no-one else to charge here meant he'd have the full weight of the law thrown on him.

Still, at least it'd help his book sales.

Trix, her job done, had returned to Whitehall after one last patronising comment at Billy, and Sutton had returned to court to find out his settlement. There was never a doubt whether he'd get it, Monroe had given him a watertight case when they solved the *Magpies* case. The problem was always how much it would be, as the Ministry of Justice was notoriously bad at paying out money for wrongful imprisonment, and it could have been anything from three quarters of a million, down to just ten grand.

As it was, Sutton was granted just under six hundred thousand, and he'd gone back to Glasgow the next day, debating how to spend it. Monroe hoped he'd open a legitimate business, but sometimes a leopard can't change their spots.

At least Sutton would be a *rich* leopard.

A week after the events, life had returned to normal. Even Billy and Andrade were back on their dates, although Declan had noticed a slight reticence on Billy's part.

'You should come back, Guv,' he said, rising and looking down at Monroe. 'You need to be there when she leaves.'

Nodding, and releasing a pained sigh as he rose, Monroe followed Declan across the courtyard.

'This is going to give me admin, and I bloody hate that,' he said.

PC Morten De'Geer stood to attention in Bullman's office.

'Bloody hell, De'Geer, sit down,' she muttered. 'You've given me a neck-ache looking up at you.'

De'Geer sat silently.

'Did you come to a decision?' Bullman asked. 'On whether you want to go for the Sergeant's exam or transfer to Maidenhead forensics?'

De'Geer went to reply, but Bullman held her hand up.

'Well, whatever it was, forget it,' she said. 'That boat has passed now.'

'Ma'am?'

Bullman pulled out a file folder.

'I've put you forward to the NPPF for the Sergeant's exam,' she explained. 'As you probably know, the National Police Promotion Framework has a, well, a framework in place for how to do this. First, you prove you've achieved competence in your current rank, which you've done. Then you take the step-two Sergeant legal examination exam; it's online, in a month, and registration's been closed since June, but I've got you on the list.'

She sighed.

'Full transparency, you've taken DC Davey's spot.'

'A month?' De'Geer looked horrified. 'I don't know if I can do that.'

'You can, and DS Kapoor's already agreed to mentor you through it,' Bullman replied, reading from the file sheet. 'The exam comprises a single examination, containing a hundred and fifty multiple-choice questions, within a three-hour duration. Questions will test candidates' knowledge and understanding of four areas, crime, evidence and procedure, road policing, and general police duties.'

She looked up with a smile.

'Multiple choice. Even you can't screw up that bad.'

'Ma'am, I'm honoured, but I'm not sure if I want that,' De'Geer admitted. 'I think forensics might—'

'Oh, yes, about that,' Bullman closed the folder, opening another. 'I'm transferring you downstairs to work as Doctor Marcos' assistant for the immediate future.'

De'Geer frowned.

'DC Davey—'

'Is on indefinite suspension, and at the moment, we don't know if or when she's coming back. And crimes won't stop, no matter how hard I pray, so I need you to step in and help. Your experience gives you enough credit to take the role, which is the same as DCI Freeman was offering.'

She smiled, but it was a tight, tired one.

'And, as you're working for Marcos, and she has this weird agreement with the higher ups, you'll be allowed not only to keep your rank as a police officer but also gain promotions.'

She stood up, holding her hand out.

'Well done, Morten,' she said. 'It's Christmas.'

Dumbfounded, De'Geer took the hand and shook it.

'I didn't want to get this through dead man's shoes,' he said, commenting on the common situation in business, where a person couldn't make progress in their careers until someone senior to them retired or died.

'We never want the promotions the way they're given to us,' Bullman nodded. 'But still we get them. Now go and see Doctor Marcos, as she has work for you already.'

BILLY SAT IN THE CANTEEN, NURSING A MUG OF TEA, AS ANJLI walked into the room.

'You okay?' she asked as she made herself a coffee.

'Andrade,' Billy muttered.

'You haven't broken up, have you?' Forgetting the coffee, Anjli turned to face her colleague, who shook his head morosely.

'I'm wondering if I should, though,' he replied. 'Everyone thinks he's a spy. Even I'm starting to think so.'

'So what if he is?' Anjli asked, sitting at the table. 'He's not getting any secrets from you. And he's helped us more than we've helped him.'

'Do you think he's a spy?'

Anjli shook her head.

'I think he genuinely cares for you, wants to spend time with you and who cares if he is or isn't,' she smiled. 'He could be sent back to Colombia at any point. Make the most of the time you have together.'

She winked.

'And besides, he brings up the male hotness quota here by a lot.'

Billy smiled in return at this.

'How are you and Declan?' he asked. 'You know I class you as the gold standard here. Monroe and Marcos, they're cute, but they seem like people holding on to each other because they're scared of what'll happen if they don't, but you and Declan, you're just right for each other.'

'I wouldn't be so sure,' Anjli leant in, lowering her voice, her smile fading. 'Since the case, he's been distant. And I know he's been talking to Tessa Martinez, his old crush. I think we're probably not going to last long. I'm currently looking for a place to live, so I can move out.'

Billy's eyes widened as Anjli turned and walked back to the coffee machine.

'Christ, Anj, I'm sorry,' Billy started. 'If there's anything I can—'

He stopped as Anjli turned around with her coffee, winked at him, and walked out, sipping at her coffee.

'You're a dick, Anjli Kapoor!' Billy yelled out after her. 'That's not funny!'

He sat back, irritated now as the echoed laughter of DS Anjli Kapoor faded into the distance.

And now, alone, he chuckled.

DC DAVEY WAS WALKING TO HER CAR, A CARDBOARD BOX IN her hands as Monroe and Declan crossed the car park to intercept her.

'You don't need to pack up your things,' Monroe took the box, placing it on Davey's car's bonnet.

'I do, actually,' Davey forced a small, sad smile. 'Morten's taking my spot, and he'll need desk space.'

'This is only temporary,' Declan stepped in. 'Monroe, me, we've both gone through this.'

'I know, and thanks, Guv,' Davey nodded. 'Thanks for everything.'

'I can give you the details of an excellent solicitor,' Monroe passed a card over. 'He owes me, so he can sort this.'

Davey stared at the card before placing it away.

'I'm not fighting it,' she said. 'I'll take what they give me. I deserve what they give me.'

'They conned you into this!' Declan snapped.

But as he said this, Davey shook her head.

'I wanted Spears dead,' she said. 'I knew, deep down, that something was going on. And I did nothing, because I wanted him to die. I wanted them all to die.'

'Wanting and acting on it are two different things.'

'Maybe,' Davey shrugged. 'But to me they're not.'

'What will you do?' Declan asked.

'Visit my family, gain some closure,' Davey nodded to herself, as if convincing herself this was a good plan. 'Maybe Ellie Reckless has a spot on her team, or I can go work with Trix, or for Johnny Lucas.'

'These don't sound like great options,' Declan frowned. 'We'd rather you were here.'

'I know,' Davey took Declan's hand, shaking it, before doing the same to Monroe. 'And boss? What I said about being called "lassie"? Ignore me. It humanises you, and people do like it.'

Monroe nodded, unable to answer as Davey took her box, placed it on the passenger seat and walked around to the driver's side.

'Tell Esme that if she hurts De'Geer though, I'll come back for her,' she winked.

And with that, DC Joanne Davey drove out of the car park and away from the Temple Inn Command Unit.

'We'll see her again,' Declan watched the car leave. 'Right?'

'Of course, laddie,' Monroe patted Declan on the shoulder. 'Us bad pennies always roll back to the source.'

He stopped, frowning.

'Who's Esme?' he finally asked, with mock innocence.

'You know, guv?' Declan walked back to the Unit, ignoring the laughing Monroe. 'You think you're funny, but you're really not.'

CHARLES BAKER HADN'T EXPECTED THE CALL. BUT, HE KNEW IT was one he had to take, if only to close the book on the whole damned thing.

He'd had his men clear out the upstairs function room of the Westminster Arms, and waited, sipping a white wine as they checked Declan for any recording equipment downstairs. Then, after a few shouted expletives, Declan walked into the room, sitting down in front of him.

'It's a busy day,' Charles said. 'You have five minutes.'

'I only need two,' Declan replied. 'I need a favour.'

Charles raised an eyebrow at this.

'Go on.'

'Your predecessor made a deal with us, and squashed all previous crimes Monroe had,' Declan explained. 'I was hoping you could do the same with DC Joanne Davey.'

'Ah,' Charles placed the glass down, and knitting his

fingers together as he placed them onto the table. 'Yeah. That can't happen, Declan.'

'Why not?'

'Monroe's actions were historical,' Charles explained. 'Davey's was part of an active case. I can't do anything until the case hits the court. And even then, I don't want to do it, as it would hurt me. I'd be seen as making rules up as I went along, and one thing I know is that people don't like PMs who do that.'

Declan stared across at Monroe.

'So nothing?' he asked.

'Sorry, I can't.'

Declan nodded, sighing.

'How's Jennifer?'

'She's coping,' Charles replied, grateful for the change in conversation. 'I'm sure in time things will be back to normal.'

'I doubt it,' Declan rose, his voice icy. 'Thank you for your time, Prime Minister.'

'Wait,' Charles rose as Declan reached the door. 'What do you mean by that?'

Declan paused, facing away as he spoke.

'I know what you did, Charles,' he said. 'Even if it wasn't you ordering it, it was your office, and that'll land on your doorstep.'

Charles frowned.

'What the merry hell are you talking—'

'Lady Justice,' Declan said as he turned back around. 'Ames didn't make the video. He almost seemed surprised when I mentioned it. Said I should look at Whitehall.'

'So what?' Charles replied. 'He was insane.'

'Yes, but I think he was telling the truth, and it reminded me of something the last time I saw Farnham-Ewing,' Declan walked back towards Charles. 'When I came to Number Ten. The video had just come out. The press were going wild.'

Declan thought back to the conversation.

'So, be real with me for a moment. Is this about the video?'

'What video?'

'The YouTube one, with Lady Justice and her weird eyes. The one that appeared tonight and gave four sets of coordinates.'

'I have no idea what you're talking about. As for you, perhaps you should stop focusing on CGI people and look for the real ones?'

'She said she didn't know what I meant when I mentioned the video,' he explained. 'But when I did mention it, I never said it was a CGI character. I just said "Lady Justice and her weird eyes." She was the one who brought it up.'

'I don't get where this is going,' Charles shook his head, but Declan could see beads of sweat forming.

'She knew the video was CGI,' he said. 'She claimed not to know it. And Ames, he hadn't made it. And that got me thinking. I know Jennifer was getting information ahead of the police from Ames and Mellor. I think she gained the details of the body parts, and instead of giving them to us, she placed them in a video. Probably one she'd been making for a while, one that was guaranteed to make you look good.'

'You can't prove this,' Charles replied softly, his voice cold.

'Ah, you see, that's the wrong thing to say,' Declan sighed. 'You could have said "I don't know what you're talking about" or "if she did, then we'll get her together". But that? Saying that makes me think not only did you know, but you probably signed off on it.'

Declan leant in now.

'Currently, I'm the only one who's looking into this, as I was the only one who heard it. But if you don't help Joanne Davey, then I'll make damn sure we not only find who made the video but also arrest them, publicly, for perverting the course of justice and give the tabloids a nice, juicy press conference.'

'Declan—'

'Don't "Declan" me,' Declan snapped. 'You had the coordinates, and you held them! You put a family's suffering out onto YouTube as a treasure hunt!'

'I did no such thing,' Charles hissed. 'And if you start down this route, you'll end your own career.'

'Not my first time,' Declan smiled. 'And as I said, it's not actually a major part of the case, just a loose and rather painful thread to pull. I could easily forget it.'

Charles Baker considered this.

'Declan, you and your team have been good friends to me in the past,' he said. 'Once the court case has finished, I'll see what I can do in relation to stopping any permanent marks on DC Davey's record.'

'No "seeing".'

'Fine. I'll squash it. She'll get the same as Monroe, if she wants it.'

'That's all I hoped for,' Declan smiled, holding out a hand. 'Good to see you, Prime Minister.'

'Once you leave this room, we're done,' Charles hissed. 'I've had my fill of blackmail, even from you. With this last favour, we're through.'

'Read you bright and clear,' Declan walked back to the door. 'It's pretty much what I've wanted for months, anyway.'

And, with Charles Baker silently gnashing his teeth behind him, Declan left the function room and headed down the steps. He knew this conversation would come back to hurt him, but in the process, he'd hopefully saved Davey from the hangman's noose.

And that was a sacrifice he'd take any day.

Reaching the street outside, he pulled his phone out, dialling a number.

'Hey, Billy,' he said as it answered. 'As our last date was interrupted, let's sort a new one out. But this time, I'll choose, yeah?'

Disconnecting, he placed the phone back and smiled.

This time, it wouldn't be somewhere expensive and out of Declan's comfort zone. This time, it would be something out of Billy's.

And, considering what something like that could be, Declan walked towards Westminster Abbey with a spring in his step, hailing down a cab, and returning to Temple Inn.

ACKNOWLEDGEMENTS

When you write a series of books, you find that there are a ton of people out there who help you, sometimes without even realising, and so I wanted to do a little acknowledgement to some of them.

There are people I need to thank, and they know who they are. People who patiently gave advice when I started this back in 2020, the people on various Facebook groups who encouraged me when I didn't know if I could even do this, the designers who gave advice on cover design and on book formatting, all the way to my friends and family, who saw what I was doing not as mad folly, but as something good, including my brother Chris Lee, who I truly believe could make a fortune as a post-retirement copy editor, if not a solid writing career of his own, and Jacqueline Beard MBE, who has copyedited all twelve books so far (including the prequel), line by line for me, as well as my other books *The Lionheart Curse* and *Paint The Dead,* and deserves *way more* than our agreed fee.

Also, I couldn't have done this without my growing army of ARC and beta readers, who not only show me where I falter, but also raise awareness of me in the social media world, ensuring that other people learn of my books.

But mainly, I tip my hat and thank you. *The reader.* Who, ten books ago took a chance on an unknown author in a pile of Kindle books, and thought you'd give them a go, and who has carried on this far with them.

I write Declan Walsh for you. He (and his team) solves crimes for you. And with luck, he'll keep on solving them for a very long time.

Jack Gatland / Tony Lee,
London, June 2022

ABOUT THE AUTHOR

Jack Gatland is the pen name of *#1 New York Times Bestselling Author* Tony Lee, who has been writing in all media for thirty-five years, including comics, graphic novels, middle grade books, audio drama, TV and film for *DC Comics, Marvel, BBC, ITV, Random House, Penguin USA, Hachette* and a ton of other publishers and broadcasters.

These have included licenses such as ***Doctor Who, Spider Man, X-Men, Star Trek, Battlestar Galactica, MacGyver,*** BBC's ***Doctors, Wallace and Gromit*** and ***Shrek***, as well as work created with musicians such as ***Ozzy Osbourne, Joe Satriani, Beartooth*** and ***Megadeth.***

As Tony, he's toured the world talking to reluctant readers with his 'Change The Channel' school tours, and lectures on screenwriting and comic scripting for *Raindance* in London.

An introvert West Londoner by heart, he lives with his wife Tracy and dog Fosco, just outside London.

Locations In The Book

The locations and items I use in my books are real, if altered slightly for dramatic intent. Here's some more information about a few of them...

Amen Court is a real place, and although I would never condone trespassing, if you accidentally turn down the street and pass the barriers without realising, you'll face the last remaining wall of Newgate Prison. Amen Court is a short distance from Paternoster Row, where monks finished their Pater Noster (a Christian prayer) on Corpus Christi Day before walking in procession to St. Paul's Cathedral. The ritual started at Paternoster Row, with the monks reciting the Lord's prayer in Latin to the end of the street. When they reached the corner or bottom of the Row they said 'Amen'. Hence the name!

They then turned down Ave-Maria Lane chanting "Hail, Mary!" before crossing Ludgate, where they chanted the Credo.

If you look up Amen Court from Amen Corner you see a row of seventeenth century houses to the right which were built for clergy to live and work in. These would have been constructed at the same that St Paul's was being rebuilt after the Great Fire. Some of the houses still have the wrought iron frames to hold a gas lamp above their doors.

Tyburn Gallows also existed, and the location of the second body's reveal is a real place, at the southern end of Edgware Road. Although executions took place elsewhere, the Roman road junction at Tyburn became associated with the place of criminal execution after most were moved from Smithfield in the 1400s. The first recorded execution took place at a site next to the Tyburn stream in 1196. William Fitz Osbert, populist leader who played a major role in an 1196 popular revolt in London, was cornered in the church of St Mary-le-Bow, and then dragged naked behind a horse to Tyburn, where he was hanged.

Broadstairs is a lovely town in the far south east of Kent, and I spent a short time living there in the nineties. And, a couple of years ago, Tracy and I went to find the 'Thirty Nine Steps', only to find some closed-off steps that lead to a very large eroded hole. So no escaping for Hannay there anymore!

The Ivy Asia is real, and is as opulent and incredible as I state in the novel. I haven't, however, seen any police detectives from TV there.

Kirkleys Specialist Cancer Hospital in Manchester doesn't exist, but is instead a fictional representation of the amazing *Christies Specialist Cancer Hospital*, and they do have a truck / mobile unit like the one I mention.

I didn't feel comfortable using their real name for a murder scene though, so created a fictitious location.

The Watford Gap Services exist, and every band I mentioned who stopped there really did. So next time you're travelling north or south, pop up onto the bridge and consider what legends also visited there.

Finally, both **Smithfields** and the **Power Plant at Wapping Wall** are real, although at the time of writing, the latter is being sold to a new developer, so may be turned into housing, as is the usual plan for these places. The rotunda with the Peace statue is actually a few yards from the location of the execution of William Wallace, immortalised by a memorial on the wall, and the location of the 'Reichenbach Fall' in the Benedict Cumberbatch *Sherlock* series, where he jumps off the roof of Bart's Hospital is literally to the right of where Declan pass while watching.

In fact, until recently, the phone box there still had messages from fans to him, scrawled all over it. As I haven't been back for a while, I'm not sure if it's still there.

If you're interested in seeing what the *real* locations look like, I post 'behind the scenes' location images on my Instagram feed. This will continue through all the books, and I suggest you follow it.

In fact, feel free to follow me on all my social media by clicking on the links below. Over time these can be places where we can engage, discuss Declan and put the world to rights.

www.jackgatland.com
www.hoodemanmedia.com

Visit my Reader's Group Page
(Mainly for fans to discuss my books):
https://www.facebook.com/groups/jackgatland

Subscribe to my Readers List:
www.subscribepage.com/jackgatland

www.facebook.com/jackgatlandbooks
www.twitter.com/jackgatlandbook
ww.instagram.com/jackgatland

Want more books by Jack Gatland? Turn the page...

DI Walsh and the team of the *Last Chance Saloon* will return in their next thriller

A QUIVER OF SORROWS

Order Now at Amazon:

My book.to/aquiverofsorrows

THE THEFT OF A **PRICELESS** PAINTING...
A GANGSTER WITH A **CRIPPLING DEBT...**
A **BODY COUNT** RISING BY THE HOUR...

AND ELLIE RECKLESS IS CAUGHT IN THE MIDDLE.

JACK GATLAND

PAINT
THE
DEAD

A 'COP FOR CRIMINALS' ELLIE RECKLESS NOVEL

A NEW PROCEDURAL CRIME SERIES WITH
A TWIST - FROM THE CREATOR OF THE
BESTSELLING 'DI DECLAN WALSH' SERIES

AVAILABLE ON AMAZON / KINDLE UNLIMITED

THEY TRIED TO KILL HIM...
NOW HE'S OUT FOR **REVENGE.**

NEW YORK TIMES #1 BESTSELLER **TONY LEE** WRITING AS

JACK GATLAND

THE MURDER OF AN **MI5 AGENT...**
A BURNED SPY **ON THE RUN** FROM HIS OWN PEOPLE...
AN ENEMY OUT TO **STOP HIM** AT ANY COST...
AND A **PRESIDENT** ABOUT TO BE **ASSASSINATED...**

SLEEPING
SOLDIERS

A **TOM MARLOWE** THRILLER

BOOK 1 IN A NEW SERIES OF THRILLERS IN THE STYLE OF **JASON BOURNE, JOHN MILTON** OR **BURN NOTICE,** AND SPINNING OUT OF THE **DECLAN WALSH** SERIES OF BOOKS

AVAILABLE ON AMAZON / KINDLE UNLIMITED

"★★★★★ AN EXCELLENT 'INDIANA JONES' STYLE FAST PACED CHARGE AROUND ENGLAND THAT WAS RIVETING AND CAPTIVATING."

"★★★★★ AN ACTION-PACKED YARN... I REALLY ENJOYED THIS AND LOOK FORWARD TO THE NEXT BOOK IN THE SERIES."

JACK GATLAND

THE LIONHEART CURSE

HUNT THE GREATEST TREASURES
PAY THE GREATEST PRICE

BOOK 1 IN A NEW SERIES OF ADVENTURES
IN THE STYLE OF 'THE DA VINCI CODE'
FROM THE CREATOR OF DECLAN WALSH

AVAILABLE ON AMAZON / KINDLEUNLIMITED

Printed in Great Britain
by Amazon